MARINOV BRATVA
BOOK ONE

KONSTANTIN

LILIAN HARRIS

Editing/Interior Formatting: CPR Publishing Services

Proofreader: Judy's Proofreading

Cover Design: Wildheart Graphics

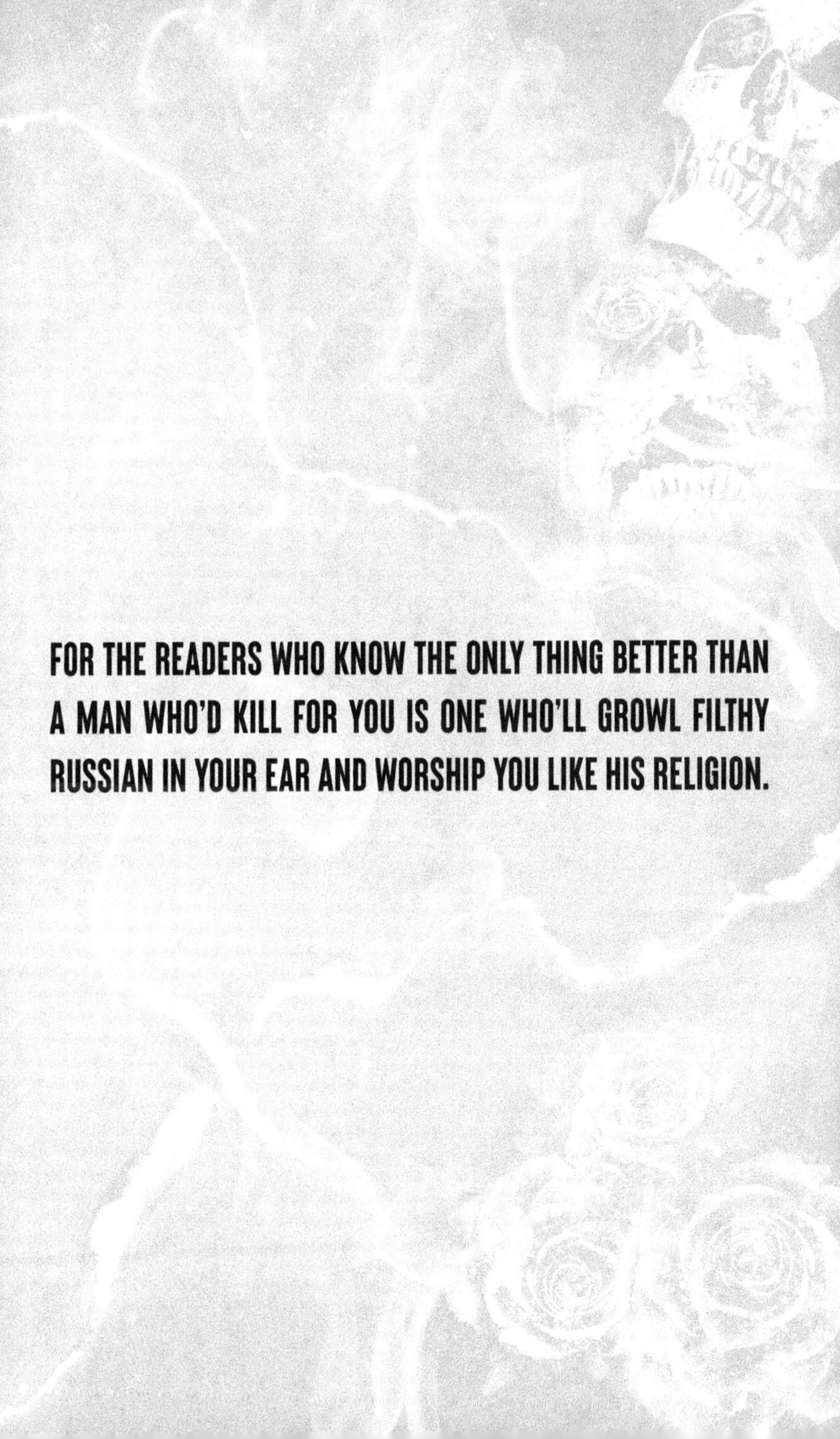

FOR THE READERS WHO KNOW THE ONLY THING BETTER THAN A MAN WHO'D KILL FOR YOU IS ONE WHO'LL GROWL FILTHY RUSSIAN IN YOUR EAR AND WORSHIP YOU LIKE HIS RELIGION.

TRANSLATIONS & PRONOUNCIATIONS

- Fionn – "Fee-yun"
- Eriu – "Air-ooh"
- Iseult – "Ee-salt"
- Tynan – "Tie-nan"
- Cillian – "KILL-ee-in"
- Malyshka – baby girl
- Dorogaya – dear
- Katyonak – kitten
- Ostorozhno, brother. – Be careful, brother.
- Moya – mine
- Malen'kaya – little one
- Vot tak, detka. Otdai mne vsyo. – That's it, baby. Give me everything.
- Lubov moya – my love
- Svolichy – bastards
- Otpusti yeyo. Boss skazal ne trogat yeyo, yesli ona popitaetsya sbezhat. – Let her go. The boss said not to touch her if she tries to run.
- Boji moy – my God
- Blyat – fuck
- Na khuy – fucking hell

ONE

KONSTANTIN

The bass hums beneath the floor, a steady pulse under the soft buzz of voices and clinking glasses. The air is thick with the scent of whiskey and temptation. My men blend into the shadows, scanning for threats, while I let my eyes wander over the room.

Some dance. Some drink. Some negotiate deals that they may regret in the morning.

And that's when I see her: sitting alone at the bar, legs crossed, a black minidress hugging her curves like it was sewn on to her skin. Thigh-high boots draw my gaze to toned, tanned legs. And that hair—long, dark, silky—would find a perfect home around my wrist.

She radiates confidence with that perfect posture. Doesn't even bother scanning the room like she wants to know who's watching her, because she knows they all are. Confidence like that cannot be learned. She was born with it.

A queen surveying her kingdom, and I am in the mood to share.

My feet are moving before I realize it. Before I even decide if they should. Something about her pulls me in, gnaws at my instincts. Like I should already know her. Like it's a sin that I don't.

What a tempting little creature you are.

As I close the distance, the angles of her face sharpen under the low light: dark lashes framing unreadable eyes, full lips painted deep burgundy as she wraps them around the straw of her drink.

It's easy to see she's the kind of woman who doesn't need anyone. The kind who makes men beg.

But I don't beg. I take.

I move nearer, every step slow and calculated. She doesn't look my way as she tilts her glass, the red liquid swirling in her hand.

When her dark eyes finally meet mine, there's no hesitation. No shyness. Only quiet amusement, like she's used to men falling all over themselves for her. And I have no doubt that is the case.

I slide onto the stool beside her, close enough to catch the faint scent of something warm and feminine. Vanilla and spice, perhaps.

"You always drink alone, or is this my lucky night?"

She smirks, lashes lowering as she takes a slow sip through the thin black straw. "I'm waiting for a friend, actually."

"Lucky friend."

Or maybe dead friend. It really depends on the level of friendship she's referring to.

Her smirk deepens. "Really? Is that your best line?"

I chuckle, signaling the bartender. "If I was really trying to pick you up, malyshka, you'd know."

She studies me, tipping her head slightly. "Would I, now?"

I lean in, forearm resting on the bar, mouth growing dangerously close to hers, and she doesn't even flinch.

"I don't play games I can't win," I tell her as my palm lowers to the top of her bare thigh, warm and velvety.

It's downright sinful how good she feels.

She exhales a soft laugh, the kind that doesn't give anything away.

A woman like this? She enjoys the chase, but she doesn't need it. Which only makes me more interested.

Her hand grazes my forearm, nails trailing over the sleeve of my dress shirt. "Neither do I."

She has no idea what she's just stepped into. No idea how risky it is to make a man like me want to learn everything there is to know about her.

The bartender sets my drink in front of me, and I lift it, watching her over the rim.

"What's your name?" I ask her.

She hesitates, just for a breath. "Tessa. Tessa Monroe."

It suits her. Smooth, refined.

I take her hand before she can pull away, pressing a slow kiss to the top of it. "Konstantin."

Her lips part slightly, and she doesn't look away. "Pleasure."

"Oh, believe me, the pleasure is all mine, dorogaya."

Her gaze flickers with something unreadable. Amusement? Intrigue? Temptation? I can't yet tell. She's like a puzzle I need to crack.

I don't let go of her hand right away, running my thumb over her knuckles. Her skin is warm, soft. A contrast to everything I am.

When I finally release her, she doesn't move. Just watches me, a mischievous gaze dragging over my body like she's assessing every inch. Like she enjoys what she sees.

A dangerous thing.

Her mouth angles up when she catches my eye.

"Oh, do not let me interrupt you. Please, keep staring. I find myself enjoying it."

She laughs. "I think I'm done now."

"And was it to your satisfaction, Ms. Monroe?"

She brushes a loose strand of hair behind her ear, and I very much would like to do that myself. "I guess you'll never know."

There's a teasing edge to her tone, and I let out a deep, dark chuckle.

"I very much doubt that." With another slow swig of my drink, I'm unable to stop my gaze from feasting on this beautiful woman. "If you need anything else, it's on me."

She arches a perfectly manicured brow. "Why?"

Because I want to keep you here. Because you're the most interesting thing in this room.

But I just shrug instead. "Consider it a welcome gift, since I'm pretty sure you've never been to this bar before and I happen to own it."

Her fingers glide along the condensation, marking her glass. "I don't accept gifts from strangers."

I won't be a stranger for long.

Gripping the edge of her stool, I pull her in, her knee brushing mine. "Then get to know me."

Her lips twitch. "Tempting."

I chuckle, finishing off my drink, then push off the bar. Adjusting my cuffs, I lean in close enough that my breath warms her cheek, my lips ghosting over her ear.

"Think about it. Enjoy your night, dorogaya. I'll see you later."

She inhales sharply when my mouth lingers, her composure slipping for the first time, and something in my chest tightens with satisfaction.

As I step back, every part of me wants to stay, which is very new for me. I don't know what it is about this Tessa that makes me want to peel back every layer and taste what she doesn't let anyone else have.

Instead, though, I walk away without looking back.

Except I don't have to.

I feel her watching me, just like I knew she would.

TESSA

He starts to disappear toward the back, and the urge to grab the nearest knife and stab it straight through his gorgeous eye is almost unbearable.

He may not know my name, but I know his. And if I play my cards right, it's going to stay that way.

The fact that I find him remotely attractive makes me sick. How the hell can I stand the thought of him anywhere near me after what he did?

But I played it cool. I don't think he had any clue how I truly felt about him.

And if I want things to work out, he can never find out.

"Okay, I'm back!" Mira's bright voice startles me from behind, pulling me back into the moment. She comes around to my side, her hazel eyes full of warmth and complete obliviousness to the war waging inside me. "Sorry. I had some stuff to discuss with the manager about my shift tomorrow, and it took longer than I thought."

Mira not only works for Konstantin at this bar, but also at his club, the one people don't know about unless he wants them to know. I'd heard rumors, but it wasn't until I met Mira that I actually learned the truth.

She slides onto the stool Konstantin just vacated, her presence replacing his, but the scent of his expensive cologne still lingers in the air, wrapping around me like a ghostly touch.

I force my muscles to relax, shaking off the residual tension curling in my gut. There's no way in hell I can afford to let him get under my skin. Not when I've spent the last month planning for this.

"No worries," I say smoothly, offering her a bright smile.

The guilt tugs at my chest, but I shove it down.

Mira thinks we're friends. She has no idea she's nothing more than a pawn in my game. A means to an end.

She was easy to follow and get close to. Young, friendly, trusting. A recipe for disaster. She doesn't have much family except for a single mother who works hard to put a roof over her head.

At least some mothers know how to love their kids.

When I "accidentally" spilled coffee on her at that café she frequents, she had no idea it was deliberate. She never questioned why I was so eager to replace it. To sit with her and chat. I made sure she saw what she needed to see: someone struggling, desperate for a job. Someone she could help.

And she did. She handed me exactly what I needed: a way in. Now it's up to me.

"So, do you really think he'll be okay with me applying for a job at the club?" I ask, keeping my tone casual.

No isn't an option. Not for me. I *have* to get this job.

"Oh, yeah!" She easily flags down the bartender and orders a drink. "I mentioned I had a friend looking to make a lot of money, and he said it was fine." She leans on the bar with a dreamy sigh. "Honestly, he's a great boss."

I nearly choke. "You're not afraid of him?"

Mira tilts her head, eyes narrowing slightly. "Not at all. All he demands is trust and respect, and that's easy."

"Yeah, for some people," I mutter.

"What?"

"Nothing." I flash another easy grin. "I'm excited, though. I never even knew a place like that existed."

"I know, right? It's crazy how he moves the club's location all the time and no one knows until they get the text that disappears once you see it."

"And is that how he mostly recruits people? Through his other businesses, like this place?"

Mira shrugs. "I don't know everyone who works at the club, but yeah, some of them come from the bars and lounges he owns."

I nod, taking another sip of my drink, even though my stomach is in a knot—not from fear, but from desperation. "I hope he likes me."

I hope he trusts me.

She scoffs. "Have you seen yourself? Pretty sure that won't be a problem. But…" She hesitates, her timbre growing lower. "Are you sure you're ready for this?"

Her words send an icy current through my chest, spreading like frost.

I force myself to hold her gaze. "I think so."

But the truth is I have no choice. This is the only way.

Mira studies me for a second, then pulls her phone from her back pocket, tapping away. Her lips tug into a smile as she looks up.

"He's waiting for us."

My fingers tighten around my glass as I set it down carefully, an eerie stillness gripping me, apprehension threading through every muscle. But I push it away.

This is it.

I have no other choice. I can't fuck this up. I have to do this. For revenge.

Konstantin will pay for what he's done.

Glancing at her, I tip my mouth up. "Let's go."

TWO

KONSTANTIN

There's a soft knock on my door, which is already ajar. When I look up from my desk, I find Mira there just as I requested.

"May we come in?" she asks.

I nod. "Please."

I close my laptop, completely intrigued by this friend she mentioned. The one who really needed money. I'm nothing if not charitable.

As Mira walks inside, I catch sight of the woman behind her, and my lips twist with dark amusement when we lock eyes.

"Ah, Ms. Monroe. So nice to see you again. I knew you wouldn't be able to resist for long."

"Don't get ahead of yourself. I'm here for the job, nothing more."

"So, you're the mystery friend." I lean back in my chair, freely letting my gaze rove down her beautiful body, wanting her sprawled on my desk so I can feast on all those curves.

"I guess I am."

Mira's expression widens as she glances between us. "Wait, you two know each other?"

"Sort of," Tessa says, her gaze still fixed on me.

"We met earlier," I add. "You may go, Mira. I've got it from here."

"Okay, sir." Her attention shifts to Tessa. "I'll wait for you at the bar, alright?" She stares at my new friend as though I'm about to eat her.

Well, that isn't far from the truth…

"I'll be fine." Tessa's eyes continue to hold mine, and my blood pumps faster, surging into my cock and making me hard as stone.

Mira nervously makes her escape and shuts the door behind her, leaving me alone with my current fascination.

"So…" I fold my arms over my chest. "You want to work at my club, huh?"

"It's why I'm here." She lets out a dry laugh.

"And you understand the sort of club it is?"

"I do. Exclusive sex club for every fantasy, catering to the uber rich and famous."

"That is correct." I beckon her with a finger. "Come closer."

She takes a step toward me, then another, a teasing smile on her face. Every muscle in my body tenses, wanting to grab her and take her bent over my desk.

The image won't leave me, and my fists curl over my thighs. If she rounds my desk, she will see how hard I've become at the mere sight of her. I cannot imagine what it will feel like once those clothes are gone and she's bare for me.

When she's only a few inches away from my desk, I look up at her tempting gaze. "You think a girl like you can handle working for a place like mine?"

"I'm not a girl. I'm twenty-six, old man."

My teeth gnaw. That sexy smirk she's wearing, that tone, makes me want to put her over my knee, tied up and at my mercy.

It will happen, Ms. Monroe. You just keep talking and see how far you can push me.

"I may be nineteen years older, but I promise, one night with me and you won't remember why you ever wasted your time on vanilla when there are far better flavors to try."

"Always so sure of yourself, huh?"

"It isn't merely confidence; it's a fact." I push my chair back and turn toward her. "Come here, little girl."

She doesn't hesitate, coming to stand right by my knees.

"Closer." My thighs spread to welcome her home.

When she glances at my obvious straining hard-on, her mouth curves. Devious woman.

My God, I want her. Want to possess her. Own her. Carve my name on her perfect skin. She's not fazed by me, and it only makes me want her that much more.

My finger hooks into the strap of her dress, and she flinches, grabbing my wrist.

"What the hell are you doing?" A flash of irritation settles in her brows.

Her touch sears into me—a brand I want poisoning my flesh, rotting through my bones, fused with her infectiousness.

I let out a wry laugh. "Inspecting my merchandise. Now drop your arms, malyshka."

Her jaw tenses, and the fact that she doesn't want to only makes me need it more.

My little temptress doesn't realize who I truly am, does she? But she will soon enough.

She does what I ordered, lowering her arms, and with my gaze locked on hers, I pull both straps down, exposing her perfect breasts, firm and more than a handful. Those pink pebbled nipples are like an invitation, daring me to come in for a taste, but that's not what this is.

If she wants to work at my club, she has to be comfortable doing just about anything and with anyone.

She glances away from me, chest rising and falling with sharp breaths she attempts to control.

"Look at me." My voice is gruff with arousal as I fight with everything in me not to take what I want.

Her eyes narrow when they lock with mine.

"We can stop right here if you wish, or…" I start to pull the dress past her chest, and her face strains.

"No. Do what you have to do."

I intend to.

"This is no place for a shy little thing like yourself."

My hand clenches the fabric of her dress, dragging it past her stomach and lowering until the first peek of her cunt appears. And my only regret is that she's not sitting on my face where I can taste it.

Her hands ball as I continue removing her dress.

"I'm not shy." But that crack in her tone betrays her.

"Don't lie to me, Ms. Monroe." I yank the dress past her thighs, my face lowering to her core and inhaling its scent as she steps out of the garment.

Her legs squeeze, and I pry them open while looking up at her, enjoying the torment on her face.

"If you have a problem with my hands on you, how will you ever handle anyone else's hands?"

The thought of anyone else touching her makes a surprising level of rage pummel through me. This is quite interesting, this possessiveness. Oddly enticing too. I'm going to enjoy this little game with her.

She grabs a fistful of my hair. "What now?"

"Now…"

I straighten, purposely letting my gaze slink down every bare curve, knowing how much she needs a proper fuck. It's basically written all over that tight face. Wonder if her cunt is just as tight and angry, like a little pussycat with sharp claws.

"You put on a show for me and let me be the judge."

"What?" She chokes on the word while I let out a bored sigh.

"The door is right there, Ms. Monroe. I'm not holding you prisoner. This job isn't for everyone."

Her fingers quiver, but only for a second, her mouth forming a thin line. "What kind of show?"

My lips wind up. *The kind I want burned into my memory long after I'm through with you.*

"Hop on my desk."

Her mouth trembles like she's about to say something, but like a good girl, she does what she's told. Climbing up, she clamps her legs shut, trying to hide from me.

Unfortunately, that won't work for either one of us.

Grabbing her knees, I slowly part them. "Spread your thighs, katyonak. Show me everything."

TESSA

His hands make me feel like my skin's on fire. Every touch sets me off, which enrages me more.

I shouldn't be turned on right now. This level of humiliation shouldn't get me off, but it does. I've clearly gone insane—or he did something to me—because I slowly let him pull my legs apart until a deep grunt escapes from his throat.

His dark eyes lock to mine, my pulse battering in my chest as he drops his attention to my core, practically licking and sucking me already. I wonder if that's what he'll do.

Would I let him? Do I even have a choice? Getting close to Konstantin Marinov is the only chance Nate has.

His large, masculine hands engulf my inner thighs, making every inch of me hot with lust. If I didn't want to stab him to death, I would've fucked him by now and enjoyed myself.

Instead, here I am, pretending to tolerate the thought of him, let alone the way he touches me. He can't know how much I truly hate him.

His gaze drags over me while his fingers trace lazy circles up and down my inner thighs.

They say he's a monster. A sadistic killer who feeds his enemies to pigs just for the thrill. But right now, he's just a man with a hard dick, and I can use that to my every advantage.

I roll my hips, tone dripping with lust. "So, what would you like me to do?"

He leans back, a teasing pull on his lips. Even while he's sitting, he towers over me. His frame is at least six-five, though I'm sure it's more. Fingers drift over his neatly trimmed goatee, eyes dark as sin, fixed on me with unsettling focus, as though he's trying to come up with the sickest thing he can make me do just to see how far I'll go.

But I'm ready. He has no idea the lengths I'll go to save my brother.

Slowly, he begins to unbutton his cuffs, dragging each sleeve up his forearms with deliberate ease, never taking his eyes off me. They roam over my skin like a touch, sparking goose bumps in their wake.

Every instinct screams at me to grab my clothes and bolt. But I'm frozen, held in place by the intensity of his gaze and the slow burn of his control.

As his sleeves roll up, ink is revealed—dark, brutal, beautiful. Thick veins of tattooed black snakes wind around his forearms, their jaws unhinged, fangs bared. They're coiled in barbed wire, vicious and alive, like they might slither right off his skin. There's no color. Only darkness, just like his soul.

I've never seen anything so dangerous. Or so mesmerizing.

"Touch yourself, malyshka. Show me how you do it when no one's there to watch."

Shit. I can't do this.

When he catches my hesitation, he scoffs and starts to rise from his seat. "I don't have time for childish games, Tessa. Sure, you're nice to look at, but I have more pressing things to deal with than sitting here waiting for you to decide whether you're actually cut out to work in a place like mine." He gestures toward the door, dismissive and cold. "Now, if you'll excuse me…"

No. I can't let this slip through my fingers.

"Give me another chance."

My blood pumps in my temples when the corner of his mouth lifts, full of dark satisfaction.

This bastard knows he's won.

"If you want to work for me, moya dorogaya, you have to be willing to do anything and everything. Are you willing?"

No.

"Yes."

"Then show me."

When he leans back in his chair, eyes fixed on me, I want to kill him.

But I can't. What a shame.

His gaze is relentless, hungry, and when his tongue drags across his lower lip, I nearly come undone.

I don't know how I'm supposed to do this. How I'm supposed to touch myself with him watching. How I'm supposed to imagine it's him inside me without hating myself for it. But that's exactly what I'm thinking, and I despise how much I want it.

My fingers drift lower before I can talk myself out of it. My body's tense, stiff with nerves, until his expression shifts.

His eyes darken, lids heavy with lust, and just like that, something clicks. That look—like he wants to devour me whole—is all it takes. It's the knowledge that I have power over him that gets me off.

I roll my clit in slow, deliberate circles, breath hitching as pleasure blooms in my gut. A moan slips past my lips when his hands land on my knees, spreading me wider until my legs press against the cold surface of his desk.

I rub faster. Deeper. Dip a finger inside with a breathless gasp.

He growls something in Russian—low, rough. "Add another finger and go slow."

I obey.

His tongue slides across his mouth, his fingertips digging into my thighs as his eyes follow every movement like a predator watching prey. Heat curls through me, sharp and dizzying, until my lashes flutter shut, overwhelmed by how badly I want to come for him.

"Don't you dare close your eyes and deny me this," he husks out, and my core squeezes at his dominating tone.

I try not to think about what he represents, the rage he brings out in me. Instead, I use that rage as fuel to the fire and I let it win.

I'm so close. My God, this feels too good. I can only imagine how rough he'd be. The way I'd fight it, the way he'd fight back.

"Fuck! I'm gonna come."

He growls, pushing my hand back, his finger replacing mine while my chest aches for its next breath.

He grazes my clit, dipping into my entrance only an inch, and I squeeze around him, causing another curse to slip from him.

"Not yet. You don't come until I tell you to."

Oh God. This is wrong. So wrong.

It's okay. You can go back to wanting to murder him tomorrow. It's been too long since you've had a man's attention. Use it.

He takes his finger into his mouth and sucks, and my need spirals when he groans while tasting me.

He reaches down to his ankle, and when his hand comes back up, it's holding a nine-millimeter, offering it to me like a gift.

"What do you want me to do with this?"

"Use it."

My eyes widen, adrenaline pumping through my veins.

"Don't worry, the safety is on. I wouldn't want you to blow up such a pretty cunt. Now, let's see how much of it you can fit."

Oh fuck, he's not joking.

My hand trembles a little as I reach for it. Not because I'm afraid of a gun—I've used plenty—but just from this insanity, this desire.

But I can't hesitate. He's this close to kicking me out of his office, and he's not the kind of man who'd willingly give me another chance.

Grabbing the gun, I grasp it tight, lowering it to my core and rolling the muzzle against my clit until the overwhelming sensation fills my entire body. My back arches, my eyes still on his as I work myself with it, so close I can taste it.

"Put it inside you. I want to watch your cunt stretch around my gun. I want to smell you every time I use it."

My head grows dizzy with insane lust, and I find myself doing just that. The cold metal inches inside me and I cry out in pleasure as I tighten around the hardness, imagining it's him.

His eyes turn molten, jaw strained so hard I'm afraid he'll crack a tooth. When my cries grow, when my wetness coats the metal and I sink it in and out, his finger grazes my clit until my back jumps off the desk.

"Need help?"

"Oh God, yes…"

I can't believe I just said that, but I'm desperate and dizzy. Right now, I don't care who he is or what he represents.

"No…" His wicked mouth lifts up. "You started, you finish."

Fuck. I hate him.

"Come on, now. Make a mess of my desk."

He pins my legs on opposite sides, and I work myself with his weapon, knowing he's probably killed over a hundred people with it. I should feel dirty at the thought, but that filth is what makes my body grow wanton, chasing the orgasm I'm craving.

My eyes fasten to his, that gaze of his dark and corrupting every inch of me. My self-hatred continues to grow for allowing this monster to do this to me, but I know deep down I like it.

When I cry out with my release, his face nears my pussy, like he's trying to smell and taste me. Like all he wants is to have me.

But I won't give him that. Not yet. I'll be the carrot dangling in front of his face until he can't resist. Until I'm the only one he wants.

That's when he'll let his guard down and let me into his world, and that's when I'll get what I want.

Konstantin Marinov is nothing but a toy I plan to play with until it breaks.

And I *will* break him, if it's the last thing I do.

THREE

KONSTANTIN

She's breathtaking, though that word alone does not even suit her.

This woman is something else, and I need to know her—every inch of her, until she doesn't know where she ends and I begin.

When she tries to get off my desk, I stop her, holding her legs apart. A blush creeps to her cheeks, which almost doesn't suit her. But then again, she's completely bare for me, a man she just met.

A little bit of shyness is good, though it wouldn't do well at my club. Nor for me.

Regardless, there's not a chance I can have her working for me, distracting me. Nor could I ever have her doing things with anyone else. I'd rip them apart with my teeth.

"Can I get dressed now?" She shifts, her breathing getting steadier.

"Not yet. I'm not done looking at you."

She huffs, her features twisting with a satisfactory level of annoyance. Doesn't she realize how excited her little temper makes me?

"Is this what you do with every woman you interview?" She angles her chin, just waiting to call me some derogatory name.

"You're the first."

A single brow arches. "And why the hell is that? What made me so *special*?" She says that last word in pure disgust.

"Well, you're not the kind of woman I normally hire." My fingers drift up her thigh, wanting to touch her, to taste that glistening pink cunt. "My normal girls, I already know from my other businesses, and usually my manager inspects them. But with you…" My mouth taunts her with a greedy smirk. "I had to do it myself."

"You're a sick bastard."

"You say that like it's a sin." My fingers take a slow swipe up her cunt, unable to resist it, and she lets out a small moan, making it harder not to continue. "But I'm not the one who fucked herself with my gun just to get a job."

Her eyes narrow, fists digging into the wood, but my laugh slips out anyway, stoking the flames I know are already rising in her.

Moya l'vitsa… *My lioness.*

"Get your damn hands off me."

She attempts to push my arms off her, but she has no chance. I could overpower her in a second. Even in her heels, she's probably only five-five, while I'm six-seven. And the fact that she's so much smaller only makes me more insatiable for her.

If she worked for me, I would barely be able to control myself or focus. All I'd do is wonder what she's doing and with whom.

Blyat. I can't hire her. I have no time for such distractions.

It's the one thing I promised myself. Attachments never end well, and if I sleep with her now, I will want to do it again and again. I can already see the effect she has on me; time spent with her will only make it worse.

I'm not naïve. I know what can happen to the heart if one's not careful, and I'm always careful.

Pushing off her, I get to my feet, giving her my back. "Get dressed and see yourself out. You won't be working for me."

"What?!" she snaps as I register her shuffling off my desk. "You made me go through all this just to deny me?"

Her tone grows even more irate, and that doesn't bring me much satisfaction now because in truth, I want to see her again, and I don't like feeling this way. My hand curls at my side just as she comes around to face me, unfortunately dressed now. My teeth rattle with the desire to tell her why I can't have her close.

"You're a real asshole, aren't you?" She shakes her head in contempt. "I'm sure Mira told you I need money to pay rent, and you just humiliate me, then toss me out? What kind of man does that?"

The kind who will never risk his heart. I remember what happened the last time I did.

"The kind who knows you don't belong in my world. I'm doing you a favor, Ms. Monroe. You'd be eaten alive. Then I'd be left cleaning up your mess, and I've got plenty of my own to take care of."

Reaching into my pocket, I take out my wallet and remove a stack of hundreds.

She stares at it, her eyes flashing with rage. "I'm not a prostitute, you fucker. Take your money and shove it up your ass."

I let out a laugh. "All I'm doing is helping you. This money isn't to pay you for such an exemplary performance, and I must thank you for that. It was definitely everything I hoped it would be."

Her slap comes out of nowhere, and a small smirk tips up one side of my face. In a flash, I'm on her, my large hand fastened around her small, delicate throat, pushing her up against the wall. I shake my head, unable to stop the way my pulse beats faster as her eyes grow with both arousal and anger.

"I will let this slide just once, Ms. Monroe, but try that again and

I will punish you until that perfect ass of yours is red and aching. Understand?"

She nears, her mouth curling into a tight, rage-filled smile. "Fuck off."

I grunt, my breath close enough to feel her lips hover just above mine. But I don't give in. I refuse to take it. Nothing good would come of it. I can feel it.

"You'll never see me again. Don't worry," she snaps.

"Don't be so sure." My knuckles draw up her cheek, and her lashes flutter as though she likes it.

Nu blyat, why can't she just hate it?

Zakrutila moyu golovu. *She's messing with my head.*

"I *am* sure. You're not someone I would ever want to work for."

The last thing I was thinking about was us working together.

Then again, she *would* be working for it…

When a grin curls on my face, she huffs, pushing against my chest with her small hands. I don't move at first, but with a harsh sigh, I back away, allowing her to slide out of my grasp.

Pity.

"I agree. Us working together would not serve either one of us. I am sorry this didn't work out, Ms. Monroe. If you find yourself in need of some money, you know where I am."

"I would never accept a dime from you."

"Suit yourself." I round my desk and settle into the chair, stuffing the money back. Opening my laptop, I refuse to look at her anymore before I keep her here permanently. "Please close the door on your way out." Pressing a few keys, I pretend to be occupied.

With a muttering curse, she storms out, leaving me there wishing I never met the enigmatic Tessa Monroe.

TESSA

My fists slam into the padded mitts Roger, my mixed martial arts coach, holds up as the sharp crack of impact slices through the air. My breath is harsh, my body coiled tight like a wire ready to snap.

I need to hit something. Hard.

"Again," I bite out, adjusting my stance.

Sweat drips down my back, my muscles burning, but it's nothing compared to the fire raging inside me.

Roger chuckles, shaking out his hands. "Jesus, Emilia, you trying to take my arms off?"

"Don't go easy on me. I'm in no mood."

He raises a brow, amusement flickering across his features. "You're never in a mood. You're a damn hurricane today. Should I be worried?"

"Just keep up," I growl, launching into another round of punches. *Left jab, right hook, duck, pivot.*

Every strike sends a jolt up my limbs, feeding my anger, grounding me in something real. Something other than *him.*

Konstantin.

The bastard played me. Made me think I had a shot at getting close. Let me humiliate myself on his desk. Let me believe for a second that I had power in that moment. Then he tossed me out like I was nothing.

No job. No way in. I'm fucked now.

I grit my teeth and throw a high kick, forcing Roger to step back.

I should've known better. Men like him…they take, they use, and when they're done, they discard.

But I'm not done. I need to find another way in.

"Alright, alright. Take it easy, killer." Roger shakes his head as he drops his hands. "I like my ribs intact."

"You done already?" I exhale sharply, rolling my shoulders and bouncing on my feet, knowing I could go for hours.

"Not a chance." He grins, but there's a flicker of something else in his expression. Concern. "You wanna talk about it?"

I grab my water bottle and take a long drink. "You're my coach, not my therapist. Now hit me."

"You're crazy, you know that?" He laughs, switching the mitts for the grappling gloves he left at the corner of the cage and slipping them on before he returns.

"Tell me something I don't know." As I throw another upper kick, my phone rings on the bench.

It could be the boss. He's probably worried Konstantin killed me or something. If he only knew the actual truth…

"Give me a sec," I tell Roger, getting out of the cage to grab my cell.

When I see the name flashing on the screen, I frown. A cold knot forms in my stomach as I swipe to answer.

"Reyes? What's up?"

His voice is tight. "Emilia, look, I hate calling you like this, but it's Nate."

The world narrows. My grip tightens around the phone.

"What happened?"

"He got jumped."

Fuck!

A breath rushes out of my lungs. "What?! You were supposed to be watching his back!"

"I know, but it happened fast. No one saw it coming, and you know he won't go to solitary."

My free hand squeezes the back of my neck. "How bad is it? When did it happen?"

"About thirty minutes ago. His face is badly bruised, but he's alright. You may wanna talk to him about solitary again, though. They'll continue coming for him."

A beat of silence rises between us.

"I've tried. He won't listen to me. He thinks he can handle it, but we both know he can't. Clearly."

Roger steps closer, his easygoing demeanor gone, replaced with sharp focus. "What's going on?"

He knows my brother well. They're good friends.

I'm already picking up my duffle bag, my pulse pounding in my ears.

"I'm coming now," I say into the phone. "You better make sure they let me in to see him, and don't tell him I'm coming."

The moment the call disconnects, I'm sprinting for the door.

"Emilia!" Roger calls after me. "What the hell is going on?"

But I don't answer him. I throw myself into the car, my hands tense around the wheel, squeezing so hard my knuckles turn white.

My brother needs me. I have to free him. I'm all he's got. And I'll do whatever it takes to make it happen.

Even if it means going back to the devil himself.

FOUR

TESSA/EMILIA

The fluorescent lights buzz softly overhead, casting a pale, sterile glow over the small windowless room. The air is thick with the sharp scent of antiseptic, mingling with something metallic.

My sneakers scuff against the tile as Officer Reyes leads me past a row of empty beds to the farthest one, where my brother lies motionless.

I inhale sharply. *God.*

Nate looks like someone took a bat to his face. His right eye is swollen shut, the skin around it an angry, mottled purple. His cheek is split, stitched haphazardly by whoever worked on him. There's a cut on his lip, dried blood at the corner of his mouth, and bruises blooming along his exposed arms, creeping beneath the pale blue blanket covering his torso. His breathing is shallow, but steady—the only sound in the otherwise silent room.

He doesn't see me at first. His good eye is barely open, gazing blankly at the ceiling, while his fingers twitch slightly where they rest on the blanket.

Reyes clears his throat as I move in closer, catching Nate's attention. His head jerks in our direction, and when he winces, my features twist with his pain.

As soon as he finds me standing there, his chest rises heavily.

"Shit," he mutters, voice hoarse. "Emilia—"

I should probably tell him to call me Tessa from now on. Then again, if he finds out what I've got planned, he'd shoot it down.

He sighs heavily, grimacing as the movement pulls at whatever pain is throbbing through his body. "You shouldn't be here."

"And you shouldn't look like someone used you for batting practice, but here we are."

"I'll give you two a few, but make it quick." Reyes steps out of the room, leaving us alone.

Nate's jaw clenches and he looks away, shifting against the pillow as if he can hide from me. As if I haven't seen every one of his wounds already.

"I'm fine."

I snort. "Yeah, you look great, Nate. Really thriving in here."

His fingers flex against the blanket, and for a moment, I see something flicker in his expression. Something like shame. It makes my throat tighten because I know my big brother. He hates this. Hates that I'm seeing him like this. That I'm seeing him weak.

He's always been my protector, my shield against the world. And now he's stuck behind bars and I'm the one trying to pull him back to his feet.

He doesn't meet my eyes when he speaks. "I told you not to come to the prison."

"And when have I ever listened?"

He's been refusing to see me the last few times, but I didn't give him a choice this time around.

I force my tone to stay light, but it's a struggle. Because beneath the thin veil of sarcasm I always wear like armor, there's a deep, gnawing fear that won't let go—that maybe, just maybe, I won't be able to set him free.

"You think I was just gonna sit around and wait for you to get the crap beaten out of you again? This is two times too many."

He exhales sharply, shaking his head. "Let the law handle this, Em. Don't do anything stupid."

I stiffen. "That's rich coming from you. The law's what got you here in the first place."

He finally looks at me, his one open eye sharp despite the pain weighing down his features. "You really think I won't get out of here?"

His words slice through me.

No…not without proof.

But I don't say that out loud. And it hurts. It physically hurts to see him here.

I swallow past the lump in my throat. "Of course you will, but I won't sit around and do nothing to help you."

Nate's a cop. A damn good cop. There's no way in hell he killed his partner, the man he trusted with his life for over five years, like the prosecutor wants everyone to believe.

But the evidence says otherwise. And now he's rotting in a prison cell, waiting for a trial that shouldn't even be happening.

"I know you," I say, softer now. "You would never do something like this. Never."

His gaze flickers, his throat bobbing as he swallows. "Then let me prove it the right way. Through the system."

I laugh, but it's hollow. Bitter. "The system's already failed you."

His eyes narrow slightly. "Emilia—"

"Have you met me?" I cut him off with a smirk. "Don't waste your breath."

His silence is answer enough. A muscle in his jaw tics, but he doesn't argue. Because we both know I won't back down. Not from this. Not from him. I owe him too much.

Being older, Nate was lucky enough to escape the hell we grew up in, running away at seventeen and making a life without me. I was only ten. There was nothing he could do to help me.

But when I turned fourteen, I called him, afraid that Mom's dealer was going to hurt me. He came over, beat the bastard half to death, and took me to live with him. He never hesitated. Never looked back.

And now it's my turn. I will get him out. No matter what it takes.

I sink onto the chair beside his bed. "I have a plan."

Nate exhales slowly, his expression unreadable. "Do I want to know?"

"Probably not."

His fingers twitch against the blanket again, and I see it: that glint of worry in his one good eye. He knows me. Knows what I'm capable of. What I'm willing to do.

He doesn't ask for details, but I see the protest on his face anyway. See the way his lips press into a thin line.

"This isn't your fight," he says.

My chest tightens. "Like hell it isn't."

He sighs, long and slow. "I don't need your heroics."

"Well, tough shit." A faint smile tugs at my lips. "You're getting them anyway."

His gaze holds mine for a long moment. And maybe it's the exhaustion or the pain or just the years we've spent holding each other up, but he finally nods.

It's slight. Barely there. But I see it: a small surrender.

"Don't get yourself killed, you hear me? And I swear, whatever plan you have, it better not involve the Marinovs."

What he doesn't know won't kill him…

I reach for his hand, squeezing lightly. He squeezes back, just as he did when we were kids, hiding in a locked bedroom while our mother raged on the other side of the door.

"I'll fix this, Nate," I whisper. "I swear."

His fingers tighten around mine, but he doesn't say what we're both thinking.

I'm in way over my head. I'm about to make a deal with the devil himself.

But Konstantin is my only way to save him.

The only problem is…I don't know who I'll be once it's over.

Or if I'll even make it out alive.

KONSTANTIN

Veronika drops the stack of applications onto my desk with a dramatic flourish, like she's just handed me something precious instead of a pile of paperwork I couldn't give less of a damn about.

"So, who was that girl leaving your office yesterday?" she asks, sinking into the chair across from me like she owns the place.

I don't look up from the file I'm skimming. "Someone who will never work for me."

She laughs, and my jaw twitches. I flick my gaze up, already irritated.

"What?" I snap, knowing whatever she's about to say will make me regret this conversation.

"Nothing." She throws her hands in the air, all mock innocence. "It's just…" Her lips press as she fights back a smirk.

"Veronika," I say slowly, voice edged with warning. "I don't have time for your nonsense. Say what you want to say, then leave."

"You're always so pleasant." She sighs dramatically, like dealing with me is an insufferable burden. "If you keep up with this moody attitude, you'll die alone."

I finally set the file down and level her with a stare. "That's the point."

Her eyes roll so hard, I half-expect her to tip out of the chair. She's worked for me long enough to know how far she can push before she steps into dangerous territory. It's been five years, and somehow she's still breathing. Impressive.

"It's all fun now, being single and fucking without commitment, but when you're pushing seventy, you're gonna want to cuddle up to a good woman."

I let out a stoic laugh. "You assume I'll be alive by then. Even sitting here right now is a miracle, wouldn't you say?"

She exhales, shaking her head like I'm some lost cause. "You're impossible. But that girl, whoever she was, the one Mira said you rejected… I saw the way you acted after she walked out of your office. You wanted her."

Of course she already knows all about the girl. She was just asking me to see what I'd say. I sometimes forget how cunning she is.

My fingers tighten around the pen in my hand. "Veronika, how about you stop talking before I fire you?"

"Please." She rises to her feet, flicking her blonde hair over her shoulder. "You're never going to fire me."

I arch a brow. "You underestimate me."

She winks, amusement dancing in her blue eyes. "Believe me, I never underestimate you. I just know you won't."

With that, she struts out of my office, closing the door behind her. I stare at it for a long moment, willing her words away.

But they don't go anywhere. Because she's right. Tessa has been on my mind since the moment she walked out of my office, and that pisses me off more than anything.

I lean back in my chair, exhaling slowly. This isn't like me. A woman gets under my skin, I fuck her, then she ceases to exist. That's the natural order of things.

But Tessa? She's lingering. Maybe it's because I haven't had my fill. Maybe after I take her, this madness will end.

I pick up my phone, scrolling until I find her social media profile. It's new, only a few months old. Strange. Most women her age have years' worth of pictures and overshared moments. But not her. Maybe she's like me and doesn't like to have her business splattered everywhere. Smart girl.

She hasn't posted anything new for a few days. A handful of pictures of her smiling—bright, warm, genuine.

That smile does something to me. Something unsettling, something I don't like.

My fingers hover over the screen. I could find her right now. See where she is. Who she's with or who she's screwing.

The thought makes something sharp and possessive coil in my chest.

I could break into her place. Take a look inside when she's not home. See how she lives. What she reads, what she drinks, what toys she uses to pleasure herself. Maybe I could wait until she gets home, then fuck her. Maybe then I'd get her out of my system and purge this fascination once and for all.

But that would be too easy. Too predictable.

If she really wants the job, if she's resilient enough, she'll come back. And when she does, I'll decide what to do with her and how to use her for my own satisfaction.

This isn't about love. Veronika doesn't know me if she thinks I'd ever seek it. I crave control. Discipline.

But love? Love is a weakness. Love gets you killed. My father taught me that lesson early, and I never forgot it. Love is nothing but a noose, and I have no intention of slipping it around my neck.

Yet as I sit here, my phone still open to her profile, I can't help but wonder.

What the hell is it about her that makes me want to ignore every rule I've ever set for myself?

FIVE

EMILIA

As I sit in the car, waiting for Konstantin to arrive, my fingers glide over my phone screen, scrolling through photos of him. Images he has no idea I've been taking. Men like him, men who see themselves as kings, never notice the little birds watching from the shadows. They're too busy basking in their own power, convinced they're untouchable.

But I've spent weeks tracking him, slipping into his world like a ghost. I know his routines. I know this bar is his preferred meeting spot for business—mostly illegal, though he's careful, hiding behind the legitimacy of his vast enterprise.

He shares his empire with his three brothers and cousins. I've been watching them too. Learning their habits. Mapping their weaknesses. When he isn't here, he's at his corporate job where he plays the CEO to his billions.

I should be working too, but work isn't an option right now. Not after my boss, Gerardo, forced me into taking time off.

"Take a step back before you ruin your career. Or worse, get yourself killed. You're too unstable right now."

Unstable. What a joke.

Yeah, my brother got arrested. And sure, maybe I've been on edge about that. Maybe I took *some* creative liberties at work. But every single one was justified.

The interrogation I pushed too far? It was because the prick had information about a child in danger. I nearly blew his head off. So what? He deserved it.

I do what needs to be done. I don't crumble under pressure.

But maybe he's right. Maybe I am unstable. Maybe I've always been. And if that's the case, there's no saving me now.

It's why I don't waste my time on relationships. Too much baggage. Too devoted to my job. Take your pick. Most men want a damsel—someone soft and fragile, someone they can protect.

I am neither. I don't need saving. From the moment my brother pulled me out of that hell, I swore I'd never be weak again. I'll have control. Or I'll die trying.

This business with Konstantin is no different. It has to go exactly as planned. He's probably already looked me up, but he'll find exactly what I want him to, thanks to my boss.

He knew I was going to do this anyway and wouldn't listen to reason, so he helped me instead. Took pity on me, maybe.

It helps that he's known me since I was five. One of the few who tried to get my mom clean.

He was a beat cop when he arrested her the first time and he put her into rehab, then took us in. He didn't have to. We were nobody to him. But he cared. And ever since, he's stuck around, maybe because he lost his own son when he was little.

Mom did get clean. But it didn't last. After she was arrested again when I was eleven, Gerardo tried to take me in, and his lieutenant shut it down. So I went into foster care, then back to her, but he never disappeared. He was always there for both Nate and me.

If not for him, my brother wouldn't have had the career he did, and neither would I. I owe him.

I also know he thinks this plan of mine will fail. But he still gave me a new identity and wiped my old one clean. If I was going to become Tessa, I needed to be her in every way.

Konstantin can't find out who I really am. If he does, I'm dead. He doesn't tolerate betrayal. I've got folders of evidence proving what happens to those who cross him. Women, men, it doesn't matter. You betray him, you end up on his hit list, and I need to stay off it.

At least until Nate is free. After that, Konstantin can do whatever the hell he wants to me.

I delete the photos of him from my phone. Not that it matters. They're backed up on a hard drive.

Minutes pass. Then I see him. He steps out of his black Royce, flanked by his guards.

Showtime.

Pushing the door open, I start toward him from across the street. The second his eyes land on me, his lips twitch, his fingers sliding his sunglasses off. When our gazes lock, I fight the reaction that slams through me.

Attraction is a deadly thing if you're not careful. And I'm nothing if not careful.

He watches me approach, a smirk curving his mouth like he's already won something. He always looks like that, like the world bends to his will and he's never had to chase a damn thing in his life.

I stop a few feet from him, keeping my expression blank. His eyes rake over me, slow and deliberate, like he's assessing every detail, filing it away. He slides his sunglasses into the pocket of his tailored coat.

"Didn't think I'd see you again, Ms. Monroe." His voice is

deep, smooth. Danger wrapped in velvet. "Guess I made quite the impression."

"Not the kind you wanna believe." I cross my arms, glancing at his men before turning my gaze back to him. One dark brow lifts, but he doesn't take his eyes off me as he gestures for his men to go inside.

They don't hesitate. A simple command, and they move like shadows, slipping through the bar's doors without a word.

Now it's just us, and my heart beats faster, as though he's got a hold of it, commanding it. And I hate that feeling of knowing he can control me, any part of me.

Konstantin spreads his arms slightly, like he's inviting me to take my best shot. "What can I do for you?"

"I want the job." There's zero hesitation, no sign of weakness, and I know he appreciates that.

His smirk deepens, and he exhales a quiet chuckle.

"You *want* the job?" he repeats, like I've just amused him more than he expected.

"I think I made myself clear."

His sharp gaze flicks over my face, lingering on my mouth before fastening with my eyes again. He takes a step closer, crowding my space.

"You're a bold thing, aren't you?" He picks up a piece of my loose hair, inspecting it in his large, dominating hand.

The thought of those hands all over my body invades my mind, like he's haunting me even while standing here. But I don't move. Don't let him see how affected I've become.

"If you want someone who's going to beg, you should look elsewhere."

He tugs my chin up, those eyes piercing into my very soul. He doesn't say anything for long, aching seconds, time bleeding until he finally does.

"I think you're the kind of woman who enjoys being forced to beg."

My core instantly tightens, my body growing warm and prickly. He chuckles like he knows exactly what he's doing to me.

The men I've slept with were boring, and there haven't been many. At twenty-six, my experience is pitiful. Way less than his, that's for sure.

He watches me for a long moment, like he's deciding how much fun he wants to have with this. Then he jerks his head toward the door.

"Come inside. We'll see if you're worth my time."

Bastard.

I step in as he holds the door for me, my heels clicking against the polished floor. I'm wearing another short dress, knowing how much he liked the last one.

The bar is mostly empty, just a few staff cleaning up before the evening rush. Konstantin doesn't stop there. He leads me straight to his large office, shutting the door behind us with a quiet click. Every inch of the room screams wealth and power: the black wood desk in the center, the plush sofas arranged like they belong in a penthouse suite, the bold artwork lining the walls. Everything here is curated and intentional. Like the man himself.

"Drink?" he offers, slipping off his coat and draping it over the chair at his desk before striding to the bar in the corner and reaching for a bottle of whiskey, the amber liquid gleaming under the low light.

I shake my head. "I don't drink."

Konstantin pauses, glass in hand, then tilts his head. "Why not?"

For a moment, I consider brushing off the question. But something about the way he's looking at me—curious, patient, like he actually wants the answer—makes me tell the truth.

"My mom was an addict. I don't want to be one."

A flicker of something crosses his face. Interest. Maybe even a hint of approval.

"You think one drink would do it?"

"I won't take the risk."

His brow arches slightly, his gaze remaining on me like he's peeling back layers, trying to see what's underneath. I hate how the attention makes my skin heat and my stomach tighten.

This attraction…it means nothing. Even if I end up in his bed, it won't mean a damn thing. It's just sex. And everyone needs that.

Konstantin smirks again, swirling the whiskey in his glass before bringing it to his lips. "Let's see if *you're* worth the risk."

He's talking about the job. But it sure as hell doesn't feel like it.

SIX

KONSTANTIN

The more I see her, the more I want her.

And that continues to be a problem.

She lowers herself onto the sofa beside me, keeping a safe distance. I almost laugh. She thinks she'll take off her clothes and fuck strangers every weekend, but she's afraid to sit next to me?

I slide closer, my leg brushing hers. When my fingers trace along her thigh, she inhales sharply, a subtle tremor rippling through her. Amused, I watch my hand nearly swallow her whole.

"You're so small," I mostly say to myself.

She scoffs. "No, I'm average. You're just a big guy. You'd probably break me."

A faint blush creeps up her face, like she didn't mean to say that out loud. My chuckle comes easily. With my other hand, I drag my knuckles down her soft cheek, and when her eyes meet mine, awareness overtakes me.

"Breaking you is something I've thought about on repeat since the moment I met you."

She sucks in a sharp breath, her nipples pebbling beneath that tiny red dress I want to rip into shreds and use to tie her to my bed.

There's so much I want to do to her. But if I let her work here and she touches anyone else, I'll get a little trigger-happy. That wouldn't be good for business.

Maybe I need a real test. To really see how much I can handle.

There's a knock on my door, and I already know from the sound that it's my personal assistant.

"Come in."

Tanya steps inside, holding a package. Her eyes flick to Tessa and widen slightly, her face flushing. "This just came for you, sir."

"Thanks."

She nods, sneaking another glance at me. Probably still hoping I'll see her as more than the help. That won't happen.

When the door clicks shut, Tessa lets out a dry laugh. "You fucked her."

Smirking, I hold her gaze. "Didn't realize I needed your approval over who I can fuck."

"You don't. But it seems to be part of your MO. Fucking your employees."

"You think you know me, don't you?"

"I do." She arches a brow, her tits practically begging for my hands.

"You'd be wrong, Ms. Monroe. I've never slept with her, and as far as you, we definitely haven't fucked. I'd remember that, believe me, and so would you." I slide my finger up the inside of her thigh, and goose bumps rise in my wake, like her body already knows who it belongs to. "That can change, though. Just say the word."

"I have no desire to fuck you. I just want a job." But there's something in her tone that makes me believe she's just lying to herself.

Whatever this is between us, she feels it too. She just prefers denial.

My touch glides up to where she's warm, wet, and tastes like heaven. But she won't give in easily. No, she wants to be chased. To fight it. Giving in would mean she's lost. I get it.

Good thing I'm an expert at games.

I pull out my phone and fire off a text, then slip it back into my pocket. If I can handle this, she can have the job. If not, we'll have to figure something else out, because one thing is certain: this woman is going to be a permanent fixture in my life, however I decide to have her.

"Do you have a boyfriend? Husband?"

Because they're already dead.

She tosses out a dry laugh. "If I did, why would I be here?"

I grin. "You'd be surprised at what kind of people work at my club."

She brushes a loose strand of hair from her face, and I have every urge to do it for her. Any excuse to touch her again.

My palm returns to her thigh as our eyes collide. The fire flickering between us flares brighter, and if I'm not careful, she'll be the one to burn me alive.

A sharp knock at the door has her turning toward the sound.

Right on time.

Veronika struts in, and as soon as she sees Tessa, she grins, giving me a knowing look.

I hate it when this woman is right. She gloats like the best of them.

"Boss. You rang?"

"This is Tessa. She wants to work at the club. I want you to interview her."

Veronika laughs, shutting the door as Tessa curiously looks between us.

This lioness doesn't realize the lion's den she's stepped into. But she'll learn. Quickly. Then we'll see if her bite is as sharp as she wants me to believe.

"An interview?" Tessa asks.

Veronika smirks. "Not the kind you're thinking."

I crack my knuckles, already hating this. "Get to it. I have a business meeting in an hour."

"You probably should've told her what to expect before I got here."

Tessa frowns, while irritation creeps up my spine. I don't want to do this, but I need to prove I can handle it. That her fucking someone else won't drive me to madness.

Because if it does, I'm in trouble.

I level her with a look. "Stand up."

Her eyes widen at my tone, but she submits, rising to her feet. Veronika stands on one side of her while I'm on the other.

"Take off your clothes, Tessa."

Her features tighten, but she doesn't hesitate. Fingers hooking into the straps, she drags them down. If I had my hand around her throat, I'd feel her pulse hammering.

My cock strains against my pants, desperate to feel her tight pink cunt around it.

This is a damn mistake. And I don't make mistakes.

Her dress drags down her body, and the more I see of her, the more my muscles fill with raging need.

When she's only in her black thong, I motion for her to lose that too.

Her brow curves. Eyes on me, she pushes it down, stepping out of it. Her in nothing but a pair of heels is the most beautiful sight. And far too dangerous.

Veronika steps forward, tilting Tessa's chin up, their eyes locking as she brushes her thumb across Tessa's mouth.

My blood boils at that touch alone. At the hunger gleaming in

Veronika's eyes.

"She's pretty. I can see why…" She lets the thought drift, knowing better than to finish it.

I drop onto the adjacent sofa, watching. A shiver ripples through Tessa, her gaze darting to me as Veronika's hand trails lower, down her sternum, slipping between her thighs with a single finger.

Na khuy. I won't be able to handle this. It's already too much.

Tessa moans—soft, breathy, her fiery gaze slamming onto mine like she's daring me to react.

I mutter a curse. I can't just sit here and do nothing. But I can't touch her. Can't throw Veronika out either. That's going to make me appear weak. I have to finish this.

"Sit," she tells Tessa, pushing her down on the sofa as she drops to her knees. "I've been wondering what your pussy tastes like since I walked in."

She pulls her leg up over her shoulder and spreads her open, a lazy fingertip feathering down Tessa's glistening core.

But Tessa doesn't look at her. She only continues to stare at *me*. She wants my attention. My hunger. My insatiable need. She thrives in it, and I can't seem to resist.

My muscles coil, indignation and lust warring inside me. No one else should be touching her, making her feel good. Only me.

She's mine!

When Veronika's mouth drops to that gorgeous cunt and she takes her first taste, I grip the edge of the sofa, practically tearing through the leather as I watch them together.

Everything inside me fractures, splinters into something feral, while on the outside, I'm still, composed, the perfect picture of control.

It should be *me* between her thighs. My mouth, my tongue, making her beg. Not anyone else. The thought of her giving that to someone else makes my vision blur. Makes me want to break something.

Or *someone.*

Tessa gasps, back arching like a damn offering as Veronika's tongue flicks and her fingers push deeper. Every sound she makes drives another nail into my restraint.

I can't fucking do this. Nu blyat, I'm losing it. What the hell is wrong with me?

I've watched women break before, but this? *She's* breaking *me.*

"Oh God, yes." Her voice comes out rough, her fingers buried in Veronika's hair, guiding her with slow, insistent pressure.

Tessa's lips wind, eyes glazed with lust, and aimed right at me.

She's provoking me. Taunting me. Playing with fire. And she knows it.

I will punish you for doing this to me. I'll make sure you never even think about anyone else's mouth but mine.

"I'm gonna come…" she whimpers, fingers clawing into the leather, body tensing like she's seconds from unraveling.

No. She won't.

"Stop. Now." The command rips from my throat, a guttural growl, raw and untamed, like something caged too long finally snapping its chain.

Veronika freezes, head turning slowly to glance at me over her shoulder, that smug little smile playing on her lips.

She knows. She fucking knows.

I was afraid of this. *Terrified* of it. If I can't stomach watching her fall apart for a woman, what the fuck would I do if it was a man?

I'd kill him. Right there. Without hesitation.

"Get. Out." The air in the room grows thick with the fury I can no longer contain.

Veronika rises, smooth and slow, like she's proud of the monster she just helped wake up. But I don't care. There's only one thought crashing through my mind now.

Tessa belongs to me. And I won't let anyone else touch her again.

Ever.

"Aye, aye, Captain," Veronika mutters with a grin, her eyes dropping to the bulge in my pants before she wipes her mouth with slow, smug satisfaction.

But I don't even see her anymore. My focus is locked on Tessa—panting, flushed, legs squeezed tight like she can shut me out after letting someone else between them.

Like hell she will.

The door clicks shut, and I move, forcing her legs apart, hands gripping her knees and spreading her open, baring that soaked cunt she tried to deny me. Her skin's flushed, lips parted, body still shaky from what she didn't get to finish. The glassy look in her eyes nearly undoes me.

"What are you gonna do to me?" she whispers, her chest rising like she can't pull in enough air.

A cruel smile crawls over my lips. "Whatever the fuck I want."

And she knows I mean it. Every depraved, filthy, unholy word.

I drop to my knees on the sofa, caging her in. One hand wraps around her throat, just enough for her to feel it, to wear the promise of who she belongs to. My other hand trails along the inside of her thigh, skimming just past where she aches the most.

"If we do this…" she roughs out. "You can't kiss me."

Rage snakes through my veins.

"That's a pity." I grab her ankle and lift it, dragging my mouth over the delicate bone before pressing a kiss to her skin. "May I kiss you here?"

My lips climb higher, up the silk of her thigh like a man scaling heaven just to defile it.

"Or here?" My mouth drops to the spot where her hip meets the top of her thigh.

She shivers, and I grin against her flesh.

She's already mine. She just hasn't accepted it yet.

"Or would you like it better if I kissed you here?" Roughly, I drag her to the edge of the sofa, locking eyes with her as I slide a finger into her.

Her body bows, craving more.

I'm dying for her. Want to bury my tongue inside her.

"Answer me. Tell me what you want."

Her fingers sink into my hair, pushing me between those thighs, her expression filled with depraved hunger. "Yes, yes, kiss me there."

With a growl, I bury my mouth between her legs.

Finally.

The taste of her hits me like violence. Sweet and sinful. Like she was made for this. Made for me. Her moan rips out sharp and raw, hips jolting, hands scrambling for something to hold as she claws into the leather.

"Oh God…"

"You like that?" My tongue flicks her clit, slow at first, then firmer, circling it while I watch her fall apart.

She nods, lips parted, panting, but that's not enough.

"Words, malyshka," I growl against her. "I want to hear it. Tell me how much you love my tongue inside you. Say it like you mean it."

Because now that I've tasted her, there's no going back.

I don't have to love her to keep her. But Tessa is mine. It's already been decided. There'll be no one else. Not for her. Not for me.

And if anyone tries to touch her? I'll tear them apart piece by piece and feed them every fucking bite.

"Shit, yes, okay. Yes, I love it…" she gasps, the confession punching through my chest like a bullet I'd gladly take again and again.

As her reward, I drag her clit into my mouth and devour her— sucking, teasing, flicking with just enough pressure before I slide my tongue into her tight, dripping hole. She tastes like sin and surrender. Like a drug I never wanted a taste of, but now that I've had it, I'm addicted.

"You like it better than her mouth?" Every wrecked word is coiled with frustration, with hunger. "Because you sure looked like you were enjoying it."

She writhes beneath me, panting, lost in it. "I was pretending it was you…"

Ona menya ubivayet. She's killing me.

Killing every last piece of logic I have left.

My jaw clenches so tight, it's a miracle I don't crack bone. This is madness. Full, unfiltered insanity, and I never want it to end.

I feed two fingers inside her, and she clamps around me like her body already accepts that I own it. My mouth stays on her, tongue flicking, tasting, possessing.

When she finally gives in to her pleasure, her body arches, spasming, crying out like she's being torn apart in the most beautiful way.

"That's it," I growl. "Squirt for me, katyonak. Like the perfect whore *I* made you."

The ferocity in her eyes only makes my cock throb harder, like she hates that she's letting me do this.

Good. Let her rage. Let her fight it. She'll still come for me.

I slam a third finger inside her, rougher now, and watch her unravel again—face flushed, lips parted, breath coming in shallow, panicked gasps. She tries to push me away, nails digging, desperate.

"I can't…"

"Yes, you can. You'll take every goddamn thing I give you and beg for more."

I thrust deeper, harder. The wet, obscene sound of her pussy echoes around us, and it only feeds the beast in me. The one that wants to ruin her, brand her, fucking keep her.

She's beautiful like this, at my every mercy, bending to my will.

Our eyes lock when she looks up at me, and it happens. Something breaks inside me.

Not rage. Not lust. Something worse. Something far too possessive and primal and dangerous.

She's not just a fuck. Not just a toy. This feels like more.

And I don't know what that means except one thing: I will never let her go.

As I drive into her this time, her walls tighten around me, her body quivering, falling apart in waves. I take it all in, savoring the sight of her submitting to her pleasure. A man could really get used to this.

But none of it solves the problem at hand. She needs a job. And there's no way in hell I'll let her work at the club.

Though I do have something else in mind…

When her body relaxes, I slip my fingers from her soaked cunt and push them into her mouth. She sucks them clean.

"Good girl. So obedient."

Her heavy-lidded eyes follow me as I stand, cracking my knuckles and releasing a slow breath.

"You may get dressed now."

I gather her clothes, handing them to her, and she rushes to slip on her panties, too eager to cover what I should've kept mine a little longer. Should've made her sit there, soaked and shivering, while I asked the questions that reveal a glimpse into who she is.

As she lifts her arms to slide the dress over her head, I catch something that causes my pulse to spike. Just a flicker beneath each arm, but it's undeniable.

My jaw tightens, but I don't say a word. Not yet.

Something in me stills, sharpening into a weapon. Because I know what I just saw. And there's only one reason marks like that show up in places people don't expect others to see.

Someone hurt her. Or she hurt herself.

And when I find out why or who…they won't touch her again. They won't touch *anything* again.

She doesn't know it yet, but whatever scars she's hiding…they belong to me now.

SEVEN

EMILIA

I can still feel his mouth on me.

Even as I sit here, catching my breath, adjusting the hem of my dress over my trembling thighs, the ghost of his tongue lingers. The warmth of his breath, the roughness of his fingers. Every part of me feels wrung out, but it isn't exhaustion. It's adrenaline. A high I never expected.

I liked it. More than I should have. And I liked knowing he was watching when Veronika touched me. Knowing it made him jealous, that it made him want me more.

I can use this. Use him.

That's all this is. All it's ever going to be.

Konstantin stands, adjusting his cuffs, the picture of control despite what just happened between us. He stalks toward the bar in the corner of his office, and as he turns his back to me, I finally take a moment to really look at him.

His shirt molds to his body, emphasizing broad shoulders and a powerful frame. The muscles in his back shift beneath the fabric as he pours himself a drink, every movement precise. Even from here, I can see the strength in his hands, the thick veins running through them.

He's built like a predator, coiled and ready, but for this moment, he's letting his guard down.

If he was anyone else, if he hadn't destroyed my brother's life, maybe I'd actually want him.

But I can't afford to think that way. Not when I know what kind of man he is. Konstantin Marinov will always be an enemy.

He turns around, glass in hand, his dark eyes locking on to me as if he can hear my thoughts. "I have a proposition for you."

A humorless laugh escapes me. "No, I won't sleep with you just because you're good with your mouth, even if you offer me the job."

His smirk is infuriating. "Fucking me? That's inevitable, malyshka. But no, that's not what I meant. I'm offering you a job."

Relief washes over me. "So I can work at the club?"

"Not exactly." He takes a slow sip of his drink, watching me over the rim. "I want you as my personal assistant."

I blink, sure I misheard. "Your *what*?"

"My secretary, whatever you want to call it. But you will be at my every beck and call." He steps closer, his presence suffocating in the best and worst way. "Anything I want. Anything I need. At whatever hour I need it."

Shit, that's not what I had in mind.

"Isn't that Tanya's job?"

His lips quirk as he approaches his desk and presses a button on his intercom. "Tanya, come in."

Within seconds, the door opens, and the short brunette steps in, her eyes bright and eager. "Yes, sir?"

Konstantin doesn't hesitate, doesn't even glance at me, before looking her directly in the face and saying, "You're fired."

Tanya's breath stutters, her eyes widening. "W-w-what?"

"Gather your things and go. You can collect your severance check from Veronika."

She stares at him, horror creeping into her features. "Did I…do something wrong?"

"No." His voice is as cold as the drink in his hand. "But I won't be needing you anymore."

The girl blinks rapidly, eyes glassy as she nods. "I-I understand."

She tries hard not to cry, tears gathering in her lower lashes before she walks out of the office with stiff, robotic steps.

I stare at him, mouth slightly open. "You're insane."

He shrugs, unbothered. "So, will you take the job?"

"You fired her just like that?" I'm still in shock. "She probably worked for you for years—"

"She was replaceable," he says simply, as if that explains everything. "I don't want someone replaceable, Tessa. I want you."

I swallow hard. "I…I don't…"

"I'd pay you well," he continues, as if I hadn't spoken. "More than you could ever imagine. But there are conditions."

Of course there are.

"You're mine. Understand?" His voice dips, becoming something darker, heavier.

His? What the hell does that mean?

As though he heard my question, he says, "You'll do what I say. When I say it. Exactly how I want it."

I should say no. I should stand up and walk out of this office and never look back.

But my brother's face flashes in my mind. Trapped. Helpless. Innocent.

He's gonna die in prison if I don't get him out, and I'm running out of options. Being this close to Konstantin gives me the best shot at finding what I need to save my brother.

Konstantin's dark eyes gleam with satisfaction. He knows he has me where he wants me. But I have him too; he just doesn't know it yet.

"Do we have a deal?" He waits for me to answer.

I force my chin up. "When do I start?"

"Tomorrow at eight a.m. sharp. I will send a car to pick you up."

Shit. I don't want this man anywhere near my place, even if the place I'm renting is a front for Tessa.

"No, thanks. I can get there myself."

I won't let him think he can make all the decisions.

His lips twitch in the faintest of smirks, as though he's expecting this. "No need to argue, Tessa. It's not up for discussion. You'll do as I say."

A laugh's trapped in my lungs. I'm not willing to let him push me around, but I feel the pressure of his words, like invisible chains around my wrists.

"Is that so?" I snap back. "I didn't realize you ran a dictatorship. I thought this was a job, not a prison sentence."

His smile is slow, deliberate, and almost predatory. "Obeying isn't hard. I expect you to follow orders without question. You'll find it's easier that way."

The command in his tone makes my teeth gnaw. He thinks he can control me. Thinks that just because he has power, I'll be a puppet. Maybe he's used to people bowing down to him, but I'm not like that.

"So, what? You want me to just jump into the back of your car like some trained dog?"

The silence between us thickens. He doesn't flinch. His gaze holds steady—cold and unyielding, like a stone wall.

"Yes." Amusement flanks his features, as if he's not only expecting this, but enjoying it.

That one word hangs in the air, and there's no mistaking the intent behind it. This isn't a request. It's an order.

I hate the way my pulse quickens at the thought of his control over me. And yet there's a part of me that almost wants to challenge him more, to keep pushing back. But I can't deny the way his presence fills the room, like a force of nature.

He's not just in charge here. He *is* the charge.

"Yes, sir," I spit out.

The smile that stretches across his face only enrages me further. It's not one of triumph. It's a look that says he knew how this was going to play out all along. That he already saw my answer written all over my face before I even said it.

"Very good." That timbre is smooth, almost soothing, like he's pleased with my compliance, and it drives me mad.

But I have no choice. This is what I have to do.

Even if it means making a deal with Satan.

KONSTANTIN

Her scent still clings to the air—sex and soft vanilla, something far too delicate for a place like this.

She doesn't belong in my world. But that doesn't matter. I'm keeping her anyway.

I lean back, watching her tug at the hem of her dress with nervous, fluttering fingers. A few minutes ago, all I could think about was the way her mouth shaped around those broken moans.

Now? Now, I can't stop thinking about the faint scars beneath her arms. Subtle, almost hidden. The kind most men wouldn't notice. Or wouldn't give a damn about.

But I noticed. And I care.

Once we're finished here, she's going to tell me exactly where they came from.

I pull out my phone and tap the screen, loading a contract template. No one works for me without one. Silently, I enter her name, then hand it to her. I don't need her ID; I already found her info.

Her brow twitches slightly as she scans the text. "Nondisclosure agreement. So I can't talk about anything with anyone?"

"Of course not, dorogaya." My mouth tilts. "That would make me a terrible businessman."

She lets out a dry laugh. "Fine."

Smart girl. Or maybe just reckless.

Her gaze drops back to the screen, until it suddenly snaps up. "Wait. This says my salary is one hundred thousand a month. That has to be a typo." She tries to hand the phone back to me. "Here, you can fix it."

I simply chuckle. "It's not a mistake."

"You're serious?"

"I'm always serious." My hand drops to her knee, fingers grazing her skin. I want her in my arms, in my bed, mine in every way. "I pay well. And in return, I expect loyalty without question."

She nods.

Ms. Monroe continues to impress me.

I could end it here. Let her walk out. Pretend this is just another transaction.

But I can't. She's already under my skin. Crawling through my veins like poison. And I won't rest until I have answers. Until I own every piece of her, even the ones she hides.

"Part of this arrangement requires your complete honesty," I say, even though it's a lie.

I don't care about my employees' pasts. Never have. Unless it concerns me or my business.

Her brows pinch slightly. "About what?"

"Everything." My hand drifts along the top of her leg, and I watch her skin twitch, goose bumps chasing my touch.

She straightens, trying to mask the shift in her breathing. "Alright. What do you want to know?"

I drag in a breath, steadying the violent hum in my chest. I don't want to scare her. But I *need* the truth. No one has a right to hurt something so perfect. I want to tear this world apart for her, but I can't show her that side of me. Not yet.

"Those marks," I say, not giving away the madness in me. "Under your arms. How did you get them?"

Her eyes drop to her lap, shoulders tightening. She's composed, but only on the surface. I can practically feel her lock up.

"I don't know how that's any of your business." She lifts her gaze to meet mine. Her voice is sharper now, but I catch the edge beneath it. The flash of shame and anger.

And it destroys me.

"If someone hurt one of my employees..." I growl, leaning forward until our faces are just inches apart. "It becomes *my* business, Tessa." My hand curls around her thigh. "*You* are my business."

She freezes, her breath stuttering for a single heartbeat. But it's enough. It's the proof I needed. She's not used to anyone protecting her. Not used to anyone giving a damn whether she bled or healed.

She's used to pain. Used to being discarded. Used to silence.

That ends now.

She doesn't know it yet, but I'll find out what those scars are. I'll drag the truth from her inch by inch, scream by scream if I have to.

And whoever left them? They won't walk again. Breathe again. I'll tear them apart, bone by bone, nerve by nerve, until they're nothing but a memory.

Because she's my property now. And I protect what's mine. With blood, with fire, with fucking war.

She turns her head, jaw clenched, like she's holding herself together with sheer force. Like if she breathes the wrong way, she'll break.

"All you have to do is give me a name. That's all it takes."

She lets out a laugh—sharp, bitter, and broken. It sounds like it clawed its way up from someplace dark.

"You'd be running through the whole damn state. There's a long list."

My body locks so tight I feel the crack in my bones. A long list. A whole fucking state's worth of people who think they could hurt her and walk away?

No.

I picture them. Each one. Cowards hiding behind silence, behind her pain. I wasn't there to stop them then, but now I will be.

I don't care if it takes years. If I have to peel her past apart piece by piece. The moment she gives me one name, just one, I'll rip through that list like a goddamn plague.

One by one, I'll wipe them from existence. Painfully. Slowly. With no one to hear their screams but me.

Because death is a gift. And I'm not in the business of giving mercy.

I take her hand in mine—small, warm, and fragile in my palm. The size difference alone makes something ugly churn in my chest. I want to shield her. Lock her away. Hide her from the world that's already taken too many pieces of her. I want to make it so no one ever touches her again without bleeding for it.

"Who did that to you?" The words scrape my throat raw and I fight to keep my voice softer, even as it goes against everything I am.

But for her? I'll bend. I'll break. I'll be whoever she needs me to be.

She doesn't answer immediately. Her eyes flick down to our joined hands, then back up to mine. Her chin lifts—stubborn, proud—but I see it. That flicker beneath the surface. Pain. Humiliation.

"No one," she says. "I did it to myself."

Time stops. And I freeze, my thoughts fractured into static.

She hurt herself? Why?!

My fingers twitch like they don't know whether to hold her tighter or tear the room apart.

She shrugs, like it's nothing. "It was a long time ago. I had a lot to process when I was young. And it didn't help that I was alone. At least until my brother saved me eventually."

A brother. So someone was there. But clearly he wasn't enough.

"Is he still around?" My composure is barely restrained.

"Yes. We're close."

"Good." My reply is short. Cold. But it barely covers what's happening under my skin.

I want to smash something. Destroy something. For the fact that I wasn't there. That someone broke her so deeply she turned on herself.

I force myself to inhale. Then I let the next words fall like a blade.

"You will never hurt yourself again." My eyes pin hers. "Do you understand me?"

Her brow lifts, surprised by the force in my tone. But I don't waver.

"If you're in pain…" I bring her hand to my lips and press a kiss to her knuckles like it's a vow etched in blood. "You come to me. I'll take it. All of it. I'll fucking rip it out of you if I have to and make it mine."

My hand finds her jaw, thumb grazing her bottom lip. I feel her breath stutter.

"Whatever you need, whatever it costs, I'll carry it. But you never turn that pain inward again. That's mine now. Do you hear me?"

She nods, barely.

"Okay," she whispers.

It's not just a word. It's a crack in her armor. A tiny, splintered opening in the walls she's spent her whole life hiding behind.

And something shifts. In her. In *me*.

"I know what it feels like to lose control, malyshka." My knuckles brush her cheek. "To need something, anything, to anchor you when the world won't stop spinning. I've been there. And I'll be your anchor. Just let me."

Our eyes collide, and what I see nearly knocks the air from my lungs.

It's me. Reflected in her. Same fire. Same buried rage. Same aching need for something real, even if neither of us knows what the hell to do with it.

I don't know what she's done to me. How she cracked every wall I've built. Why I want to wreck her and worship her in the same breath.

But I know this: I will protect her. And anyone who tries to take her from me will learn just how far I'm willing to go to keep her.

EIGHT

EMILIA

Margo, my therapist, jots down notes like she always does during our sessions, while my mind is still on the events from earlier today.

Konstantin's words continue to ring in my head. The way he looked at me like he has any idea what I've been through, like he's experienced the same shit.

But there's no way he knows. He can't. A man like Konstantin has never known what it means to truly suffer, because he's the one who makes everyone suffer instead.

I put him out of my mind, or I try to. I don't have the luxury of being distracted, not when my brother's life is on the line.

The most important thing is I got the job.

That's what matters. Not what happened between us. Not the way my skin still burns from his touch. Not the way he speaks like he owns every secret I've spent years hiding.

What matters is that now, I have access. To him. To his office. To everything he doesn't want anyone to see.

If he's the one who framed Nate, if he has the evidence tucked away somewhere, hiding behind encrypted files and private safes, I'll find it. I have to. Failure is not an option. It never has been.

Because Nate is rotting in a cell for something he didn't do. Because I owe him everything. And this is the only way I know how to repay him.

I didn't even suspect Konstantin at first. Not until my boss helped me dig into Tim, Nate's partner, and found the rot—trail after trail leading to payoffs, suspicious case closures, connections to the Russians, to other low-level crime syndicates. Then I learned from a source on the street that there were rumors that the cop was gonna talk to the feds and my brother's partner conveniently ends up dead.

But Konstantin isn't stupid. If he's keeping evidence, it'll be well hidden. I realize I may be grasping at straws and I may find nothing, but I have to try. If I can bring the prosecutor the evidence that Konstantin was the one who ordered a hit on Tim, then my brother can go free.

Luckily for me, I have an IT friend at the bureau who can hack just about anything. Riley started at the FBI around the same time I did. Brilliant, fast-thinking, and dangerously good at anything involving a keyboard. She's cracked data that's taken full task forces weeks to access.

And more importantly? She adores Nate. Always has. But he never saw her that way.

Once she knows what I'm doing, she'll help me. I know she will. She won't even blink before jumping in headfirst.

All I need is a sliver of data. A single file. One connection. And the rest will fall into place.

I just have to be careful. Konstantin may play the part of the seductive monster with ease, but I know better than to let my guard down. He's charming, yet lethal, and definitely not someone to underestimate. The man's always watching.

And if he even suspects why I'm really here? This game I'm playing won't just cost me my career. It'll cost me my life.

"So, about that dream…" Margo says gently, pulling me out of my spiral.

My eyes snap to hers, the calm behind her red-trimmed glasses anchoring me for a second. "Yeah, sorry. What about it?"

I definitely zoned out. Worse than usual.

"I was asking how long you've been having it again?"

I exhale, jaw tight. "A few weeks. It started up again right after Nate got arrested."

That dream. That fucking dream.

Except it's not. It's too vivid. Too sharp around the edges. It feels like a memory I should already know. Like it's right there, just behind a locked door I can't kick down.

"I keep seeing it. Same closet. Same gunshot. But the faces are always gone, like my brain won't let me see what I'm supposed to."

"You were young. That's normal," Margo reassures me.

"I know." I shake my head.

I had to be under seven. But Nate swears nothing like that happened. And my mom? She doesn't remember either. Then again, she was always high, so I doubt she would.

"Maybe it is just a dream," I add. "Maybe my mind's playing tricks on me."

But…something in me knows it happened. I felt it. That kind of fear? You don't invent that out of thin air.

"Have you recalled any more details?"

"No." My voice comes out flat. Defeated. "Same every time. I'm in the closet. Two men yelling. My mom's crying. One man gets shot. I can still hear the gunshot like it just happened—like it's happening right now in this room."

I press my fingers to my temples, squeezing hard.

Come on, come on. There has to be something.

Shutting my eyes, I force myself back into the scene. Back into the dark, into the cold floor under my knees. The closet door cracked open just enough for me to see Mom's bedroom. The shouting. The sound of someone begging. A flash. A bang.

And then…

Nothing.

No face. No eyes. Not even a goddamn jawline. Just that same hand reaching toward me. A man's large hand, maybe blood on the knuckles, maybe not. My child self reaches for him…then it's all gone.

Fuck!

"Somewhere inside me, I know I need to remember. I just don't know why."

That feeling, it gnaws at me. Like the memory alone could unravel everything.

Margo nods thoughtfully. "Emilia…I know you've been coming here for a while now, and I know we've hit walls with this memory. Traditional talk therapy can only go so far with certain kinds of trauma."

"So, what are you saying?"

"There are other strategies we can try. Have you ever considered hypnotherapy?"

"Like…hypnosis?"

"In a clinical setting, yes. With trauma-informed guidance. It's not like the movies. You're not unconscious, not out of control. You're relaxed. Your mind becomes more receptive, and sometimes, those buried pieces? They start to surface."

I sit there, chewing on the idea.

"Alternatively, you can explore EMDR, or somatic processing. Both have shown results in uncovering repressed memories, especially those tied to early trauma."

"What exactly is EMDR?" I fidget with the hem of my sleeve. "And somatic processing? I've heard the terms, but…"

She smiles, calm and reassuring. "EMDR stands for Eye Movement Desensitization and Reprocessing. It's a method where a therapist uses bilateral stimulation, usually guided eye movements or taps, to help the brain reprocess traumatic memories. It doesn't erase them, but it can reduce the emotional intensity. Sometimes it helps unlock pieces of those memories that got stuck."

"Okay…" I nod slowly. "And the other one?"

"Somatic processing is more body-based. It's focused on the idea that trauma doesn't just live in the mind; it lives in the body. So instead of just *talking* about what happened, it helps you tune into the physical sensations connected to those memories. Sometimes that's where the missing details are. Trapped in tension, posture, or how your body responds to certain triggers."

I absorb her words, trying to picture myself doing either of those things. Sitting still while my eyes follow a finger. Letting my body lead the way instead of my head.

It sounds…weird. But nothing else has worked, and if there's even a chance that one of these methods could help me remember what happened that night—who was in that house, who pulled that trigger—I should take it.

Because this dream isn't just a nightmare anymore. It's a key. I don't know to what, but I know it means something.

"Would it work?"

"There are no guarantees. But if this is something real, if your mind is trying to protect you from it, it might be the only way to find the missing pieces."

My fingers knot in my lap, the burden of it all bearing down. "I'll think about it."

"Well, let me give you a card for a friend who specializes in all of these things, and you can decide what to do with that."

"Alright." I take the card from her outstretched hand.

I'm not sure what's holding me back. Maybe it's fear. Or maybe my mind is protecting me for a reason.

Because whatever's buried there…it was never meant to be dug up.

NINE

EMILIA

The sun is already pushing through the slit in my curtains when I blink my eyes open. It spills across my face in soft gold, and for a second, I forget where I am.

But then I roll over and see the time: six thirty in the morning. In a little bit, I'll have to come face-to-face with Konstantin all over again.

This is gonna be a fun fucking day. I can feel it…

Groaning, I swing my legs over the side of the bed and pad toward the shower. The pipes in my tiny two-bedroom home creak to life as steam fills the bathroom. My muscles ache, not from sleep, but from everything else. From what Konstantin did to me. What *I* let him do.

I step into the hot spray, letting it scald my skin, hoping it will wash away the memories still clinging to my body. It doesn't. I stay under the water until the steam clouds the mirror and the heat seeps into my bones.

Eventually, I force myself out, toweling off quickly, then dry my hair before stepping into the hallway. That's when my phone pings and a message lights up the screen.

KONSTANTIN

My driver's waiting for you outside. Don't rush.

TESSA

He might be waiting a while.

KONSTANTIN

We both know you're worth waiting for.

I fight the smile as I toss the phone on the bed and take my time getting ready. His charm won't work on me. Not in this life, and not in the next. And I sure as hell am not about to let him think I'm scrambling for him. He may be my boss, but I'm in charge.

Grabbing my black pencil skirt and pale blue silk blouse, I slip into them before sliding into a pair of black pumps. The outfit's modest, but sharp, the kind of thing I wore working bureau cases.

Adding a touch of makeup, I dry my hair and curl the ends just a little before flipping my head over and running my fingers through the strands. With my purse in hand and my peacoat on, I finally step outside, the morning air slightly chilly.

The black sedan parked at the curb is definitely expensive. I think it's a Bentley of some kind, with windows tinted so dark I can't see a thing.

I lock my front door, slipping my keys back into my bag. Just as I turn to head down the steps for the car, the front door next to mine opens.

"Morning, Tessa," says Caleb, my sweet, kind-of-flirty neighbor.

He's probably in his early thirties, and if I was into the whole "bring him to meet your mom" vibes, I'd have already fucked him. But I don't have a mom who'd give a shit, and the kind of guys I'm normally into are definitely not what people would call sweet.

"Hey." God, I despise small talk, especially with people I'm deceiving.

He jogs across his lawn toward me.

Great…

"You're all dressed up." He grins. "Got a big day or something?"

I shrug, trying to stay casual. "New job."

His brows lift. "Congrats. You celebrating tonight? Maybe I can take you out. I know this really low-key place—"

The back door of the Bentley swings open so fast, it makes both of us jump.

Konstantin steps out, to my utter shock. Black suit. No tie. Shirt open at the throat. But it's his gaze I'm more concerned about. That lethal brutality in it, aimed at poor Caleb, like he might put a bullet between his eyes for simply existing.

This day is getting better by the second.

He stalks toward me, slow and sure. When he gets close, he leans in and presses a kiss to my cheek, but I can feel his anger coming out of him in waves.

Well, this is bad. Psycho Bratva kingpin is about to get real crazy.

"I didn't know you were here," I tell him, while his glare remains on my poor, innocent neighbor. I start to turn to Caleb, fumbling for something to say. "This is my b—"

"Boyfriend," Konstantin cuts in, smooth as silk, while his arm curls around my hips.

My eyes widen slightly at him, but his expression is filled with amusement, like he's daring me to fight him on it.

Caleb's smile drops. "Oh. Cool. Well, congrats on the new job."

He retreats fast, and Konstantin watches him with his nostrils flaring.

"Why did you just say that? You're insane," I mutter.

He sucks in a long breath before he turns to me, fingers gripping my jaw as his face drops closer. "You haven't even seen the tip of the iceberg."

I can feel the truth of his words, like they're living and breathing.

"So get in the car, Ms. Monroe…" His mouth lowers to the curve of my ear, palms tightly rounding my hips. "Before I show you exactly what I'm capable of."

Pretty sure I already know everything this man is capable of. Nothing would surprise me. He's a soulless monster while, to the world, he pretends he has an ounce of decency.

His fingers thread through mine, and a rush of warmth skates up my spine. I hate how good it feels to be held so protectively, especially by the likes of him. I grit my teeth against the comfort it brings, like my body is playing for the wrong team.

He leads me toward the car, opening the door in the back, and I slide in before he follows. Once we're both seated, the driver takes the car down the road.

I turn toward him. "So, are you gonna explain why in the hell you called yourself my boyfriend? Don't you realize how inappropriate that is?"

Konstantin reclines, spreading his knees, those dark irises roving down my body. "If anything, you should be thanking me."

I laugh. "And why's that?"

"Well, it seems as though I was saving you from what looked like a tragically boring relationship. And you're not the kind of girl who thrives on boredom, are you, Ms. Monroe?"

I glare. "That was still not appropriate. You're the furthest thing from my boyfriend."

He sighs, as though this conversation is beneath him. As he draws closer, his fingers trail up my thigh, slow and measured. "I think you seem to be forgetting one thing."

I quirk a brow in question, and his mouth tips up.

"You belong to me."

"As your assistant. Not your girlfriend."

His chuckle drips with darkness. The kind of sound that seduces and scars. He leans closer, mouth brushing my ear, the scent of him doing terrible things to my resolve.

"I love this skirt, by the way." His tone turns gruff. "But if you wear that blouse again, I might have to fuck you across my desk just to get it off."

My breath catches, thighs clenching on instinct. But the way he brushed past our conversation doesn't go unnoticed.

The bastard smirks again. "You're blushing, malyshka."

I force my voice steady. "I don't blush. But know one thing. I'm here to work. That's all."

He cups my chin, turning my face to his. "This is fun." His thumb swipes my lips. "Watching you pretend you don't want me."

My jaw tightens beneath his touch. Because he's not wrong. My body responds to him like it has never learned how to resist. No man has ever made me feel like this, like I'm losing control.

But that doesn't mean he gets to have all of me.

I have a mission. A brother to save. A truth to uncover.

And Konstantin? He's the villain in this story. The kind of man who burns everything he touches. The kind of man who doesn't just destroy lives; he plays with them first, and I won't be his next toy.

No matter how good he looks in that suit, no matter how badly I want to give in and let him ruin me, he'll never have the part of me that matters. Not my loyalty. Not my heart. And certainly not my trust.

If I end up in his bed, it won't be because I love him. It'll be because I chose it.

When it's over, he'll still be the same ruthless man. And I'll still be the woman who walked into hell for her brother and never let herself forget why.

KONSTANTIN

The Bentley glides to a stop in front of my building—a monolithic tower of glass and steel that reflects the city back at itself. Clean lines, black and silver. Cold to most, but to me, it's cathedral.

The doors unlock, and I don't wait for the driver. I round the car and open hers myself. She steps out slowly, her heels clicking against the concrete.

Her eyes trace up the building, lips parting like she's actually impressed. "You own this whole building?"

"Every floor, top to bottom. Even the café downstairs that sells overpriced croissants."

She lifts a sassy brow when she catches my smirk. "How humble of you."

Of course, she's not at all amused. Not that I expected her to be. It'll take more to crack that armor around her. But I have all the time in the world.

"Come, let me show you where you will be working."

I guide her through the lobby, my hand on her lower back. She tenses beneath my touch, but doesn't pull away, which naturally pleases me.

The elevator opens and we step inside. She doesn't speak, simply content staring ahead as we climb to the top floor. Though I don't miss the way her reflection watches me in the polished steel, and I would pay any money in the world just to know what she's thinking.

As soon as the door parts, the floor secretary greets us with a polite nod. "Good morning, sir."

We head left, down a long corridor that leads to the heart of my empire: my office. I let her in first, observing as her gaze sweeps across the room. It's massive, intentionally so. A symbol of power that I wield freely over those who need the reminder that I'm always in charge.

A black velvet sofa rests against one wall, while my desk dominates the center of the space—a massive slab of polished obsidian, clean and cold.

I lead her toward the glass-paneled door on the right that opens to the small office within mine.

"That's your workspace." My hand rests across the small of her back. "Close enough that I can see you at all times."

She lets out a snicker, but doesn't step out of my touch. I watch her look around her new space, her gaze swimming past the black desk, already installed with top-of-the-line tech.

"Everything you need is here. Your credentials are in the drawer."

My hand draws up and down her arm from behind as her breath hitches. Every muscle in my body tenses as this proximity, this need for her claws at me, ripping through skin and bone.

But I won't take her. That would be too easy. This game we're playing is a lot more exciting. For both of us.

"You're part of my world now, Ms. Monroe. Let's see how well you can handle it."

I register her audible exhales, the way her skin prickles the more I touch her.

I feel it too, katyonak.

"I'm sure it won't be that difficult." Her perfect mouth curves at the corner as she glances at me from over her shoulder.

I let out a harsh laugh, tipping her chin up between two fingers. "You like goading me, don't you, Tessa?"

Spinning her around, I push her up against her desk, winding her hair around my wrist. I let out a groan as I yank her head back, making her eyes glaze over.

"When we finally fuck, Ms. Monroe, I won't hold back."

Her chest rises and falls heavily, her lips parting in a harsh sigh. "You make it sound like I'd be easy. Like I'd let you have me."

"No…" I shake my head. "You're like a safe I'm going to enjoy cracking." My knuckles feather across her chin. "And when I do, you'll be on your knees begging me to give you what you have been long denied."

She swallows heavily, her eyes locked with mine, her throat bobbing.

"We're supposed to be professional." But her voice betrays her, filled with quiet desire, the same that's coursing through me.

"But that's not what you want, is it?" My body presses against hers, every inch of her melding with mine, and I know she can feel my straining erection against her stomach.

Her cheeks flush, her body needy as her gaze flickers between me and the floor. I could have her right now, legs spread, my cock buried so deep she forgets every other man who dared to touch her.

My mouth lowers to hers, a growl escaping from deep in my throat. Her hands grab my biceps, and my lips brush hers just as the intercom on my desk goes off.

Nu blyat.

"Sir, you have a meeting in fifteen with the new investors. Just wanted to remind you," the secretary we passed earlier says.

I practically grunt like an animal at the disruption.

The line goes dead, and the last thing I want to do is leave the comfort of this woman.

It's a strange thought, to feel some odd comfort in her arms. But unlike her, I don't live in fantasy or denial. I don't pretend what I feel means nothing.

Only weak men deny what's in front of them. Fear is not something I have, not like most people. I'm not afraid of whatever is happening between us. If anything, I'm intrigued. I never thought I'd ever experience such a…phenomenon.

After all these years of being unaffected, truly unaffected, I know this woman is different.

She's something more. Something important. A bigger part of my destiny. I just haven't figured out how.

And God help whoever tries to get in the way when I do.

Those eyes suck me in, the need in her body calling to me, but I can't miss the fucking meeting. Ms. Monroe will have to wait. For now.

It's a good thing we have all the time in the world.

Pulling back, I head for the doorway, glancing back at her. "Just so we're clear, I expect my coffee at my desk as soon as you get in."

"Let me guess. Black, no sugar, like your soul." That mouth curls like the feisty temptress she is.

I'm on her in a blink of an eye, fingers curled around her slender throat, pushing her almost flat on the desk.

"I should have you on your knees for that, forcing every inch of my cock into that mouth until you're gagging and clawing for air. But it's your first day…" I drop my mouth to her cheek and leave a gentle kiss there. "So I will excuse this insubordination."

She flusters as I back off, straightening her skirt, fingers running up to her neck where my hand just was.

If that's too much for her, I don't think she'll be ready for what I have in store. That only amuses me.

"Oh and as far as your duties, you'll go where I go. That includes this office, the bar, the club. Sometimes we'll have to travel. You're mine in every way."

Her eyes narrow. "Travel?"

"Mm. Business trips. Maybe a private island or two." I smirk. "We might even have to share a bed."

She rolls her eyes. "And here I was hoping for a luxury suite *without* a caveman in it."

I laugh—deep, genuine. She's sharp. Witty. Keeps me on edge in a way I shouldn't enjoy as much as I do.

I step closer, crowding her again—like I can't help being everywhere she is, like I need to touch her every chance I get. It's a sickness, this intensity, this lust…if one were even to call it that. But what else is there?

Reaching for a loose strand of hair, I inspect how soft it is, how perfect. "You don't like the idea of sharing a room with me?"

She lifts her chin. "Not at all, considering how difficult it is for you to keep your hands to yourself."

God, she has no idea how tempting she is when she's like this.

"Never know. You might actually like it."

"Doubtful," she scoffs.

I let out a wry laugh. Her witty tongue shouldn't turn me on, but it does. Everything she does hits like a shot of good vodka.

"I have to go. But if you need anything, you come to me." My knuckles caress down her cheek—so soft, I'm almost undeserving of it.

Almost.

When I step out of her proximity, she turns away from me, staring out of the floor-to-ceiling windows at the view of New York City beyond us.

I step behind her, palms across her hips as I look out with her, the city buzzing and unaware of the predators that lurk around every corner. "What do you see when you look out there?"

She shrugs. "People. Problems. Chaos."

"I see power." I lean in just enough that my breath stirs her hair. "Everyone plays a role, serves some sort of purpose. Some of them just don't know it yet."

She stiffens slightly. I like that. I like the way her body reacts before her mouth can catch up.

"And what role do I serve?"

I run a finger lightly over her shoulder, a feather of a touch. "We'll figure that out together, I promise. But I want you ready."

She turns to face me, her expression unreadable, but her body leans in, drawn toward me like a tide she can't fight.

"Ready for what?" she asks.

I reach up, fingers brushing a strand of hair behind her ear, letting my touch linger. "Anything."

Her eyes cling to mine with charged silence and thick with everything unsaid.

This thing between us…it hums beneath my skin, electric and alive. Whatever this is, it's not a spark. It's a fuse.

And we're seconds from detonation.

TEN

EMILIA

He walks out of my office and into his, getting ready for the meeting he's about to head into, which will give me the perfect opportunity to get to know my new surroundings. But I don't know how much time I actually have, considering I have no idea where this meeting will be or for how long. And if I had to bet, I'd say he's watching me through secret cameras installed all over his office.

I have to be smart. There's no way I can simply head for his desk and log in to his computer. There has to be a reason.

But nothing says I can't get comfortable in my new space. Walking toward his desk, I glance at the glossy desktop, a leather planner sitting neatly in the corner, but I pretend I'm simply looking out at the beautiful view of the city.

With my cell in hand, I tap out a message to Riley without looking like I'm doing anything out of the ordinary.

Window open. Storm may pass through. Will send weather updates when possible.

Translation: I got the job. I'm in. Will send info when I can. Seconds tick by before she responds.

Bring an umbrella.

I exhale slowly. If I can't save Nate, his life is over. He'll probably be killed in prison. The thought of him dying is like a razor blade to my heart. My brother is all I have left of the fucked-up family I was born into.

My eyes close, and I see Nate taking me for ice cream when he was like fifteen and I was around eight. Those days were the times when I forgot how awful my life was. When I actually had fun.

It would be another two years before I started cutting, when the pain of my existence became too much to bear.

I was one of those kids who enjoyed going to school because life at home was worse than anyone could imagine. When I was around ten, the men my mother brought home would try to touch me. Others hit me for fun, slapped me around when I said something they didn't like. But Nate was always there, defending me. He was the only normal I knew.

My mind races, replaying the day he saved me, when he nearly killed that man. If he hadn't stepped in, I might not have made it out alive.

AGE FOURTEEN

The cigarette burns low between Lloyd's fingers, the ash curling like a slow, deliberate threat. I feel his eyes on me as I move in the kitchen, him on the sofa while my mom is laid out on the floor. Drugged up, not dead.

I think...

"Get me a beer," he slurs, eyes glassy, that ugly grin spreading over his face like grease.

I nod, forming a barely there smile, my stomach twisting as I open the fridge and remove the cap before walking up to him.

When I try to hand him the beer, he grins at me, his dirty fingers lingering on the top of my hand. "Can't be this pretty and not expect me to look."

My heart beats faster.

Run. Just run and don't look back.

But where can I go? Nate has a life. He has a job. I can't make myself his responsibility.

As I inch away, my pulse thuds against the thin skin of my throat. When I try to take another step, his hand snatches my wrist and the beer falls on the floor, spilling across the carpet.

Crap. My head grows lightheaded when he gets to his feet.

"Now look at the mess you're gonna have to clean up."

"Uh, it's okay. You-you can sit. I'll clean it." I rush for the kitchen to get paper towels.

"Oh I know you will." He crowds my space, his fingers inching up my stomach as I'm backed into the counter.

His laugh is like acid on my skin. "Don't be so scared. Your mama likes it. You'll learn to like it too."

His hand reaches toward the hem of my tank top, fingers thick and cracked from whatever work he does when he's not trying to touch girls like me.

And something inside me snaps.

When I notice the glass ashtray on the counter, my hand moves without thinking. I grip it, swing it, and feel it connect. Hard.

The sound is sickening. Something wet and solid all at once.

"You little bitch!" Blood spills from the side of his head.

Not waiting a second longer, I bolt toward the door, sprinting out of the house as fast as I can. I don't wait to see if he's chasing me. I can't afford to.

The pounding of my heart drowns everything else as I push myself harder. Only when I'm on the city bus, twenty dollars from Mom's purse in my pocket, do I let myself slow down.

A small cry escapes when the bus pulls away, and I press my face against the cold window, trying not to sob. But by the time I reach Nate's apartment, the tears are already drying on my cheeks.

I bang on the door. Fist after fist after fist.

Please be home!

And when it finally opens, he takes one look at me and goes completely still, eyes filled with rage.

"What happened?"

"He tried to touch me. Mom's boy-boyfriend." I will my heart to stop beating so fast. "I hit him, then I ran here. I'm sorry!"

"Em." He grabs my shoulders and looks right at me. "I'm your big brother. I'm the one who's sorry. This ends today."

Relief washes over me, and I throw my arms around him, finally letting out all the suppressed emotions, crying against him as he holds me for I don't know how long.

When I'm calmer, he grabs his keys from the foyer and growls, "Get in the car."

I know where he plans to go and what he plans to do. I should try to stop him. But I don't want to. And once Nate's made up his mind, there's no stopping him anyway.

He drives fast. The kind of fast that makes the tires scream when he brakes in front of the house. He kicks the door open without a word, and we step inside.

Lloyd is still on the sofa holding a rag to his head when his eyes connect with Nate's, then mine. And for the first time since we met, there's real fear in his eyes.

"Go pack your shit. You're done here." Nate doesn't look at me as he says that, his attention on the man who tried to hurt me, and I know what's gonna happen as soon as I head for my room.

I don't watch the whole thing, but I hear it. The grunts. The smack of fists against bone. The begging. And when I finally come back out, a duffle over my shoulder, Nate's knuckles are split and bloody, his chest heaving.

Lloyd is on the floor next to Mom, his face bruised and unrecognizable.

"You're with me now. No one's gonna hurt you again." He takes the duffle from me and we head back into his car.

Maybe this hell is finally over. No more filthy hands reaching for me in the dark. No more needles in the cushions. No more Mom screwing random guys in the kitchen.

Just me and Nate.

After I got out of there, I thought I could forget that part of me, but that never happened. We can't outrun our past. Scars are lullabies for the broken, always singing the name of the person you tried to kill inside you.

My phone buzzes, ripping me out of the past. When I find Konstantin's name on the screen, I force myself to focus.

KONSTANTIN

Need you to log on to my computer. Use code Lev459821 to get in, then open the folder named Odessa Holdings that's on my desktop. There's a spreadsheet. Send me the account number at the top.

> **TESSA**
> On it.

The leather of his chair sighs beneath me as I sit. I tap the keyboard, and a password prompt appears. I type in the code, knowing exactly who Lev is just as the computer grants me access.

And just like that, I'm inside. I locate the folder he mentioned, open the spreadsheet, and send him the account number.

> **KONSTANTIN**
> I should be done here in thirty, then I'll need some additional spreadsheets prepared. Think you'll be able to handle that?

> **TESSA**
> I think I can handle anything, sir.

I add that last part on purpose, knowing how much he liked it when I did it last time. And him liking me is the goal here.

> **KONSTANTIN**
> Keep calling me sir and I will have to give you a promotion.

> **TESSA**
> Are you really that easy to please?

> **KONSTANTIN**
> You'll have to wait and see.

I laugh to myself. He'd lose his mind if he ever knew how easily I was able to deceive him. Konstantin is the kind of man who prides himself on having the upper hand, but it's men like him who fall the hardest.

Knowing I don't have much time before Konstantin gets suspicious about why I'm still on his computer, I click through a few folders, feigning normal activity. One folder catches my eye.

Consulting.

It sounds innocent, but nothing about this man ever is. Inside are subfolders labeled in all caps.

VULTURE.
CINDER.
THORNHILL.

I click on one. Access denied.
Then another. Same result.
A message flashes.

Access requires secure authentication.

My heart skips. I grab my phone and snap a few photos of the file tree and the lockout screen. Then I text Riley under the desk, hoping the boss doesn't see it on his cameras.

EMILIA

Just found something. Sending now. Tell me what I'm looking at.

It takes less than a minute before my phone buzzes.

RILEY

If I had to guess, it looks high-level military grade. Possibly custom-built, but I won't be sure unless I'm in.

I glance over my shoulder. The office is still quiet. No sign of Konstantin.

EMILIA

What do you need?

RILEY

There's a tool I can use to piggyback into his terminal so I can try to bypass this. Like a remote backdoor access. It's government-developed, so it won't trigger his security or show up in his logs. But you have to install it manually. From his computer.

Shit. This better be quick. If he catches me, it's goodbye Emilia.

EMILIA

Okay. Send me the link.

I get it in seconds.

RILEY

Type it into his browser. Once you open it, it'll run silently. You won't see anything on the screen. Just give it ten seconds, then shut the browser and erase everything. I'll handle the rest.

EMILIA

Got it.

RILEY

Text me when it's done.

I copy the link into Konstantin's browser, my nerves thundering. One unexpected return to the office, and I'm done for.

The screen stays blank. I count to ten, then close the tab and erase the history.

EMILIA

Done.

RILEY

I'm in.

I'll start unpacking what I can. But, Em, this may lead to nothing. I want you to prepare for that.

EMILIA

Just find what I need.

ELEVEN

KONSTANTIN

The boardroom is empty now.

The last investor left ten minutes ago, but I haven't moved. I'm still seated at the head of the table, elbows resting on the glass surface, eyes locked on the screen in front of me.

On her.

She's still sitting at my computer after I messaged her for the account number, a few minutes longer than necessary. I'm sure she decided to do a little sightseeing.

I don't blame her. I would've done the same thing. Curiosity is survival.

Or sometimes death. All depends on how many buttons one pushes before they find themself blown to bits.

For her sake, I hope it doesn't come to that. I think I'd miss her. She's sharp. Tough. Doesn't cower. And that makes her irresistible.

I'm not even sure if she'll make a good assistant yet. Not like

Tanya was. But I never once had the urge to press my body against Tanya's just to hear the way her breath caught.

That was actually a good thing. Now, I can't seem to think of doing anything else. Tessa makes me crave things I have no business craving. Makes me restless in a way I've never been.

That's exactly why she's here. I know it's a mistake to let her get under my skin the way she's managed to. But I'm curious now. And curiosity can get a man killed.

The smart thing would be to end this. But I don't want to. Not even a little.

And that's the real problem.

I push up from my seat and move down the corridor, my footsteps silent against the marble. Entering my office, I find her seated at her desk. She turns slightly at the sound of my approach, but she doesn't rise as our eyes connect, and something in me tightens.

"I'll be needing those spreadsheets now." I place the manila folder down on her desk, crowding her from behind. My hand brushes her shoulder, and she flinches.

"Meeting go well?" She flips the folder open, her tone dry like she doesn't actually care.

"Better than expected."

As I lean over, my mouth near her ear, the scent of her shampoo invades my senses—a sweet drug I never intended to get addicted to. Reaching around her, my hand covers hers as I guide the mouse across the screen to pull up the file she'll need. Her breath hitches, making a smile tug at my lips.

"Let me show you where the templates are."

"Okay." She clears her throat, every tiny hair on her arm rising the more my hand remains there.

"Once you finish…" My lips brush the shell of her ear. "…we'll have lunch."

Or preferably, you'll be my lunch, dinner, and dessert.

I can't seem to forget how good she tasted, how much I want that again.

"Lunch with the boss on my first day?" She quirks a brow from behind her shoulder. "Should I be honored or concerned?"

"Both." I offer her a small grain of truth. "I haven't decided yet." Straightening, I spin her chair until she's facing me, my fingers curling under her chin. "Depends how much more of that mouth you think I'm going to tolerate before I put it to better use."

Her eyes glint. "I'm sure I can handle anything you give me, Mr. Marinov."

My cock throbs. She doesn't know who she's playing with.

I grab a fistful of her hair and lean in, my mouth grazing hers. "Don't do that, Tessa. You have no idea how close you are to setting me off."

Her gaze flicks to my hard-on straining against my pants. "I have a pretty good idea."

I nearly lose all semblance of control, ready to take her bent over this desk. My jaw tightens as I mutter a Russian curse, tearing my hand away from her like it burned me.

"Spreadsheets. I expect them in an hour."

Then I walk out because if I don't, I'll remind her exactly who she's dealing with, and I won't be gentle.

EMILIA

The restaurant is quiet and opulent as the hostess leads us to a small table in the corner, the glow of candlelight spreading across the crisp white tablecloth. Konstantin pulls out my chair, eyes dark and unreadable, but the heat simmering beneath them coils between us, thick and electric.

He feels it too. And it's going to ruin us.

The table is set on a terrace overlooking a lush floral garden, the scent of jasmine and roses drifting in the air. A tiny waterfall ripples in the background as I settle into my seat, his palms stroking down my arms, and I shiver from his touch, my eyes closing for a beat as I let the warmth of his palms sink into my marrow.

"This is a nice place," I tell him as his fingers drift away and he takes his seat across from me.

"I'm glad you approve." His smirk could drop the panties off of any woman in the room. "I wouldn't want you to think I was cheap. It wouldn't bode well for my reputation."

Right. Except I already know his true reputation: a psycho in an Armani suit.

Before I can respond, a man in a chef's coat approaches with a bottle of wine. "Mr. Marinov. Good to see you."

Konstantin nods, gesturing to me. "This is Tessa, my new assistant."

His eyes line with mine, dark gaze lingering, like he meant to say something else.

But of course he didn't. I'm only his assistant. Nothing more.

The chef offers a polite greeting, describes the seven-course meal, and pours us each a glass of wine, before slipping out of view. I'm almost tempted to have a taste, but I won't. I'll never go down that hill. It's not worth it.

I lift my glass of ice water, taking a slow sip.

"Shame I don't drink. Seems like it's allowed on the job." A teasing grin flashes over my lips.

His laugh is low and warm, feathering over me like a ghost. "That's alright." His fingers graze mine from across the table. "You'll find there are other perks to working for me."

"Perk. Is that what we're calling it these days?"

His gaze pins me. "Life's too short not to enjoy it, Ms. Monroe."

He draws his hand back, eyes distant for a beat. "We're all a ticking time bomb, one way or another."

The air shifts. It's the way he says it, like he's already seen his own death.

I shouldn't care. But something unsettling takes root in my chest.

I start to wonder what his childhood was like. I know his mother died when he was very young and his father was a psychopath, but did his father ever love him? Did he feel an ounce of the affection I was never given as a child?

And why do I suddenly feel sad?

Fuck, Emilia. Stop it. Don't humanize him. Focus on the important things. Like keeping your identity intact so he doesn't chop you up into little pieces for his piggies to enjoy.

I wonder if I'll ever meet them. I bet they're cute.

A server approaches with the first course, interrupting my thoughts. When I pick up my fork and take a bite, Konstantin watches me intensely, like his life depends on it.

"It's really good."

He laughs, the sound like a mixture of whiskey and a slow-burning fire, warming me from the inside. "You sound surprised."

I shrug. "I'm a simple girl. I've never done fancy."

Because I couldn't afford a simple meal growing up, let alone one like this.

"If you'd prefer something less ornate, I can make that happen next time."

"Next time? You plan on taking me out for lunch on a regular basis?"

His mouth thins, but he doesn't answer me as he starts to eat. Watching him, I wonder what he wants from me exactly.

Is this just about sex? Probably.

According to everything I've found on him, he's never had a girlfriend. Not one. Which is strange, considering the women in his world wouldn't bat an eye at what he does for a living.

As we finish our first course, the second is brought out.

I won't lie, I could get used to this. When I pop a piece of tender steak into my mouth, I practically moan, and his features grow with satisfaction.

"I'm happy to see you enjoying yourself, Ms. Monroe."

As I'm about to respond, a woman's heels click against the stone terrace, blue eyes staring right at Konstantin, not trying to hide how much she likes him.

She's tall. Elegant. Blonde. Exactly the kind of woman I'd picture him with.

You don't stand a chance.

I don't want *a chance.*

Liar.

The diamonds on her wrist sparkle when they catch the light, her attention zeroed in on him. But he doesn't notice her. Not at first.

Not until he glances at me and catches the flicker in my gaze.

My throat tightens as his eyes remain on hers, and I start playing images of them together and I hate every damn second of it. I don't care who he's slept with or flirted with or whispered dirty things to in Russian.

I don't.

But when her eyes drop to his mouth for a beat too long, it feels like a knife twisting in my stomach, and I stab my fork into the next bite like it insulted me.

"Konstantin," she purrs, like he's her pet. "I thought that was you."

He sets his wineglass down with deliberate calm. "Nadia."

His jaw tenses, while I start to wonder who she is and how many times he's fucked her and where.

She doesn't spare me a glance, eyes devouring him instead. "It's been too long. We should catch up."

"I'm in the middle of a date," he says flatly.

That catches me off guard, my heart drumming faster.

"A…date?" She blinks, like the words don't compute.

He gestures toward me with an outstretched palm, giving her a look that could melt steel. "Yes. Meet my girlfriend, Tessa."

Girlfriend…

The word punches through me, and this sudden desire to be just that comes out of nowhere.

Her gaze cuts toward me, expression filled with thinly veiled disgust. "Oh."

"Hi there." I arch a single brow.

Nadia stiffens, her mouth snaking into what could be described as a smile…by some…before she flicks her attention to Konstantin.

"I see. Well…I won't keep you." She flings her hair over her shoulder.

"You already have." His words cut, and she stiffens, tension creeping through her.

She hikes up her chin. "I'll see you around."

"Doubtful," he replies without a shred of emotion. It almost feels like a threat.

She's visibly seething as she turns her back to us and starts away.

When she's gone, I set my fork down. "Was that your ex?"

His mouth thins. "Far from it."

It's none of your business.

"Well, either way, I really think you need to stop calling me your girlfriend. People will start to believe it."

His expression darkens as he leans in. "It's inevitable, Ms. Monroe. I'm just getting you used to the idea."

I let out a wry laugh. "Look, if this is about sex…" My voice drops so the other tables don't overhear. "Maybe we should just get it over with. That way you can be done with whatever interest you have in me."

"You think I just want to fuck you?" His lips curl as he leans in, close enough that every nerve in my body sparks to life. "Net, katyonak. Of course I want to see you on your knees—begging, crying because you can't take another orgasm."

His hand grips mine, thumb drawing circles on my skin with rough tenderness. "But that's not all this is. You're the kind of woman I want to savor, Tessa. Slowly. Thoroughly. Again and again. Until you ache for it. Until you can't breathe without it. Without *me*."

I swallow hard, wanting everything he just described.

He's dangerous. Arrogant. Criminal. Yet here I am being a whore for the enemy.

My lips wind into a smirk. "Bold of you to assume I'd be the one begging."

Amusement flickers beneath the hunger breeding within his gaze.

"Oh, you will. And when you do, you'll say my name like it's a prayer…or a curse. Either way, you'll mean every fucking syllable."

My pulse skips, hand gripping the glass a little too tight.

This is exactly what I wanted, right? To make him want me, crave me. Until I've infiltrated every facet of his life.

Except I wasn't supposed to feel this out of control of my own body.

"So, are you going to tell me who Nadia was?" I quickly change the subject, though the thought of that woman makes me want to punch something.

He sighs, like he'd rather talk about anything else. "We slept together. Once. Years ago. Her family runs in my circles, and she thought there'd be wedding bells, but I've never been one to desire marriage and I told her so."

I'm surprised he gave me all of that. A man like Konstantin doesn't strike me as the open-book kind of guy.

"So you never plan on getting married?"

He shakes his head. "There's no need."

"Me too."

His brow pops. "And why is that?"

I laugh. "I need a reason, but you don't?"

"Fair enough." The sides of his eyes crinkle with his genuine smile.

"I'm sure your bed's never empty, though. How many women are you sleeping with right now? One? Five?"

The image flashes through my mind: some faceless woman wrapped in his sheets, laughing at something he said, touching what I shouldn't care about. But I do.

He squeezes my hand. "Right now? I'm hoping it'll be you. No strings, of course. For either of us."

My core tightens and I reach for my water, the cool glass the only thing keeping me grounded. I shouldn't even be entertaining this. But it's been so long. And that mouth… God help me, the things it did to me.

"You feel it too." He drags his thumb over my knuckles. "Don't lie to me."

My throat dries. That voice could drag me straight to hell, and I'd beg him to take me deeper.

If he hadn't destroyed my brother's life, would I want him? Could I actually fall for someone who kills without blinking, who rules with fear and violence?

I don't want to know the answer. But deep down in the darkest, most broken parts of me…I think I could. And that makes me just as twisted.

"No." It's barely a whisper.

His smile is murky and knowing. "You lie."

He lifts my hand, brushing a kiss against my knuckles. My lashes flutter from the sensation, from the warmth of his breath.

"And I don't like liars."

"Maybe you're the one lying to yourself." My gaze holds his, daring him.

"I am," he says, low and raw. "But not about this."

His words swim with a husky baritone, dripping with meaning that I don't understand. What is he lying about?

"You want me," he goes on. "And I want you. That's a fact. Denying it doesn't make it any less true."

A part of me wants to run. His presence is overwhelming, suffocating in the most maddening way.

He doesn't just take up space. He owns it. And somehow, without touching me, he already owns this moment too.

"How long's it been?" His words are etched in unsatiable hunger.

"What?"

His mouth curves. "Since you were properly fucked."

Heat pulses straight to my core. My God, this isn't fair.

"That's none of your business." It comes out breathless instead of indignant, and I hate that.

"Ah…" His eyes narrow. "So never."

He's not wrong.

"Shame." He presses another kiss against my hand—soft, unhurried—and I feel it everywhere. "I could have you crying my name by dessert, if only you'd stop pretending you don't want it."

I stare at him over the rim of my glass, refusing to let him see how deep he's already gotten under my skin.

"Think about it," he adds, voice dipping to a gruff whisper.

My fingers tighten around the glass.

"Unless you're afraid you'll just keep coming back for more."

I meet his stare and force a smile that doesn't reach my eyes. "Don't flatter yourself, Mr. Marinov. You're not that unforgettable."

He laughs, completely unbothered. Like he already knows I'm lying.

The worst part is, deep down, I know if I let him have those parts of me I've never let anyone else see, I'll never want to walk away.

And there's no coming back from that.

TWELVE

EMILIA

The next morning, the car glides through the city streets while I'm tucked into the backseat beside Konstantin, every inch of his body a magnet to mine even as I try to pretend he's invisible.

Thank God Caleb wasn't out front when he came to pick me up. One run-in was more than enough. Hopefully after seeing the possessive beast that showed up at my door, he got the message loud and clear.

Konstantin sits close enough that his scent—wood, spice, leather— wraps around me, making it impossible to ignore him. I can feel his stare, heavy and greedy, burning into my skin.

But I refuse to look. The less attention I give him, the better. He likes the chase. He *lives* for it. And if he thinks I'm just another easy game, he'll be very disappointed.

"We have a very busy day ahead." A strong hand lands on my

thigh, like he doesn't need permission to touch me.

If he was anyone else, I'd have broken his hand by now.

When I glance over, I instantly regret it. His navy suit molds to his body like a second skin, stretching over hard biceps and a broad chest I have no business thinking about. One of those arms could easily pin me down while he…

I shift in my seat, crossing my legs and squeezing. He catches the movement, his eyes gleaming. God help me, it only makes me hotter, and all I feel now is the shame that comes after I get these thoughts about the last man I should ever want.

"I left a list on your desk last night," he goes on. "I expect it to be completed before the end of the day."

"Won't be a problem, sir." I let my mouth curve into a faint smile just to needle him.

His nostrils flare, and his gaze drops to my lips without even trying to hide it. I shift again, desperate to relieve the ache blooming low and deep in my core.

In the next second, his arm slides around my waist, dragging me further into him with startling force. I'm flush against his side, the heat of his body searing straight through my dress. His hand cups my jaw, thumb grazing the corner of my mouth.

"Does your rule about no kissing still stand, or will you finally let me taste you?" he murmurs, rough enough to sandpaper my willpower away.

I blink up at him, the memory of what I told him slicing through my haze of desperation.

No kissing. Kissing is too intimate. Too dangerous. Kissing is for people who mean something.

Konstantin means nothing.

"It stands," I whisper, but it sounds like a lie even to myself.

"Ty ubivayesh menya." He fists my hair with a growl, a low and primal sound rumbling straight through my limbs.

My thighs press tighter, but it's useless. I'm already burning for him.

I tell myself it's the lack of sex. The adrenaline. The deceit. But deep down, I know the truth.

It's him. Konstantin Marinov is a living, breathing addiction.

And the worst part? He knows it too.

The soft clack of keys fills the silence of Konstantin's office as I work through the latest task he texted me: compiling an updated list of hotel acquisitions and sending it to some offshore account managers for review. Easy enough…especially considering the span of his empire.

Casinos. Hotels. Investment portfolios sprawling across half the damn world. All tied together neatly under the pristine name Marinov Global Holdings.

If only people knew what kind of bloodstained hands held the reins. The monster beneath the suit. The one who smiles in one breath and stabs you through the heart with the next.

As I focus on the screen, movement outside the glass catches my eye. Three men pass by, walking in a tight formation like a pack of wolves.

And I know immediately who they are: Aleksei, Kirill, and Anton. Konstantin's brothers. They're unmistakable. Tall, sharp-eyed, all of them carrying the same dark, dangerous air Konstantin wears like a tailored suit.

Their eyes zero in on me, like they've found their next target. Aleksei's eyes narrow as he jerks his chin toward the door, signaling for his brothers to follow him.

They have no idea I know just as much about them as I do about their older brother.

Like the way Aleksei murdered a rival gang member only to get away with it.

Or the way Kirill tucks in his nine-year-old son, Lev, with the same hands he uses to murder a home full of people. The child whose mother left him when he was two after he was diagnosed with autism. But some people aren't meant to be parents. I know that well.

Anton, though? When you stare into his brown eyes long enough, it's like there's no soul within them. Like it's been drained out of him, or maybe he was born without one.

Maybe they all were.

All I know is, if they ever find out, any one of them wouldn't hesitate to put a bullet through my head.

As soon as they march inside, I'm ready for whatever questions they have coming my way. It's why they're here, I'd bet anything. They stop just short of the desk, and I offer them a polite smile even while my insides twist with vitriol.

The whole family is poison. Not one redeeming quality about them.

"Who are you?" Aleksei demands, his Russian accent thick with his contempt.

"Hi there." *Asshole*. "I'm the new personal assistant. And you are?" I tilt my head innocently, pretending I don't wanna run them through the meat grinder.

Kirill steps forward, the skull and rose tattoo that spills from the base of his neck to the side of his head flexing with the clench of his jaw. "Where's Tanya?"

I shrug lightly. "Mr. Marinov just hired me. You'd have to speak to him about that." I flash a fake smile. "I'm just following orders."

For a moment, none of them move. Aleksei's glare rakes over me, thick fingers sliding through his perfectly coiffed strands, but I don't dare flinch. It's what they want me to do.

Anton says nothing, though. He doesn't need to. His dead-eyed look tells me everything: he's already imagining a dozen ways to bury me if I ever slip up.

Aleksei steps closer to my desk, knuckles tapping once against the edge.

"You won't last long," he says, cool and detached.

I don't plan to. Just need enough time to do what I came to do.

"Thanks for stopping by." I throw on a sweet, syrupy expression, and his eyes turn violent.

It almost seems like he'll say something, but then they all turn and march out, their footsteps heavy against the marble floor.

I force myself to breathe normally, waiting until they're out of sight before leaning back in my chair. Hopefully I don't end up dead by sundown. I know exactly how cruel each one can be. How much blood stains their expensive shoes.

But it's all worth the risk. And when Nate walks out of that prison a free man, I'll disappear from Konstantin's world like a ghost.

Stick to the plan, Emilia.

And whatever you do…

Don't fall for the devil holding the keys to your brother's freedom.

KONSTANTIN

From my office, I watch the security feed on my laptop, arms crossed loosely over my chest as my brothers corner her like a pack of hunters sizing up prey. Tessa doesn't flinch.

I like that. Very much.

My eyes zero in on Aleksei as he leans in and stares like he's ready to skin her alive. But she doesn't let him get to her.

My mouth curves. A woman like her would belong perfectly in my world.

The fact that I'm making life plans where Ms. Monroe is concerned is very…unusual. But I'm not one to fight destiny. I let it take me where it's meant to go, and if she's where I belong, then I will welcome it.

The door opens without a knock, and I already know who it is. Aleksei strolls in first, followed by Kirill and Anton. They each take a seat around the conference table, and Aleksei's eyes narrow, like I'm hiding something.

"Kto ana?" *Who is she?*

"What do you mean?" I give him an indifferent stare. "Just a new girl I hired. Is that a problem?"

Kirill sneers. "So you fired Tanya for no reason? Without even saying a word to us? She's not just some girl. Don't give me that shit."

Of course there was a reason, but they don't need to know that. They'll think something's wrong, that I'm losing my touch. Because I'd never have done what I did, hired some girl I knew nothing about, just because I couldn't get her out of my mind. Even the thought makes me sound pathetic. And I'm far from it.

Leaning in, I glare at him. "I do not owe any of you an explanation. In case you've forgotten, *I* run this family." I slam a curled fist into my chest. "Me. Do not question my decisions again."

Aleksei's and Kirill's anger simmers in their irises. They hate to be reminded that I'm in charge of every aspect of our enterprise. I call the shots, and everyone else obeys. Anton simply stares, his dark eyes giving nothing away. But I know what he's thinking.

Are you investigating her? Is she a threat?

The rest of the world may not be able to read him, but we can.

Rising up, I head for the bar on the far side of the room, pouring myself a drink before returning to my seat.

"She's someone who caught my attention." I meet their gazes one by one as I take a long sip of my vodka. "And when something catches my attention, I keep it close until I decide what to do with it."

Aleksei raises a brow. "That's a dangerous game, brother."

I smile—an easy, lethal curve of my mouth.

"When have you ever known me to play it safe?" I take another drag of my drink. "And speaking of danger, are you still following that prosecutor? What's her name again?"

"Fiona." Kirill chuckles darkly under his breath, leaning back against the chair.

"Ah, yes, the lovely Fiona. How is she?" Of course I know her name. We all do. "Is she still trying to put you in prison, or has she moved on to murder?"

Aleksei's anger radiates from every pound of flesh.

"What do you plan to do with her?" I ask. "Continue to stalk her? That isn't polite, brother. Maybe invite her to dinner. So she can properly meet the family."

His laugh escapes like a threat, a smug look on his face. "I know her every move before she does. And when I finally play my cards, she's not going to see it. Because that woman…" He cracks his neck with a faraway look as though he's picturing her. "She will get what's coming to her. I'll make her pay for it with blood."

"You sound like you have a crush." Kirill laughs with a cold stare.

"She's the last woman I would ever touch." Alexsei's jaw clenches like he's ready to rip Kirill's head off…and I just had this office cleaned.

"Kogo ty obmanyvayesh?" he scoffs. *Who are you kidding?*

"Enough of that. Love will wait. We have business to discuss." My tone sharpens.

"I don't love—"

I cut him off with a single stare. He groans, but shuts up. Because they know exactly why I called them all here.

"Do we have a plan to take out the DeLuca crew yet?" My vision darts between them.

A beat of silence follows. We all want them gone. Erased, like they were never here to begin with. They shouldn't even be as big of a problem as they have been in the past few months. They're only a small-time New Jersey operation, and we were getting along just fine until they pissed it all away.

Encroaching into territories they have no business touching. Unprovoked attacks on Marinov-aligned businesses that I know they're connected to. Missing shipments. Whispers of alliances being formed with our other enemies.

Kirill's mouth tightens. "We're working on it."

"Work faster. I want it done soon, and I want them to know it was us." I roll the words slowly over my tongue.

Anton speaks for the first time, voice low and flat. "It will be done."

The mere fact that the DeLuca crew is still breathing down our necks like they think they have a shot? Unacceptable. But this also has to be done right, and I know my brothers will get it done.

"They're like weeds." I adjust my cuffs. "Cut them once, they grow back uglier. You want to kill the root, not the leaves."

Aleksei's mouth tips up into a cold grin. "You want us to dig deeper?"

"Yes." I lean back, threading my fingers loosely. "I want to know exactly who they've been talking to. Who's bankrolling them. Who's got delusions of grandeur."

Because someone does. And if it ties back to anyone bigger, anyone stupid enough to think they can challenge us? Well…they'll be dealt with the same way we deal with everything else.

Ruthlessly. Efficiently. Without mercy.

Anton gives a short nod, rising to his feet while Aleksei pushes off his chair, already pulling out his phone to start making calls.

Kirill lingers a second longer, his eyes flicking toward the door before they zero in on me.

"She's pretty," he says almost idly. "Let's hope she's not as fragile as she looks."

"She's stronger than you think." I lean forward, zeroing my attention on him. "And if any one of you touches a hair on her head, I promise you won't live to regret it."

Kirill's mouth curves into something dark. "Ostorozhno, brother. It almost sounds as though you like her."

He strides out after the others before I can get a word in.

But that's not what this is. I don't just *like* her. I'm infatuated, and that is quite the predicament.

When the door clicks shut behind them, I turn back toward the monitor showing the live feed of my office. Tessa's still there at my computer, completely unaware of the danger she's in, what my brothers are truly capable of.

But if they touch her, it'll be the last thing they ever do.

THIRTEEN

EMILIA

"**W**hy the hell have you not been at work?" my friend Fiona snaps through the phone before I can even say hello. "First you rent a new place, now this? What's going on?"

I sink into my couch, letting the cushions swallow me. Every muscle in my body aches. Konstantin had me running nonstop today, like his personal schedule was a war campaign and I was his foot soldier. I sure as hell could've done without the heels.

"Emilia!" Fiona's voice cuts through my haze. "Are you even listening to me?"

Shit.

I press a palm to my forehead, trying to come up with a response that doesn't include, *I'm working sort of undercover for the Bratva boss whose brother you tried to put in prison.*

That would go over *so* well. If I had a choice, I wouldn't have even told her about my new place, but that would be impossible to keep from her.

"The boss told me I needed some time to cool off. You know how rough it's been after what happened with Nate." The lie tastes sour on my tongue.

The silence on the other end says everything. She knows me too well. Knows when I'm hiding something. And Fiona's the last person I want digging too deep.

Before I can change the subject, a knock rattles my front door.

"Hold on. Someone's at the door."

"It's me. Open up."

My stomach dips. Of course it is.

I hang up and drag myself to the door, already bracing for the lecture I know is coming. Fiona doesn't let things go. Especially when it involves me doing something reckless. But she should be kinda used to it by now. She's known all the shit I'm capable of since college.

But I can't let her try to stop me like when we were younger. I've already gone too far. I *have* to finish what I started, no matter the cost.

The knock has barely faded when I open the door, and there she is: Fiona Clark, all fire and fury and ready for war. It's no wonder defense attorneys hate her. She has a reputation of being a hard-ass in the courtroom, and out of it too.

Her green eyes narrow the second she sees me, arms crossed over her chest, long brown hair cascading over her shoulders like a weapon.

"Gonna invite me in." She doesn't even bother making it a question.

I step aside, and she walks in like she owns the place, heels clicking with every step, her entire body radiating with suspicion. She heads straight for the leather couch, but doesn't sit down. The silence stretches, heavy and expectant.

"Tell me what's going on," she finally says. "And don't lie to me,

Em. If it was just time off, you would've said something days ago."

She's right. I tell her everything. Or I used to.

I force a dry laugh. "It's nothing, really. Gerardo just thought I needed a break. Said I was being too reckless lately. Nate's case has been eating at me." I flash her a small smile. "Not that we can talk about it, since you're technically the enemy."

She doesn't even crack a smirk.

"Don't do that." She finally sits. "Don't deflect. We may not be able to talk about the case, but I'm still your friend. And I know you, Em. You wouldn't be okay with the time off. Not unless you were doing something with it. Something risky."

Her eyes bore into me, seeing too much. I hesitate as I lower to the loveseat opposite from her. Lying won't work. Not with her. She'll dig until she finds the truth.

Fiona isn't just a prosecutor. She's a bloodhound when something smells wrong.

"I'm undercover… Sort of…"

Her eyes flare. "What the hell does *that* mean?"

I lift a shoulder. "It's not officially sanctioned."

She leans forward. "So that means what, exactly?"

"It means I'm doing what no one else will. I'm getting close to someone I think can clear Nate's name. Someone who may be tied to the murder."

Fiona goes still, ice in her eyes. "Who?"

I hold her gaze. "You know who. Konstantin Marinov."

Silence detonates between us, heavy and crushing.

Her mouth parts, then clamps shut again. "You're joking."

I don't say anything. I just hold her gaze.

"You're pulling one on me because of how pissed I've been about losing Aleksei's trial, right?" She laughs, but it's hollow. "No, but seriously, what are you doing?"

"I told you the truth. Konstantin's most likely involved in what happened to Nate. And I'm going to prove it."

She shoots to her feet like she's been slapped, pacing in front of the couch, her heels snapping against the hardwood.

"Are you insane?" She pushes her hair behind her shoulder. "Emilia, please. Don't do this. Find another way. Anything but that!"

"If there was another way, do you honestly think I wouldn't have taken it by now?" I say sharply, cutting through her panic. "If you've got something better, Fiona, by all means, let's hear it."

Her mouth opens, then shuts again. She runs a hand down her face before collapsing back onto the couch like her body suddenly can't hold her up. Because she knows. There isn't another way.

Getting up, I sit beside her, my fingers curling gently around hers. "I know what I'm doing."

"No, you don't," she whispers, and it hits harder than a scream. "If you did, you wouldn't be using yourself as bait in a fucking shark tank. These aren't just criminals, Em. They're brutal. They don't feel the way we do. They'll gut you without blinking."

"I'm doing what needs to be done." The words slip out quieter. "You know that better than anyone. You fight like hell to put away the guilty and protect the innocent. That's all I'm doing. I'm trying to save my brother."

Her stare turns intense, a war behind her eyes. Pain. Fury. Something helpless and hollow.

Finally, she exhales and leans back. "You're not going to stop no matter what I say, are you?"

A small smile tugs at my mouth. "Of course not. And FYI, I'm Tessa now."

She glares. "God, Tessa, you're just as stubborn as Emilia."

"Takes one to know one."

Her lips twitch, but it fades fast. "Fine. But promise me one thing."

"Don't die?"

She sighs. "Fine, two things. Promise me you won't sleep with

Konstantin or any of them."

"What?" I scoff. "Are you crazy? Of course I wouldn't sleep with him. Why would you even think that?"

Okay, maybe he went down on me. But that's not the same thing.

Fiona crosses her arms, glaring at me with a gaze that could pierce through steel. "Because even though I hate them, I have eyes, and those Marinovs are nice to look at. But they're the definition of toxic. And Konstantin is the worst of them. Don't let him crawl under your skin."

"Don't worry. That won't be a problem."

What a liar…

I deflect, fast. "Speaking of problems, are you still seeing Aleksei everywhere you go?"

The shift in her body is subtle, but telling. "Unfortunately. I mean, it's not everywhere, but it's enough. I even had to be careful coming here, make sure he wasn't following me."

I raise a brow, the realization settling in. If Aleksei makes any connection between her and me…well, that would be a serious problem.

"I know what he's trying to do," she adds. "Scare me. But I don't scare easily. It's just annoying now. I go out with coworkers, and he's already there. I stop for coffee, and he's in line ahead of me. I turn my phone off every time I leave the office. I sweep for trackers. Nothing. But still, it's like he just *knows.*"

I hate the way that makes my stomach twist. If that jerkoff does anything to Fiona, not even Konstantin will be able to save him.

"You need to be careful. Seriously. I'll keep an eye out too."

"No," she says quickly. "You handle *your* psychopath. I'll handle mine." She settles beside me and grabs my hand again, her grip tighter now. "But promise me, Em. Don't let your guard down. Not even for a second."

"Don't worry. That'll never happen."

The sun filters through the tall windows of Konstantin's office, casting golden lines across the polished floors.

I sit behind my desk, chewing slowly through a Caesar salad I barely taste. My fingers tap lightly against the wood as I skim over a list of scheduled meetings, trying to look busy while my brain whirs with a thousand thoughts. Mostly about Konstantin. About last night with Fiona and how worried she is.

All I need is a little more time for Riley to do her magic. And if she finds nothing, I'll have to find something else of his for her to hack.

He has to be connected to Tim's murder. It all makes sense.

My phone buzzes against the desk, cutting through the silence. I glance down and find Gerardo's number there, and my pulse kicks up. He wouldn't be calling unless it was necessary.

God, I hope it's not something with Nate.

I know he's doing what he can for my brother. He's always been one of the few people I can depend on, the closest thing to a father either of us ever had.

"Hey." I try to keep my voice low in case Konstantin has listening devices around the office.

"Hey, kid. Can you talk?"

I glance toward the office door. "Yep, but I only have a few minutes because I'm working."

"Got it. But you're alone, right?"

"Yep."

"Alright, listen. There's something you should know. There's been talk that the DeLuca crew's making moves against the Marinovs. A war is coming, and I need you to be careful, got it?"

"Yeah. I'm good."

"In and out, you hear? I won't be able to protect you if there's a fallout. You understand, right?"

"I know." I can't say more, and he knows that.

He releases a sigh. "I don't want anything to happen to you, and I already regret this."

"Too late for that." I laugh.

"Mm-hmm. Just watch your back. I know you're loyal to your brother. But don't get too close. These men, especially Konstantin, they have a way of pulling people in until they can't escape."

"Don't worry so much. It's not good for your heart."

He snickers. "Yeah, yeah. You sound like my wife."

"Well, maybe try listening to her for once."

"I'm getting off now." He's silent for a beat too long. "If you need anything, anything at all…"

"I know. Thank you."

"You bet. Nate is like a son to me. And you? You've always been my daughter."

I clear my throat, hating the flood of emotions rising deep within me. "Gotta go."

"Alright, speak soon."

Just as I'm about to stab another soggy piece of lettuce, Konstantin steps into his office, heading for the door separating us. Tailored black suit, no tie, black shirt unbuttoned. It's just enough to distract the rational part of my brain.

His eyes find me immediately, dragging over me like a slow caress. A smirk tugs at the corner of his mouth.

Caught checking out the boss again. I don't even bother pretending I wasn't.

"How are you today, Ms. Monroe?" His voice is a decadent drawl. "Tragic, really, how little I've seen of you this morning."

I meet his gaze evenly. "But look at you. You somehow managed to survive."

My lips curve at the corners, and his smile widens, unapologetic and cocky. I hate the way my body lights up in response—tightening low, burning hot.

I need this to stop. I need him to stop being…*this*.

"Do not worry." He steps closer, his presence swallowing all the space between us. "We'll make up for lost time tomorrow."

I blink. "And what makes tomorrow so special?"

He lifts his hand, brushing a strand of hair from my cheek with maddening tenderness, and I feel it in every inch of me. Like lightning crackling beneath my skin.

"We'll be flying out together on my private jet. Bright and early." His tone dips lower. "Pack light."

My stomach drops.

Perfect. Just what I need: a day trapped in the sky with the man I'm supposed to be manipulating, who already seems to have complete control of my body without even trying. At least here, I have grounding. Safety nets. Distance. That won't be the case wherever he's taking me.

"Where are we going?"

"Chicago. I have meetings. You'll be assisting me. And of course…" He leans in just enough for his breath to skate across my lips. "You'll be available for anything else I may need at any hour of the day."

A single brow shoots up. "Professional things, I hope."

He chuckles—dark, rich, and thick with meaning. "That depends entirely on how long you plan to keep pretending there's nothing between us."

I'm halfway to a retort when he backs away, his eyes dragging across my face like he's memorizing every inch.

"Go get some rest, malyshka. You're going to need it."

His stare lingers like a brand, and by the time he turns away, I'm painfully aware that this tightrope I'm walking is fraying fast.

FOURTEEN

EMILIA

The jet is sleek and black, waiting on the tarmac like a predator in a suit. Looks like it has something in common with its owner.

Konstantin's hand grazes mine as he silently takes my suitcase, the brush of skin sending a current through me. I climb the steps with his presence right behind me, heat prickling down my spine. There's a sound—low, primal—and I can't tell if it's him or the jet growling to life beneath us.

Once I step into the cabin, I'm surrounded by pure luxury.

A bright-eyed blonde in a tailored uniform greets us at the top of the steps with a practiced smile. "Welcome, Mr. Marinov. Ms. Monroe. May I get you two anything to drink?"

Before I can answer, Konstantin's voice slides in, smooth and razor-sharp. "I'll take care of her."

He presses up behind me, his hand resting lightly, yet possessively against my hip like he's staking a claim. A rush of heat radiates through my chest, furious and unwanted.

I'm not his. I never will be. But my body hasn't gotten the memo.

Not when his palm lingers a second too long. Not when his lips are so close to my ear, I feel the brush of his breath.

"Take a seat," he demands.

And suddenly, I'm not sure if the tightness in my chest is nerves… or anticipation of what's to come.

The scars on my arms throb, like they want to remind me that he knows my secrets, the ones I never talk about. I hate that he does, that he forced me to give him something I wasn't ready to, but it doesn't change anything between us.

I slide into one of the white leather seats, crossing my legs and meeting his gaze with the kind of calm I don't quite feel. It's a challenge. A performance. Like I belong here. Like his world was always meant to be mine.

His mouth lifts slightly, and there's something in his eyes that sharpens. Something that says he sees more than I want him to.

Then I stupidly wonder again if anyone's ever loved him. Truly loved him. Would someone miss him if he disappeared? Cry for him? Ache for him like he was worth mourning?

Would anyone miss *me*?

Sure, Nate would. Gerardo and Fiona too. Maybe even Riley. But that's not what I mean. I want someone to miss me like their world's been ripped apart. I want to be remembered so deeply it ruins them.

I'll never have that, will I?

I drag in a long breath. Is this what happens when someone's starved for affection? They start craving it from the most dangerous people?

But falling in love, having a family of my own, is absolutely not in the cards for me. I'm far too messed up for that. With the kind of mother I had for a role model, I'd be a disaster.

A bitter laugh scrapes the back of my throat. Guess therapy's been working better than I thought. At least I can recognize how fucked up I am.

"What's so amusing?" His voice slices through my thoughts, dragging me out of the spiral.

He stands at the minibar, pouring himself a drink. His eyes lift, catching mine across the cabin. The moment our gazes collide, it's like he's commanding me in place without even touching me.

"Nothing." I push my hair away from my face and sit straighter.

His smile curves, slow and knowing, like he can read the lie right through me. "You drink coffee?"

Only when I'm being seduced by a Bratva kingpin.

"Not usually. But I'll have one. Splash of cream, one sugar."

He lets out a low chuckle, rich and smooth, the sound curling through me like a thick vine. As he pours from one of the silver pitchers, the scent hits me first: rich, bitter, and far too inviting. With both drinks in hand, he turns and settles beside me, closer than necessary, and offers me my cup.

Our fingers brush, barely a graze, but it sparks something low and hot inside me, undoing the control I've been clutching to like a lifeline. His eyes latch on to mine, and I swear he can feel the shift inside me.

I bring the cup to my lips, desperate for a distraction. The warmth of the coffee grounds me, the bitter strength of it anchoring me just enough to pretend I'm unaffected.

But it still tastes like him. Dangerous. Addictive. Impossible to ignore.

He continues to watch, like he's trying to memorize the way I react to every little thing.

The seatbelt sign dings softly overhead, and within minutes, the jet lifts into the sky with barely a tremor. I force a slow breath through my nose, keeping my posture composed while lowering my mug.

Nothing bad is going to happen. It's just a trip. He's not taking me somewhere to kill me.

Well, at least I hope not…

But to be on the safe side, I sent messages to both Riley and Gerardo before I left. If anything happens, they'll know where to look.

"Relax, Ms. Monroe." His palm, warm and heavy, settles on my thigh like it belongs there. "Are you nervous?" Thick fingers cinch around my flesh. "If so, I have a few ways I can help."

"I'm sure you do." I sound composed, but my body is a traitor, a pulsing need unfurling from the weight of his touch.

I glance down at his hand, broad and possessive, and silently thank myself for not wearing a dress. Or maybe curse myself. It's hard to tell the difference right now.

He shifts slightly, angling toward me with an ease that feels more like a stalk than a gesture. "It's a short flight. We'll be in Chicago soon. You'll sit in on the meeting, take notes. And after that…" His eyes glint. "The evening is ours."

I should ask what that means. What *his* version of "ours" includes. But the words catch in my throat when his gaze drops to my mouth, remaining there like he's already tasted it.

Then slowly, his thumb sweeps across my lower lip.

Awareness ignites within me. The move is both intimate and greedy. Like he's claiming space he hasn't earned, but fully intends to take.

"Just enjoy yourself," he murmurs. "Don't fight it so hard. It's not good for you."

"And you know what's good for me?" I try to come off indifferent, but his fingers grip my thigh tighter, and suddenly the silence between us thickens, humming with something unspoken.

"Of course I do. I know everything."

I should pull back. Say something sharp and deflect. But I don't move. I stay perfectly still, every nerve lit up as his mouth hovers over mine, close enough that one breath would erase the space between us.

The plane suddenly jolts, a sharp burst of turbulence throwing me off-balance, and I surge forward.

His arms are around me in an instant—steady, firm, anchoring me like he's done it a hundred times before.

But it's not the strength of his grip that undoes me. It's the way he's looking at me. Like I'm his.

"You alright, katyonak?" The affection in his tone hits me hard as he tucks a loose strand of hair behind my ear.

Kitten. That damn word again. I looked it up the last time he said it. I told myself I hated it…but something about the way he says it makes my chest hit with a twinge.

"I'm fine." I shift slightly, putting space between us as I reach for my coffee, but it does nothing to douse the wildfire burning under my skin.

I shouldn't want him. It's a betrayal to everything I took an oath to stand against.

But the truth is, I can't deny the way he makes me feel.

And the scariest part? I'm starting to think I don't want to.

KONSTANTIN

The elevator opens directly into the penthouse suite of the hotel, perched on the top floor with unobstructed skyline views. The space exudes sophistication: dark marble floors, black velvet accents, and gold-trimmed furniture.

But none of it compares to the woman stepping in beside me. Strong. Mysterious. Inescapably alluring. And apparently, she's exactly what I'm looking for. Or so my heart tells me.

Life is a funny thing. One second, I was fine being alone. Then she appeared, and suddenly, I could see it: waking up beside her, fighting for something more than vengeance and blood.

But love in my world? It's no different than death. It costs you. Destroys you.

And if I claimed her, *truly* claimed her, things wouldn't get easier. They'd get worse.

Still, I've never been one to flinch from fire.

And Tessa Monroe? She's the most dangerous flame I've ever touched.

Her heels click against the floor as she walks in, her eyes taking in the space with a mix of awe and apprehension.

She doesn't trust me. She's smart not to.

But that doesn't stop her eyes from drifting to me when she thinks I'm not looking. And I witness the battle within her. Like she's despising herself for wanting something she knows is wrong.

But I see it. I see everything. That flicker of hunger she tries to bury beneath all that stubborn resolve.

She wants me. Maybe not with her mind, but her body knows what's good for her.

That's the unfortunate thing about attraction. It's primal. Uncontrollable. It doesn't ask for permission. And no matter how hard you fight it, once it takes hold, it drags you under.

My attention zeroes in on her, those tailored dress pants clinging to her curves like they were stitched with my hands in mind, just begging to be stripped off. But now isn't the time to imagine all the ways I'll have her on her knees. That will have to wait.

"Where's my bedroom?"

I gesture toward the narrow corridor with a flick of my wrist, while my men roll in our luggage. "Let me show you."

She follows close behind, but the second I open the door, she brushes past me like she can't wait to get rid of me. I laugh to myself at the absurdity of it.

"Thanks. You can go now." She pops an irritated brow.

I step in further, my finger trailing up the bare skin of her arm. "I would…" My lips twist. "But that's going to be difficult…since this is my bedroom too."

She stops cold, her eyes popping wide. "I'm sorry, what?"

I move in closer, our bodies aligned like puzzle pieces meant to break, my fingers curling around her nape with just enough pressure to remind her who's in control. Her lips part, pupils flaring in response.

"Don't worry, this bed's big enough for the both of us. Though the last thing you'll want is to get away from me, I promise." With my other hand, I brush her cheek with my knuckles, enjoying the feeling of her soft skin too much.

It's like I can't stop touching her, like I'm a desperate man. She tries to mask the way I affect her, but the goose bumps racing across her skin speak the truth she refuses to voice.

"There's absolutely no way I'm sleeping in the same bed as you. You're my boss, and I'm your assistant. That's all this is, and that's all it'll ever be."

I laugh, low and dark, before grabbing a fistful of her hair and tugging her head back until her chest heaves.

"That's exactly what you are. My assistant. Mine to command. So when I say we're sharing a bed, that's exactly what will happen. And if you don't like it?" I lower my pitch to a dangerous whisper. "The door's right there. Walk through it and lose the job you were begging me for. The choice is yours."

She grits her teeth, her body coiling with her displeasure.

"Fine." The word might as well be a curse with the way she said it.

I chuckle to myself. Of course she'd give in. What choice does she have?

When I loosen my grip, I savor the pink flush on her cheeks, the way her lips stay parted like she's still catching up.

"Good girl." A smirk pulls at my mouth. "I knew you'd see

reason."

She exhales hard, a sound closer to a snarl than a laugh.

"It's for your own safety. I have enemies. They wouldn't hesitate to use you to get to me."

"So this is for *my* benefit, huh?" Sarcasm drips from every word as she glares like she's not sure whether she wants to slap me or drag me closer.

I'd welcome either.

"Of course. Everything I do is for your benefit." My gaze trails down the length of her body, and I can't help invading her space again, both hands gripping her hips and dragging her flush to me. "But if you want the complete truth, I want you in my bed. I want to feel your bare skin on mine. I want to own every sound you make. Every look. Every damn heartbeat. You're so far under my skin, I'm bleeding for it."

The smallest shift gives her away. A twitch in her jaw. Her spine straightens like a blade, and I know she feels this. Every inch of her is on edge, and I like knowing that it's because of me.

Her defiance flickers behind those fierce, firelit eyes, but it's starting to crack. Because this thing between us? It's stronger than her resistance. It's hunger in the form of a slow, unraveling surrender, and she's starting to realize it too.

I don't want to want her. It'd be so much simpler if this was just about sex. But I can't escape this. I don't even want to. And that's a deadly recipe for the both of us.

I step back, undoing the cuffs of my shirt one by one, and she turns her back to me almost too quickly, like I can't see through the paper-thin armor she's wrapped herself in.

I want to break through it. Shatter every piece of control she's gripping to.

"Look at me," I demand.

She doesn't move. So predictable.

"I said *look at me.*" My tone sharpens, daring her to disobey.

Slowly, she turns, her chin high, breaths shallow. Every inch of her is tight with tension, ire…and need. I see it all. She can't hide from me.

"Come closer." I beckon her with a finger, wishing she was naked with a collar and leash around her neck.

The image in my mind is so vivid I can taste it. Her crawling to me like the good girl I know she'll become.

Her tongue darts out to wet her lips. "What do you want?"

Every muscle in my body twists. I want her hands on me. I want her surrender.

"Take off my belt."

She freezes. "Excuse me?"

"You heard me." I take a step forward, erasing the last breath of space between us. My voice dips to a warning. "Take. Off. My. Belt."

Her eyes thin, that fire flaring. "I'm not your servant."

"No…" The heat between us practically vibrates. My hand feathers against her hip, deliberately slow. "You're not. But you *are* mine. I own you, Ms. Monroe. Now do as you're told and take off my belt."

A beat of silence passes. Then, with our eyes locked, her hands rise. And with disdain written all over her features, she finds the buckle and starts to unfasten it. Not because she's obedient. Because she wants me to know she can play this game and still stay in control.

She tugs the leather free with a smooth pull, and I see it in her eyes: Ms. Monroe is just as addicted as I am.

And I haven't even touched her yet.

I take the belt from her hands, slipping it behind her neck and pulling her in. "That wasn't so hard, was it?"

Her smile is fiery as her fingertips graze my abdomen, igniting the very core of me. She begins undoing the button of my trousers before dragging the zipper down, then lowers my pants until they're pooling around my ankles. I step out of them, my cock straining beneath my boxers, and I know she sees it.

Her pupils widen, face flushed. Her hands hover over my biceps, like her body begs to hold on to me for dear life.

"You're not done yet. The shirt too." I drop the belt onto the floor, wanting to tie her to the bed and use it on her perfect skin instead.

She'd never need to hurt herself again, not when I could give her everything she's searching for. Every high. Every low. Every desperate ache. I'd be the one to give it and take it away.

When she bites her lip, I find the war inside her. She craves this with the same intensity that she resents it.

But the heart is a selfish thing. It doesn't weigh logic or fear. It goes after whatever it desires. And resistance only sharpens the hunger.

Her hands slide up my chest, fingers working each button with deliberate slowness until my shirt parts and she pushes it from my shoulders. Those eyes clasp to mine like a challenge that I willingly accept.

I watch her face the entire time. Watch the way her breath falters, how her gaze drinks me in even as she tries to stay composed.

I lean in, my mouth grazing her ear. "You have no idea how much I enjoy your hands on me."

And how much I wish I didn't.

Before she can respond, I step back, walking off to grab fresh clothes from my suitcase.

When I turn around, I find her rushing into the bathroom. The soft click of the lock fills the air; my lips twitch into a grin.

Run all you want, katyonak. But no matter how hard you try, you'll never get away from me.

FIFTEEN

EMILIA

The thought of sleeping next to him tonight makes my thoughts spiral.

You'd better not fuck him or I'll kill you.

Yes, I occasionally threaten myself with bodily harm. It works. For the most part.

This time, though? I'm not so sure.

He walks up beside me as we head toward the conference room in some fancy hotel, his masculine woodsy cologne invading my nostrils without permission like everything else about him.

The hallway leading there is silent but for the muffled echo of our steps. His hand cups the small of my back, the heat of it searing through the thin fabric of my dress. I hate that I like it. Hate that I want more.

Everything about earlier in the hotel room slams into my mind. The way he demanded that I undress him, the way he looked at me as I did, like he wanted to take every little bit of me until there was nothing more…

I wanted that. I still do. And I hate myself for it. Instead of being loyal to my brother, I'm fantasizing about screwing the man who put him in prison.

"You remember everything I asked of you?" Konstantin's voice breaks the silence as we get closer to the meeting room.

I nod, glancing at him for a moment. "Take notes. Don't get in the way. Keep my mouth shut. Did I get everything?"

He chuckles. "You make it sound like a punishment."

"Only because it's coming from you."

His smirk bends like a blade, and I feel every inch of it crawl down my spine just as the doors swing open and we enter. The conference room is all glass and marble, a powerful combination of menace and opulence.

At least ten men turn to look at us, all in expensive suits, all carrying the same air of entitlement and danger. Two seats wait at the head of the table.

I falter.

Konstantin leans in, his mouth grazing the shell of my ear. "You belong here. Right next to me. Don't let them intimidate you."

But that's not what this is. I can't afford the risk of being outed. I've been involved in too many cases related to the Mafia and other criminal organizations, and depending on who these men are, they might have crossed paths with me. If one of them has, I'm fucked.

I force my feet forward, and his hand slips through mine, giving me a surprising reassuring squeeze. He lets me go just as I slip into the chair beside him.

"Gentlemen, welcome. I know some of you have traveled a great distance to be here, and that is not overlooked."

They nod solemnly while I uncap the pen on the table and open the leather-bound notebook waiting for me too. I start to write the moment one of them speaks, discreetly looking at every face and not recognizing any of them.

Relief washes over me. My cover is safe. For now, at least.

The meeting drones on, words like capital, expansion, and equity buzzing around the marble table. Countries are named. Figures are tossed into the air like poker chips.

Then I feel it.

His hand.

It lands on my thigh without warning, short-circuiting my brain.

I inhale sharply, trying to keep my expression neutral while my eyes are on the paper in front of me, pretending I can still take notes while every nerve in my body locks on to the man beside me.

Konstantin doesn't so much as glance at me. His gaze is steady, fixed on whoever's speaking at the far end of the table, like he's actually interested in logistics and offshore accounts and political red tape. But his fingers move with purpose, creeping beneath the slit of my dress, dragging higher.

Every inch of exposed skin he touches burns.

I shift subtly, trying to push his hand away without drawing attention.

Big mistake. He tightens his grip on my inner thigh, fingers digging into the soft flesh like a silent command.

Don't move. Don't fight me.

But a part of me doesn't want him to stop.

The atmosphere in the room turns suffocating, like it's pressing down on my chest. I've trained for danger. I've dealt with criminals. But nothing could've prepared me for this—being touched under a table in a room full of men who would probably gut me if they knew who I really was.

Then he slides my panties to the side, and I nearly choke on air.

His fingers brush my clit—featherlight, testing, teasing. My thighs tremble. My lashes flutter as I fight to keep from making a single sound.

One breath too deep, one glance too quick, and they'll all know. They'll see it. The way he touches me. The way I react. The way I melt for him while I hate it.

I grip the edge of the notepad tighter. Words blur. My pen drags over the paper, illegible and shaking.

Then he pushes two fingers inside me, and I nearly drop the pen.

The pressure is slow at first. Gentle. But God help me, I want more. I crave it. My teeth sink into the inside of my cheek, biting hard.

Across the table, someone clears their throat. A man begins to speak again. The words swim past me like white noise.

Konstantin's fingers thrust rougher. More insistent.

I move in my seat and try to push him away, but he only takes me deeper. Like a silent warning that he's in charge.

I'm soaked. My body clenches. My thighs quiver violently under the table, desperate for release, for relief. He turns his head slightly, just enough to catch my eye, and the look he gives me is pure sin.

Oh God, this isn't happening.

My body is screaming. And there is no hiding it anymore. I'm going to come in front of a room full of dangerous men, and I'm powerless to stop it.

Konstantin drives his fingers deep once more, curling them inside me, and my toes curl as a sharp gasp escapes before I can catch it.

The pen slips from my fingers, clattering against the table.

One of the men pauses mid-sentence. Another older one narrows his eyes from across the table. His gaze drops to the table, like he's noticed the rhythm of my breathing. The flush in my cheeks.

But Konstantin doesn't care. He keeps going.

His fingers are slick with me, pushing deeper, circling my clit again with that maddening precision that has me riding the edge of oblivion. Every breath I take is labored, my body drawn so tight I could snap.

And when I'm almost on the verge, shaking silently in the leather chair, I want to slap him. I want to scream. I want to climb into his lap and beg him to do it again.

"This isn't a fucking whorehouse, Marinov," the same older man barks, slicing through the meeting like a blade. "Have some respect."

The room stills while I freeze, heat creeping to my face.

And for the first time since this began, Konstantin's hand stops moving. It rests right where it is: possessive and bold between my thighs.

His lethal gaze zeroes in on the man. His face doesn't twist. His posture doesn't shift. He doesn't even blink. He simply smiles. That cold, amused, dead-eyed smile that chills the room.

"Did you just call her a whore?" he asks quietly, almost conversationally. Like he's discussing the weather.

The man leans back slightly, not an ounce of fear. "What I meant was, maybe this isn't the time for that."

"And you think you have the authority to tell *me* what I can and cannot do?" Konstantin's voice is smooth, yet soaked in gasoline.

"No, I just—"

A flash of movement comes before I register it.

One second, his other hand is on his lap. The next, he's holding a gun.

The sound doesn't register, not right away. Not until blood spatters the marble floor. The man slumps back in his chair, eyes still open, a neat hole drilled between them.

The room explodes into stunned silence. Not a breath, not a scrape of a chair.

My body kicks with adrenaline from the shock of it all. He just killed a man. Just like that, in front of the entire room. This is Konstantin Marinov in all his glory.

And the craziest part is he's still completely calm. As if he didn't just shoot a man in cold blood five seconds ago.

He returns the weapon back to its holster, fingers still inside me. His gaze sweeps over the rest of the table, lingering, daring someone to say something just so he can do this all over again.

"I was getting tired of hearing him speak. Wouldn't you say, gentlemen?"

A mumbling sound of agreement comes from them as one man clears his throat. Another fidgets in his chair like his bladder's about to give out.

Konstantin turns to the man who had been speaking before the interruption. "Please. Continue. I promise there will be no more disruptions." His gaze wanders around the room, as though in a silent warning.

The man tries to gather his thoughts. His mouth opens, but his voice comes out weak, cracked. "Uh…r-right. As I was saying… the expansion into Macau would require at least twenty million upfront—"

Konstantin nods, once again engrossed in the topic for a few minutes before his mouth finds my ear.

"I'm sorry I had to do that in front of you. But if anyone disrespects you ever again, I'll kill them slower. I want them all to know what it looks like when a woman belongs to me."

He's insane. And also kind of romantic?

No, murder isn't romantic.

But isn't it, though?

I've clearly lost my mind. Only an insane person would find this romantic.

His fingers stroke my clit once more, gently now. Teasing. Soothing.

Another man starts to speak, and my eyes roll back.

I doubt any one of them would be stupid enough to say a word. Ever again. Terror clings to the room like humidity, thick and choking.

But not to me. Because beneath the chaos, something else curls in my chest. Something dark and twisted.

Something that feels like gratitude.

For once, someone didn't just protect me. They avenged me.

How many times did I wish someone would do that growing up? That someone would kill the monsters who hurt me when I was younger? But no one ever came. Not until that last time when Nate took me away.

He doesn't care about you, Emilia. You're nothing to a man like Konstantin Marinov. And you don't want to be.

But even as I tell myself that, the way he touches me makes me forget why this is wrong. Slow, possessive circles at my entrance are like a silent command that he still owns me in this moment.

And my body? My traitorous body doesn't care what my mind screams. It winds tighter and tighter, desperate for the release only he can give.

Every breath I take is shallow. Every nerve is pulled taut. He works me expertly, like he knows exactly what I need and how to hold it just out of reach until I'm nearly weeping for him.

The room fades. The voices around us become muffled noise. The tension, the danger, the obscene audacity of it all…it rattles through me like a raging earthquake.

My thighs tremble. My breath stutters. My eyes flutter shut for half a second too long, the pleasure dragging me under like a riptide.

My climax rips through me in a blinding rush, and I cling to him, my fingers digging into the hard muscle of his thigh.

My jaw clenches, holding in the scream that wants to tear free. My body jerks once, twice, hips straining against his hand as I ride it out in pure silence. His head tilts toward mine, his breath a wicked brand against my skin as he pulls his fingers away with a soft, wet sound.

"You're perfect when you come for me." His lips brush the shell of my ear. "Don't hide it. Let them all see you're mine."

I'm not yours! I want to scream out loud, but I'm too far gone.

His hand returns to my thigh and he keeps it there, like a chain. And in this moment, with his scent all over me, my body still shivering from the aftershock, I know one terrifying truth.

If I'm not careful, I won't just belong to him. I'll *want* to.

142

SIXTEEN

EMILIA

We return to the hotel room, and my back is to him as I open my luggage.

My fingers hover at the zipper like they're trying to remember how to work, like I'm just another woman shaken by what happened. Nervous. Fidgety. Quiet.

That's how someone who saw what I did would behave. Someone normal. Someone who isn't used to watching a man get shot in the middle of a business meeting like it's just another line item on the agenda.

Okay, fine, so maybe that's the first time I've witnessed a death during a meeting, but I've seen quite a few murders in my line of work. Even committed one.

His footsteps are slow behind me, his palm landing on my forearm, heavy and warm. "Do you want to talk about it?"

I almost laugh. Is this a joke? Does the murderous Bratva boss want to unpack my feelings now? Maybe offer a shoulder to cry on? It's absurd.

But maybe this could be my way of getting to know him better, and anything I learn is a potential weapon that I intend to use.

I slowly drop my hands away from the suitcase and turn. He's standing just inches away, his eyes heavy with something that feels too close to softness, which is quite the opposite of what he is.

This man is cruelty in its finest form. He's never been soft with anything in his life.

My gaze wanders down his large form. His suit jacket is gone, hung neatly in the walk-in closet, and the top buttons of his crisp white shirt are undone, revealing a sliver of the chest that made me lose my mind just hours ago.

My attention drags lower. His belt. That expensive diamond-encrusted gold watch. The strength in his arms. It all gleams in the dim light. He exudes power and he knows it, so why is he looking at me like he'd protect me from the world if I asked?

When I glance up and meet his stare, the shift is instant. The room seems smaller, the tension louder, the draw between us impossible to ignore.

No matter how much I tell myself to fight these feelings, he's still the man who pulled a trigger without blinking.

And I'm still the woman who liked it.

"Was that…uh…normal for you? To do that?" My voice comes out shaky, discomfort woven through each word, making a show of unease.

His lips press into a thin line. "You mean do I normally kill people in front of my assistants?"

I nod once, keeping my gaze guarded, trying to look like I'm in over my head.

"Surprisingly, that was my first time." A half-grin spreads across his face while his fingers rise to graze my jaw. "But I'd happily do it again for you."

"I don't want you to."

His expression doesn't change. "That really isn't up to you."

The words strike me like a slap, yet when his touch falls away, I sense the absence like a cold draft, part of me irrationally wanting it back.

He takes a step closer, his presence eclipsing everything. "I know you're not a stupid woman. You know who I really am. What I really do behind the pretty façade of this empire I've built. Don't you?"

My throat tightens. I nod again, slower this time.

"Then say it." His tone dips lower. "Tell me what I am."

Shit.

Panic flutters in my chest. Is this a trap? Some twisted loyalty test I'm destined to fail? A tremor races through my limbs, and of course, he notices.

"This isn't a test." His fingertips glide up and down my hand. "I promise you. I just want us to be honest with each other."

I hesitate for only a second before whispering, "You're…you're Russian Mafia."

His grin spreads—slow, seductive, and treacherous, the glint in his eyes saying he enjoys hearing me admit it.

"Maladetz." He leans in, the heat of his body stirring the air between us. "And how does that make you feel, working for someone like me?"

"Not great?" I cringe a little. "Terrified?"

His chuckle bursts out. "There are no wrong answers here."

"May I ask a follow-up?"

"Of course. You can ask anything you want, dorogaya." With a twist of his hand, he gestures for me to continue, the gentleman in the devil's skin.

"Do you…kill a lot of people?"

His eyes flash with humor. "Maybe more than others in my

position. I haven't really crunched the numbers. I could if you'd like."

"No, that won't be necessary." I glance down for effect just as he chuckles again, like it's all so casual.

But nothing about this is funny. Not to the girl who once feared for her life every night in a roach-infested home, and definitely not to the woman who puts men like him behind bars.

"Don't you worry sometimes?" I go on, watching him closely, wanting to know the man inside, wanting every bit of him.

"About?" His thick brows furrow.

"That you're next in line…to die?"

That makes him pause. "All the time."

The honesty in his answer knocks me off-balance. I expected arrogance. Invincibility. Not this brutal, quiet truth. And it shakes me more than I want to admit.

Because maybe he's not just a monster wrapped in expensive suits and bloodstained power. Maybe he's just a man, one who walks with death at his back just like I do. And somehow, that makes him even more dangerous.

Not because he kills without thought. But because, if I'm not careful, I might start seeing the man beneath it all.

And that…would be the most dangerous thing of all.

KONSTANTIN

I didn't intend for her to see that side of me this quickly, but it was bound to come out sooner than later. Better for her to get used to it now. I am who I am, and there's nothing she can do to change that.

The lights are low, the hum of the city barely reaching the penthouse as I step out of the bathroom in nothing but boxers and a white T-shirt.

She's already in bed, back propped against the pillows, legs curled under the sheets. But her gaze lifts when she sees me. It flickers over my chest, my arms, then down. Subtle, but not subtle enough.

Her mouth parts. "You're not going to put on pants?"

I shrug. "This is what I normally wear to bed. You'll have to get used to it."

She mutters something, turning away with a roll of her eyes, but the flush on her cheeks betrays her. Irritating this woman and turning her on are my current favorite pastimes.

I cross to my side of the bed, making sure my gun is right on the nightstand before flicking the bedside lamp off and settling beside her.

The silence lingers, both of us on opposite sides of the bed. But all I can think about is holding her close, chasing the rhythm my heart only finds when she's beside me.

I lean in, mouth brushing her bare shoulder, unable to stand another second without touching her.

"Goodnight, katyonak." My lips stay pressed a second too long, desperate to hold on to something I shouldn't want.

She inhales sharply, almost imperceptibly, but I hear it. Feel it in my bones. She's trying not to react, but her body always gives her away.

I roll onto my back, staring up at the ceiling. But sleep doesn't come. Every hour that ticks by is torture. All I can think about is her. How she tastes. How she sounds when she comes. What it would be like to have a woman in my life.

Then a soft rustle of fabric catches my attention, followed by a sharp hitch in her breath.

I turn toward her silhouette in the dark. She's on her side, but her legs shift, the softest whimper escaping.

Blyat.

She freezes when I slide closer as though I didn't just catch her. My arm wraps around her waist, hand gliding down until I grip her wrist inside her shorts.

My mouth finds her ear. "You need help?"

"I—"

"You should've told me you were aching for it."

"I-I'm not…" Every syllable is a blatant lie.

"Shh." I press a kiss to the pulse beating in her throat. "Let me help you."

She hesitates for a moment, but doesn't stop me.

I guide her fingers first, make her move them the way I want. Slow. Deep. Controlled. Her breath turns ragged, body trembling.

"Were you thinking about me while you were fucking this sweet cunt, or do I need to murder someone else tonight?" Pushing her hand away, I take over, fingers replacing hers.

She's soaked. Needy. Desperate.

"You're dripping wet. This better all be for me."

When she doesn't answer, I force three of my fingers inside, and she cries out, nails digging into my forearm.

"Answer me before I lose my goddamn mind and go on a killing spree, Tessa."

"You…I was thinking about you."

Sweet relief. It's what I thought, but hearing her admit it is something else entirely.

I work her gently, my thumb stroking her clit, before I go harder. Her hips arch into my hand as she tries to stay quiet, but fails miserably.

She's out of her element, losing control like this. But she'll soon learn how much better things can be when she relinquishes her control to me.

"That's it," I groan, my fingers sinking in and out of her tightness. "Come for me."

When she moans, I thrust deeper. "Yes, just like that. That's my good girl. Let me hear how much you like it."

There are so many things I want to do to her—at my club, in my home—but this… This is enough right now. She's like a baby bird who needs tending to before I let her fly.

With another flick of my touch, she shatters around me, breathless and shaking, her walls quivering.

"Fuck!" She grips my arm tighter, nails clawing until it almost hurts.

But I welcome the pain, refusing to stop until she's climbing for the second time.

"Please, oh God, I can't do that again."

"You will give me another." I pin her arm with my free hand and take her harder, slamming into her with brutal force until she's twitching, screaming my name.

"Konstantin!"

I let go of her wrist and grab her throat, grinding my cock into her ass before her second orgasm slams through her, soaking the sheets beneath us.

"I promise the next time you scream my name like that will be with me inside you."

Her breathing turns labored, her body growing limp against me.

My cock is a painful weight against her, but I grit my teeth, knowing nothing else will happen tonight.

Wordlessly, I gather her in my arms and carry her out of the dark room and into the other bedroom.

I catch the weighted look in her eyes before she sags against me, her cheek to my chest, and I swear my heart twitches.

"Go to sleep, katyonak." I lay her down on the mattress, even while my body aches to take what it wants.

"Why?" she breathes.

"Because if I don't stop now…" I growl. "I'll fuck you so hard you'll forget why you ever wanted to resist me. And we both know you're not ready for that."

Even in the darkness, I feel her eyes on me—trapping me, saving me, doing things to me no woman has ever done before.

I should make some attempt to fight it. But I don't. Because there's nothing I want more than her.

SEVENTEEN

KONSTANTIN

She sleeps like she didn't just watch me blow a man's brains out and barely blink.

Yet she's breathing steadily beside me. Like I'm not the nightmare people pray they never meet.

My arms are still wrapped around her, spooning her from behind, her body warm and soft against mine. My palm rests in the center of her chest, and I feel the slight jerk in her fingers, little signs that she's dreaming.

I've never held a woman like this. Never stayed after. Never *wanted* to.

It's always been about the act. A release. A transaction.

But this? This is something else.

And every day, I discover myself through her. It's more than a gift. It's cathartic. I don't think she realizes how much she's given me in such a short period of time.

I bury my nose in her hair, letting her scent ground me. She smells like vanilla and skin and something like peace, laced with ruin. My chest tightens, the weight of her against me almost too much to bear.

If she knew I was still awake, knew I was holding her like this, she'd shove me off in a heartbeat. So I keep still. Just a man holding a woman in the dark, pretending the world outside doesn't want to eat us alive. And for a few minutes, it works.

Until the floor creaks a close distance from outside of our room.

Someone is inside the penthouse, and I already know my men stationed outside are dead. I curse myself for not hearing them come in.

That's what happens in my world. Enemies lurk everywhere, trying to rip every shred of peace I have.

My instant worry is for her, the beautiful angel in my bed, and how I can best protect her.

"Tessa." I shake her. "Wake up."

She stirs, but doesn't open her eyes.

"Tessa, wake up and grab the gun in the drawer beside you."

Her lashes flash open. "What?"

I tilt my head toward the sound. Another thud.

"Gun. Now," I whisper. "Can you shoot?"

"Yeah." She blinks quickly, grabbing the handle of the drawer. "My brother taught me."

That's a relief. She needs to know how to protect herself.

I slide out of bed, silent on my feet, while she gets to her feet, gun in hand, her body tense. Grabbing her hand, I kiss her knuckles, staring deep into her eyes like this may be the very last time I get to look into them, and the thought rips me apart.

"Get in the closet." I point to the walk-in. "And stay quiet."

"What the hell is going on?" she breathes as another creak comes closer.

"Someone's come for me." The Glock is already in my hand. "I don't want them finding you. Get the hell inside and don't come out, no matter what you see or hear."

She hesitates, like she wants to argue.

"Tessa. Go. Now!" I keep my voice low, wanting the element of surprise.

She scrambles to her feet, disappearing into the closet on the far side of the room. The soft click of the closet closing is the last thing I register before the bedroom door rattles.

I wait behind the portioned wall, silent, still. The need to rip apart whoever dared to walk in here is overwhelming. Whoever they are, they won't leave this room alive. And when I have their bodies, I will send bits and pieces to whoever sent them.

When the door bursts open, three—no, five—men rush in, all in black. Ski masks. Gloves.

Is it the DeLuca crew? Have they really become this stupid?

I will find out soon and make them all pay.

With a growl, I squeeze the trigger once from behind the wall, dropping the first man before his boot crosses the threshold. Blood sprays across the white carpet.

Another dives behind the couch. I roll toward the dresser and fire again, hitting his leg, then crouch down and roll again before firing into his skull.

A third swings his weapon toward me, and I charge him before he can pull the trigger. My shoulder smashes into his chest, and we hit the floor. He struggles. But he doesn't stand a chance. I snap his neck and shove him off me, panting through my nose.

Two more left. Two more bodies standing in the way of me keeping her safe.

My adrenaline pumps through me, her face appearing before my eyes.

No one is going to hurt you again.

One of the guys charges, swinging a blade, and we collide. I grapple with him, slamming him into the edge of the dresser. My fist connects with his jaw, and he kicks my leg out before we go down together.

I can't see the last man.

Where the fuck is he? The bastard was just here.

All I can think is that Tessa better still be in that fucking closet.

Because if she isn't, I'll tear apart this entire hotel and everyone in it to find her.

And I won't stop there.

EMILIA

My breaths are shallow, though not out of fear. This isn't my first rodeo, and it won't be my last.

Yet here I am, trapped in a closet, sidelined like some helpless kid, while he gets to have all the fun.

If he knew who I really was, who trained me, what I've done… maybe he'd stop treating me like something breakable. But of course that's not possible.

Through the thick slats of the door, I catch glimpses of the chaos. Konstantin moves like he was built for war. Outnumbered, but far from outmatched.

He fights with precision, power, like the odds don't even matter. Like a man who's had to claw his way out of hell before.

I'm almost impressed.

Whoever these men are, they came to take him out, and I need to know why and who they are. Maybe this is that DeLuca crew Gerardo mentioned.

I don't care what happens to Konstantin. If he dies, I won't cry, not that I ever do. But he *is* entertaining in a maddening, overbearing sort of way. And I do need him alive…at least long enough to get the evidence that can clear Nate.

Sure, Riley could probably dig it up on her own, even if Konstantin was six feet under. But keeping him alive? That's just better for my plan.

When one of the men moves behind him, raising a gun, he doesn't see it. He's too busy choking the one in front of him.

Shit.

Before I can think, I slip out of the closet, gun raised. My feet hit the floor with barely a sound, and I shoot the jackass and the man Konstantin is close to murdering.

Not bad at all, Emilia.

Konstantin spins, his eyes wide, and the silence that follows is louder than the chaos.

Blood is everywhere, the stench of gunpowder hanging thick in the air, but all he sees is me.

I lower the weapon, my heart pounding from the adrenaline while he stares at me like he's never seen me before. Like I've just grown horns or wings.

Maybe I should've pretended I'm not a good shot, but it's too late now.

He walks toward me, that lethal, hungry look in his eyes.

"You saved my life." There's shock in the timbre of his deep, husky voice, like he can't imagine little old me saving the life of the big, powerful man the rest of the world fears.

"Seems like I did." I smirk, trying to brush it off. "I'd ask for a promotion, but you already pay me too damn much."

But he's not smiling. Just keeps coming closer until he's right in front of me. His hand slides into my hair, yanking my head back. And with a growl, he crashes his mouth with mine. No warning or permission. Nothing but primal thirst and hunger. Everything that is Konstantin.

I should push him away. Remind him of the rule.

No kissing. No falling for the enemy.

But I don't. I kiss him harder, my free hand yanking at his shirt, needing his skin on mine, needing to forget why I should hate him. Because right now, all I want is this. Him. The taste of him. The way his body pushes into mine like a storm I can't stop.

The gun slips from my fingers, his falling beside mine with a louder clank, until we are just two bodies, desperate to get lost in each other. My arms wrap around his neck as he lifts me in the air, pressing me into the wall, mouths devouring, teeth clashing.

He groans into our kiss, hands everywhere, tearing at my clothes, shredding the tank top, yanking my shorts down. I fumble with his boxers, shoving them off his hips until I feel him, hot and hard against my stomach.

Reaching for him, I can barely wrap my fingers around his thick cock, and every inch of me aches to feel all of that inside me.

He pins me to the wall with the strength of his body while he wraps a hand around my throat, just enough to remind me who's in control.

"Moya." The single possessive word rips out of him as he slams savagely inside me.

And the world disappears. All that's left is this. The way he fills me. The way he fucks me like he owns me. Over and over until I don't recognize myself, until I beg and plead for more. Like I'm his and he's mine and nothing else matters.

The blood. The fear. The rules. Gone.

His eyes lock with mine, his body pounding into me until every sensation within me is because he allows it. Pleasure crashes over me like a tidal wave, and my nails claw into his shoulders, needing an anchor as my body shudders, my pussy rippling around him like it wants to keep him inside me forever.

He doesn't stop. He drives into me harder, faster, the sound of skin against skin pushing me closer, my body winding tight until I'm trembling on the edge again.

I almost forget he's not even wearing a condom. A part of me knows I should care, that I should be worried about consequences, but I can't think of anything I want more right now.

"Oh God, Konstantin, harder!"

He gives me everything, unleashing the side of him I knew was there. And I somehow come to envy every woman who has ever had this with him because I want him all to myself.

His eyes never leave mine as his hips thrust deeper, pounding until the picture on the wall shatters to pieces.

And as I shatter right along with it, screaming his name, I know this changes everything…yet somehow nothing at all.

EIGHTEEN

KONSTANTIN

With my mouth on hers and my cock still buried deep, I lower us to the floor, away from the shards of glass, and press her beneath me, wanting it slow this time.

Her pulse still thunders against my palm as I pin her wrists above her head. Her chest rises hard beneath mine, her mouth parted as if she doesn't know whether to gasp or scream my name again.

This woman saved my life for reasons that don't make sense. And now I'm taking hers, inch by inch.

I stare into her eyes, in awe of her, still not sure why she risked her life to save me. What did I do to deserve it? And how in the hell can I repay her for that?

I don't ever let debts go unpaid, and this one is no exception.

Blyat. She could've gotten hurt!

Rage storms into my veins. I can't make the dead suffer again, but the ones still alive? I'll make them wish for death.

But for now, my focus is her. This enigma of a woman I can't seem to rip out of my head.

Still buried inside her warmth, I circle my hips into her pussy, and her eyes roll back. The way she cried out my name, how good it felt to hear it… I need that again.

"Look at me, malyshka." I tighten my grip on her wrists, my hips slamming into her with maddening need as soon as she gives me those eyes. "You don't get to look anywhere else when I'm fucking you. Understand?"

Her sultry gaze sinks into mine, glassy with blazing intensity, but she doesn't dare to turn away.

"You saved my life…" My mouth drags along her neck. "Risked your own. Why?"

I need an answer more than she realizes. I need to understand why she would do this when in one second, she could've been dead.

The very thought of her lying on the ground with blood pooling around her makes me furious all over again. She shouldn't have done that for me.

Her thighs tighten around my hips, her gaze narrowing, and I fuck her harder when she doesn't answer, grinding into her deep until she's clawing at the floor, moaning like I'm both heaven and hell.

"Tell me!" I growl, throwing her legs over my shoulders and dropping my weight on top of hers, giving it to her until her cries echo through the walls, through the blood painted on them. "Why did you do it, Tessa?"

Thrust.

"Why?!"

"Oh God, fuck…please…"

Her eyes pinch shut, her back arching, and I take a nipple between my teeth, biting and sucking it until she hisses in pain, yanking my hair in her small fist.

"Because…" She groans. "You're my boss and you pay well."

My laugh rolls across her flesh right before I catch her wild gaze. "Is that the only reason?"

Is it not because you feel what I do right now? Is it all in my head? Have I gone crazy?

Because I refuse to believe this right here is one-sided. That I'm lying to myself, seeing what I want to see instead. Because no matter what I tell myself, I know there's more between us than maybe she even realizes.

"What other reason would there be?" Her nails score up my back, drawing a picture of her pleasure that I want permanently etched on my skin.

As I grab her jaw, my mouth drops lower, feathering across her lips. "Don't ever put yourself in harm's way for me again."

"And what happens if I do?"

She kisses me slow, and I growl, my cock jerking inside her, wanting to take her like it's a punishment.

"If you do…" My fingers curl around her throat, squeezing until her eyes turn heavy-lidded, a moan slipping out. "I will punish you."

"This doesn't seem like much of a punishment, sir."

"Blyat, ty svodish' menya s uma." *Fuck, you're going to drive me to insanity.*

My teeth grind, pumping into her with punishing strokes, and her eyes are on me through it all.

"This is not a game, Tessa." My body stills. "It is my job to protect you, not the other way around."

"That sounds pretty sexist, if you ask me."

That bite in her tone? I crave it like sin. She doesn't even know how rare it is, how rare *she* is. I'll keep her safe if only to hear her challenge me again.

"Not sexist, just protective. There's a difference."

"Mm, if you say so, Marinov."

"I like it when you're agreeable." My lips skim hers, my hips thrusting slow and deep until a breathy sigh escapes her.

"Don't get used to it." She throws her arms over my shoulders.

I chuckle, my mouth lowering to her throat, kissing up her neck. "I wouldn't dream of such things."

Her fingers slip into my hair, and for a moment, it's like she's breathing life into me, feeding something human I thought died a long time ago.

Her walls clench around me, and I groan, increasing my pace, wanting to forget all the blood and violence that is my life and live in this moment. Live in her. With one brutal thrust, I take her hard, my mouth ravaging hers, enjoying the way she groans into our kiss, her hand gripping the back of my head, wanting more.

Words may lie. But bodies don't. And hers is telling me everything I need to know. She wants this. Wants me. It's up to me to make sure she never forgets why.

I slow down just enough to feel every tremor, every tremble in her body that tells me she's mine.

She has no idea how much more I plan to take. How deep I'll carve myself into her life, into her flesh. Tessa Monroe belongs to me. She has from the start, and it's time she knows that.

I flip her over, dragging her to her knees on the blood-slick floor, reminding her that she's in this now.

My hands wrap around her hips, and I drive into her again—deeper, harder, my fingers biting into her skin like I'm branding her from the inside out. She gasps, her forehead dropping to the floor, but I catch her hair and pull her back up.

"No hiding," I grunt in her ear. "I want every sound. Every shiver. I want everything. Ti moya." *You're mine.*

She pushes her hips into me, wanting more, and I give her all of me.

"Say it. Say you're mine. I need to hear it." The desperation claws at me.

She mutters a curse when I slow down, her voice a ragged whisper. "I'm yours."

I know she doesn't mean it, though that makes no difference. Willing or not, she's not going anywhere.

I wind her hair tight in my fist and drive into her over and over, fingers working her clit until she breaks, moaning my name. Her body convulses, pussy clamping around me like it was made to keep me inside her.

"Oh God, yes!"

"Tessa!" I slam into her once more, and everything inside me detonates.

My release tears through me like rage, coating her walls, until every man who dares to touch her knows who she belongs to. With one last slam of my hips, I collapse over her, arms caging her in, breath ragged at her ear.

The world is quiet now. Except for the sound of her heart beating against mine.

But soon my world will erupt in blood once again. Because when I find the men who sent those bastards, they won't die because they came for me. They'll die because they could've hurt *her*.

For that, I'll tear their world down, brick by brick, until everything around them crumbles.

NINETEEN

KONSTANTIN

Two hours later, Tessa's back in bed and in my arms where she belongs. The blood's been washed from our skin, the penthouse clean like nothing ever happened.

There were no witnesses either, not that it matters. I own this place. If I want silence, I get it, no matter what.

And just as I suspected, the men I had stationed outside the suite were taken out before they could call for backup.

But those svolichy who came for me made one fatal mistake: they revealed their connection. DeLuca crew, just as I thought. Their tattoos gave them away, like a signature on a death warrant.

Once I told my brothers what happened, they went straight for DeLuca's last known hideout. But just like cowards, they'd already vanished.

Not to worry, though. They will be found. And once they are, I won't just give them the mercy of a clean death. I'll tear them apart, bone by fucking bone until they're begging to die.

Tessa shifts, her bare body warm against me, her breathing steady, but she's not asleep. I can feel the thoughts racing in her head as clearly as if she was speaking them out loud.

"Are you going to tell me what's going on in that pretty head of yours?"

Her gaze lifts to meet mine, shadowed with worry. "I was just wondering why we're still here and not on the plane going back home."

"You trying to run from me that fast?" My fingers draw a slow path up and down her spine, trying to memorize the feeling of her. To make this moment last as long as I can.

Her body fits against mine like it was made for this. Made for me. I never thought a man like me would ever find this. Someone who makes me feel…something. But she does.

"What if more come?" Tessa exhales sharply.

At that, I cup her chin. My thumb drags gently across her bottom lip, and her breaths stutter.

"Are you afraid?"

Doesn't she realize I'd protect her with my own life? Kill any man or woman who dares to even wish her harm?

"Yes," she whispers, and the sound of it guts me.

Not because she's weak. Because she's trusting me enough to admit it.

But no one should've ever made her feel this way in the first place.

I swallow the anger that surges up at the thought of her in danger, push it down, and let my touch speak what I already know. I'd die before I let anything touch her or scare her again.

I kiss her forehead, slow and soft. "I won't let anything happen to you. Not now. Not ever."

She closes her eyes like my vow does something to her. Like maybe she needs to believe in something or someone. And maybe she's starting to believe in me.

But then she pulls back just enough to break the spell.

"You don't know that. You don't even know me," she whispers.

My fingers tighten on her jaw, just enough for her to feel the steel beneath the softness. "Maybe that's true. But I know enough. Enough to destroy anyone who touches you. And I'll burn the world down before I let it take you from me."

Her breath hitches, and I know it's not from fear. It's the war inside her. The one she's losing.

"You may be scared of the monsters out there." I grip the back of her head and press my forehead to hers, letting the darkness rise between us like smoke. "But they're the ones who should be terrified of what I'll do once I get my hands on them."

She pushes back to look at me, her brows drawn tight, and I know she feels this.

In a flash, I flip her beneath me, pinning her there with the heaviness of my stare and the pressure of my hips. I brace myself on one forearm, while the knuckles of my free hand drift down her cheek, soft enough to make her lashes flutter.

"Though maybe I should thank them too. After all, if they hadn't come for me, I wouldn't have had you against the wall with my cock buried so deep you'll feel me for days."

She groans when my lips brush hers.

"And you definitely wouldn't have let me kiss you either."

"It was just the adrenaline…" she breathes, practically moaning against my mouth. "We can't repeat this. It's just a one-time thing."

"Adrenaline?" My tongue traces the curve of her lips. "That's all this is? You feel nothing for me?"

My cock presses against her wet core, hard and thick, the friction unbearable. She fights a gasp, her hands flying to my back, nails raking down my flesh like she wants to tear her way into me.

"What do you want me to say?"

"The truth, Tessa."

I trail kisses along her jaw, nipping at the soft places that make her squirm. I stop just before her mouth, my exhales brushing her lips but never giving her what I know she wants again.

"You're my boss…" she tries, but her voice falters, hands pulling me closer.

"That's not what I asked," I growl. My fingers curl around her throat as my eyes burn into hers. "Do you feel something when I touch you? When I look at you?"

I push closer, the tip of my cock nudging against her entrance, hot and heavy.

Her lips part, eyes shining, defiant and drowning all at once. She wants to lie.

But I won't let her.

"God damn it, Tessa, just say it!" My hips circle, my thickness dragging against her center, teasing us both with what we could have. With what I *need* to take.

She groans, her fingers digging into my back, thighs squeezing around me, hips rocking forward like her body's already made the decision for her.

"Fine! Yes…I feel it, okay? Happy?"

"Entirely." My smile widens right before my mouth crashes down on hers, devouring her confession with a kiss so hungry, so intoxicating, it tastes like a war I have no intention of losing.

She moans against me, and I swallow the sound, our tongues clashing as I drive into her with one hard, claiming thrust. She arches beneath me, a cry escaping as I fill her completely, every inch of her mine again.

"This," I grunt against her mouth. "This is what you wanted."

She doesn't deny it. Can't.

"You need to stop fucking me without a condom. I may be on the pill, but I don't trust you." Her nails work into my scalp as I piston into her harder, deeper, every stroke punishing and reverent all at once.

"I will never wear a condom with you, so get used to it."

"Oh God!"

I slam into her again, and her body tightens around me, warm and slick and everything I've been craving my entire life. And as I fuck her into the mattress, I know one thing.

I'll never let her lie to me. Not when the truth sounds like this.

"Are you gonna tell me about your scars?"

Her question comes out of nowhere, cutting through the quiet as we lie tangled together, our bodies sweat-ridden and satisfied.

For a second, I say nothing. I barely think about those scars anymore. Not really. When you can't see them, it's easy to pretend they don't exist. Like the pain is a ghost you've outgrown. But it never really leaves. It just settles deeper into your bones, into the parts of you no one else can touch.

I don't mind the scars. They're a part of me. A roadmap of the life I survived. But she wouldn't understand that kind of life. And the last thing I want from her is pity.

"What do you want to know?" I draw her in tighter, her sweet, floral scent curling around me.

"How did you get them?" Her brows furrow, her curiosity turning into something that feels a lot like concern, and I very much like seeing it.

I've never even had a woman ask about them before, like they just assume I got them because of the life I live.

Her fingers tenderly trail over the raised scars etched into my back. Like I'm something fragile. Like I could break.

The thought is laughable, but I'm strangely enjoying it. Because for the first time, I want someone to see what's beneath the monster and stay.

But I don't know how much to tell her, how much of myself to reveal. The more you give to someone else, the weaker you become—or at least that's what my father taught me. A long time ago.

"I was a boy. Around ten when I got my first scar."

"Who did that to you?" Her gaze drips in anger.

And I find myself smiling, because I can't remember the last time someone gave a damn.

Her fingertips trace another scar at the center of my back, gentler now. Like she senses something heavier is coming. Something ugly. Something far too broken to ever fix.

I exhale slow, the memories pushing against my lungs.

"My father," I tell her, confessing something I haven't told anyone. Never had a reason to.

She stills. "Your father gave you those scars?"

I nod once. "He believed pain builds men. That beating it into us every day would carve out the weakness…until we stopped crying."

"Jesus Christ." She shakes her head, letting out a heavy exhale as I continue.

"He was obsessed with shaping perfect heirs. Soldiers. Kings. He used to lock us in the cold cellar for days. Barely any food. No light. He'd pit us against each other in fights. Tests of strength, he'd call them. Over time, we stopped crying, stopped feeling."

My gaze finds hers, my hand cupping her cheek. "Or maybe I just convinced myself I did."

"I understand." She curls against me, her palm sliding over my chest like she wants to protect something already shattered.

I stiffen at the tenderness.

"Don't," I say roughly. "Don't feel sorry for me."

Her brows pull together. "I don't."

"Good. Because I don't hate him. Not for that. That was nothing compared to what he did when I loved someone."

She drags her head back, staring intently.

"My father liked to kill things." My knuckles drift across her jaw, my gaze following my movement.

"Liked…as in, he's dead?"

I nod. "He'd say fear and love make you weak. That enemies see it and use it against you. That when you love someone, they will destroy you. Or be destroyed because of you."

Her features twist and tighten like she's bracing for the worst of it.

"At the time, I didn't want to be like him. I was young. Hopeful. I wanted…love. What kid doesn't? And after my mother died when I was eight, I craved it until he carved it out of me."

Tessa sits up slightly, waiting for the rest of it like it's about to punch through her rib cage.

"I met a girl named Katya back in school when I was sixteen. She was sweet. Looked at me like I was more than a weapon. Like I mattered. When he found out I cared for her, he made sure I'd never make that mistake again." My voice flattens, becomes something hollow as the memories take hold. "He caught us one night. I snuck out to meet her at her parents' farm, and he was already there… waiting. He brought us both back to my house."

Tessa's lips part, but no sound comes.

"She cried. Begged for him to let her go. But I knew if I asked, he'd just make it hurt worse. So I said nothing as he slit her throat in front of me."

"Oh my God," she whispers, cupping her mouth.

"And he made me watch. Made me stand there while her blood soaked the dirt."

"I'm so sorry," she whispers, grabbing my hand and squeezing it.

"Don't be." I bring the top of her hand to my lips. "That was the first time I learned what love costs. What it destroys." I pull her in by the back of her head, my grip a little too tight. "I swore to never cross that line again."

But now I want to.

She sags against me, her arms winding around my back as we lie together in the aftermath. Neither of us says anything for a while, and I understand that what I just gave her is a lot to process.

But that's who my father was, and I swore that I would never become like him. That I would never have children and do what he did to me to someone else.

I was born from a monster, and I'm bound to create one too.

But Tessa doesn't pull away. She doesn't run. She stays in my arms. Her fingers trace one of the old scars like it means something now. Like it's not a flaw, but a story she's willing to carry. And that does something to me. It lodges deep in my chest, somewhere between ache and fury, and it terrifies the hell out of me.

So I don't say another word. I don't thank her. Don't ask what she's thinking. I just hold her against my chest. Like maybe if I keep her close enough, long enough, the dark won't find her.

Not like it found Katya.

Not like it found me.

TWENTY

EMILIA

I can't help it. I actually feel sorry for the devil.

Maybe because now I sort of understand him, and a part of me hurts for the child that died the night he lost the girl he loved.

His story is heartbreaking. The blood. The violence. The brutality carved into his bones since childhood.

It's no wonder Konstantin Marinov became the man he is. We're all shaped by what raised us, aren't we? Twisted by it. Hardened by it. At least partly. And from what I've seen, he and his brothers were born in fire and forged in hell. That, I can appreciate.

My mother enjoyed beating me too, the few times she was sober enough to actually realize I existed. The uninvited twinge in my chest resurfaces, but I shove it back down. Lock it in the box I always keep sealed.

Now isn't the time. I have a job to do.

Getting close to Konstantin is working. Too well.

The silence between us stretches like an open wound that refuses to close.

I haven't said anything else since he told me what his father did. Since he let me glimpse into the darkness still clinging to the corners of his soul.

Lying against him, curled into the crook of his body, my head on his chest, I listen to the thuds of his heartbeat beneath my cheek, and for a second, I imagine it tethered to mine. Like we're two people born into hell, connected in that way.

I let out a sigh, enjoying the feeling of his arms around me, forcing myself to forget who he is and let myself sink into it, pretending this is something real. Something good. Something that won't end in disaster.

At the very least, I got multiple mind-blowing orgasms out of it. Small victories.

"I'll have to meet your brother sometime," Konstantin slices through my thoughts. "To thank him for teaching you to shoot like that." He looks down at me, intensity brewing in his eyes. "When will I get to meet him?"

I shrug, keeping my tone easy. "Not sure. He's not around much. But next time he visits, I'll be sure to let you know."

Good luck with that…

"Please do." His gaze pins me. "I'd love to know more about him…and the rest of your family." His fingers trace a slow path along my arm, sending a pulse of heat through my veins. "Seems only fair I learn more about yours."

Shit.

Of course he'd want something from me in return. A man like him always wants more.

I don't want to tell him anything. But I have to give him something true, something that makes him feel like he's connecting with me.

Pulling back just enough to stare up at him, I start at the beginning.

"I never met my dad. Not even once. Just knew him from stories my mom told when she was drunk. Which, spoiler alert, was most of the time." I let out a wry chuckle.

But he doesn't return my dark sense of humor. His brow tightens instead, and I don't like to see that look in his eyes, the one that tells me he actually cares.

"She wasn't a good mother." I clear my throat. "Alcohol turned to pills. Pills turned to drugs. And I learned pretty fast how to stay quiet and disappear."

He takes my hand in his, and it would be sweet…if he wasn't also a psycho killer.

Who's also got a romantic side, Emilia. You can't forget that.

"What else?" His question pulls me back.

"She'd hit me sometimes. Maybe not as bad as your dad. Still, it hurt." My lips lift, soft and strained, shaped by the ache of the memory. "I cried. A lot."

His palm cups the side of my throat, a thumb tilting my chin up when I glance away. Those deep eyes search mine, and my stomach flips, my heart beating faster. My body drowns in this sense of warmth and affection.

I hate this. It shouldn't feel this good to have him care. The way he touches me, stares into my eyes, it forces me to continue.

"She'd scream over things I didn't do just to have a punching bag. And the men she brought home…"

My throat closes, and I have to look away. But he doesn't let me, holding my jaw prisoner and forcing the eye contact I want to avoid. It's too much.

"What did they do?" The words escape him like a threat, and a sane person would fear him right now, but I don't.

He wouldn't hurt Tessa.

Now, Emilia? She doesn't stand a chance.

I drag in a long, tired breath. "Some would hit me. Others…tried worse."

His nostrils flare, jaw clenching.

"Don't worry. I learned how to fight back. Not always well, but enough to escape."

"You never should've had to, katyonak." Leaning in, he presses his lips to my forehead, and something cracks open in my chest.

The sting behind my eyes is instant, sharp. I bite it back, but the warmth of him remains like a promise I don't know how to trust. When he pulls away, his gaze finds mine again—fierce, unwavering, like he's holding the weight of my past with me and daring me to keep going.

"When things got bad, I'd sneak out. Crash at friends' houses until whoever she had there left, only to be replaced by someone else the following day."

His eyes grow lethal, carved from fire and ice. I can feel the heat radiating off him.

"My life was a mess," I say with a dry laugh, flicking my hand like I'm tossing the truth away before it can sting.

But he doesn't flinch, doesn't let up. Just keeps watching, waiting. So I exhale and give him more.

"My mother was arrested a few times, and I thought maybe I'd finally be free of her, but after being sent to foster care, the system dumped me right back into hell. To say I don't trust the system is an understatement. It wasn't until I turned fourteen that my brother took me in. He left as soon as he could, but I think…I think he always meant to come back for me once he could take care of us both. He was the only safety I ever knew growing up. When we were kids, he'd stand between me and her, take the beatings so I didn't have to. He was my shield. My anchor. My rock."

Konstantin's face twists into something haunted and raw. He cradles my face in both hands and kisses my cheek. My eyes drift closed, and I soak it in like it's the only moment that's ever felt real, like it's something to treasure.

"Do you know the names of any of the men who hurt you?"

The question stuns me. Of course I can't tell him that. If he decides to go on a little expedition and find them, he'll also find Emilia. Can't have that.

I push back, trying to read his expression, but all I see is rage.

"No, but there was this one guy. He was a real asshole. Lasted months with my mother when the others were gone in days or weeks. He'd come into my room when I was sleeping…." I choke on the rest of it. Hate that I'm giving him this part of me.

"Did he…" He can't finish the sentence.

"No, but he definitely tried."

He grinds his teeth, his entire body stiff and ready to break something.

"My brother gave him a beating the last time he attempted to touch me, and that's when I left for good."

"And you don't remember his name?"

I shake my head.

His lips curl into something cold and predatory.

"Whatever you're thinking…" I press my hand to his chest. "Don't. You're never gonna find him."

Not that I'd mind if you actually killed Lloyd…

"Of course I will." His eyes burn into mine. "No one gets to hurt you and live, Tessa. That's a promise."

A chill shoots down my body.

God help me, some twisted part of me likes it. Not just the possessiveness, but the ferocity. The certainty. The way he says my name like it's already tattooed on his soul.

If only this was real. If only he wasn't the reason my brother is rotting in prison.

Maybe in some universe, we could have been something.

I force the thought down.

Don't be stupid, Emilia. He's the enemy. The man you're here to take down. He doesn't even know who you are.

Still, the words echo in my head.

No one gets to hurt you and live.

God, why does that sound so damn sexy?

TWENTY-ONE

KONSTANTIN

The door to my office closes the next day with a quiet click, sealing me in with the only men I trust. I settle into my leather chair, eyes locked on my brothers.

Aleksei leans against the edge of my desk, arms crossed, eyes cold and unflinching as always. Kirill sprawls in one of the leather chairs like he owns the place, a wicked grin tugging at his mouth as he flicks his knife open and closed with rhythmic precision, while Anton stands by the window, hands clasped behind his back, blank-eyed, watching the city like he's calculating which building to blow up first.

"I want an update," I tell them. "What have we learned since the attack?"

Aleksei is the first to speak. "The two she killed were high ranking. Word is, DeLucas want her blood for it."

"How do they even know about her?" My fist curls.

I will destroy them all for even thinking they could kill her.

"Maybe they had you followed," Kirill offers.

That's not likely.

"What else do we know?"

"They moved their location again," Aleksei continues. "Went underground. Every contact we've leaned on says the same thing. But the word on the street is clear."

Kirill picks it up. "They want her blood and won't rest until they get it. There's even talk of a bounty."

I slam a fist on the desk, sending pens scattering to the ground. "Find them and bring them to me. Every last one of them!"

"Trying," Aleksei says calmly. "But they're ghosts right now."

"You're telling me none of you can hunt down a nest of fucking roaches?" My temper continues to unravel. "If anything happens to her…" My voice carves through, sharp and unforgiving. "It's on every single one of you. And I don't forget."

"You're serious." Anton tilts his head, eerily still, his gaze narrowing. "Why is she not dispensable? Why do you care? She's not family. She's not necessary."

"She saved my life."

Of course, that's not the only reason why, but Anton of all of them would never get it. He hasn't understood connection since the night our father slammed a bottle across his skull and left him unconscious for hours. Whatever emotion used to live in him died then. After that, he just…stopped feeling. Stopped caring. A perfect killer.

Sometimes I envy that. The simplicity of not giving a damn.

"She's useful," I add. "Not that I need to justify anything to any of you."

"Of course not," Aleksei replies, throwing his hands in the air.

"She shares your bed. Of course she's useful." Kirill laughs.

"Enough!"

Anton tilts his head. "You'd go to war for her?"

"I'd wage a thousand wars to keep her safe, even if it was just for an hour."

The room goes silent, all eyes on me. The man I was before I met her would laugh. To go to war for a woman never crossed my mind until now.

Kirill flips the blade closed. "Nu da. Never thought I'd see the day Konstantin caught feelings."

"That's not what this is," I grit out.

"Like hell it isn't," he adds, smirking.

My eyes cut toward him.

He holds up his palms. "Hey, I'm not judging. She's beautiful. Deadly. I'd probably catch feelings too."

My eyes narrow. "Call her beautiful again, and I'll rip your tongue out. You focus on the crew. Leave her out of your mouth."

"So sensitive." Aleksei laughs. "How exactly do you plan to keep her safe?"

I let a small, sharp smile play at the corner of my mouth. "Don't worry about that."

Kirill raises a brow. "You've already planned it out, haven't you?"

"Of course."

They don't need to know anything. Not yet. But I've thought of the perfect way to ensure her absolute protection.

If DeLuca wants her blood? He'll have to go through me.

And I don't break. Not for anyone.

EMILIA

Without Konstantin near me, it's like I can finally breathe again. Like his presence doesn't cling to my skin or coil around my ribs like a vise. I needed space, real space, to remember who I am and why I'm doing all this.

My home is too quiet as I walk inside after having a run. No scent of his cologne in the air, no low murmur of Russian-accented commands, no flicker of that glinting stare watching me like I'm both prey and prize.

I kind of miss it.

See, no! Don't do that!

Fuck. I'm never this pathetic.

I take a long sip of my water before grabbing my phone and making the call I've been dying to make.

I haven't seen Nate for a couple of weeks, not since this whole operation began. The guilt weighs on me like an anchor around my throat, but it's been impossible to get away and I can't risk one of Konstantin's men following me.

I tap Reyes's name. He hasn't called, which is hopefully good news. The phone continues to ring, but he finally answers.

"Emilia…hey… What's up?" His voice cracks slightly, the nervous energy laced through his words, and I immediately know something's wrong.

"You tell me. Why do you sound like you're scared of me? What the fuck happened to Nate?"

Silence presses into my chest. Something's wrong. I can feel it.

"Reyes, I swear to God if you don't start talking right now, I'm gonna—"

"There was an incident two days ago."

My stomach instantly free-falls. I picture my brother dead on the floor, blood all around him.

No, no, he's fine. I expected shit to go down again. He's okay…

"What kind of incident?" I keep my voice steady.

"He was jumped in the yard while working out. Three guys. Skinheads. We think it was planned."

I go cold. My fingers tighten around the phone. "Is he okay?"

"He's alive. Got stabbed in the leg, but the blade missed anything vital. He's stitched up and recovering."

I can barely swallow past the lump rising in my throat. "Why the hell didn't you tell me?!"

"I wanted to, but he told me to keep you out of it. Em, I'm sorry. Being caught between you two hotheads isn't a place I wanna be, but I'm trying, alright?"

My chest rises and falls with long, shallow breaths. "Let me make it clear. When he tells you not to tell me shit, you tell me shit. Got it? Because if this happens again, I will make sure you lose you goddamn job! We understand each other?"

Blood rushes to my head; I can almost hear it in my temples.

"Yeah, okay. I'm sorry. You'll know everything from now on."

"Good. 'Cause remember, in exchange for you protecting him, I keep your little secret about supplying the prisoners with drugs." Heat flashes through my veins. "If that's too much work for you, I can let your boss know what a bad boy you've been."

"Jesus, alright. I'll do better. You think I wanted this to happen?" His tone grows sharper.

For a second, it sounds like he has a pair of balls. The fucking coward.

"I don't care what you wanted. I care about what you're getting done. We won't have this conversation again."

"Yeah, fine."

"So, what happens to Nate now? Are they gonna put him in solitary?"

"Yep. They're gonna have him in there for a few weeks, and he's got no choice this time."

I hate that I'm relieved that my brother will be locked in a box, cut off from everything. But at least he'll be safe.

"Do me a favor," I tell him. "I want you to pass him a message from me."

"What is it?"

"Tell him…" My throat tightens as I close my eyes. "Tell him I'm doing everything I can and I'll never stop until he's free."

Reyes is quiet for a beat. "You've got it."

I hang up and let out a shuddering breath.

Nate can't stay in there. I know deep in my gut that if he does, he'll die.

When I call Riley next, she answers immediately.

"Tell me you have good news." I release a sigh, desperation digging into me.

"Wish I did."

Fuck!

"I need something, Riley. He can't go on like this. He was attacked again."

"Oh, shit. Is he okay?"

"He's alive. And the good thing is they're gonna put him in solitary for a while. But he won't last in there forever."

She blows out a harsh exhale. "I know, and I'm trying. I've dug through everything on Konstantin's laptop, and I'm sorry to say but there's nothing that points to evidence tampering or Nate at all. The man's paranoid as hell and smarter than most, and believe me, he made it difficult to comb through everything. But you have me, so…"

"Okay, Miss Cocky." I let out a laugh. "Tell me what else we can try. Where else we can look."

"Well…" She pauses, like whatever she plans to say next is even more dangerous.

But thankfully, danger is my middle name.

"Tell me."

"Okay, but it might be hard."

"I don't care."

She scoffs. "Of course you don't. Alright, so as long as you can get your phone close to his, I can access it and see what I can find there. Or if you can somehow get near another laptop, maybe a private one, then we can try that too."

I press a palm to my forehead, the weight of everything crushing me. "I'll do it. We work pretty closely together, and having my phone near his won't be a problem."

"Okay, but it will be risky because the program runs for about ten minutes and he can't be using his cell at the time."

"I'll take care of it."

My hand slides through my hair, gripping it with frustration. "Fuck, maybe he's keeping the evidence in some damn safe at home or something. But how would I get in there?"

"I'm guessing he won't just let you snoop around in his mansion of death?"

"I've never even seen it."

I guess I need to get closer to him, secure some way inside, but how?

"So other than his phone, you're out of options," she says softly.

"There's always plan B…"

There's a pause. A beat too long. Then Riley exhales.

"Em…"

"What? Framing him is a viable plan. He won't play ball otherwise. If I make him believe that he could be put in prison for that cartel boss's murder, he'll give me what I want. He won't want a war with them either. Once he gives me what I need, whoever actually killed that cop goes away, and so does the evidence I'd have on him."

"That's reckless and you know it. That man…he'll kill you without blinking. There'll be nothing stopping him once you tell him what you're up to."

Sure, she's right, but it's a risk I'd be willing to take.

"I don't care what he does to me, because if I'm dead, you'll give the bureau everything you need to frame him. If I can't free Nate, then I'll make sure that the man who put him there rots for the rest of his life."

She lets out a sardonic chuckle. "Of course I'd do that for you, 'cause I know if I don't, you'd haunt me for the rest of my life."

"You bet your ass I would." My mouth curls. "I owe you. You're a good friend."

"I know. Now go and get me that phone. I'm texting you the program you need to install on your end. When you're ready, you run it on your cell and the program will do the rest."

"Okay. Thanks. Speak soon."

I end the call and toss the phone onto the table with more force than necessary. It skids across the surface, but I barely notice. My feet start moving before I can think, pacing back and forth like a caged animal, breath shallow, pulse thundering in my ears.

The pressure builds in my chest, fury and helplessness coiling so tightly it feels like I might snap in half. The room shrinks around me, the walls pressing closer with every second. I rub my arms and flick the elastic band on my wrist, trying to use the breathing techniques the therapist taught me to help ground myself.

But nothing helps. My mind spirals, needing to center all this pain and frustration.

A familiar ache pulses beneath the faint, silvery lines hidden on my arms.

They burn—not from pain, but from memory. From temptation. The need creeps in like a ghost. A quiet voice whispering that if I just let the blade kiss my skin, the storm inside will finally break.

I know better. But that doesn't stop me.

I rush into the bathroom, hands trembling as I drop to my knees and yank open the cabinet under the sink. The chaos in my head screams louder with every heartbeat. I dig past bottles and towels until my fingers brush the box filled with disposable razor blade refills—the ones I should've tossed, but didn't.

The light catches the metal as I open the box, glinting like a cruel invitation.

I stare at them, and I swear I can feel my past staring back at me.

None of this is going the way it was supposed to. I wasn't supposed to lose focus. Wasn't supposed to forget who I am or crave the way Konstantin's body feels wrapped around mine like armor I never asked for. But now I miss it like air.

And that terrifies me.

My fingers close around the razor, my palm trembling as I lift it. I lower myself to the cool tile floor, the silence of the room pushing in around me like a scream I can't release.

I press the dull edge against the faded lines on my arms, those reminders of darker days.

My body tightens. My throat closes.

I swore I was past this. That the girl who needed pain to breathe was long gone.

But here I am again, staring at a blade like it has answers.

This mission wasn't supposed to get personal. I was supposed to infiltrate, manipulate, gather evidence, and walk away unscathed.

But Konstantin Marinov isn't just anyone. He disarms me with a look. Wraps me in warmth and hunger. Makes me feel safe when I know I'm anything but.

He touches me like I matter. Holds me like I'm already his.

And part of me wants to believe it. Wants to believe the possessiveness in his voice is protection, not control. That the way he watches me, listens to me, kisses me…it's not just a game.

But it is. Because he's still the one who destroyed my brother. The man who plays judge, jury, and executioner behind closed doors. The Bratva king with blood under his nails and power in every word.

And I'm playing him like a violin.

Except now I don't know who's being played anymore.

I press the razor a little harder. Just enough to feel the cold bite of steel.

You're stronger than this, Emilia. Don't do it. You've come so far.

My other hand curls as I stare at the blade for long, drawn-out seconds.

FUCK!

I drop the blade on the floor, breathing so fast my head grows dizzy. I won't do this to myself again. I won't become her.

Running a hand down my face, I pick up the blade and the box with the rest and I toss them in the trash.

I can't go back there. Not ever.

I have to believe Nate will make it. That I can resist Konstantin long enough to outplay him before the spiral pulls me under, before I forget why I'm here and let him burn away what's left of my soul.

He may hold me like I'm his, but he's still the man who put my brother in a cage.

And no matter how tangled my feelings get, how deep I fall, this mission doesn't change. I *will* free Nate.

Because love is a luxury. Survival is a choice.

TWENTY-TWO

EMILIA

The night is silent. The kind of silence that feels heavy, pressing against the walls of my home.

I lie in bed, the soft hum of the fan the only sound. Sleep has been elusive lately, my mind a whirlwind of plans and fears. Tonight, however, exhaustion finally claims me, and I drift off.

But good things never last.

A sudden noise jolts me awake.

The hairs on the back of my neck prickle with unease as I try to listen for the sound again. It was low, a creak of some kind. Hell, it could be the floorboards. The house is pretty old. Still, my hand slides beneath the pillow, fingers wrapping tight around the grip of my gun.

The bedroom is swallowed in darkness. No moonlight. No streetlamps outside. Just a void closing in from all sides.

But as my eyesight adjusts, I swear I see something.

A shape in the far left corner of the room. Broad. Motionless.

My thumb clicks the bedside lamp on. The warm glow floods the space, and I nearly drop the gun.

Konstantin Marinov is seated in the leather armchair like he owns the place. Black dress pants, black loafers, the top few buttons of his shirt undone like he's just stepped out of a boardroom. Except it's midnight, according to the clock on my wall.

His eyes are calm. Patient. Hungry. But it's the black leather gloves on his hands that send a fresh spike of fear through me. Because gloves mean no fingerprints. And if he's here to kill me, he wouldn't want to leave evidence behind.

I steady my voice, gun still in hand. "What the *hell* are you doing here?"

His mouth curves into that signature smirk, the one that makes my nipples pebble beneath my thin white tank top—and God help me, I make no move to hide it.

"I apologize for startling you, Ms. Monroe," he drawls, words thick with dark amusement. "I only came to make sure you're alright. The DeLucas—the ones behind the hotel incident—are still out there. And I'd hate to lose such a…valuable employee."

"I'm alive. You can go now."

Please get the fuck out of here because you make me suffocate.

"I think what you meant to say is, 'Thank you, sir, for watching over me.'"

That's definitely not what I meant.

He rises slowly, like a panther about to pounce. "And you're welcome, by the way."

Presumptuous asshole.

"As you can clearly see, I'm fine, so you can leave. Breaking into my home in the middle of the night isn't just inappropriate. It's insane."

"Are we back to pretending the other night never happened?"

The closer he gets, the heavier the thud of his footfalls becomes, and the more I contemplate whether shooting him between his eyes right now would be all that bad.

"The other night was a mistake. A one-time mistake. That's all."

"Mm." He settles beside me, removing one of his gloves with slow precision. "No, malen'kaya. That was just the beginning."

Reaching out, his fingers brush a few strands of hair from my face. The gentleness is terrifying and alluring all at once. It's what makes him so much more dangerous. Powerful.

How can he so easily be both monster and man in the span of a breath?

"Look, you need to go," I whisper, but the words lack conviction, thin and useless against the tension crackling between us. "I need sleep. Okay?"

But he makes no attempts to move, fingers lingering on my skin, dragging heat through every nerve, making my stomach twist and my pulse thrum like a warning I'm too tired to fight. All I want is to close my eyes and give in, to stop resisting this dangerous pull between us.

But I can't afford that. Not with him. Not when everything I am is built on keeping him out.

And the more he touches me, the harder it becomes to fight whatever this is.

"I'm sorry, but I'm afraid I can't do that," he says. "Your safety is not negotiable."

"I can take care of myself. In case you forgot, I took care of you too."

His stormy laughter rattles through the walls. "I will admit, you can handle yourself with a weapon." His hand slides to my jaw, and my breath stutters. "But luck runs out. Next time, you could be outnumbered. And I won't risk that." His fingers tighten just slightly, eyes searing into mine. "Not with you."

Not with me?

The words resonate, sharp and disorienting.

Why?

His gaze dips to my mouth like he wants more of what he's already tasted. My skin hums, alive with anticipation, every inch of me pulled taut with desire.

"Why do you even care what happens to me?" The question slips out, barely a breath.

A slow smirk curves his lips, equal parts threatening and devastating. "Now, that's the million-dollar question." His thumb glides across my lower lip, sending a tremor down my spine. "I don't have an answer. All I know is you're the only brand of poison I want bleeding through my veins."

He leans in, so close I can taste his breath, mint-laced and maddening.

"And when I want something, I grip it with a tight fist until it's either mine or dead."

"You're such a romantic," I whisper, even as my body begs me to stop pretending I don't want to be his.

A flicker of amusement flashes in his gaze. "That's what they tell me. Now be a good girl for me and go get dressed."

I jerk back, eyes turning to slits. "I'm sorry, *what*?"

The trace of playfulness in his expression vanishes, replaced by something colder. Sharper. Deadly.

"I suppose I should clarify what's about to happen."

My spine straightens, every nerve sparking to life. "What are you talking about?"

"There's only one way to guarantee your safety."

"And that is?"

"You move in with me."

I laugh, harsh and disbelieving. "Yeah, no. I'm fine right here. If you're feeling protective, get me a bodyguard. Hell, post a sniper outside my window if it helps you sleep, but I'm not moving in with you."

The back of his hand glides down my cheek. "It seems you're under the impression this is a negotiation." His tone hardens. "At no point did I offer you a choice, Ms. Monroe. Now get dressed before I decide to do it for you."

"You're fucking insane!"

"Yes, and?" His eyes gleam with zero remorse. "Would you rather I not care? Leave you here to die? The DeLucas have a bounty on your head. Do you think I have no conscience?"

I scoff. "Do you really want me to answer that?"

On top of everything else I'm dealing with, I now have the DeLucas to worry about? Great…

Konstantin, of course, is too calm about it all. Like dragging me out of my bed in the middle of the night is perfectly rational. I guess for him, it is.

He exhales slowly, like I'm the one being unreasonable. "In case you've forgotten, my men were murdered while we slept. I won't let you be next. You saved my life, Tessa. This is how I repay you."

I clench my jaw. "I never asked you to, so consider us even. You don't owe me anything."

His smile widens, slow and dark, like I'm some unruly pet refusing to heel. The arrogance radiating off him could suffocate a room.

"Go put on some clothes," he goes on. "We're going home."

I bristle. "I *am* home. *You* are trespassing."

His features spiral with cold fury. "Get dressed. Now."

I cross my arms, blood boiling, my chest tight with anger and something else I don't want to name.

"No." I refuse to waver. "Leave."

For a heartbeat, silence stretches between us like a loaded gun. I can feel it—the moment the tension shifts.

What is he going to do? Grab me? Force me?

I hate him. I hate that a piece of me *wants* him to do it. Wants the control, the fire, the possession that only Konstantin knows how to deliver.

But that's the problem, isn't it? He's not just dangerous to the people chasing me. He's dangerous to *me.*

Because if I'm not careful, I might stop resisting. I might start letting him win.

He mutters something low and sharp in Russian, too fast for me to catch, before stalking straight to my dresser like this is his home, not mine.

My stomach knots.

Yanking open the top drawer, he pulls out a pair of black leggings and a cotton tank top.

I freeze. "How the hell did you know where those were?"

He doesn't answer.

My blood turns cold.

Shit.

He's been here before.

When? How many times? Was I asleep? Has he touched my things? Watched me?

He could've planted a bug. A camera.

A shiver rips down my spine, but I shove it down. I sweep for bugs every night. I scrub every inch of this place. I would've found something.

Wouldn't I?

Still, I can't be sure anymore. I have to be careful from now on. That is, if I ever come back to this place. God knows I'll probably end up dead in his mansion. Probably fed to the pigs I'll never get to meet.

When he tosses the clothes into my lap, waiting for me to strip, a bitter laugh escapes me.

"Turn the hell around, Marinov, and stay like that until I tell you otherwise."

His gaze dips to my mouth and lingers. That arrogant smirk tugs at the corner of his lips as he towers over me, like temptation in human form.

"I like it when you're bossy," he murmurs.

A pulse of need tightens in my core, unwelcome and infuriating. God, I hate that he can do this to me. That my body reacts even while my mind screams danger.

I roll my eyes, and he finally turns around, giving me his back. But even facing away, he radiates control.

Still, this…this is good. It might look like I lost this round, like I gave in, but this is the opening I've been waiting for.

What if he didn't do it?

The thought hits like a tsunami, slamming into me with no warning or mercy. My fingers freeze against the hem of my shirt.

What if you're wrong?

No. That's not possible.

Is it?

I squeeze my eyes shut, chasing away the doubt sinking its claws into my gut. I can't afford to believe in that. I can't afford to believe in *him*.

Not when Konstantin Marinov is the monster I've built this entire mission around.

But monsters aren't supposed to kiss like he does. And they're definitely not supposed to make you feel like maybe, just maybe, you're not alone in the dark.

"You can look now."

He turns, eyes gleaming with satisfaction, then casually pulls out his phone, types something, and slips it back into his pocket like this is just another day for him.

Not even a full minute later, two of his men walk into my bedroom, rolling in a black suitcase like they're bellboys at some luxury hotel.

My mouth drops open. "Are you kidding me?"

One of them heads toward my dresser.

"Don't touch my underwear," I snap, glaring.

Konstantin smirks, utterly unfazed. "Don't worry, malyshka. I'll handle that personally."

"This is insane," I mutter under my breath.

"This is *good*," he corrects with a wicked grin, pulling open the top drawer.

Without shame, he begins placing my bras and panties into the zippered pocket of the suitcase, as if it's the most natural thing in the world, while his men head for the bathroom, carrying a duffle.

My face burns, but I refuse to give him the satisfaction of seeing me flustered. Still, the way he handles my most personal items, like he already owns every inch of me, sends a twist of desire and dread curling in my stomach.

The men return from the bathroom and give Konstantin a nod.

He extends his hand to me, and I just stare at it for a second, like maybe if I blink hard enough, I'll wake up and this will all be some bizarre fever dream.

But it's not.

With a resigned sigh, I place my hand in his, and he leads me out of the house.

As I lock the door behind us, something cold and final sinks in my chest. My nerves tighten with every step down the stairs, each echo of our footfalls slicing through the quiet of the night.

And when I spot the black Rolls-Royce SUV waiting at the curb, it hits me.

I'm not just leaving my house. I'm leaving my life.

And walking straight into the belly of the beast.

Konstantin opens the passenger door, but before I can climb in, he steps in behind me, his body pressing against mine. He plants his hands on the roof of the car, caging me in, heat radiating from him like fire, licking at my skin and curling into my spine.

Then his mouth—God, his mouth—dips low to the shell of my ear, his breath fiery and deliberate. "I haven't been able to stop thinking about you.”

My eyes close, soaking in the moment like it's the only thing I've ever wanted to hear.

He waits, like he wants me to say it back. Like he needs me to.

But I won't. Even if it's the truth.

“It's alright, Ms. Monroe. One of these days, you'll reciprocate.” His lips graze the crook of my neck, and I almost groan in pleasure.

“Don't hold your breath,” I whisper, letting my head fall back against the hard plane of his chest. “You might be waiting a while.”

He laughs, a low, dark sound that feels like sin itself. “You'll find out soon enough that I'm a very patient man.”

And somehow, that scares me more than anything else.

His fingers trail along my hip, dipping lower, until they press between my thighs, right where I'm already throbbing for him. One thick finger drags upward, rolling over my clit through my pants with expert precision, like he already knows my body better than I do.

“Ty moi ray i moi ad.” Every syllable is rough and revering.

He rubs me with maddening control, his pressure devastating me, and I nearly cry out. But before the sound can tear from my throat, he pulls back and opens the car door all the way, like he didn't just unravel me with one hand.

He helps me in, his touch now infuriatingly polite, the ghost of his fingers still burning against me.

I try to gather myself, to reclaim some scrap of dignity, but it's useless. My body has already sold itself to the darkness.

And the worst part? I'm not sure I want it back.

Less than an hour later, we reach his estate, an endless stretch of land extending in every direction, wild and empty. The car glides down a long, double-laned road flanked by towering trees that shield whatever's lurking beyond their shadows.

When we reach a sharp curve, the path opens to a towering iron gate. Two guards stand on either side, rifles slung over their shoulders like an unspoken warning. They don't hesitate when they see him. Just a nod, and the gate swings open.

We roll forward again, deeper into his world, until the trees give way to a mansion so large it looks more like a compound. It spreads across the land like it owns it.

I don't know why anyone needs that much space. But I guess I'm about to find out.

He definitely has a taste for grandeur. Towering white columns sculpted into angels flank the entrance, their stone eyes casting judgment even in the dark. Two of Konstantin's men stand guard at the front, their postures rigid despite the late hour.

It's just past two in the morning when we pull into the circular drive, headlights washing over a collection of colorful sports cars already parked outside. Of course he has an entire fleet.

He steps out and rounds the car, opening my door like we're on a date and not whatever twisted arrangement this is. Ever the gentleman.

"Welcome home, Ms. Monroe," he says, offering his hand. "I hope it's to your liking."

I take it, ignoring the way his touch sends a shiver up my arm. "It'll do."

He chuckles low, and we start toward the massive doors.

One thing's painfully clear: if I'm supposed to uncover something in this fortress, I'm going to need more than a plan. I'm going to need a miracle.

The moment we step inside, I notice the lights are on. Every single one. Which is strange, considering the hour. I assume he has staff, but shouldn't they be asleep by now?

We move through the grand entry into a sprawling den, the gleam of a chandelier spilling light across the polished floors. And that's when I see them.

Three men are already there. Two of them are dressed in black from head to toe. Clean-shaven, broad-shouldered, sharp-eyed. They look a lot like Konstantin. Same height. Same imposing, dangerous aura.

But it's the third man who makes my breath hitch. He rises slowly from one of the velvet chairs. Older, shorter, kind-looking…and unmistakably wearing a priest's collar.

What the hell is a priest doing here?

My instincts scream that something isn't right. Every part of me itches to turn and bolt. But I already know there's nowhere to go.

"What's going on? Why is there a priest in your den? Who are those guys?"

No one answers.

Then Konstantin takes a step forward. A step closer to the end of my life as I know it.

Because he's either gonna kill me…or much worse.

"They're witnesses," he says casually, like we're talking about a birthday party.

"Witnesses to what?"

His smirk widens, dark and predatory. "Our wedding."

The words hit like a fist to my chest.

I stumble back, pulse roaring in my ears. "You're out of your goddamn mind!"

"There's no need for dramatics, Ms. Monroe." His tone is maddeningly calm, while I'm anything but. "This is the only way I can ensure your safety. As my wife, you'll be untouchable."

"This is insane! You can't do this."

"Why not?" He stalks forward, eyes burning with command. In one swift move, he grips my chin, forcing my face up to his. "Who's going to stop me?"

"I don't want a husband," I grit out. "Especially not one like you."

His gaze flares at that, something vicious twisting in his expression.

"You could do worse." His thumb glides ever so slowly over my mouth. "And let's be honest…you've already had worse."

His arm wraps around my waist, dragging me flush to his chest. I feel every hard line of him, every ounce of power.

"So let me tell you how this is going to go. Father Pasha will marry us. And my cousins, Maksim and Dmitri, will serve as witnesses."

Konstantin's grip tightens.

"You will stand beside me and say yes. Because if you try to run, you won't get far. And if you disobey…" He leans in, mouth brushing the shell of my ear, words dropping to a deadly whisper. "I'll chain you to me like my favorite accessory, so tight you'll forget what freedom ever felt like. You choose, Tessa."

His words echo like a gunshot in my skull. This isn't protection. This is ownership.

But as I look around—at the priest calmly flipping pages in his Bible, at the two cousins watching like this is their Friday night entertainment, at the guards posted like gargoyles, I realize…

There's no way out.

My fingers twitch at my sides. My stomach flips.

Think, Tessa. Think.

I could scream. I could make this difficult. But what would that get me? A tighter leash?

Or worse, him deciding I'm too much trouble to keep breathing.

I swallow while my heart won't stop hammering.

But the truth punches through the chaos: this might be the best move I have.

If I'm his wife, I'll have more access. I can use that.

Even if it means selling a piece of my soul in the process.

Fine. You want to drag me into this hell? I'll walk in smiling and burn you from the inside out.

"You're an absolute psycho. How the hell do you think forcing me into this is how you protect me? What world do you live in?"

"Are you really asking me that?" His knuckles roll down my cheek, and I almost wonder what kind of husband he would be.

A savage in the bedroom and a saint outside of it? At least to the woman he loves.

Except he doesn't love you. Sure, maybe he cares, but you'd be as good as dead once he learns who you are, so enjoy this marital bliss while you can.

"This is what I want," he says, voice low and final. "And whether you admit it or not…a part of you wants it too."

"No, I don't." My glare narrows.

He steps closer, crowding my space, dark eyes burning with ruthless certainty. "It doesn't matter. This is happening, because I need to keep you safe. And I'll do it with or without your permission."

"You're an asshole even when you're trying to be chivalrous. You know that, right?"

"You'll soon learn it's all part of my charm, Mrs. Marinova."

Why did that just sound so good?

Oh my God. Fiona and Gerardo are gonna lose their shit once I tell them about this.

I glance over at the priest and his cousins as they discreetly move to the far end of the room, giving us space.

"Will you grant me a divorce once the DeLucas are dealt with?"

"Sure," he replies smoothly. "Unless, of course, you find yourself enjoying this marriage."

I laugh, sharp and bitter. "Yeah, that's never going to happen."

He tsks under his breath, a playful but dangerous glint in his eyes. "Such little faith." His thumb lightly traces my chin, and without warning, his mouth hovers closer. "I could be a very good husband, you know."

His lips brush against mine, and the world tilts, the last of my resistance slipping away. My hands instinctively find his biceps, solid and frustratingly addictive. I want to rip his shirt off and climb him like a tree…which would be bad, considering I suck at climbing and would probably fall flat on my ass.

Still, I bet he'd catch me and tuck me against his broad chest…

Focus, Emilia. Jesus.

"How is this marriage going to work?" I push off of him. "If you think you're going to have me followed or chauffeured around like some rich bitch, think again."

He laughs. "Fine. Please, wife, enlighten me on what you'd like this marriage to look like."

The moment he calls me "wife," it hits me like a physical force. My heart skips a beat, a rush of heat flooding my body.

It's just a word, but the way he says it, so possessively…it sets something in motion inside me. Something I'm not sure I'm ready to confront.

"I don't want to be followed."

"That's fine." He shrugs.

"Really?" This can't be that easy.

"Yes. There are other ways."

Here we go…

"What other ways?"

"I can always put a GPS in you."

"I'm sorry, *what*?"

"How else can I keep you safe?" He gathers my hand in his and kisses the top of it.

"This is insane."

"You keep saying that. But it doesn't have to be bad for you. All your life, you didn't have anyone protecting you, not really. I know you've come to depend on yourself, and that's important. But now you have me. You have a whole family who would die for you. Don't you want that?"

Yes…

He makes it all sound like a fairy tale, like he'd give me the family I've always wanted to have, but we know that fairy tales are all a lie.

"None of this is real. Once you've taken care of my death threat, I'll just be your assistant again. I don't mean anything to you."

A crooked smile spreads on his face. "You underestimate the power you have over me." He kisses the tips of my fingers, and that sweet gesture, those words, send a shudder through me. "You'll have everything you could ever want. Just behave, and the rest will go smoothly. And imagine how fun it will be when I'll get to enjoy seeing you at work, then every night in my bed."

His bed…

God, there's no way in hell I'll ever be able to resist him.

"I'm still working for you?"

"Of course. You'll have some time off to adjust to your new life, but there's no one better than you."

I stare into the eyes of the monster I can't escape.

This is a nightmare. But I have to play along. For Nate. Let Konstantin think he owns me. Because the truth is, the closer he pulls me in, the more power I have to destroy him.

Yet the more power he has to destroy me too.

TWENTY-THREE

KONSTANTIN

I watch her from the corner of my eye. Arms crossed tightly over her chest, hair still tousled from sleep, and defiance gleaming in those sharp irises of hers.

Not exactly how most women imagine their wedding day, but to me, she's the epitome of perfection. My angry little viper of a bride.

She shifts beside me, just enough to put distance between our bodies, but not enough to stop me from feeling the heat radiating off her skin. I catch her glancing at the door, probably calculating if she can outrun my men.

Of course, she can't. That would only delay the inevitable.

"I never dreamed of getting married," she snaps, loud enough for everyone to hear. "Let alone in a mobster's house, dressed like I just rolled out of bed."

I bite back a smirk, taking her hand in mine. "You'll make it up to me on our honeymoon."

"You wish." She tries to pull her fingers free, but I tighten my grip, not letting her go.

Not now. Not ever.

Dmitri laughs under his breath, turning to Maksim. "Dayu tri dnya, prezhde chem ona yego zarejit." *I give it three days before she stabs him.*

Maksim snickers. "Pozhaluysta. On prosto poprosit yeyo sdelat' eto snova, no medlenneye." *Please. He'd just ask her to do it again, but slower.*

I shoot them a look, and those smirks vanish instantly.

"What?" Dmitri flips a hand in the air. "We're just happy for you."

Father Pasha clears his throat as he begins the ceremony.

"We are gathered here today under the eyes of God to witness the union of this man and this woman." Each word is thick with a Russian accent as he continues the sacred lines.

I never saw myself getting married, but if I ever did, it would be to someone like Tessa—strong, smart, capable, and utterly breathtaking too.

She exhales. I can feel the tension in her fingers, the way her body fights every spoken word.

My blood drums with possession. This may not be real, but it's ours, and I will remind her of our vows every chance I get. Because they mean something to me, no matter how we got here.

The priest continues guiding us through the vows. When he asks me if I take this woman to be my lawfully wedded wife, I answer without hesitation.

"Da." *Yes.*

Tessa says nothing at first. Then, after a long pause, she mutters, "I guess."

Gripping her jaw, I turn her face to mine. "That's not an answer."

She lifts her chin, ferocious as ever. "Fine. Yes."

"Good girl," I whisper.

She grits her teeth. Her defiance is so beautiful.

When it's time for the rings, my cousin passes me a box, and I slide the engagement ring first, a large five-carat round stone. She stares at it, the glistening diamond no comparison to the beauty of her eyes.

"This is…nice." She glances up at me, and my smirk curls as I slowly slip the platinum band onto her finger, covered in diamonds.

This doesn't have to be pretend.

Her hand trembles slightly, but she doesn't pull away, her eyes wild and searching as she stares up at me.

"By the power vested in me by the Orthodox Church and the laws that govern our people…" the priest says. "I now pronounce you husband and wife."

There's a beat of silence.

Then he adds, "You may kiss the bride."

I don't hesitate.

My hand wraps around the back of her neck, fingers threading into her hair as I drag her mouth to mine. The kiss is brutal, possessive. An unspoken vow sealed in hunger and fire.

I kiss her like I own her soul, like every breath she's ever taken has led her here, to this moment. To *me*.

Her lips soften beneath mine, and for the briefest second, I sense her surrender.

I pull back just enough to see the wreckage I've left behind. Her lips are swollen, stained a deeper red, pupils dilated with confusion, rage, and something darker. Something that mirrors the chaos I feel every time I look at her.

This isn't just the beginning of her end. It's the start of a war.

And I'll fight to keep her. No matter the consequences.

EMILIA

I don't remember walking out of the den. One second, I'm standing beneath that chandelier with a priest declaring me married, and the next, I'm moving through the halls like a ghost in my own life.

Mrs. Marinova.

The name sits in my gut like a stone I can't swallow.

But now I'm his—at least until I can break free.

Konstantin walks beside me, a slow, confident stride as though he's leading me to the life he's already planned. His hand rests lightly at the small of my back, a reminder of how much power he has over me.

"You'll get a tour tomorrow," he says, as if we've just moved into our first home instead of me having been forced into this marriage. "I'll introduce you to my staff. Show you the grounds. And you're free to go wherever you like on the estate, of course. Unless I tell you otherwise."

"And why would you do that?"

His eyes cut to me, a faint smirk pulling at his mouth. "Sometimes there are…things you don't want to see. People you don't want to hear scream."

Of course. As if I could forget about my new husband's murderous escapades.

Once we reach the master bedroom, he lets me inside, revealing a massive, black-upholstered bed that dominates the room, the kind with an oversized headboard and a mattress that looks softer than clouds. The curtains are a muted gray, the walls a rich charcoal, and everything smells faintly of cedarwood.

My luggage is already there, sitting like a quiet threat in the corner.

"Welcome to your new bed," he says, as if it's a gift.

I don't answer. Instead, I grab my clothes and head for the bathroom, locking the door behind me. Though I know it wouldn't stop him if he really wanted to get in.

Quickly changing into an oversized tee and a pair of shorts, I brace myself on the edge of the sink, breathing deep. I glance down at my left hand, the large engagement ring catching the light with every slight movement. The diamond sparkles, almost mocking me, its brilliance too much to ignore. I turn it slightly, watching the way the light bounces off its facets, feeling the weight of it on my finger. The wedding band, encrusted with diamonds, sits snug against it, like an anchor and a shackle all at once.

You just have to survive this.

But I know he won't make it easy.

When I return to the bedroom, my thoughts scatter like ashes.

Konstantin's shirt is gone, revealing a body sculpted with lean muscle, every inch of him hard and defined. His snake tattoos slither up his arms and down his rib cage, a reminder of the power he holds. His black boxer briefs dip low on his hips, and I can't tear my eyes away.

Of course, he notices.

A smile pulls at his mouth. "Don't be shy. You can look. You can touch. I'm your husband now, after all."

"I'd rather not," I lie, swallowing thickly and walking to the opposite side of the mattress.

"Suit yourself." He chuckles low in his chest.

His phone is on the nightstand on his side of the bed, and I know there's no way I can do what I need tonight. He'd wonder why I placed my phone beside his when I have a nightstand on my side.

I slip beneath the covers, trying to ignore how soft the sheets are, how good the bed feels, how much I don't hate being here. Turning away from him, I force my eyes closed, trying to make myself forget that he's still here.

He flicks off the lamp, plunging the room into darkness just as the mattress dips behind me. Then a heavy, warm arm slides around my waist, and before I can stop him, Konstantin pulls me against his chest. His bare skin brushes my back, lips lowering to the curve of my neck as he kisses me there.

"I know you don't trust me yet," he whispers. "But you will."

The words sink into my skin.

"Goodnight, Mrs. Marinova."

I lie there, staring at nothing. His breath warms the back of my neck, his hand resting heavy on my stomach.

I should hate this. I should pull away. But I don't want to.

Because this thing between us, whatever it is, is getting harder to fight. And the longer I stay in this bed, in this house, in his life, the harder it will be to let him go.

TWENTY-FOUR

EMILIA

A soft stream of sunlight breaks across my face, warm and golden, coaxing me from the deepest, most peaceful sleep I've had in years.

For a second, I forget where I am—wrapped in silk sheets, head sinking into a pillow that smells faintly of his cologne.

And that's when it hits me. I've tied myself to a monster, and this is his castle.

When I glance to my side, the bed is empty. A folded note sits on the pillow next to mine, thick ivory paper with something scrawled in bold handwriting.

JOIN ME FOR BREAKFAST, MRS. MARINOVA.
-K

I stare at the words for a moment, my stomach tightening.

Mrs. Marinova.

It still doesn't feel real. The ceremony, the kiss, the way he looked at me as if he'd claimed something more than just my name. Like he'd claimed *me*. My skin tingles at the memory.

My gaze drops to the rings on my finger, their cold brilliance a reminder of the promises made, the ties that bind me to him. It's strange how something so beautiful can also feel so deadly, each gleam like a warning I can't escape.

I climb out of bed and head to the suitcase, removing a floral dress from inside, something soft and feminine that falls to my knees. I'd much rather wear something black, something that reflects how I truly feel. But if I'm going to play this game, I have to follow his rules, even while I hate every minute of it.

The winding staircase feels endless as I descend. Framed paintings line the walls. Nature scenes, dense forests, wolves howling under full moons. Power and beauty. A reflection of the man who lives here.

At the bottom, a guy waits, gun holstered, back straight.

"Good morning, Mrs. Marinova. The boss waiting for you. I show you where."

"Alright." I follow him past the foyer and into an expansive kitchen with gray cabinetry, white marbled counters, and pendant lights glowing like low embers.

A long oak table anchors the room, piled high with food. Konstantin sits at the head of it, his phone in one hand, a porcelain coffee cup in the other. He looks devastatingly relaxed, the crisp white of his shirt rolled at the forearms, veins visible as his fingers scroll lazily. But the moment he sees me, his posture shifts. The phone lowers; his lips curl into a slow, deliberate smirk; and something in my chest stutters hard.

The way he looks at me…it's too much. Too intimate. Like I'm something precious he doesn't intend to let go of.

And for a split second, I let myself wonder how it might feel if this was real. A husband whose eyes soften when I entered the room. A man who smiles like I'm his world.

My heart squeezes at the thought, because I know better. I know exactly what this is: a velvet-lined trap that tightens every time I exhale.

"Careful, Mrs. Marinova. That dress might start a war," he drawls, low and rough, thick with something that makes my pulse flicker.

He rises from his seat like a man with purpose, closing the space between us in three measured steps. His fingers brush my waist before his arm curves around my back, pulling me in. His mouth dips to my ear, breath warm and unhurried against my skin.

"Good morning, my beautiful wife."

My heart does that stupid thing again every time he calls me that, like it's flipping in my chest.

Stupid heart.

"Morning." I slide my hand up the solid column of his neck and tug him closer, unable to stop myself, like he's controlling every inch of me.

My lips graze his jaw, and he lets out a low growl, the vibration seeping into my chest. He follows as I turn toward the table, but before I can reach the nearest seat, he pulls out the one beside his. I hesitate, but his fingers slide along mine in a slow caress. When I look up, his gaze has darkened, burning through every layer of my restraint. It roams my face, my lips, down the slope of my neck, like he's memorizing me.

I force myself to clear my throat, to break whatever this is. When I finally lower into my seat, he slides in beside me, his hand falling to my thigh beneath the table, firm and possessive.

And just like that, I forget how to breathe.

Before I can process the heat spreading through me, footsteps echo softly against the tile. An older woman enters the kitchen, her gray hair swept into a low bun and a warm smile lighting up her face.

"Oh, hello! It is pleasure to meet you, Mrs. Marinova.

Congratulations!" Her Russian accent is hard to miss.

I stand to greet her, offering a quick glance at Konstantin, silently asking who she is.

"This is Arina, my chef. She prepared our breakfast."

"It's nice to meet you," I tell her, still trying to wrap my head around how domestic this moment feels. "Everything smells incredible."

She smiles warmly and squeezes my hand. "I make blini with red caviar, syrniki with powder sugar. Is Russian pancake. And pirozhki with egg and onion. You eat, yes?"

"Sure, I'll try everything." A grin grows on my face.

I've never tasted any of that before, but my mouth waters just from the aroma. As I take my seat again, Arina pours me a cup of coffee while Konstantin leans forward and begins piling food onto my plate.

"Whoa…" I laugh, eyeing the generous portions. "That's way too much. If you keep feeding me like this, I won't fit into this dress you seem to like so much."

His gaze darkens as it sweeps over me. "That's perfectly fine. I prefer you without it anyway."

My mouth falls open, heat blazing across my cheeks as I throw a pointed look toward Arina, who's facing away from us, washing something in the sink.

He barely blinks. "Don't worry, she's seen and heard worse."

I don't doubt that for a second.

Trying to ignore the thrum beneath my skin, I focus on my plate, letting the steam and scent pull me in. I take a bite of something buttery and soft, and the taste is so rich, so unexpectedly good, that a quiet sound slips out before I can catch it.

His attention sharpens instantly, zeroed in like a hunter. "You like it?"

"It's amazing."

"You enjoy." Arina wipes her hands on a towel, her smile soft as she heads toward the hallway. "I go."

"Thanks again," I tell her.

She nods once and disappears, leaving behind a silence that suddenly feels thick. Only the clink of cutlery fills the room as we both enjoy our breakfast. My attention flicks toward his plate for a moment, where his phone sits beside his coffee.

This might be the best chance I have.

If I can get to the bathroom, launch the program Riley sent, then bring my phone back and place it close enough to his, the sync should begin. All I have to do is make sure he doesn't use his phone for ten minutes. How hard can that be?

I clear my throat. "Where's the bathroom?"

He glances up, his fork pausing mid-air, eyes narrowing just slightly. "Just through there." He lifts his finger toward the hallway behind him. "First door on the right."

"Thanks." I attempt to keep my movements casual as I rise.

Each step away from the table feels like walking a tightrope. I can feel his stare trailing me as I disappear down the hall.

Once inside the bathroom, I lock the door and launch the program, the screen flashing once before going completely black. Exactly what she said would happen. Still, I can't stop my nerves from clawing through me.

What if it doesn't work? What if he somehow realizes what I'm doing?

Fuck, I need to stop. I'll only make myself crazy with worst-case scenarios.

My pulse crashes in my ears as I flush the toilet and run the water, giving the illusion of normalcy. Catching a glimpse of myself in the mirror, I force a breath into my lungs.

Don't blow this now.

When I return to the kitchen, I attempt to keep my pace natural.

Konstantin looks up as I approach, and for a moment, his gaze sharpens, like he's reading the thoughts right off my subconscious.

"Find it okay?" he asks, tone easy. But his eyes…they're not.

"Yeah." I smile, quick and tight, and slide into the seat beside him.

My phone rests on the table, inches from his, close enough to start the sync. I grip my coffee cup, fingers stiff, every cell in my body wound tight.

He reaches for something, and my stomach drops as his fingers brush the edge of his phone. I brace, ready to scream into the fucking void.

"I need to go back to my apartment sometime today." My words come fast, too fast. "There are a few things I forgot."

His hand stills as he leans back in his chair, attention swinging fully to me. The moment stretches.

"That's fine." He lifts his cup to his mouth. "I have business to handle this morning, so your bodyguards will take you."

Bodyguards. Plural.

Of course. Not enough that I have to cover my tracks from one. Now I'll get to have fun with more of them.

My hand curls beneath the table. "When will I meet them?"

"You already have." He smirks slightly. "Maksim and Dmitri. They're the only ones I trust with your safety, aside from my brothers."

He turns his attention back to his coffee, the phone remaining untouched, exactly where I need it.

About seven more minutes. I just have to act normal.

"Speaking of your brothers…" I swirl the last of my coffee. "How come they weren't at the ceremony yesterday? Do they not approve of your choice of wife?" The amusement in my tone is anything but subtle.

His jaw tics. "Don't worry about them."

I smirk. "Sounds like a yes."

"Their opinions don't matter to me. And they shouldn't to you."

"I guess it shouldn't, since we won't be married for long."

He just cuts into a thin pancake like I didn't speak at all. "You'll see them tonight at dinner. And I promise they'll be on their best behavior."

The way he says it, there's no doubt in my mind that "best behavior" is not a suggestion. It's an order. And if one of his brothers steps out of line, he'll handle it. No matter the blood they share.

He sets his fork down. "Before I forget, I have something for you."

Rising from the table, he crosses to a drawer, returning with a long black jewelry box.

"What's that?"

"A wedding present." He places it in front of me.

When I look inside, I find a thin bracelet, delicate and glinting with small diamonds. The kind of thing you'd expect to find in a vault, not casually slid across a breakfast table.

"That looks insanely expensive. What if I lose it?"

"I'll get another." He lifts it from the case and clasps it around my wrist.

The metal is cold. So is the pit forming in my stomach.

"You should know…"

My gaze snaps to his, heart racing. "Know what?"

"It has a tracker."

I jerk my hand back. "Are you serious right now?"

"Very." A devilish grin stretches across his face. "Since you were so against the GPS implant, I thought this was a reasonable compromise."

A dry, cutting laugh slips from my throat. "A reasonable compromise? Wow."

"I understand this feels extreme to someone like you," he says, calm as hell. "But in my world, this keeps you safe. If you're ever separated from my men, this will ensure I know where you are to get to you."

"So you're going to stalk me now?" My eyes narrow.

"Do you have something to hide?"

Too much.

"That's not the point. I have a life. Outside of this…whatever this is."

He leans closer, his tone softer—almost gentle, but carrying quiet dominance. "Your life is now my life, dorogaya. Get used to it."

He lifts my hand like it's fragile, precious, and kisses my knuckles. The warm press of his lips sets my mind on fire, making me forget why I was just pissed at him. A shiver ripples through me, shamefully pleasant.

It shouldn't feel good. It shouldn't light a fuse inside me or make my stomach flutter like he's more than just a monster in a suit.

I clench my jaw. I wish I could hate him properly, but he somehow slipped beneath my flesh and rotted me from the inside.

His grip doesn't loosen. Instead, his thumb moves in slow, steady circles over my skin, a soothing motion that somehow tightens every muscle within me.

"You should also know…" he says, almost conversationally. "If you decide to take it off, it has an electric shock mechanism."

I blink at him, yanking my hand away.

"Wow. This just keeps getting better. Tell me more." My fingers squeeze at my lap.

He reaches into his pocket and pulls out a small, black remote.

What the hell?

"I control it." And with the click of a button, he adds, "Now it's on."

"You're fucking nuts."

He returns to his breakfast, like this is normal. "And yet here we are. Now finish your food. After that, you can return to your apartment."

I stare down at the bracelet, a trap masquerading as a gift.

The longer I look at it, the tighter my chest becomes. It's a pretty little prison, wrapped around my wrist.

That's okay, though. I may be his prisoner now, but I won't stay one for long.

TWENTY-FIVE

EMILIA

The second the SUV pulls up to my apartment building, I'm already reaching for the door handle.

"We will wait here," Maksim grunts from the front seat as I get out, rushing up the stairs.

As soon as I enter my home, I turn the lock into place, heart thudding. Not because I'm scared, but because if I don't hurry, they may come knocking.

When I dial Gerardo, he answers almost immediately.

"Hey." His voice tightens. "Everything okay?"

"Sort of. A lot's happened since we last spoke."

"Did he do something?" His tone shifts instantly to protective, and I can't help but smile.

As a kid, I used to wish he was my real father. It was one of the many fairy tales I dreamed up, along with living in a giant mansion with a prince who adored me.

Well, I did get my mansion...but I definitely got the villain instead of the prince.

"Yes and no," I tell him. "There was a shooting. It happened during a work trip. The DeLuca crew found us and tried to kill him."

"What?" His breath quickens. "You didn't get hurt, right?"

"No, I'm fine. But I saved his life by taking out two high-ranking guys. Now there's a bounty on me."

Silence stretches between us before he speaks again, his voice low with frustration. "Damn it, Emilia. This is exactly what I was afraid of."

"You think I planned this?"

"No." He sighs, weariness bleeding through the line. "But you know I can't help you with this. If the bureau finds out I let you do any of it—"

"I'd never rat you out."

He exhales sharply. "I know that, kid."

"There's more." I pinch the bridge of my nose.

"Oh, come on. What else could there be?"

I take a moment before I say it. "He made me marry him."

A long, dreadful silence wedges between us. "He *what*?"

"I didn't have a damn choice. He said it's for my protection, and now I'm living with him."

"Jesus Christ, Emilia!"

"I'll be fine. This is good."

"Good?" He lets out a dry chuckle. "Only you would call what you just said good."

"I'm closer than ever to finding what I need."

"You're out of your goddamn element. I never should've let you do this."

"Too late."

He says something under his breath. "Just be careful. I don't have to tell you what would happen to you if he finds out what you're really doing."

"He won't." I grip the edge of the counter. "But please…just watch out for Nate. I won't be able to see him for a while."

"You have my word. I'll only contact you if something is wrong."

"Thank you. Talk soon." I end the call, then immediately phone Riley.

"Hey!" she says. "So happy you called. Great work, by the way. I got into his cell."

Relief hits me.

I fucking did it.

"But that's not what I wanted to talk to you about…" Her voice trails, and I don't like it.

"What is it?"

"So, I was going through Nate's partner's stuff again and found encrypted monthly wire transfers tied to some offshore account. This time, though, I traced it back to the DeLuca family, not the Russians."

I freeze. "So, what the hell does that mean? He was taking money from both of them?"

"Seems that way."

"What the fuck was he up to? How dirty was this guy?"

"As dirty as they come."

My head starts to spin and I back up against the wall for stability. "Maybe he crossed the DeLucas and got killed for it. Maybe it wasn't the Russians."

What I really want to say, though, is *maybe it wasn't Konstantin.*

It's like I'm grasping for any sign that he isn't involved. Like somehow that would make him a good person or give me permission to be with him.

"It's possible, yeah. If he was working with the DeLucas and their relationship went sour, they'd get rid of him. It's too soon to know for sure, but I'll keep digging."

"Okay. I have to go. Do me a favor and only call me if it's an emergency. I'm gonna have constant eyes on me."

"What happened?"

I take a deep breath, bracing myself for the absurdity of it all. There's no way to explain how absolutely insane all of this is without it sounding like a bad joke or one of those Mafia romance novels where the girl falls for the big, scary guy who forces her to marry him.

"Long story short, I killed someone in the DeLuca crew, and now they want me dead for it. So, my boss decided it would be best if I became his wife instead. Now I'm living with him."

There's a pause. A long, heavy silence that makes me want to laugh but also cry. Because of course this is my life now.

"Holy shit…" she says, disbelief clouding her voice.

"Yep." I let out a shaky laugh, rubbing my temple. "I can tell you where to send a wedding present if you'd like."

"How the hell are you gonna get out of this?" she whispers, her tone still laced with shock.

Dropping the back of my head against the wall, I close my eyes. "He promised me a divorce once he kills the crew."

There's more silence, and I can practically hear her mental wheels spinning.

"And you believe him?"

I can't help the small laugh that escapes. "No, I don't, but what choice do I have?"

She lets out a weighty sigh. "Yeah, I get it. Just don't do stupid shit and keep your head down."

"Don't worry. I'm trying not to let the whole 'my husband is a Mafia boss and I'm his prisoner' thing set in. It's really starting to cramp my style."

I can almost picture her rolling her eyes on the other end of the line before she lets out a laugh. "I can definitely see how that would be a problem."

"Do me another favor."

"Anything."

"Can you fill Fiona in? She'll kill me if I tell her."

Riley's laughter is lighter this time. "I'll handle her. You stay safe, okay?"

"I will. Thanks."

As soon as the call ends, I delete the call log and stuff my phone into my handbag.

Then I grab a duffle and toss in a few other clothes his people couldn't fit in, just enough to make the visit look legit.

Because if Konstantin even suspects what I'm doing, I won't just be married to a mobster. I'll be buried by one.

KONSTANTIN

"I can't believe you married her." Aleksei takes another puff of his cigar, the scent of leather clashing with the bitter sting of cigar smoke.

"I did." My gaze lands on each of my brothers. "And all of you will be your best selves when you see her for dinner tonight, or I'll have your heads."

"You really care about her, don't you?" Kirill eyes me intently as he leans against the wall.

I ignore him, glaring at each one of them. "Tessa is off-limits. Do you all understand? You disrespect my wife, you disrespect me."

Aleksei flicks his ashes into the tray on the desk in my study. "We understand, brother. The help is now your wife."

"Watch your fucking tone!" My fist connects hard with the desk, my anger vibrating through me.

The smirk fades from his face, irritation lingering instead.

Kirill raises his glass and cuts in before things can get ugly. "Vso normalna." *Everything's fine.* "We'll all be on our best behavior. If she matters to you, that's enough for us."

Aleksei nods once. "Yeah, all good. We will protect her with our lives, if that's what you want."

"That's exactly what I want." I rise, heading to the bar in the corner, needing a drink. "Now, tell me what you've got on the DeLucas."

Aleksei's mood intensifies. "They've got someone on the inside. A cop."

I glance at him over my shoulder. "Name?"

"Don't have one yet. They're keeping his info well-guarded. All we've heard so far from the ones we spoke to is that whoever this cop is, he's in deep with their organization, and only the top lieutenants in the crew know who he is."

I return to my chair. "That's not news. Cops have been dirty since the beginning of time. Why should I care about this one?"

"Because this one isn't just helping them," Kirill adds. "This one might be leading them."

That gets my attention. "You really think this cop is the one running things?"

He gives a small shrug. "If not running, then pulling strings. Explains a lot, no? Why they've been bold lately. Why they keep testing us and aren't scared of consequences."

It does make sense. The DeLucas used to know their place. Then suddenly, they started reaching into territories they'd never dared to touch before. Contracts we had locked down began to slip. Rumors of suppliers switching sides. It wasn't desperation; it was arrogance. The kind of arrogance that only comes when someone powerful is whispering in your ear.

A cop. Someone who could cover tracks, redirect investigations, give advance warnings. Someone who made them feel invincible.

I sit back, processing it all. "Find him. And when you do, I want him alive. I want to know who else he's working with, what he knows."

Kirill nods. "We're already looking. He won't stay hidden forever."

I glance at the time, then fix my brothers with a look. "Be back here at seven sharp."

Kirill grins, that dark humor lighting up his face. "I swear I still can't tell if you're joking or if you're actually serious about her."

"I'm always serious. Especially when it comes to what's mine."

Anton watches, his eyes searching, as if trying to grasp what it's like to care for someone.

"Seven," I repeat. "Don't be late."

They get up, one by one. And just like that, the room empties. But the remnants of what we just discussed remain.

If there's a cop helping run the DeLuca crew, then he's their shield. If that shield cracks, so does everything they've built.

And I plan to be the one holding the hammer.

TWENTY-SIX

EMILIA

Konstantin's brothers walk in for dinner, along with Kirill's son, Lev. The greetings are brief, just polite nods. None of them meet my gaze for more than a second. And something about their silence feels off.

Maybe Konstantin told them not to talk to me so they don't say something they shouldn't. Or maybe they really don't like me—which is fine, because the feeling's mutual.

My gaze shifts to the quiet nine-year-old boy, his dark curls falling softly around his forehead. His eyes remain fixed on the floor, and his small hand nervously grips his father's large one.

Kirill leans down, whispering something to him, and only then does the boy glance up at me. His soft "hi" barely reaches my ears before his gaze falls back to the floor.

My heart swells and a lump forms in my throat. Something about him tugs at me, though I can't quite put my finger on what it is.

Maybe it's because we both had mothers who decided we weren't worth the effort, or because we were both born into circumstances we didn't choose. Whatever it is, the urge to hold him, to wrap my arms around him and tell him it's okay and his mother's lack of love doesn't define him, overwhelms me.

Konstantin's arm falls over my shoulder as he whispers, "That's my nephew, Lev. He has autism."

Of course, I already knew that, but I pretend I didn't, nodding in acknowledgment. "He's sweet."

"He's a great boy."

Glancing up, I catch Konstantin's eyes. There's a tenderness in them, a quiet adoration as he watches Lev, his expression filled with something raw and pure. And in this moment, seeing him like this—so open, so vulnerable in his love for this child—makes it just a little harder to hate him.

"Come, let's eat," he tells everyone, pulling me out of my thoughts.

Grabbing my hand, he leads the way to the opulent dining room, a long table set with more food than any one of us could ever stomach. The meal progresses beneath the awkwardness of an uncomfortable silence, broken only by the sound of silverware clinking against porcelain.

None of the brothers offer much in the way of conversation, their attention focused elsewhere. It feels like I'm invisible to them, an unimportant detail, and I don't know why it pisses me off so much. I can't stop glancing at Konstantin beside me, sitting at the head of the table, composed with a quiet sense of ease surrounding him that I can't quite grasp.

Does he notice how weird things are? Does he even care?

He looks over at everyone, his palm landing on my thigh, giving it a little squeeze. It's then I know he did notice, and that quiet gesture puts me a little bit at ease.

"I'm glad we can all be here," he says. "And I'm very happy you all have had the privilege to meet my beautiful wife." Picking up my hand, he kisses the top of it, and shivers run through me. "I also wanted to take this opportunity to announce that in three days…"

I lift my glass of water and bring it to my lips.

"We'll have a reception here at the estate to celebrate our marriage."

The cup almost slips from my grasp, my mind catching up with his words.

"Oh, wow… Great," I mutter.

The thought of some fancy reception, surrounded by strangers, makes my skin crawl. I didn't sign up for this circus.

The brothers offer a congratulations that seems less than enthusiastic before Kirill says, "We must drink to the happy couple."

His grin spreads, but there's something sinister beneath the façade, his tattoos making him seem even more deadly.

"That's a good idea." Konstantin nods as one of the waitstaff starts pouring each one of us a shot.

When she's about to pour me one, he shakes his head, and she returns to her spot in the corner of the room.

Kirill picks up his shot glass in the air, and everyone follows. "Za zdorovya i schastya. It means to health and happiness."

His eyes go to mine, and I offer a small smile before they all swallow their drinks and pour another round. After that, it seems the air of awkwardness melts away. Even Anton looks at me, though it's like he's assessing me, which doesn't make me feel any better.

Konstantin's mouth drops to my ear. "You didn't seem thrilled about the idea of a party. Do you not like parties?" His fingers lazily glide up my thigh past the hem of my red pencil dress, discreetly slipping between my thighs. "Maybe I can change your mind."

My breath hitches as he slips a single digit past my panties, and I suppress a moan, shoving his hand away without catching the attention of his brothers.

"There are children present. Behave," I whisper, and he lets out a deep-chested laugh.

"It's hard to behave when you're dressed to kill, Mrs. Marinova. Is that your intention? To kill your husband before you've had the chance to fall in love with him?"

My eyes slip to his, his words unnerving me.

"You are so beautiful." His gaze sinks into mine, the quiet before the storm. The beauty before it's washed away in the aftermath.

Because he has no idea how right he is or how many times I've dreamed of killing him, but now the thought seems almost painful.

His thumb caresses my cheek. "Eat. Your food is getting cold."

But neither of us seems to be able to look away, and all I want is to kiss him and tell him that I'm sorry.

Even when maybe it's the last thing he deserves.

After dinner, we move to the den. The fire crackles in the background, though the room still feels cold.

I stand against the back of a sofa, an iced tea in hand, watching as Konstantin kneels on the floor beside Lev. They're working together on a puzzle, Konstantin's large hands guiding Lev's smaller ones with absolute tenderness as he whispers to him, things I can't make out from here. There's something about the way he is with the child that softens the edges of his hard exterior, just for a moment.

My chest tightens as Lev hands him a puzzle piece and Konstantin kisses his knuckles before placing the piece where it's supposed to go. And stupidly, I start to imagine if we had a family. If this was our child he was playing with.

What would that even be like? To have a family of my own. People to love, and who love me back.

Here I go, getting sucked into fairy tales again.

But sometimes it's just easier to get lost in something instead of being forced to face your own reality.

The more I watch them together, the harder it becomes to look away, and the more I realize that Konstantin is nothing like his father. The man in front of me is gentle, patient, protective. He's good to the people he loves.

And if he can be different, maybe there's hope for me to be different too. Maybe there's a chance that I could be a good mother, despite all the ways I've been failed.

I close my eyes for a moment, letting the thought settle in.

Someone clearing their throat startles me, and when I peer to my left, I find Kirill there, standing beside me with an intensity that matches his presence. His eyes flicker briefly toward Konstantin and Lev before turning to me.

"I've never seen my brother with a woman the way he is with you." There's a fondness there, twined with the hard edge of his voice.

"Well, that's good, then." My gaze meets his, a quick smile flashing on my face.

He nods with a tilt of his mouth right before he whispers, "Just know, if you hurt him, I'll kill you with my bare hands."

The words hit like a swift punch, delivered with the kind of calm certainty that sends a chill down my spine. Without another word, he walks away, leaving his threat hanging in the air.

This is just further reminder that the danger I'm in isn't just from one side. It's everywhere.

And it's only a matter of time before it catches up to me.

TWENTY-SEVEN

EMILIA

The soft hum of the television fills the den as I sit on the couch, eyes glued to the screen while Konstantin is in a meeting.

But my mind is elsewhere. Like on the party we're supposed to host in two days, and that nagging feeling that I'm nowhere near finding anything to help Nate.

I tried to snoop around the house earlier, but Konstantin's men are everywhere and it felt like an impossible task. At this point, I won't find shit for Riley to hack.

Anxiety tightens through my muscles, each breath growing harder to take.

I can't fail. I won't let Nate rot inside, but with every passing day, that's exactly what I'm doing. Failing. The weight of it presses down on me, a crushing force in my chest.

I take long breaths, hoping the chaos will quiet before I spiral into panic. Instead, I think of last night. Falling asleep in Konstantin's arms, somehow feeling at peace. Funny how the mind can make you feel safe even when you're in the arms of your enemy.

A set of footsteps echoes, and I sit up straighter and run a hand down my face, wondering if it's Konstantin.

Before I can wonder long, he steps in with a man covered in tattoos on every visible part of his skin, his face framed by the metal ring in his nose.

Who is he, and what is he doing here?

Konstantin says something to him in Russian as they both look over at me, and it gives me this eerie feeling I can't put my finger on.

A maid enters, carrying a chair before placing it in the middle of the room.

"Come, Tessa. Sit." Konstantin pats the leather upholstery.

Another spike of unease rolls through me. "Why? What's going on?"

"Sit, Tessa." His features harden, and I know arguing won't help.

Reluctantly, I stand and sink into the chair, hoping this isn't where I get executed. The man with the tattoos steps forward, his eyes scanning me briefly.

"This is Boris," Konstantin explains. "He is here to give you a tattoo."

My heart skips, my eyes widening. "A *what*?"

Konstantin doesn't even flinch at my shock.

"A tattoo," he repeats, as though it's no big deal. "A small, black circle with a red club in the center, right here…" His fingertips glide up the back of my neck as he peers at me with that cold, unflinching stare. "It's for your protection. This way, my enemies will know you are mine as soon as you show them that mark."

I swear this man does everything with the guise of protection. If it wasn't so annoying, it might actually be romantic.

"No." The word bursts out of me. "I don't want it."

The last thing I need is to have a piece of him etched on my skin forever. Or until I can pay to get it removed, which I really shouldn't have to do.

But Konstantin doesn't give me a choice. He steps closer, his fingers brushing my hair from the back of my neck.

"It's necessary." His voice softens, almost gentle, but the finality in it is unmistakable. "Trust me."

"I don't trust you at all."

He laughs, a cold, grated sound. "It doesn't matter, malyshka." His hard knuckles draw down the side of my face, making my skin crawl with both desire and apprehension. "I get what I want."

I don't have time to argue further as the artist moves behind me, preparing his tools.

Konstantin's fingers intertwine with mine, his grip firm as the needle starts its work, piercing my skin. The sting is sharp, but the pressure of Konstantin's hand in mine is strangely comforting.

It's funny, really. Or maybe not that funny. But the feeling of the needle going in, sharp and relentless, the small punctures to my skin, reminds me of something familiar.

Every time I used to cut, that moment of pain, that second when the blade would sink into my skin, was a relief. And this? It feels similar. That same burning sensation, but this time I'm not in control, and I hate it.

Every time the needle hits, I want to scream, but I don't. Instead, I stare at Konstantin, my eyes filled with anger and something else too. Something I hate to admit.

"It's almost done," Konstantin says. "I'm sorry if this is causing you any pain."

How sweet is that? He's sorry when he's the one forcing me to do this.

Time drags on as the artist works, the ink settling on my skin, marking me to the man I swore I'd hate. But now that hatred has somehow morphed into more of a strong dislike.

They do say marriage takes work, right?

When the man finishes, Konstantin's gaze shifts to the tattoo, his expression tightening briefly before he leans in, his breath warm against my ear. "It's perfect."

The artist shows it to me through a mirror, and thankfully, it's small. The man covers it up and steps back while Konstantin takes my hand, helping me to my feet. My skin is tender, but I can handle the discomfort.

Once we're alone, Konstantin's eyes rake over me, the ferocity of his stare lingering as it glides over my skin. "If you're feeling up to it, I'd like to take you shopping."

I frown. "Shopping for what?"

"The party. It's time to get you a wardrobe worthy of my wife."

A sigh escapes me. "That's not necessary. Keep your money. I'm happy with my own clothes."

He gives a slight chuckle. "That's thoughtful of you to worry about my finances, but I assure you, I have plenty to spare." A smirk tugs at the corner of his lips. "And you, katyonak, need to look the part. Otherwise, people will start talking."

I roll my eyes, but it doesn't stop him from leading me out of the house and toward the back of the SUV. One of his men sits at the wheel, another in the passenger seat. The engine whirrs to life as we pull away from the estate, his powerful hand cupping my knee, and I find an odd comfort every time he touches me.

When we finally arrive, it's at a place that feels like it was made for people like Konstantin. Expensive, high-end, every corner of it designed to scream wealth and power.

"Mr. Marinov, I'm so happy to see you," the woman at the front desk practically purrs, her eyes lighting up when she spots him.

Her greeting is laced with too much enthusiasm, and my irritation spikes immediately. The thought of grabbing the nearest stiletto and stabbing it through her eye is strangely tempting right now.

But Konstantin doesn't even spare her a glance. His features remain tight, authoritative, as he strides past her without breaking his pace.

"Do you have everything I asked for?"

"Of course, sir! We have all the pieces for your…uh, wife…in the back." Her eyes flick briefly toward me before quickly returning to him, sending him a gaze drenched in lust.

The woman's stupidity is almost unbearable. Does she have a death wish?

Tension builds in my chest, but Konstantin's fingers tightening around my hand draw my focus back to him.

"She's nothing," he says, loud enough for her to hear, the words cutting through the air like a blade.

The woman goes pale, her face reddening.

"I-I swear I wasn't—" she stammers, but he cuts her off before she can dig herself deeper.

"You don't speak unless you're spoken to."

Her eyes pop wide at the lethal tone of his voice, and a small smile tugs at my lips.

The woman clears her throat and steps back, visibly shaken, her hands clasped in front of her white blazer.

Konstantin's arm slides around my back, tugging me close. His front presses against mine, the heat of his body making me warm all over.

"I must say…" His voice drops low and gravelly, his mouth grazing my lips. "I'm relieved to find you so jealous, Mrs. Marinova. I was starting to think this marriage wasn't going to work."

I throw my arms over his shoulders, a grin tilting. "Tell my husband not to be so full of himself. I wasn't all that jealous."

He laughs, a low, satisfied sound that sends a jolt through me. Before I can respond, his lips are on mine, gentle, yet urgent. A soft kiss that sparks something deeper.

A groan slips from him as he shifts back, his eyes darkening. "Come with me."

Before I can react, he grips my arm, pulling me toward the back of the store and yanking me into an empty changing room. My chest rises rapidly as he watches me, his gaze turning predatory, the air crackling between us with something unspoken. Then, without warning, his lips crash to mine, urgent and possessive.

I'm barely able to catch my breath, our mouths colliding with such force that it's like we're fighting for dominance. He groans into the kiss, his fingers threading through my hair, gripping the back of my head with an intensity that makes my pulse hammer. This kiss…it's wild, almost violent, like we're both on the edge of something we can't control.

Every second he pulls me deeper into his spell, my body responds, aching, desperate for him. His hands are everywhere, ripping at my clothes, each touch pushing me closer to the brink.

My fingers work quickly to undo his belt, dragging his pants down with urgency until his cock springs free. And in one swift motion, he lifts me in the air, my back flat against the wall, the heat between us burning hotter with every second.

With a growl, he grips a handful of my hair, his eyes on mine as he thrusts into me with punishing force.

"Oh God, yes," I gasp, my voice breaking on the edge of a moan.

I try to stay quiet, try to be good, but he drives into me harder until silence is no longer an option.

"Louder, Tessa," he roars against my ear. "Let her hear you. Let the whole damn world know I'm yours and you're mine."

His fingers slip between my thighs, stroking my clit with merciless precision. Pleasure builds like fire licking up my spine, twisting until I'm on the edge of something I can't contain.

Each thrust sends me spiraling faster, deeper, until I'm clawing at the wall for balance.

My orgasm tears through me like a storm, wild and consuming. "Yes! Konstantin, oh God!"

"I'm the only God you're ever going to need."

His hand closes around my throat, my pleasure enhancing the tighter he squeezes. My cry echoes through the room, body trembling, nerves on fire. Every part of me his.

With a guttural grunt, he explodes inside me, driving into me with a vicious, relentless force, giving me every inch of himself. It's raw, feral, and I can't get enough.

As the storm inside us slowly fades, his breathing is heavy and erratic as he lowers me just enough, his forehead pressing into mine. "S toboy ya zabyvayu, kto ya takoy."

The sound of his tortured words hangs in the air between us, making my heart stutter with curiosity and a strange ache.

"What does that mean?" I ask in a barely there whisper.

He pauses, his hands tightening around my hips like he's afraid I'll slip away. "That with you, I forget who I am, Tessa. And I've never been one to forget."

His words hit harder than I expected. My stomach flips, a wave of vulnerability crashing through me.

In this moment, I know without a shadow of a doubt that I'm in deeper than I ever thought possible. And there's no turning back from whatever we've become.

Hours later, I'm finally done shopping and that sales associate who had goo-goo eyes for my husband suddenly can't even look at me.

Might have been the five orgasms she had to listen to before we finally made our appearance. Poor thing.

My lips wind up as I grin at her. "Thanks for all your help..." I glance down at her name tag. "Gwen."

"Of course." She can barely get the words out. "Have a good day, Mrs. Marinova. Mr. Marinov."

"We will." I grab his hand as we exit the store together, his men carrying our bags for us.

He stops midstride, turning to me. His gaze lingers, and for a moment, I forget how wrong we are, because nothing about this feels wrong at all.

"You're beautiful and ferocious, moya l'vitsa." His palm cups my cheek, thumb rolling over my skin until my lashes flutter.

"Does that mean lioness?"

"Yes. It's what you are, especially when you have those sharp claws out the way you did in the store. I like it." His lips fall to the corner of my mouth, and my hand instinctively wraps around the back of his neck.

"That's sweet," I tell him as he backs away, staring into my eyes.

"You know…" he says, tugging my chin in his tight grasp. "If my enemies ever heard me being described as sweet, they'd laugh."

"Oh, trust me…" I rise up on my toes to kiss him. "I completely understand."

He groans, kissing me hard, and I surrender to this mind-bending passion between us that only gets stronger with each day. By the time we come up for air and head into the car, I don't even know what time it is.

As we drive back to the estate, I ask to stop at a convenience store, needing something to drink.

"Take this. It has no limit." He hands me a credit card.

"Aren't you coming with me?"

"Of course I am. But this is yours. I've been meaning to give you your own card."

"Oh. That's generous."

I could refuse, but I know he'll just insist, so I reluctantly take the black card from him.

"We're married, remember? What's mine is yours." His mouth curls in that insanely sexy way that has me getting all goo-goo-eyed for my husband too.

When his phone starts ringing, he stares down at the screen, his face hardening.

"If you have to take it, go. I'll be fine in the store alone."

He hesitates, but whoever it is on the other line calls again. "Alright. One of my guys will stand by the door."

"Okay."

I step out of the SUV and head inside, getting lost in the aisles as I pick up drinks for him and me when someone approaches from behind. My fight-or-flight instinct rises when I glance back to find a tall, thin man who was definitely just staring at my ass.

I head for a different aisle, but he follows me, and all my thoughts zero in on either killing him or running out before I do.

"Hey there," he says, leaning into me from behind.

Instinctively, I step out of his way, but the man isn't deterred.

"You look good enough to eat."

Ew.

His hand reaches for my waist, brushing against it, and I flinch, my mind instantly taken back to my days as a child and the men my mother brought home.

I flip around and step into him. "Get the fuck away from me, asshole, before I kill you."

Instead of retreating, though, he laughs, which is pretty much how every one of her boyfriends treated me. A helpless little girl they could do whatever they wanted with.

When he touches my hip, I'm suddenly not in a convenience store anymore. I'm back in my mother's house, with men I didn't want trying to touch me in ways they shouldn't.

Before I can stop myself, I grab his throat and flip him over, slamming him into the shelves while everything falls to the floor. My heart pounds, my exhales quick and ragged, but I don't let go. My arm stays wrapped around his throat, cinching until his airways are cut. His arms flail in panic, trying to break free, but I'm stronger.

Not talking now, are you, bitch?

"It's okay, malyshka," someone says.

I don't realize it's Konstantin, not at first. Not until he says it again, his gentle hand on my arm, coaxing me to relax.

"It's okay, malyshka. I'm right here."

Gradually, my mind begins to clear and my breathing eases, a little less frantic.

"Good girl." His voice is soft and soothing. "I've got you now."

When I release the man, he stumbles to his feet, inhaling with quick spurts. "You-you-you fucking psycho bitch!"

But before I can react, Konstantin is on him, grabbing him by the throat.

"Where the hell do you think you're going?" He lifts him off the ground. "Do you know who this woman is?"

He doesn't even raise his tone. He doesn't need to. This calmer version is more terrifying.

"She's my *wife*, and you touched her."

The man stammers, "L-l-look, man, I'm sorry. I-I was being stupid. I l-learned my lesson."

"No, you did not. But you will, I promise you that." Konstantin grins, cold and predatory. "You see, you broke a very sacred rule of mine. Do you know what that is?"

He shakes his head, panic rising.

"You touched what belongs to me. And for that, you deserve to be punished, don't you think?"

When Konstantin drops him to the ground, the man tries to back away, but Konstantin's two men are right behind him.

"Fuck. I-I just thought she was pretty, that's all. I didn't know she was married, I swear."

"Next time, don't think. Clearly, your mind is your worst enemy." Konstantin shifts his attention to me, his gaze hardening. "Which hand did he use to touch you?"

"His right." My teeth grit, my chin rising.

Whatever happens to this asshole is his fault.

Konstantin pulls out his gun from the holster at his waist in one smooth motion. "Hold out your right hand."

The man hesitates, his body trembling like a leaf.

Konstantin's gaze locks on to him, cold and unyielding. "Do it. Now. Or I will take your entire arm. It's your choice."

"Fuuuck, man! Come on," he pleads, but a second later, he obeys, holding out his hand.

Without hesitation, Konstantin fires, the low sound of a gunshot ripping through the man's palm. Blood spills from the wound as his scream cuts through the silence.

"You should be grateful." Konstantin's mouth winds. "Normally, I'd have a chainsaw in my trunk. I forgot it today. I won't forget next time." He grabs the collar of the man's shirt as blood continues to drip to the ground. "Say a word about this to anyone, and I'll cut off both your arms *and* your legs. Understand?"

"Mm." The man nods.

"Good. Now go get that looked at. You wouldn't want to bleed out, would you? That would be a real shame."

As we start to head for the exit, Konstantin turns back around, points his gun at the man, and pulls the trigger. One clean shot straight through the head.

Holy. Shit.

I didn't see that coming.

"You didn't think I'd let him live, did you?" He takes my hand and kisses the top of it, his demeanor relaxed, as if he didn't just murder a man. His gaze softens, a tenderness that always catches me off guard no matter how many times I see that side of him. "Are you okay?"

A lump rises in my throat.

"I don't know." I give him the most truthful answer I can.

His fingers tighten around mine. "I will never leave you alone again."

"I'm not helpless, Konstantin."

My hand reaches up, fingers brushing against his cheek. I need to touch him, to make him realize how much I appreciate the way he stood up for me. His eyes close, his fingers reaching for my wrist and gripping tight, like he wants to keep me there for as long as possible.

"I know you're not." His words are thick with emotion, each one heavier than the last. "But I'm your husband, and I'll always protect you. It's my job."

With a sigh, I lower my face against his front, and he wraps his arms around me, pulling me in tight, like he'll never let go.

"Let's go home, malyshka." He presses a kiss to the top of my head.

We make our way to the counter, and he places a thick wad of bills down.

"This is for any damage. My men will handle the cleanup."

The cashier nods, his face instantly shifting into a mask of respect, though I have a feeling he's the owner.

"It's no problem at all, Mr. Marinov. You have a good day."

I glance at the cameras above us, knowing full well they're not recording.

As we head back to the car, I wrap my arms around his bicep. The quiet between us stretches, thick with unspoken words, and I can't deny it anymore.

I'm falling for him. Hard. Fast.

The realization claws at me, terrifying me. Because I know I'm already too far gone, too tangled in him, to protect whatever's left of my heart.

TWENTY-EIGHT

KONSTANTIN

Guests shuffle into the grand entryway two days later, their laughter and voices bouncing off the marble floors. But none of them really interest me, my eyes constantly flicking toward the stairs, waiting for Tessa to walk down.

She's been quiet since the day at the store, understandably shaken, and I blame myself for taking that business call. If I hadn't, no man would have laid a finger on her. It'll never happen again as long as I live.

Every time I close my eyes, I can't get her expression out of my head. The way she looked while she choked the life out of him, like she wasn't really there. I don't even think she heard me calling her until I touched her.

My fingers curl at my side. Whatever she's been through, it left an impact, and I will do everything I can to give her a better life.

More guests begin to pour in, drawing my attention, and soon, the

Quinns appear at the entrance. Tynan, head of the Irish family, steps inside first with his wife, Elara, on his arm.

"Congratulations." There's a hint of amusement as he says that. "Can't say I ever expected to see you tie the knot."

Elara quickly elbows him, offering a warm smile in contrast. "What he means is, we're truly happy for you. We can't wait to meet her."

"Bolshoye spasebo, dorogaya." *Thank you very much, darling.*

Tynan's brother Fionn and his wife, Amara, follow with their congratulations, more genuine and polite. Then their youngest sister, Eriu, steps in with her husband, Devlin.

"A bloody congratulations, you fecker," Devlin says with a sharp grin, slapping me on the back hard enough to jar bone, while Eriu laughs, clearly amused.

And then Iseult Quinn-Marino struts in with her husband, Gio of the Messina crime family, right beside her. Her eyes lock on to mine as she strides toward me, that trademark smirk playing at her lips. I pity any man or woman who underestimates her. She's a force, the oldest sister in the family, and one of the deadliest assassins I've ever encountered.

"Well, well, well, Konstantin," she drawls, her tone laced with mockery. "Never thought I'd see the day you got married. I could've sworn you'd die alone. I was almost getting sad for you. Almost."

A grin spreads across my face as I approach, wrapping my arms around her before greeting Gio with a nod. "You flatter me, dorogaya."

She steps closer, her smile ice cold. "I'll offer my condolences to your wife as soon as I meet her."

"She'll enjoy that."

"Oh, then we'll get along so well." Her eyes sweep the room. "Where is she, anyway? She's like a mythical creature. One has to see her to believe she's real."

Laughter ripples through the room, mine included.

"She's getting ready. Should be down soon. In the meantime, head outside. There's food, drinks, and more than enough to keep you entertained. I promise she'll make her rounds."

"Can't wait."

Then Cillian Quinn steps through the doorway with my cousin, Dinara, on one arm and her sister, Tatiana, beside them.

"My girls." I pull them both into a quick embrace.

They used to live under my roof, but everything changed when Dinara married Cillian and Tatiana decided to live on her own, which has been good for her.

"It's nice to see you too," Tatiana says warmly, while Dinara fixes me with a glare.

"A phone call would've been nice to let your family know you were getting hitched."

"She's not wrong," Kirill chimes in from behind us. "We didn't even know until after."

"It all happened fast," I say, brushing it off. "But let's not dwell on the past. Go and enjoy yourselves."

Dinara's eyes narrow. "I know you're just trying to get rid of us."

"Can you blame him?" Cillian scoffs.

"Never thought *you'd* ever defend him." Fionn laughs.

"Me either." I grin. "But I told you one day we'd become good friends, Cillian. And look at us now."

I slap him on the back, earning a scowl.

"Too much?" A smirk settles on my face.

"Yeah, a little," he mutters.

"Alright, alright," I chuckle. "I'll learn to keep my excitement to myself next time."

"All jokes aside…" Iseult says, her smirk softening just enough to pass for sincerity. "I think I speak for all of us when I say we're happy for you, Konstantin."

I incline my head. "Spasebo." *Thank you.*

"But…" She tilts hers, one brow lifting. "I do wonder…"

"Wonder what?"

Her eyes gleam. "How much did you have to pay the poor woman to get her to say yes?"

Before I can fire back, Fionn cuts in with a grin. "Please. He didn't pay her. She was thrilled to marry him…right after he put a gun to her head."

A few laughs ripple through the group.

"That's not *exactly* what happened."

Cillian snickers. "Which part? The gun or the marriage?"

"Well…" I shrug. "Let's just say the courtship was…persuasive."

Tatiana shakes her head, laughing. "You're lucky she hasn't stabbed you in your sleep yet."

"There's always tomorrow." My mouth tips up.

That earns another round of laughter.

But it all fades, every sound melting into background noise as something inside me shifts. I feel her before I see her. As if some invisible thread pulls my gaze toward the stairs.

And there she is. Standing at the top, haloed by soft, golden light, wearing a white gown of silk and lace that hugs her body like it was made just for her. Those luscious waves are half-pinned, dark curls cascading down one shoulder, and for a moment, I forget how to breathe. She doesn't look like she belongs here, yet she owns the space, casting everyone else into shadow.

But it's her eyes that tear me wide open, that burning gaze cutting through me like it's carving something deep into my soul. I can feel the weight of her stare, like she's searching for something—some hidden part of me I've buried. And in this instant, I feel exposed.

For the first time since I can remember, the vulnerability I've spent years running from creeps in, and that's when I remember what my father once said. That love is a weakness.

But he was wrong. There's power in it too.

And in her eyes, I find that power.

It's then I realize something I'll never admit: I'm not in control anymore. And it's the most alive I've ever felt.

I start toward her as she begins her descent, one step at a time. By the time she reaches me, I'm already taking her hand. She places it in mine without hesitation, and I pull her in, not giving a single fuck who's watching. My lips find her cheek, warm skin that smells like vanilla and danger.

"I think my heart forgot how to beat," I murmur against her skin.

She turns her face, her smile jerking at the corner. "Might want to get that checked, husband. Doesn't sound normal."

A laugh rumbles out of me, unfiltered and real.

"Nothing about this is normal." My thumb brushes across her cheek. "But for the first time, I don't want it to be."

Her eyes meet mine, holding me in place, and the world outside of her doesn't even exist. She's the only thing that makes sense in this mess, the only thing worth holding on to. And somehow, for the first time in a long time, I find myself hoping.

Not for peace, nor for power. But for a future that includes her.

EMILIA

The night air is cool against my skin as I sit beside Konstantin, his palm heavy and possessive on my thigh.

He's always touching me, no matter where we are. It's as though he needs to make sure that I'm real. And I realize I like it. Maybe it's that quiet protectiveness, the ownership, the claim. Whatever it is, I don't want him to stop.

Guests dance and laugh as I scan the scene from our long table beneath the stars, the estate sprawling out before us like a kingdom.

A good few hundred people have gathered for the reception, enjoying the endless food and entertainment. Glittering vases with hanging Swarovski crystals adorn each table. Acrobats twirl and flip, suspended in the air like circus performers. It's hard to believe all this is for us.

Us.

It seems strange to think of Konstantin and me as an *us*, but for all intents and purposes, that's exactly what we are.

A sharp pang hits my center, the betrayal crashing into me. Because that's what this is. I'm betraying my brother by even allowing myself to think of Konstantin as anything other than the enemy.

But what if I had it all wrong? What if he didn't do it? What if I've built this entire mess on a lie?

Does that change anything? I'm a fed, he's a criminal. What future can we possibly have together?

"Are you enjoying yourself?" The question cuts through my thoughts like a blade.

Startled, I turn toward him. "What? Oh…yes. Everything is beautiful."

His gaze sharpens, as if he can see straight through to my subconscious.

Then, just as quickly, a tight and unreadable smile tugs at his mouth. "I'm glad. I want to make you happy, Tessa. I want to give you everything you could ever want."

My heart twists in my chest, caught somewhere between longing and confusion. Who could possibly say no to that?

But I know better. Nothing he offers comes without a cost.

And I don't mean the billions he has. I mean the kind of price that can't be measured in money. Only in the pieces of yourself you lose trying to survive someone like him.

But I want him. My God, no matter how wrong it may be, I want Konstantin Marinov with every fiber of my being. And if there's a way that I can keep him and save my brother at the same time, I'll take it. Because being with him has been more than I ever thought it would be.

My pulse skitters, and I take a long drink of ice water to cool the fire rising in my body.

"This dress is beautiful on you." His fingers lazily roll up my thigh.

I glance down where his touch brushes the delicate lace. It fits like perfection, hugging my body in all the right places.

"I hope so. It cost you thirty grand."

He chuckles, the sound low and rough. "I'd give it all up to have you."

His fingers tug at my chin, gripping tight, and a jolt of heat runs through me.

"Every penny I have," he says, slower this time. "Just to keep you."

A tight knot forms in my stomach, twisting painfully.

"Then you'd be poor," I try to joke, but my voice is too thin. "And trust me, that's no fun either."

He leans in, his forehead brushing mine, hand still wrapped around my jaw like he's anchoring me to him. "I'd be the richest man alive with you beside me, moya lyubimoya."

The words don't just knock the air from my lungs. They crack something open inside me. Because beneath all the fear and the lies, beneath the badge and betrayal, a part of me aches to believe him.

And that part—that foolish, reckless part—might be my undoing.

His eyes search mine as he pulls back, devouring every flicker of hesitation.

"What does that mean, lyubimoya?"

"My love," he answers softly.

My heart stammers like it doesn't know what to do with that.

"Does that word scare you, Tessa?" His thumb brushes over my lips, sending a current through me that makes my skin burn in its wake.

"No," I whisper.

Yes.

He may not have said he loves me, but this? This is as close as he's ever come. And the prospect of him ever loving me… I don't know what to do with it. I don't even know what love means, let alone from someone like him.

"Just so you know, I don't need expensive things to make me happy."

A flash of a smirk pulls at his lips, but his eyes burn with something more. "I still intend to give you the world, Mrs. Marinova. Whether you want it or not."

I want it. With you.

But I don't say that. Instead, I let the hunger in his eyes swallow me whole as he leans in and crushes his mouth to mine.

The world falls away. The party, the people, the music…it all disappears when his lips devour me, greedy and full of promise.

It's not just a kiss. It's a declaration. A brand. And I let it consume me.

When we finally break apart, I'm breathless. Drunk on him.

"I thought you two were going to start undressing right here." Iseult cuts through the fog like a knife.

I turn to find her and Gio beside us, two glasses of wine in her hands.

"You have impeccable timing," Konstantin mutters, his tone clipped as he keeps his arm tightly wrapped around me, like he's daring anyone to try to take me.

"Don't I always?" She grins, handing me a glass. "Here. Hydration is key. You'll need it to survive tonight."

A laugh escapes me. "I actually don't drink."

Her eyes widen. "Oh. Well, lucky me." She raises both glasses. "Double the fun."

My grin spreads. I like her.

Settling into the empty seat that was occupied by Aleksei earlier, she throws a leg over the other side, eyes twinkling. "So, tell me about yourself. What do you do for work?"

Something that could get me killed if you knew the truth.

"I'm Konstantin's assistant. That's how we met."

She lifts a brow. "Interesting…"

"Yeah… For someone who didn't have a lot of options, I guess I haven't done so bad." I swallow hard, tamping down the flood of memories threatening to surface.

"So, life liked to knock you around a bit, huh?"

"Sometimes." I shrug, feeling Konstantin's eyes on me. "I didn't come from much. A shitty mom. No real stability. I did what I had to do."

She leans back in her chair, eyes sharp. "And look at you now."

"You should see her with a gun," Konstantin cuts in, full of pride.

Iseult perks up, her expression lighting with interest. "Really, now? Do tell…"

I shift in my seat, a little uneasy. "Yeah. My older brother taught me."

Iseult's lips curve into a sly, dangerous smile. "Well, then I think it's only right we test your skills with a little shooting contest."

My eyes widen. "Wait, what?"

Before I can fully process, her gaze flicks to where her siblings have gathered nearby, mischief dancing on her face.

"What's going on?" Fionn asks, brows raised.

"My wife just challenged Mrs. Marinova to a shooting match," Gio pipes up, sounding far too amused.

Fionn lets out a bark of laughter. "That sounds like my sister."

"Come on." Iseult shrugs. "It'll be fun."

Konstantin chuckles beside me. "I say we do it. What's a wedding without a few bullets between friends?"

Honestly? It does sound fun. And it's not like this will somehow out me as a fed just because I know how to hold a gun.

"Alright." I get to my feet. "Let's do it."

Iseult throws her hands in the air. "That's what I'm talking about! Let's go, people."

Gio's eyes trail her body with open admiration. "You with a gun and five-inch heels? Sexiest damn thing every time."

She elbows him, but there's affection in the move. "Behave."

He groans with a smile. "That's how she says she loves me."

I laugh. "No judgment here. Whatever works."

They're chaotic, a little unhinged, but honestly? Kind of adorable.

Konstantin takes my hand and leads the group to the far edge of his estate, away from the lights, the laughter, and the rest of the wedding guests. With the grass beneath our shoes, we move through the lit-up path. One of his men steps forward on command, lining up empty glass bottles along the fence line. Eight in total—four for me, four for Iseult—set at a distance that's clearly meant to impress.

Iseult flips her bright red hair off her shoulders and pulls a sleek pistol from the holster strapped to her thigh, hidden beneath her long black dress. Her grin is razor-sharp as she rolls her neck and flexes her fingers. She lives for this, doesn't she?

Konstantin hands me his weapon. The metal is cold and unforgiving, like the world I've chosen to infiltrate.

"Four shots. Four targets. One winner." His gaze bounces between us.

The tension tightens around me like a noose. I'm incredibly competitive. I don't lose.

Iseult stands at one end of the line, posture flawless, her gun already raised and waiting. I steady myself on the other side, heels planted, grip firm.

"Ready?" Konstantin's voice rings out.

We both nod.

"Go."

My breath slows. I block out everything. The brightness of the lights above, everyone's stares. Just me and the bottle.

We fire at the same time.

Glass shatters in unison.

She turns her head, smirking. "Nice shot."

"You too."

"I never miss," she tosses out, like she's trying to make me nervous, but I only admire the cockiness about her.

"Neither do I." My mouth curls.

We fire again. Both bottles shatter cleanly.

Then two more.

Only one bottle remains for both of us.

She turns her head, flashes an arrogant smile, and fires. The bullet goes wide.

And she misses.

Whoops…

I try hard to hide my grin, but fail miserably.

"Fuck!" she hisses, the gun falling to her side.

Now it's my turn. I take one steady breath, center the target, squeeze the trigger, and…the glass explodes.

A low whistle escapes Gio. "She's gonna be pissed."

"She's dangerous when she's pissed," someone mutters behind him.

Iseult shakes her head, pacing once in frustration before spinning to face me. "How the hell can you shoot like that? Shit, are you a cop or something?"

My pulse stalls for a fraction of a second, but I force a laugh. "I sure as hell hope not. Don't think that'd end well for any of us."

She narrows her eyes at me, then snickers like it's all just a joke. "Rematch? I think you owe me one."

I start to answer, but Konstantin cuts me off, a hand winding around my hips.

"How about you let my bride rest? That's enough for tonight. Wouldn't want people wondering where we've gone."

He plucks the gun from my hand and slides it into his holster.

His palm presses gently against my back as we begin the walk back to the glowing lights of the reception. I glance over my shoulder at Iseult, her eyes still sharp and calculating.

They're all watching me. The most dangerous people in the world.

Sooner or later, one of them is going to figure out who I really am.

And when they do, I won't see the bullet coming.

TWENTY-NINE

EMILIA

The soft glow of the moonlight filters through the curtains, casting a gentle light across the room. It's late, the silence of the night wrapping around me like a blanket. The aftermath of the party still pulses through me, a mix of exhaustion and adrenaline that refuses to fade.

I stand in front of the dresser, applying lotion to my hands. The silk of the nightgown Konstantin bought for me feels smooth against my skin, its white sheen gliding over me like a whisper. The fabric clings to my curves, soft and delicate, and there's something about the way it makes me feel: exposed, yet adored.

From the corner of my eye, I catch him in the reflection of the mirror, standing just behind me with nothing on but a pair of boxers riding low on his hips.

His presence fills the space, the air filled with intensity as his eyes trail over my body. He says nothing, just watches me, and in his gaze, there's a mix of admiration and something more. Something feral.

"Did you have a nice time tonight?" He comes closer now, pressing into me from behind, his hands snaking over my arms.

The contact is comforting, but it also stirs something deep inside me.

"Yes," I manage while I try to tame the way my body wants his. "It was a great party."

A slight chuckle rumbles from him. "I know you enjoyed it." His palm slides to my hip, fingers digging into my needy flesh. "But I think there's something else on your mind."

I let out a breathy moan, my head falling back against him, unable to control the shiver that runs through me. The way he touches me— the slow, deliberate way his hands explore my arms, my waist—it's as if he's trying to own every inch of me without saying a word.

And I let him. Every part of me wants to be owned by him.

His lips drop to my neck, warm and tender at first, then pressing harder, his teeth grazing my skin. A low growl vibrates in his throat, pulsing through me. Slowly, his hands slip up, the silk of my gown slithering up my legs.

"Konstantin..." My voice comes out in a whisper, a mixture of hesitation and longing.

"Shh," he murmurs against my skin, his exhales hot and soothing. "Don't worry, malyshka. I'll take care of you."

My arms rise as he slips the gown over my head, tossing it on the floor before his mouth finds the sensitive curve of my shoulder.

I turn slowly, and his eyes lock on to mine with an intensity that steals my every thought. He doesn't speak, his gaze roving from my face down to the length of me.

"You are so beautiful," he says, his timbre husky and rough. "It's like I see you for the first time every time."

His words sink deep, and I get lost in the way he looks at me, like I'm the only thing that matters in this world.

His hand skims up my back, pulling me toward him, and I can't stop myself. My lips crash into his, hungry and desperate, a kiss that speaks everything I can't say out loud. His grip tightens as he lifts me effortlessly, my body trembling with anticipation as he carries me to the bed and throws me onto it, his large form hard and heavy over mine. His mouth hovers over my lips, his cock rocking into me until a moan escapes.

"Tell me you want me. That you want us." His desperation bleeds from every syllable, rocking through to my core.

"I do." My hands cling to his bare back, to the warmth of his skin against mine. "I do want you, Konstantin. I want this."

He groans, the sound rough and raspy, before his lips capture mine, fierce and hungry. His mouth moves down my body, leaving a searing trail of fire across my skin, while his hands roam, worshipping every crevice. When his tongue finally finds its way between my legs, I gasp, arching up toward him instinctively, wanting more.

"Oh God, yes." My hands clutch his hair, nails working his scalp as he brings me to the brink of pleasure.

He forces his fingers inside me at the same time, causing me to quiver, every cell in my body pulsing with need. His tongue is relentless, working my clit, sinking into me while his thumb works my center before he sucks my clit into his mouth. My eyes roll back, every part of me unraveling, the need spiraling inside me until I can't hold back anymore.

"Konstantin, oh God!"

Waves of pleasure crash over me as I come undone, but he doesn't stop, his palms holding my thighs open as he flicks and sucks with commanding pressure. My nails dig into his scalp as I try to steady my breath, but he's persistent, his mouth working me until I'm gasping, my body writhing beneath him in desperation once again.

This time when he looks up, his fingers thrusting hard and fast, I lose all ability to utter a word, the sound of my wetness filling the room as the most intense orgasm takes hold, ripping through me until I practically shed tears.

"Vot tak, detka. Otdai mne vsyo." The guttural way he says that, it sends another wave of pleasure splitting through me.

Finally, when my body comes down from the high, he pulls away, kissing his way back up my body. His erection is hot against my entrance as he pushes his boxers down, and I want to feel every thick inch of him.

The back of his hand strokes across my cheek. "You're the sweetest thing I've ever tasted."

When I groan, he kisses me, his tongue snaking with mine, forcing me to taste myself before he pulls back in a rush. And before I know what's happening, he enters me in a forceful thrust, his size stretching me, causing a burn to rip through me. But I like the pain, want more of it.

The stretch, the feeling of him…it's everything I've craved. I gasp as he moves, slow at first, his rhythm building with intensity. Every thrust sends shockwaves through me, my body responding to him like it always does. Like it's desperate and filthy for him.

He lifts one of my legs over his shoulder and drives hard into me. And there's nothing soft in the way he takes me. He's wild, possessive, as if he's staking his claim on me all over again, and it feels like everything I've ever needed. My nails scrape up his back as I pull him closer.

"Don't stop," I gasp, my body trembling, needing more. "Please don't stop."

He growls, his other hand gripping my throat as he pounds faster.

"I'll never stop," he says, his words sharp, his voice rough with desire. "You're mine, every inch, and I'll keep reminding you of that."

His mouth falls to mine, kissing me savagely, the position making every one of his thrusts even deeper. All I feel is this—his body against mine, the wildness of it, the urgency.

And when I finally come again, the pleasure explodes through me, overwhelming and all-consuming. He lets out a guttural grunt, his muscles going rigid as he follows me, spilling inside me in hot, relentless bursts.

I never imagined sex could be this good. This real.

He collapses beside me, pulling me into his arms, his chest rising and falling in tattered breaths. My head's dizzy, my body still humming with the aftermath of what we just shared.

"I like watching you lose control, malyshka." His hand brushes through my hair as I rest my head against his chest.

"You're good at…" I can't seem to finish the sentence.

"Fucking?" He chuckles. "Yes, I *am* quite good."

"Shut up." I laugh, smacking his chest with the back of my hand.

Then his smile fades, eyes dimming. "I can't wait to teach you more. To show you all the ways your body was made to be touched. To be owned."

My gut tightens, but he doesn't say more, only pulls me closer, his arm snaking around me. As we lie tangled in each other, the world around us fading into nothing, a thought flickers through my mind.

Maybe this is how it was always meant to be: us finding each other in the most unexpected of ways.

KONSTANTIN

I lie in the dark, her head resting on my chest, the steady rhythm of her breath against me grounding me in a way nothing else ever has.

Her warmth, her closeness…it's everything I never thought I wanted. For so long, I thought I was unbreakable, impervious to anyone or anything that could make me feel something more than the cold, calculated existence I've built.

But here she is, making me question everything I thought I knew about myself, and I can't remember a time I've felt this…happy. It's not even a fleeting happiness. This feels real, rooted, like something I can hold on to.

A part of me, one I've buried deep under layers of distrust and indifference, feels complete with her by my side. And lately, she's made me want things I never even knew I was capable of wanting.

A family. A future. Maybe even love.

For the first time in my life, I'm not terrified of the idea of having a child. I never thought I was cut out to be a father. Growing up, I was shown what it meant to be a monster, not a man. My father made sure I knew how to break, to hurt, to dominate, but never how to love.

But with Tessa, something's shifting inside me. The idea of having a child with her, someone who could show me what love actually looks like and teach me how to be better, how to be more than just the product of my past… It doesn't scare me anymore. Not like it used to.

She shifts slightly as I peer down at her, her eyes connecting with mine. I trace the line of her hair, the delicate strands slipping between my fingers.

The question escapes my lips before I can stop myself. "Have you ever thought about…having kids?"

Her body stiffens. "Uh…why?"

"It's just, I've been thinking about it lately, A family of my own. I swore after my father I'd never even consider it, but now…" My knuckles brush down her cheeks. "Now everything is different."

Her lips flutter, brows furrowing.

"Konstantin…I…" She glances down, her head shaking, her fingers playing with the fabric of her nightgown. "I wouldn't be a good mother." Her laugh is small, almost sad, and it tears me apart to hear it. "My mother wasn't much of a role model. I…I don't even know the first thing about being a mother, let alone a good one."

Relief fills me at her confession. Because she didn't say she'd never want to have a family with me.

"The question wasn't if you'd be a good one, which I know you would be, Tessa." I cup her chin and tilt her face to me. "I asked if you've ever thought about having a family. With me."

Her eyes grow wide, and she swallows roughly, unable to answer.

"I get it. My father was never much of a father, as you know. He showed me what I didn't want to be, yet somehow became, so I never wanted kids either. But now…" I pause, considering what I'm saying. "Now, with you…I'm not so sure anymore."

Her palm falls across my shoulder, fingers tightening against my skin, her features tortured and full of quiet pain. I kiss her forehead, my mouth remaining there for a few seconds before I pull back, trying to soothe the fear in her.

"We can figure this out together." The conviction in my tone surprises even me.

"And what if we can't?"

I pull her closer, my lips brushing against her temple. "All we can do is try. Our child would have the best parts of each of us." My fingers caress softly down her arm. "And the worst parts too, probably."

A small, genuine laugh tumbles from her. "Yes, probably."

She fastens her gaze with mine, something tender flickering there, something that grips tight around my heart and won't let go. Lifting her hand, she brushes the stubble along my jaw with a slow, thoughtful stroke.

"I think you'd actually be a good dad." The honesty in her tone rips something open in me.

With a groan, my mouth lowers and I kiss her, gently at first, before the kiss deepens, the intensity rising between us.

"Fuck…" My forehead slants against hers. "Go to sleep, Tessa." Every word is rough with desire. "Before I keep you up all night."

She chuckles, and I sense the tension in her ease as she nestles into me, her head resting on my chest as I reach over to turn off the bedside lamp, plunging the room into darkness. She burrows into me, her breaths calming me as she drifts off.

I lie awake for a while after she falls asleep, just listening to her steady exhales, thinking about everything. About her. About us. Wondering if there really could be a future for us and what this would mean for the future of my empire.

Then, just as I start to close my eyes, a low groan slips out from her lips. Her body tenses, stirring a bit as she mutters something I can't make out. She must be having a dream or a nightmare.

I hold her tighter, trying to calm her, my hand running up and down her arm. "Tessa. It's just a dream. It's okay."

But the groaning continues, growing louder, more frantic. She starts mumbling, but I can't make out the words, though the distress in her voice is clear. I flick on the bedside lamp, a warm glow cutting through the dark.

"Tessa." I shake her gently, trying to pull her from whatever hell she's trapped in. "Wake up."

Her eyes flutter open. Confusion floods them at first, her exhales quick as she sits up. When she blinks again, reality clicks back into place. Still, her chest heaves like she's run miles. And all I can do is hold her, tighter than before, as if I can chase away whatever shadows tried to steal her from me.

"Are you alright?" Tugging her to my chest, I lay us back down.

She sighs and relaxes against my chest, her hand finding its way to my bicep.

"It's just a dream," she says, her voice still shaky. "One I've been having since I was younger. Except…" She can barely get the words out.

"What is it?"

She peers up at me, gaze searching mine, like she's trying to decide whether to trust me with whatever it is she's holding back.

"I promise, whatever you have to say is safe with me."

For a moment, she closes her eyes, her lips trembling as if the words are too heavy to say out loud.

"I don't think it's a dream," she breathes, barely audible. "Whatever I'm seeing…I think it actually happened. And now my mind's trying to make me remember."

I gently trace her arm, trying to relax her. "What is it about?"

She pauses, her mouth pressed into a thin line. "I was little, hiding in a closet. Two men were arguing, one shouting at the other while my mother cried in the background. Then suddenly, I hear a gunshot. It was so loud. I can still…" Her lashes flutter shut. "I can still feel my fear. See myself covering my ears, thinking it was all over."

She drags in a shaky inhale as she continues. "When the door opened, I thought the man would kill me. But instead, he reached for me. And I went with him even when I didn't want to. That's it. That's all I remember."

A cold knot tightens in my stomach as her words sink in. My mind races, trying to piece it together. If one of those men hurt her, I'll make them suffer for what they did.

The fact that she could've been hurt… It fuels an intense desire to protect her, to shield her from everything, to make sure nothing ever hurts her again.

"And you think all of that was real?"

She nods, and I can see how much she believes it. "It feels like it's connected to something bigger. Something I can't remember, but need to." She pauses, her eyes getting lost in thought before her attention returns to me. "My shrink thinks I should see a hypnotist. Do you think that's stupid?"

I consider it for a moment. "The mind's complicated. If it helps, why not? You have nothing to lose."

She finally relaxes, the tension in her body easing as a small, uncertain smile tugs at her lips.

"Okay. Maybe you're right. Maybe it'll help." She pats my chest. "Good chat," she adds, her tone a little lighter now. "I'll make the appointment."

"See how well this marriage is going already?" A smirk twitches at my lips.

She elbows me in my stomach, and I chuckle, playfully grunting.

"Ouch. You're tough for a tiny thing."

"I'm not tiny," she snaps, narrowing her eyes at me.

My grin widens, relishing the way she challenges me, the fire in her. "Yes, I remember. I'm just a big guy."

Before she can speak, I flip her beneath me, caging her in with my body. My weight hovers just above hers, every muscle throbbing with need.

"What are you doing?" she breathes, the sound catching as I roll my hips between her thighs, aching to be inside her, wanting to make her forget everything that makes her hurt.

"Breaking you." My words are barely more than a growl against her throat, my hand slipping between us, feeling the warmth of her cunt, how wet she is for me already.

I slide my curled fingers inside her, teasing her just enough to make her squirm. Her nails claw into my back, dragging me closer as I kiss along her jaw, lingering there, tasting her skin. I grab her hips, flipping her onto her stomach and pulling her legs apart, holding her open and helpless. Rising on my knees, I catch her gaze from over her shoulder.

One brutal thrust drives me deep into her pussy, and the sound she makes shreds what's left of my control.

The room explodes into motion. Filled with grunts, gasps, the sharp slap of skin against skin. We're chaos and hunger and passion, clashing like we were built to destroy each other and love each wrecked piece in the aftermath.

She arches beneath me, wild and furious, and I match her with every ruthless stroke.

This isn't just sex. It's war. It's worship. It's everything I've ever craved.

And everything I never thought I'd have.

THIRTY

EMILIA

I lean back in the chair at the hypnotherapist's office, shaking my head at the conversation from last night.

Kids. I can't believe he asked me if I wanted them. With him. And I can't believe I actually considered it.

But I meant what I said. I can't be someone's mother. There's no way another human being would benefit from me mothering him or her. I'd ruin them the way my mother ruined me.

Right now isn't the time to think of the future, though. My brother's freedom. That's the priority. Once he's out, then Konstantin and I can figure out what we are to one another.

My leg bounces as I wait for my appointment, wondering what she'll be like and if she'll actually be able to help me. It's hard to ignore the way my muscles tighten in anticipation.

The door creaks open and she steps out, greeting me with a warm smile. Her blonde pixie cut frames her round face, softening her features.

"Ms. Hayes, please come in." She motions toward her office.

Her eyes seem kind, and there's an easy calm about her that makes me feel like everything will be okay before we even speak.

Getting to my feet, I follow her into the office, unease rising in my stomach, though I'm doing my best to push it down. She gestures to the chair across from her desk, and I settle into it, my hands folded tightly together on my lap while she gets a notepad and pen.

"So, what brings you in today?"

I hesitate for a moment before answering. "I've been having this dream… I've had it since I was a child."

Her eyes don't waver as I tell her all about it while she takes notes.

"I need to know if it's just a dream or if it's something from my past, something that actually happened. I need to remember the details, but regular therapy hasn't helped with that, so here I am."

She nods, understanding written across her face. "Alright, let's take it slow. I'm going to guide you through the process. Just relax and let the images come to you. Trust that your mind will show you what's necessary. You're in control."

I take a deep breath, trying to steady my nerves. She asks me to close my eyes, and I do, trying to block out the tension in my body while I focus on my breathing like she says.

A minute later, my body starts to loosen, the tightness in my chest easing just a little.

"Now, I want you to focus. Go back to the moment in the closet. Envision it in your mind. Don't be afraid."

It takes a minute, but my thoughts start to race as the memory begins to rise to the surface, little by little, and I feel as though I'm there.

"What do you see?"

"It's…dark. Narrow. The air smells old, damp." My voice falters. "I hear her—my mother. She's screaming through the walls, her cries breaking between words. She's begging someone to stop."

A sharp breath catches in my chest.

"There are men there. I hear them too. Their voices are muffled, like they're behind a thin wall or just out of reach."

"You're doing great, Emilia. Stay with it. Try to focus on what they're saying. Can you make out the words?"

My mind reaches into the haze, sifting through the echo of voices like scattered puzzle pieces. They blur, bleed together, until one breaks through the fog.

"One of them says… 'You need to stop. You can't be doing this to her.'"

My skin tingles, a nervous flutter rising in my stomach.

Who is he talking about? Me? My mom?

"That's excellent, Emilia. Keep going. Can you hear anything else?"

A beat passes. The memory stretches deeper. Words filter in, growing clearer.

"Another man laughs. It's cold…like he enjoys what's happening. He says, 'You're threatening me?' His voice…it turns sharp. Like he's about to snap."

Every instinct in me screams that something terrible is coming.

"Then he says…" The hairs on the back of my neck stand up. "'You just never learn, do you?' And then…oh God."

"You're safe, Emilia. You're just remembering. They can't hurt you now. What happened next?"

A tremor runs through my body, the words scraping out. "A gunshot."

It rings through the memory, crackling in my skull like a lightning strike. A piercing sound that vibrates through my bones—impossible to forget, impossible to outrun.

A shudder creeps over me, the sharpness in my lungs, the choking fear of a little girl who can't move, can't escape. My hands involuntarily tighten into fists, clinging to whatever I can. I'm frozen, stuck in the dark, still that terrified little girl trapped in the corner of that closet with hands against her ears and tears rolling down her cheeks.

I can see it all clearly. The tiny space. The cramped, suffocating air. The musty smell of dust and old wood.

The hypnotist cuts through the panic. "Do you hear anything else?"

The question bounces through my mind, pulling me back to the memory, forcing me to focus. The room grows colder as I strain to hear something, anything that might lead me to the truth. The silence presses in like a trap, like I'm slipping deeper into something I can't escape.

Then I hear it.

"The door. It's opening…and-and there's a man there."

The darkness in front of me begins to part, a sliver of light cutting through the void. There, in the space between the shadows, I see the outline of a figure—tall, broad—standing in the doorway.

"Can you see his face?"

His presence feels familiar. *Too* familiar.

I freeze. My body locks up, every muscle screaming, but I can't move. My chest tightens as the figure steps closer, his silhouette sharp against the light. Then his voice, calm but unmistakably familiar, says my name.

"No, I-I can't. But I'm trying. He knows me. He says, 'It's okay, Emilia. You're safe now.'"

"Concentrate on him. What does his face look like?"

I close my eyes tightly, pushing against the darkness, trying to make him out.

His words should be comforting, shouldn't they? But they're not. The hollowness of the room around me is like a thick fog, and it's growing thicker. Then he begins to fade…

No! Nonono!

I try harder, but the harder I strain to focus, the farther he pulls away. It's like trying to catch smoke with my bare hands.

"Focus, Emilia. Look into his eyes," the hypnotist encourages.

But it's all too distant, too far from where I am. I try with everything I have, the pressure in my chest growing as the space around me distorts, like I'm losing my grip on reality. The figure flickers in the darkness, fading into nothingness, his face just out of reach.

And then, just as quickly as it appeared, the image disappears entirely. The room grows cold, and I feel nothing but emptiness.

"Fuck!" My eyes fly open, and the world feels a little too bright. "Why the hell couldn't I see him? I was so damn close!" My anger radiates through me.

The therapist leans forward, her eyes filled with quiet sympathy. "Take a deep breath. You did well for your first time."

"I just need to remember. I know it's important." I run a hand through my hair, frustration building in the pit of my stomach.

It's like I'm so close, but the pieces keep slipping through my fingers.

"The more we work through this, the more you'll remember. Just be patient."

I let out a small snicker.

"Not very patient, are you?" Her grin is infectious, lighting up her face as she watches me.

"Not even close."

"Well, you will learn to be, because the mind is a tricky thing. Be kind to it."

"I'll try."

"Good. We'll schedule another session for next week. Same time, yes?"

"Yep. I'll be here."

As I get up to leave, a strange sense of relief mixed with uncertainty hits me.

There's so much more to uncover, and for the first time, I believe like I can actually get there.

I still sense the aftershocks of the therapy session as I step into the house, but I push it all aside, focusing on the familiar comfort of home.

It's strange how much this place, this life, is starting to feel like mine. And honestly, that should terrify me, but it doesn't.

As I slip off my shoes, the weight of the day settles in my shoulders. But then the sound of footsteps catches my attention and Konstantin appears in the foyer, his presence filling the space as it always does.

My eyes follow the lines of his body and the way his gray sweats hang low on his hips, the way that white T-shirt clings to him. My God, it's almost unfair how good he looks.

"How did it go?" He approaches, gaze sharpening as he tugs my chin with his firm grip, pulling me in just enough to feel his chest press into me.

"It actually went well. I remembered some things, but not enough yet."

A small smile tugs on his face as his thumb brushes across my bottom lip. "See? I told you it was worth a try."

"Yeah, yeah. Stop gloating." I elbow him, and he chuckles, crouching over playfully.

"Come. I made you something." His hand slips into mine, the heat of his fingers sending a jolt through me. He presses my knuckles to his lips, his gaze smoldering with intensity.

"Oh, yeah? And what's that?"

"You'll see, my impatient wife," he says, each syllable deliberately dragging through the air.

That last word hits me harder than it should, creating a tightness in my stomach, and I can't deny how much I love how it sounds coming from him.

The savory aroma drifts through the air as we step into the kitchen. Pots and pans simmer on the stove, the sounds of a meal in the making filling the space.

Konstantin pulls out a chair for me, always the gentleman. "Sit."

Once I do, he moves to the stove, stirring something in the pot. My gaze stays rooted on him, roaming over his body, every inch of him suddenly more captivating than the meal he's preparing. He looks so domestic, and it's all kinds of sexy.

"You cook?"

He glances over his shoulder, offering me a flirty smile. "These days, men cook, Tessa."

"Haha, you're hilarious." I roll my eyes. "I'm aware of that, but I just didn't picture you as the cooking type."

The playful stare he shoots me tells me he's enjoying this too much. "Just because I'm handy with a gun doesn't mean I can't handle a kitchen, Mrs. Marinova."

With a smooth motion, he turns off the stove, crosses the room, and moves my chair so I'm facing him. His hand settles around my throat, fingers tightening just enough to send a surge of desire through me.

"If you stick around long enough…" He pushes up my chin with his thumb. "You'll find I've got more tricks up my sleeve."

He drops his lips to mine and kisses me slow, every pull of his mouth against mine sending my pulse fluttering. When he pulls away, I'm breathless, my skin still tingling from the feel of him.

He arranges the food, placing the platters at the center of the table, then sets two plates and small bowls for us before taking his seat at the head, with my chair positioned to his right.

The dishes are unlike anything I've seen before. Rich colors, bold textures, the kind of food that makes your stomach ache with anticipation. My eyes settle on a steaming pot filled with something dark red, like blood.

"What's this?" I ask as he pours some into my bowl, then fills his own.

"Borscht. It's a Russian soup with beets and other vegetables. You're going to love it."

I hesitate for a second, eyeing the unfamiliar dish, then dip my spoon in and taste it. The flavor hits me immediately. Savory and tangy.

"Wow. This is incredible."

He watches me closely, satisfaction flickering in his eyes as I take another bite. "Good. I'm glad you like it."

With every taste, his attention never leaves me, waiting for my reaction as I try the other dishes. Only when he sees that I'm enjoying it does he eat.

As I cut into a piece of chicken, his hand slides up my thigh. "Come sit on my lap. Let me feed you."

I freeze. "What? No, I'm fine here."

His smirk deepens. "That wasn't an invitation, katyonak. Now come." He pats his thigh.

A grin pulls at my lips as I catch the challenge in his eyes. I stay seated, continuing to eat, while he watches me, nostrils flaring and his mouth twitching with amusement.

"If that's how you want to play it."

Before I can react, his arm curls around my back and he's sweeping me into his arms and lowering me right onto his lap.

"Konstantin!" I gasp, laughter bubbling up from my chest. "What are you doing?"

"When I tell you to do something, you do it. Simple." His fingers graze my chin, sending heat rippling through me. "And if you don't, I'll help you. That's what a marriage is." Awareness creeps up between us, the hungry way he looks at me only deepening. "Now, isn't this much better?"

"No."

Yes.

He chuckles softly, leaning to my lips, his tongue breaching the entrance.

His groan of satisfaction stirs something deep inside me, sending a clawing need spreading to my core, making me want him badly enough to beg. His rock-hard erection pushes into me, causing a rush of need to surge through me. I shift, desperate to ease the fire he's ignited.

He laughs. "It likes you. Quite a bit."

"I'm a bit of a fan too." A small smile tugs at my face.

His eyes darken, heavy with desire, as his hand slides into my hair, gripping me with a possessive force.

"Eat, moya l'vitsa..." His voice drops low, his breath hot against my ear. "Before I make a meal out of you."

A breathy moan escapes my lips as my fingers curl around his bicep, the electricity between us undeniable. He lifts the spoon to my lips, feeding me from his bowl while his cock continues to press against me, sending waves of sensation through my body. Each bite feels more personal, more intense, charged with a raw energy that mirrors the way he looks at me.

The tension thickens, an electric current running through the space between us, drawing us in even tighter. His presence is suffocating in the best way, making it impossible to ignore the way my pulse quickens each time his fingers brush my skin or when his eyes lock on to mine.

He pulls back slightly, his voice turning raspy, almost teasing. "I bought you something for tonight. It's hanging in our bedroom."

My brow furrows. "What's tonight?"

"I have a meeting at my club, and I need my assistant there with me." The sensual undertone in his words sends a shiver down my spine.

"The infamous club." The curiosity I've had about it bubbles to the surface, and before I can stop myself, the question slips out. "Will you show me around?"

He arches a brow, clearly surprised at my eagerness. "I was hoping to."

Nerves stir in my stomach, but it's not fear. It's something else, something thrilling. The idea of stepping into that world, seeing what he's been hiding, intrigues me more than I care to admit.

A part of me wonders what he might make me try. And if I might actually want to.

THIRTY-ONE

EMILIA

Konstantin's SUV silently glides on the road as we drive to the club, while I glance at my reflection in the tinted window.

A strappy red gown clings to my skin, my body accentuated by the soft, luxurious fabric. Gently, I adjust the intricate gold lace mask he gave me that sits on the bridge of my nose, the anticipation of this evening taking over. It's one thing to have heard about a place like this, but a whole other thing to experience it.

When the car pulls to a stop, the hum of the engine dying away, I peer over at him, face concealed by a simple black mask as he types something on his cell. Surveying the industrial building in the middle of nowhere, New Jersey, I have no idea what's waiting for me inside.

He exits first, coming around to open my door and giving me his hand as I step out. The heels on my feet don't add enough inches to come close to his towering height, which both intimidates and excites me.

More than a dozen cars are already parked as we approach the door, where a man in a red devil's mask taps away at his laptop.

"Boss," he greets Konstantin.

"Privet. This is my wife. Tessa, this is Igor."

"Good to meet you." The man nods, his accent thicker than Konstantin's.

"You too."

As we head through the glass doors, he presses a button for the elevator, and we ride up in silence. His hand slips into mine, and he brings my knuckles to his lips. I love when he does that.

The elevator opens, revealing a hallway with a coat check area before we head toward two double doors. The moment we step inside, the atmosphere shifts. Low, colorful lights bathe us in a seductive glow, the music thumping through the speakers with an erotic rhythm.

"There aren't any guests here yet," he says over the music. "It won't open for another hour."

I glance around, eyeing the people in masks and red collars. "And who are they?"

He pulls me closer, his palms tugging my hips as he stares into my eyes. "That's my staff. This is what Mira does." His lips brush my ear as he leans in. "What you would've done, if I hadn't found it impossible to picture you with anyone but me."

My arms slip around him, my fingers grazing his back. "Is that where your genius idea of making me your assistant came from?"

A smirk pulls at his lips, the heat in his gaze scorching me where I stand. "Yes, but my true brilliance came when I made you my wife."

I raise a brow, my lips curling playfully. "I think you're overestimating your brilliance."

His laughter vibrates through me, deep and raspy. "I think you're *underestimating* it, katyonak."

Something flickers in his irises. A flash of something darker, more intense. But it disappears as quickly as it appeared, leaving me questioning if I even saw it.

"Come. I want to show you around." His fingers slide into mine but he makes no attempt to move.

"Whatever you say, *sir*."

He catches the seductive note in my tone, and with a low groan, his mouth takes mine, urgent and all-consuming. A deep, primal sound slips from him as he drags me flush against him, his hand fisting my hair as he kisses me with an intensity that leaves me breathless. I melt into him as his fingers tangle in my hair, the other hand gripping my jaw and tilting my face as he deepens our connection.

With the masks on, everything is heightened. Every urge, every desire.

He pitches back, longing clouding his eyes, his lips still curled in a devilish smile.

"What was that for?" I breathe.

"I like it when you call me 'sir.' Keep doing that."

"Yes, sir." My giggle fades as I watch his nostrils flare, his grip tightening around me, the heat between us intensifying.

He mutters something under his breath as he leads me down into another section of the club.

"So, what exactly will I see here?"

His grin widens. "Just about everything. Every fantasy you can imagine."

A surge of warmth shoots through me, the thought of what I might witness or even experience making my body tingle with heightened anticipation. Stepping out of my comfort zone is tempting, and if I'm going to explore, it's him I'd want to test every boundary with.

We stride down a narrow hallway, the walls lined with fine art and plush, elegant furniture that gives the place the air of a luxurious home.

Except it's not. It's a sex dungeon.

My gaze shifts to a room with rings hanging from the ceiling, a tray of toys in the corner, and another with a metal bar attached high up. We pass more rooms, and I can't seem to look away from the equipment on display, my curiosity drawing me deeper into this strange, intoxicating world.

When we stop in front of another area, his eyes shift toward me as I stare at the bench in the center of the room, leather straps attached to the arms and legs. I know exactly what it is: a spanking bench.

My body instantly ignites, like it knows exactly what I want before I do. Thoughts race through my mind, imagining how it would feel to be strapped to it while he touches me, takes me hard and deep from behind.

"Do you want to ask me something?"

It's like he can read my thoughts, and I wonder if he knows exactly what I'm imagining.

Keeping my composure, I say, "Have you ever done that to a woman?"

His lips drift into a faint smile. "Yes."

My stomach tightens, my jaw clenching as I try to push away the knot of jealousy twisting inside me. It's irrational, I know. But it doesn't make it go away.

"Did you like it?"

His knuckles graze my cheek, gentle but electric, and my breath catches. "Yes."

My chest tightens even further. "Did she?"

He chuckles, low and seductive, the sound wrapping around me like a thorny vine. "Ask me what you really want to ask me, Tessa."

His hand slides around my back, pulling me into him, his hard body pressing against mine.

Suddenly, the words stick in my throat. My body pulses, aching for what I can't bring myself to say. But he doesn't need my words. He feels it dripping from my skin, written in the way I tremble beneath his gaze.

His mouth lowers to my ear, breath hot and wicked. "Do you want me to slip off this dress and restrain you, malyshka?"

The way he says it, low, lethal, makes my body grow taut.

"Do you want me to leave my mark on your skin?" he goes on. "Shall I do it with my palm…or the whip I favor most?"

His hand grips my hip hard before pushing me backward until my spine hits the wall with a soft thud. I gasp as he leans in, his body caging mine, dominance rolling off him like a deadly touch.

"I can lock the door…" His lips brush my cheek. "…and it'll be just us. Or…I can leave it open. Let them all watch what it looks like when you give in. When you surrender completely to me."

My throat dries, every inch of my skin burning with untamed and reckless desire.

"Do you want the pain, Tessa? The pleasure?" His fingers slide down, inching beneath my dress. "Do you want to let go and give me everything?"

Maybe? Yes? God, stop making me feel so damn good.

He finds me bare beneath the silk of my dress, his fingers slipping between my thighs. My moan breaks free before I can swallow it, head falling back against the wall as he circles my clit with devastating slowness.

This is so unfair…

"I want to watch your skin turn red beneath my palm." He pushes a finger inside me, and need swirls like a storm. "I want to watch my whip kiss your skin. Hear you beg for my cock. Beg me to fill your tight little cunt until it hurts. Until you're ruined for anyone else."

A second finger joins the first, and my body clenches around him, desperate and greedy.

"I want to test every one of your limits. Tear through them until there's nothing left but animalistic need. Then give you more than you ever knew you needed. I want it all with you, Tessa. Only you."

My hand flies to the back of his neck, dragging him to me like I'll shatter if he doesn't kiss me right now. He lets me take the lead, my mouth grazing his, exhales skimming over those lips I crave too much, and then I crash into him, rough and reckless, unable to stop the way I want him, like I can't breathe without him.

This isn't just lust. It's ravenousness. Obsession-rivaling madness. The kind of craving that claws at the edge of sanity. The kind I always thought was fiction.

I'm so glad I was wrong.

Before I even realize what's happening, we're in the room, his hands hot against my skin, cupping my breasts with a possessive hunger that has me gasping. His fingers pinch my nipples hard enough to sting, and I welcome it.

I need the pain. Need the edge, the release. He knows that now. Knows exactly how far I'm willing to go.

Maybe I've lost my mind, but deep down, I know this desire is something I've always lived with. And right now, it feels like the only sane thing I've ever done.

His fingers slide down my back, finding the zipper of my dress, while the other hand reaches for the door.

"Leave it open," I whisper, the command slipping past my lips without thinking.

He grins, a slow, satisfied smile, before his hands cup my cheeks, pulling me into his gaze. The tenderness of his touch catches me off guard, and before I can react, his lips brush mine with a slowness that drives me wild.

The kiss deepens, like he's savoring something sacred. And in this moment, everything else fades—the noise, the confusion, the uncertainty of everything we are.

All I feel is him.

When he pulls back, his gaze lingers. Dark. Intense. Burning through me. As if he's trying to memorize every part of me from the inside out.

And I let him. Because whatever this is, whatever we're becoming, I don't want it to stop.

"I need you to pick a safe word. If at any point you want it to end, all you have to do is say it."

The thing he's offering, control wrapped in consent, presses against my skin. Tension coils in the space between us as I consider it. Am I really doing this? Here? With him? In front of—

Before I can fully grasp what's happening, his hand is on my back again, fingers trailing down my spine as the zipper hums in the stillness of the room.

With every slow inch, my skin spreads with goose bumps as the straps slide from my shoulders, fabric slipping down my body. His gaze follows the movement, until the dress is pooled at my feet.

"Have you chosen your word yet?"

I nod. "Lioness."

A small smile flickers across his face. Without another word, he takes my hand and leads me to the bench, each step heavy with the promise of what's to come.

"Let me help you up."

In one smooth motion, he lifts me, positioning my body with my knees bent, elbows resting on the cool leather, my chest pressed against the surface.

Vulnerability wraps around me like a second skin as he begins with my ankles, locking them in place before moving to my wrists.

I'm completely spread open. Exposed, restrained, trembling beneath the growing anticipation.

He steps away toward the armoire, opening it to retrieve something. When he turns, he's holding a red leather whip. Chills explode across my skin as he drags it slowly up my spine, the leather like a teasing caress, down the curve of my back, tracing every inch with expert precision.

My breath stutters as it slips lower, gliding between my thighs, brushing over my clit. A sharp jolt of need shoots through me before he strikes my thigh. Hard.

Instead of pain, a wave of surrender rushes over me, my muscles tightening as my mind and body fight to keep up with the rush of sensations.

"More, sir."

My back arches, submitting completely to him as he rains a series of strikes across my skin, each one sharper, deeper. The sting of pain twists into something else, something heady and addictive. My body burns with the desire for more.

"Good girl." He hisses as he lets the whip glide up my back. "You take it so well."

Then a deeper strike lands and I cry out. "Thank you, sir."

Another strike comes, then another, before his hand softly feathers over my throbbing flesh.

"I think you need a little more of a challenge," he adds, his voice a low growl.

What the hell does that mean?

And why does the thought thrill me more than it terrifies me?

He drops the whip on a nearby table, and the sharp clatter makes me flinch. Then he's at the armoire again. This time, when he turns around, there's nothing in his hands…except a black silk blindfold.

And that just makes me sweat even more.

"Remember your safe word." He slips the blindfold over my eyes, and the world goes black.

Instantly, everything heightens. Sound, touch, the racing of my pulse echoing in my ears.

Warm fingers trail down my spine, dipping lower, sliding between the cheeks of my ass, then teasing my entrance. I arch into the touch, needing it deeper.

But he avoids my clit entirely, stroking everywhere else until I'm clawing the leather, all my attention on the fact that I want him to touch me there. I squirm, the need building, nerves fraying. Then… nothing. His hands disappear, and every inch of my skin throbs in anticipation.

When something hot drips onto my back, I wince, the feeling satisfying as it cools against me.

Before I can ask if it was wax, a sudden, powerful vibration jolts across my core, like from a toy. My nails dig into the leather beneath me, a cry ripping from my throat.

"Oh God—"

A deep chuckle resonates from behind me, his warm breath teasing my neck. "Your pussy's soaked, and I haven't even gotten to the best part."

The vibration intensifies, rolling through me with savage precision. My body bows, teetering on the edge.

His name rips from my lips. "Konstantin…please!"

But mercy never comes. The pressure lessens, the teasing pull of the device retreating just enough to drive me mad.

My hips jerk, chasing the sensation, but he offers nothing but the slow, exquisite torture he knows how to deliver so well. Fingers tangle in my hair, pulling tight while a warm palm strokes over the curve of my ass, deceptively gentle, until the sharp crack of a slap rings out. I jump, a whimper slipping free.

"It's too bad you can't see the crowd you've drawn." His words are low and rough. "Your perfect cunt on display, and they all know it's mine. Only mine."

He spanks me harder, soothing the sting before striking again. And again.

My body shudders beneath him, on the edge of release, the pleasure too much, yet not enough.

The vibrations return between my legs, circling my clit in maddening slow rolls. My walls clench, needing this to end, to feel myself come undone.

"Please, please, let me come, sir," I plead with everything I have, and knowing we're not alone makes it even hotter.

"Give me everything. Don't hold back." His hand curls around my throat while the toy drives me to the brink before he pulls it away.

"No, no, please, sir…"

His deep, raspy moan ripples through me. "I like the sound of you begging."

A hand cups my center, grinding into me before slapping my pussy. The pulsating desperation makes me dizzy. I hear the metallic jingle of his belt, and my blood pumps violently in my veins, hoping he fucks me and fills me.

But instead, a strike lands sharp and hot against my thigh.

"Yes, God, yes!" My voice breaks with pleasure. "Again."

"Again what?"

"Sir. Again, sir." The words quiver out of me. I've never felt this much pleasure before.

Another blow comes, harder this time, biting into my other thigh. The belt lashes over my ass, the backs of my legs, each strike driving me higher and pushing me closer to that edge.

"Your skin…" he groans behind me. "The most perfect shade of red, katyonak."

Something loops around my neck, pulling my head back. I can't see him, but I don't have to. I can feel the feral heat in his gaze.

"Please…I need it."

"What do you need?" His breath ghosts over my ear. "Say it."

"I-I need to come, sir."

"Then come." With a growl, he drives his cock into me in one brutal thrust, and my body arches, stars bursting behind my eyes.

He pulls the belt tighter, his grip fierce, his pace ruthless.

Every time he rams into me, I cry out, unable to control myself. I shudder as the wand returns, pressed mercilessly at my clit. The orgasm rips through me, shattering, uncontrollable, as I squirt all over him, legs shaking, vision going white at the edges.

"That's it, come on. More." He slams into me. "Show me how you belong to me, wife."

I can't stop. My body won't let me. The more I come, the more I need to again. My hips move on instinct, seeking another release.

He laughs knowingly. "Don't worry. I'm not stopping. Not until you beg me to. And even then, I'll keep fucking you until your body breaks beneath me. Because that's what you need."

And he's right. I never knew how badly I needed this. Not just to come, but to let go. To surrender completely. Not to share control, but to hand it over entirely. To lose myself in the wreckage and be reborn through it.

I needed more than just a fucking. I needed to be wrecked. Needed the pain to cleanse both my body and soul. And that's what he's giving me.

His body punishes mine with perfect rhythm, unforgiving and skilled. When the wand returns, another climax detonates through me, even harder than the last.

And if Mira or his brothers are watching? I couldn't care less.

All that matters is this. Him. The way he breaks me apart and puts me back together.

Over and over again.

THIRTY-TWO

EMILIA

The air inside the club still feels thick, buzzing with the energy of what just happened between us.

Konstantin's hands are gentle as he helps me slip my dress back on while I try to ignore the eyes of the people passing by, their gazes drawn to us.

The fabric of my gown settles over my limbs, and he drags up the zipper, his fingers brushing my skin with tenderness.

Every touch, every small movement, is like a thread tying us together in ways I'm still trying to understand. I can't ignore the rush of heat that pulses through me once he faces me, those eyes intense and unwavering, as though he's searching for something deep within me.

For a moment, time seems to stand still, the world outside disappearing completely. Then, without breaking our gaze, his lips gently brush mine—soft, yet full of unspoken desire, like he's savoring every second. His palm cradles my cheek, and the warmth of his touch sends a wave of emotions through me.

When he drags himself back, he lifts my knuckles to his lips, sending a jolt through my body before leading me into the hallway. But as we move forward, a woman suddenly rushes toward us.

She's barely dressed, a corset around her midsection, her breasts only covered by jeweled pasties, a black, lacy thong around her hips. But it's when I see her red collar that I know she works here. She looks briefly at me, as if uncertain about saying something in front of me, but Konstantin doesn't give her the chance to hesitate.

"Tessa is my wife now. She knows everything." His tone leaves no room for argument.

The woman meets his gaze, then looks at me again, her own concern evident.

"It's Mira," she says, and I instantly realize it's Veronika behind that mask.

"What about Mira?" The question slips from me without thinking.

I may not know her well, but I don't want to see her hurt.

"She's in trouble." Veronika's vision flicks toward Konstantin. "It's Billy. He hurt her."

Who the hell is Billy?

Konstantin's jaw clenches, and I can feel quiet rage within him, waiting for the right moment to explode.

"Where are they?" Konstantin's hand tightens around mine.

"The guys have him in a room. She's getting cleaned up by the girls."

I don't like the sound of that.

"Who's Billy?" I ask aloud this time.

"He's a local politician," he tells me. "Someone who thinks he's above the law. But tonight, he's going to learn the hard way what happens when you hurt my business or my people."

And I know without a doubt tonight will be a reckoning.

We move quickly toward Mira, entering the back room where she waits. The moment I see her, my heart drops.

She's sitting on a plush chair, a robe wrapped around her body, face bruised on both cheeks, blue and bloody, her eyes swollen from crying. She's trembling, but when she sees Konstantin, her face softens slightly, like she feels a bit safer with him here.

"Oh God, Mira." I rush to her side, kneeling down in front of her. My heart aches as I reach out to touch her arm gently. "I'm so sorry this happened to you."

She stares at me. "Tessa?"

Lowering my mask, I offer her a small, sad smile. "Yeah, it's me."

She sniffles, tears rolling down her face as she throws her arms around me.

"It's okay, I've got you." I hold her tightly, feeling Konstantin's gaze burning into my back.

When we finally pull apart and I rise to my feet, his eyes are on me, his expression unreadable, but something in them softens as he watches me comfort Mira.

"Don't worry," he says, his voice laced with violent intent. "I'll take care of him for good."

A quiet promise of revenge and protection. And I can't help but feel moved by his unwavering need to avenge those he cares for, even when it's in murderous ways.

After a few moments, we leave Mira to rest, and Konstantin leads me to where Billy is. The walk to his room feels like it takes an eternity; the anticipation of what's about to happen has me excited. Nothing makes me happier than seeing a fucker who touched a woman get what's coming to him. Unresolved trauma and all that.

When we step into the room, Billy is sitting in a chair, five men with black masks surrounding him, guns in their holsters. His mask is gone, leaving nothing but an old, shriveled-up face who thought he could beat Mira without consequences.

"Konstantin…" He laughs nervously, trying to stand up, but the men push him back down, and his smile immediately vanishes.

Konstantin moves toward him, circling him slowly. "What did you think you'd accomplish by touching one of my employees, hmm?"

"Look, it-it's a misunderstanding. She wasn't listening, so I had to teach her a lesson. You know how it is."

In an instant, Konstantin whips out his gun and smashes it into Billy's jaw, blood exploding from his lip.

"Fuuuck!" His chest rattles as he wipes the blood away. "We don't have to do this. I'll never come back here, I promise."

"Of course you won't." Konstantin's laugh is cold and vicious. "That's a given. You took advantage of your membership, hurt one of my people, and now you're going to answer for it."

Billy opens his mouth to speak, but before he can say anything, Konstantin moves with terrifying speed. He slams Billy's face against the desk over and over, the sound of impact filling the room. Billy groans, his hands instinctively coming up to protect himself.

Konstantin doesn't stop. He shoves Billy to the ground, driving his face into the floor with relentless force.

A normal woman would wince, or maybe even cover her eyes, but I'm not a normal woman. I'm enjoying this a bit too much.

"Your membership's revoked." Venom drips through every one of his words.

And as he pulls out his weapon, Billy raises his arms in the air, his face barely recognizable.

"Please, please, you don't have to do this."

Konstantin laughs. "But I do."

A single bullet to his forehead, and it's over. I'm supposed to feel something, but I feel nothing but relief.

He steps back, signaling for his men to take the body out of the room. "Make it look like a mugging gone wrong."

One of them nods as the rest drag Billy away, leaving me alone with my husband.

He stands tall, his back to me, body heaving. Wordlessly, I step forward, wrapping my arms around him from behind and holding him tight. He doesn't pull away, instead clasping my hands in his fiercely, as if he's afraid to let go. He brings my knuckles to his lips, kissing each one with a tenderness that clashes with the violence I've just witnessed.

And in this moment, as we stand here in the aftermath of everything that's happened, I realize just how deep I'm falling for him. How far I've come from the woman who walked into his life wanting to destroy him to now praying he isn't involved in my brother's case.

THIRTY-THREE

KONSTANTIN

The next day, I can't stop thinking about how she wrapped her arms around me, like she was silently telling me she accepts who I am. Like she won't walk away once the DeLuca business is finished.

I want to believe I don't have to force her to stay, that she'll want to, but I don't know if we're there yet.

When I step out of my car, the scent of earth and shit fills my lungs as I approach the pig farm, miles away from the house. The three men are already waiting, their bodies trembling, their knees in the dirt, my brothers and our men all waiting for me.

The hint of blood and metal clings to the air as I circle them, tied to the fence, arms bound tightly behind them, their faces pale in fear.

I grip the knife in my hand, its steel catching the faint light. The chainsaw rests on the ground beside them, gleaming with a deadly promise.

One of them starts to speak, his body shaking.

"I-I don't know the n-name of the cop," he stammers, eyes wide with terror. "Th-the boss doesn't t-tell us any of that."

I tsk under my breath, taking a step forward. "It's in your best interest not to lie to me. You know what happens when I lose patience, right, my friend?"

He squirms, glancing at the chainsaw with obvious fear.

The second man starts to plead. "P-p-please, please, we swear we don't know anything. We're j-just street-level guys. DeLuca only t-tells us what we n-need to know." His words crack, desperation dripping from each syllable.

I don't believe them. Not for a second.

"And that hit on me at the hotel." I flip the knife in my hands, continuing to walk around them. "Was that the cop's idea or the boss's?"

The third man shifts uncomfortably, his eyes flicking between me and his two companions.

"Don't fucking look at them." I rush toward him, the tip of the knife inching near his eye. "You look at *me*."

He shudders with a nod.

"What the fuck did you want to say? And it better be the truth."

"Y-yeah, o-o-okay."

"Speak!"

"The hit, that was DeLuca. But…"

"But what? Nu blyat govori!" *Fucking talk!*

Sweat coats his forehead, face a mixture of terror and uncertainty. "The-the hit wasn't meant for you."

I stop, my body stiffening. "What do you mean?"

When he doesn't say anything, I press my shoe into his hand. The man begs me to stop, but I don't. I press harder until I swear a bone cracks.

"All I heard…"

I step off his hand, and he pants heavily.

"All I heard was that they were after some woman. The one who killed the two lieutenants."

"I already knew they were after her. That's not a surprise."

I grab the chainsaw from the ground and drop the knife, ready to end them all. The sound of the saw revving up fills the space between us, the noise ringing in the silence of the night.

"Wait!" The man cracks in terror. "You don't understand! They wanted her dead *before* she killed them."

My body locks in place. "What?"

"Please, I'm telling you what I heard. DeLuca put the hit on her. He wanted her gone."

Every muscle in my body tightens. "Do you know why?"

I back away, staring at him for long seconds. The silence stretches between us as I wait for him to give me answers I need.

His face pales as he stares at the saw. "I-I don't know that…but if you let me go, I can find out."

I shake my head, the edges of my mouth curling into a smile that's anything but comforting. "No need. I'm more than capable. But thank you for the offer. You are far too kind. Now, with that…"

The chainsaw roars to life once again.

"Your usefulness has come to an end."

His eyes widen in realization, but it's too late. Before he can say another word, I bring the saw down with precision, the blade cutting through his neck. His scream is short, and his head hits the ground with a soft thud.

The other two men wail vainly, their bodies jerking in their restraints as they beg for their lives, imploring me to spare them.

But I won't. Everyone who works for DeLuca will die.

I bring the chainsaw to the second man, slicing through his neck with brutal force. The roar of the saw nearly drowns out the screams of the remaining man, but with a single pull of the lever, his head is severed from his body.

Crimson splatters across the ground, painting the dirt beneath us a deep red.

They knew what they were getting into when they crossed me.

I step back, wiping the blood from my forehead as I shut off the saw, the silence hanging heavy in the air.

Aleksei steps forward, watching me carefully. His expression is unreadable, but there's something in his eyes that tells me he's thinking about what just happened. Thinking about *her*.

"Why would they want her dead? What does she have to do with the DeLucas?" The undercurrent of his tone is unmistakable.

Tension builds in my body, my muscles growing stiff, my jaw clenched, and for a moment, I don't speak.

"I don't know yet." I cut the distance between us, staring right at him. "But I will find out. And when I do, *I'll* deal with it. You stay out of it. Ponyatno?" *Understand?*

His mouth jerks. "Da, ponyatno. But you know what must happen if she somehow betrayed us, right?"

My fist tightens around the collar of his shirt, my teeth grinding. "If you even think about touching my wife, I'll kill you just like I killed them."

Aleksei laughs, and it's cold. Sinister.

"You've lost it, brother." His voice is laced with mocking amusement. "Maybe losing her is exactly what you need to become who you were before."

His words hit a raw nerve deep inside me, snapping away my control. My fist crashes into his face, the impact sending him stumbling backward. The pain in my hand is nothing compared to the rage boiling inside me.

Aleksei recovers quickly and lunges at me, throwing his own punch and knocking me to the ground. Our fists fly, bodies slamming into the dirt, each of us trying to overpower the other.

As I land a punch to his gut, Kirill and Anton step in, pulling us apart before things escalate.

"Okay, you two had your fun. Now stop this shit." Kirill drags me back.

My chest heaves as I stare down at Aleksei, lying on the ground with a bloody grin. I can still feel the rage pulsing through me. Because I meant it.

I'd kill my own brother if he ever dared to hurt the woman I care about.

Turning around, I don't look at any of them as I walk away. There's nothing left to say.

And as I make my way back to the car, needing to see my wife, I know I will have to work even harder to protect her from everyone around us.

I won't let anyone touch Tessa. She's mine. And I will do whatever it takes to keep her safe.

For the rest of my life.

EMILIA

I wait for Konstantin to leave, the heavy door closing behind him as his footfalls fade down the hallway.

The house settles into the familiar quiet I've come to recognize. His men are scattered, doing their jobs, leaving me with a rare moment of solitude. But today, it feels like there are fewer of them than usual. Probably busy helping my husband with his…extracurricular activities.

Glancing around, I find one of his men by the foyer, his back to me as I flip through channels on the TV. Maybe this is my chance to go snooping to see if I can find just one more thing for Riley to go through.

I texted with her earlier, and she's at a dead end for now. I hate knowing there's nothing I can do from here.

Getting to my feet, I pretend I'm on my cell, staring at the screen as I start down the hall, feeling his man watch me as I move around.

I step into the guest bedroom first, one of many in the house, and continue moving through each room quietly, pretending to familiarize myself with the space. But there's nothing useful inside—no computers, no devices I can access.

Next, I slip into his study, the one room that feels more like him. Shelves line the walls, old leather-bound books stacked high, the desk perfectly organized, everything in its place.

A single lamp casts a soft light across the polished wood. I pace around, my fingers trailing along the edges of his things, but nothing stands out. No laptop. No sign of anything that could help me. Even the drawers are empty. Damn it.

I stand there for a moment, knowing there are cameras everywhere, watching every move I make, even if I can't see them. So I have to be careful.

Walking out of the study, I enter a game room next. Arcade games line one side, and the centerpiece of the room is a large pool table. I strut around the table, my fingers brushing the edges, the polished wood cool beneath my touch. The sharp click of the pool balls echoes in the room as I pick one up, idly rolling it between my fingers.

But then it slips from my hands and skitters across the floor. I lean down quickly to retrieve it when something under the rug catches my attention. My foot grazes it first: a slight bump beneath the fabric.

What the hell is that? Access to some secret dungeon where he keeps souvenirs from his victims?

Crouching down, I lift the corner of the rug, the fabric heavy in my hands. Pulling it back inch by inch, I flip it over until I find…a handle, a metal latch fastened to the floorboards like a hidden storage compartment.

My fingers tremble slightly as I grip it, but it doesn't give right away, refusing to open. But with a quiet grunt, I pull harder and it finally shifts, the floorboards groaning in protest as a large section slowly rises.

A wave of excitement floods me as my eyes land on the yellow envelopes stacked inside. Dozens of them. This is it. The breakthrough I've been waiting for. Something that could maybe help Nate.

But suddenly, the sound of footsteps grows louder.

His footsteps.

Fuck!

Panic jolts through me as I slowly shut the compartment, the low thud echoing louder.

The door handle begins to turn.

Oh God!

I scramble to fix the rug, my fingers shaking as I try to smooth it out. Every second stretches into an eternity, the rush of adrenaline making my head spin.

Straightening up fast, I move toward the pool table like nothing's wrong. My body quivers with nerves as I pretend to line up a shot, my heart racing just as the door creaks open.

Konstantin.

His eyes meet mine, cold and calculating. For a moment, he just stands there, watching me with that unreadable expression. And then a smirk slowly spreads across his face, like he knows exactly what I was doing.

"Having fun?" he asks, his voice smooth, laced with something dark and playful.

But it's the blood that catches my attention first. His shirt is torn, crimson staining the fabric in large patches. His face is bruised, the cut on his lip still fresh, and there's a deep gash along his cheek.

"What the hell happened?" I ask, rushing over to him. The concern is instant, the anger and fear for him rising within me.

"Just a little sparring between brothers." His mouth tilts up.

I take in the state of him and my brow curves. "That looks like more than just a friendly fight."

"Are you worried about me, moya l'vitsa?" His voice is smooth like whiskey as his hand reaches up, fingers grazing my cheek and sending a shiver through me.

"I am." The words slip out before I can stop them. I don't even try to hide it.

His gaze sharpens, the smirk curling at his lips as he watches me, studying me like I'm a challenge he can't resist. Then, without warning, he leans down, his lips brushing against my ear, his breath hot on my skin.

"So make me feel better, then."

The air between us crackles, like a storm ready to break.

"How shall I do that?" My finger trails down from his chest, dragging slowly until it reaches the outline of his hard erection.

He stiffens under my touch, making a wicked thrill race through me.

"I'm sure you can come up with something." His voice pulls with something low and rough, a growl barely hidden beneath the surface.

There's that hunger again—the same hunger that pulls me in and forces me to give in, even when I know it will consume me. His eyes are on fire, dark with need, and for a moment, the world around us disappears. It's just him. Just us.

I can't escape the pull. And I don't want to.

Before I can second-guess myself, I drop to my knees in front of him, holding his gaze without breaking it. My fingers go straight to his belt, his jaw tensing as I unbuckle it with teasing precision.

"Blyat," he growls, his hand tangling in my hair like he's already unraveling.

I tug the belt free, his zipper following. When my fingers stroke over him through the fabric, his cock jerks—hard, heavy, and barely restrained.

"How many times have you imagined this?" My lips graze the skin just above his waistband. "Me on my knees. Wanting to please you and suck you dry."

He mutters something in Russian.

"Too many times to count, malyshka." His voice is heavy with arousal as he brushes his knuckles along my jaw. "I've imagined your mouth wrapped around me, your eyes watering while you fight to take more. The way you'd sound while you struggled to make it fit, to breathe with every inch of my cock stuffed down your pretty throat. I've thought about the way I'd fuck you after, hard and fast, bent over this very pool table."

His grip tightens in my hair, tipping my head back while his gaze devours mine, hunger and control swirling in every line of his face. "And most of all, I've imagined how good it would feel when you begged me to do it all over again."

My core throbs, wanting all of that. When I yank his pants and boxers down, his thick hard-on springs to life.

My fingers wrap around him, barely able to meet, and when he shudders at my touch, a thrill of dominance pulses through me. *I'm* the one who's making the ruler of the underworld ache like that.

He watches my every move, eyes intense. Wanting, waiting for me to taste him.

I close the distance between us, my lips barely grazing his hardness, my gaze locked on his as my body hums with need. Seeing him like this, overcome with desire, makes everything burn hotter.

His body tenses as soon as the tip of my tongue traces the crown of his cock, a soft hiss escaping him. Fingers slip into my hair, pushing me down until I swallow him whole.

"Fuuuck!" A harsh, guttural growl escapes him as he keeps me trapped around him while I savor every inch.

His hand in my hair guides me deeper, but I don't need it. I know exactly what I'm doing. His length hits the back of my throat, and when I gag, he groans.

"That's it. Take it all, katyonak. Every inch of me is yours."

My mouth tightens as I bob my head, his cock twitching against my tongue. My eyes stay fixed on him as he tilts his head back, his hand tangled in my hair, his body tense with power. He looks like a god in every sense of the word.

The taste and feeling of him fills my senses. The way he groans, the way he can't stop himself from pushing his hard-on deeper. Every inch of him is a promise of things to come, and I'm not sure I can wait for it.

The faster I suck him, the tighter his fingers tangle in my hair, his control undoing with each flick of my tongue, each hollow of my cheeks around him.

He groans, low and guttural, the sound dragging desire straight through me. I lick along the length of him, slow at first, then faster—relentless, greedy. His hips jerk, and when I take every thick inch, he curses sharply in Russian, his whole body straining under the pressure until he spills down my throat, his grip tightening like he needs to anchor himself to reality.

He doesn't pull away. He keeps me there, wrapped around him, until he's given me every last drop. And even then, I want more. My lips are swollen, breath ragged, but I stay right there, licking along his crown, tasting every trace of him.

A deep rumble vibrates in his chest, and with a swift movement, he pulls me up, his grip stealing my breath before his lips smash into mine with a force that leaves me breathless.

This isn't just a kiss. It's a possession, wild and intense, driven by a desperate hunger.

His tongue meets mine, tasting himself, and it only drives him to kiss me harder. My hands clutch his bloodied shirt, gripping on to him as I begin to lose myself. His kiss overtakes me like he's starving, like I'm the only thing that can sustain him, and I kiss him back with a depth I didn't know I had, surrendering every part of myself.

My back slams against the pool table, and before I can even process it, he lifts me effortlessly, laying me back against the smooth surface. The chill of the table contrasts sharply with the heat of his body as it presses into mine, his hands exploring every inch of me, tracing every curve he's memorized.

He pushes up my dress, his mouth leaving a trail of heat down my throat, his breath tattered against my skin. His hand rests on my stomach, his palm warm and steady.

"I'm not done with you yet, malyshka. Not even close." And from the fire in his eyes as he stares down at me, I know he means every word.

The next moment, he's pulling me to the edge of the pool table, my legs falling open beneath his touch as he tears my panties to shreds. His mouth wraps around my clit, sucking hard, his fingers thrusting inside me, and I lose all ability to think or do anything besides feel.

I bow beneath him, a moan slipping past my lips as he flicks his tongue around me, driving me higher with nothing but his fingers and his mouth, undoing me piece by piece.

My hands grip the end of the table, heart racing. It's too much. Not enough. I can't think. I can only feel—the sharp rush of pleasure, the burn of throbbing need twisting inside me.

My head tips back as his tongue grazes faster, teasing me to the edge before he slows. The faint scrape of something against my thigh makes me blink down just in time to see him with a pool stick in hand, a slow, dangerous smile growing as he strokes it.

"What are you—"

The words barely leave my lips before he slides the stick inside me, the sudden rush of sensation crashing over every nerve, overriding my thoughts and stealing my breath. My legs tremble uncontrollably, as if I'm caught in the wake of a tidal wave I didn't see coming.

And when he pushes it further into me, my body answers before I do, writhing beneath his touch, chasing the release only he can give me. He thrusts the stick into me, and my walls clench, need spiraling, wanting more.

I reach for him, needing him closer, needing more, but he's already ahead of me, already working me deeper, faster, taking me beyond my limits with ruthless precision.

My cries echo as he teases me, slowing down the tempo, my core dripping for him.

"Please don't stop. I need more." My voice is nothing but a wrecked plea.

"Then take it." He forces more of it inside me, fucking me with it while the thumb of his other hand strokes my clit. He's not gentle, the way he punishes me, the way he elicits every moan, each one of them his.

When I come, it rips through me like lightning—a harsh, electric pulse that leaves my body shaking. I cling to whatever I can hold on to as the aftershocks roll through me, his name the only thing I remember how to say.

He doesn't give me a second to recover. The stick hits the floor with a loud clatter, and then he's on me, the tip of him nudging into me as his body presses against mine, his eyes fixed on me like I'm the only thing that matters. His hands grip my hips, and in one hard thrust, he's inside me.

My gasp is swallowed by his mouth as he starts to move, slow at first, then faster, rougher, until all I can do is beg for mercy that never comes. His rhythm is punishing and perfect. There's nothing gentle about it, which is what I need. Every thrust sends me closer to the edge again, every kiss deeper, more consuming.

I can't think. I don't want to. I want to drown in him.

He mutters something low in Russian, sweat slicking his skin, his hands possessive on my waist as if he's anchoring himself to the very depth of me.

I reach up, fingers threading through his hair, and whisper, "Harder, baby."

His teeth snap, chest rising higher before he pumps his hips even faster. The sound of skin on skin fills the room as he drives us both to the edge, until I'm begging without shame, until his mouth finds my neck and he groans, "Tessa," like it's the only word he's ever known.

When we come together, it's violent. A quiet explosion that leaves us tangled, breathless, and utterly undone.

THIRTY-FOUR

EMILIA

I wake up with the remnants of what we did last night still clinging to me. The bed feels colder now, and I roll over to find the spot beside me empty, a slight dip in the mattress where Konstantin should be.

The man is always the first one out of bed. Does he even sleep?

Swinging my legs off the bed, I'm still wrapped in one of his oversized T-shirts, the one he gave me to sleep in, and the scent of him clings to my skin.

Getting to my feet, I grab a pair of shorts from the dresser and quickly slip into them before heading down the stairs.

As I reach the last step, my eyes catch something: several pieces of luggage sitting at the foot of the stairs.

Is he going somewhere? An emergency work thing?

Am I going with him?

Curiosity spirals in my gut as I head toward the kitchen, making out the soft clink of something, and as I enter, I find Konstantin at the breakfast table pouring himself a cup of coffee. His usual commanding presence fills the room, and when his eyes lift to meet mine, he offers a small, almost imperceptible smile. One that feels both distant and unreadable.

Maybe I imagined it?

"Good morning," he says, the deep rumble of his voice making my stomach flip. "Have a seat."

I hesitate for just a second before walking toward him. When I sit down, he rises to pour me a cup of coffee and places a plate in front of me, the food steaming. But his silence only makes my anxiety worse.

Why is he being so quiet? What's going on?

I peer down at the plate, then back up at him. "Are you going somewhere?"

He pauses, his gaze briefly drifting to his plate as he chews slowly. When he finally meets my eyes, he says nothing, and the silence stretches between us, making my nerves flare even more.

"No," he finally answers, his tone flat. "*We* are. I packed for you while you were asleep."

The words hit me like a punch to the chest, and I don't understand why. Maybe it's because he caught me snooping in the game room and now plans to kill me under the pretense of some trip. Or maybe I'm just overthinking it.

Come on, Emilia. If he wanted you dead, why bother with the theatrics? He could easily do it right here.

Then again, Konstantin loves theatrics.

I force myself to act casual as I take a sip of my coffee. "Where are we going?"

His eyes narrow, then his lips curl into a sly smile. "On our honeymoon."

I freeze, every muscle locking up.

Honeymoon? This makes no sense. Who goes on a honeymoon at the last minute?

"Did you think I wasn't going to treat my wife to one?"

The stiffness in my chest is suffocating, but I try to push it down. "Why didn't you tell me yesterday?"

His mouth winds up. "I wanted it to be a surprise."

Well, consider me surprised.

"And where are we going?"

"You'll see." He picks up his fork, digging into his meal, while my mind spins with doubts and questions.

But I don't have a choice but to go, do I?

"Eat." His command slices through my thoughts. "We leave in two hours."

Two hours? Jesus!

All I can do is grab my fork and stare blankly at the food, fighting the anxiety rising inside me and the nagging feeling that something's not quite right.

The hum of the private plane fades into the background as I look out the window, watching the darkened clouds stretch across the sky beneath us. The flight's too long, and with every passing hour, a tension grows inside me, gnawing at the edges of my mind.

Konstantin has barely said a word, and the silence is deafening. I still wonder if he looked through the cameras after our pool table session and saw me snooping. What else could it be?

I tried to text Riley after breakfast a few times to give her a heads-up about my trip, but each time, there he was, watching me. It was as if he knew I'd try to make a move, like he was waiting for me to slip.

Now, as his private plane descends into Nice, France, I'm even more afraid of what's waiting for me.

The plane touches down smoothly, the engines whining as we roll to a stop. Konstantin's men shuffle out of their seats, gathering our luggage, while I glance at him beside me. His expression is impassive, and when our eyes meet, he says nothing—just a slight smirk as he rises, gesturing for me to walk ahead of him.

The cold night air hits me as we step off the plane and into the waiting cars. The faint smell of the Mediterranean lingers in the breeze, but the tension in the air is suffocating. I try to shake it off, but it follows me like a shadow.

We drive through winding roads, the lights of the city fading into the distance as we approach a sprawling estate, nestled high above the sparkling coastline of Villefranche-sur-Mer with the most stunning view of the south of France, the Mediterranean stretching out in an endless expanse.

I can't believe this is real. It's breathtaking. I try not to stare, but the castle looming ahead is impossible to ignore, surrounded by acres of lush greenery. The staff is already waiting for us, dressed in black uniforms as they greet us with practiced politeness.

"Do you own this place?"

He turns to me, flashing that familiar Konstantin smirk, effortlessly charming. "Yes, and I hope you like it."

"I do." My smile that follows feels forced.

I don't know what's going on inside his head, and I don't like it.

We enter the home, the gray marble floors gleaming under the soft glow of chandeliers. His men carry our luggage up the stairs as we follow, the silence between us palpable.

When his guys open one of the doors and leave our luggage, we move in after them, stepping into a spacious bedroom where a sparkling chandelier hangs from the ceiling, casting soft shadows across the room.

Walking past the large bed, draped in rich, dark linens, I head for the floor-to-ceiling glass doors, which lead out to a terrace that overlooks the garden and the shimmering waters below.

The view is insane, but it doesn't ease the growing anxiety gnawing at me.

Why are we really here?

When his hand rests on my shoulder, I flinch, startled by the sudden touch. Clearing my throat, I turn to him, forcing myself to look him in the eye, pretending I'm fine.

"Are you okay?" he asks, his voice low, almost concerned.

I should be asking you that.

Instead, I nod quickly, my words coming out too fast. "I'm just tired."

He doesn't seem convinced, but he doesn't press the issue. "Then we should get some rest. We have a big day ahead tomorrow."

"What do you have planned?" The question slips out, my curiosity getting the better of me.

A half-grin tugs at his lips. "I wouldn't want to ruin the surprise, malyshka."

Oh, please, ruin the surprise. I don't even like surprises.

"Can't wait."

I turn my attention back to the view outside, trying not to imagine whether we'll be lounging by the glistening pool below or if he's planning to drown me in it. Or maybe toss me off a cliff.

Though I was kind of hoping to try some French food before I die...

Eh, maybe there's still time.

THIRTY-FIVE

KONSTANTIN

The sun glints off the Mediterranean, casting its golden hues across the water, but I can't seem to focus on anything other than her. She's leaning over the side of the boat, her hair whipping in the breeze, and for a moment, I let myself watch her without interruption. She's beautiful, perfect in every possible way, and all mine.

I don't approach her immediately, letting the sound of the water crashing against the hull fill the space between us, wanting to hold on to this view of her just a little longer.

When I've had my fill, I step up behind her, the soft swish of my shoes on the deck the only sound that follows. Her body jerks when I come close, like she's waiting for me to do something, but she doesn't look back, her eyes locked on the horizon.

"How are you enjoying yourself so far, Mrs. Marinova?" I easily mask the frustration that's been gnawing at me since before we even flew here.

Something doesn't sit right. Why did the DeLucas want her dead? What is she to them?

"It's beautiful here." She finally glances over her shoulder, forcing a smile that does nothing to erase the obvious stiffness in her body.

I know she knows I'm not my usual self. I haven't hidden it. Let her wonder. The more nervous she gets, the better chance she slips.

Her eyes flick to me quickly, a tense energy surrounding her like a flame. My fingers run up and down her arms before I tug on her hips, spinning her around.

"Tell me something…" I continue to touch her, craving the contact.

"What?" Her mouth jerks into a barely there smile.

"Had you heard of the DeLucas before I mentioned them?" The question hangs in the air while I watch her closely.

Her face remains neutral, though her posture goes rigid almost instantly.

She's hiding something.

"No. Should I have?" A soft smile spreads, appearing with little effort.

I can't tell if she's lying. But I don't press.

"No. Don't even worry about it. Probably a mistake." I lean down, close enough that my breath brushes against her ear. "An associate of theirs mentioned he might have known you. I told him he must've been wrong."

She laughs, but it doesn't sound right. It's too sharp, too high-pitched. "Yeah, I don't think that name rings any sort of bells. Sorry."

She throws her arms around me, resting her cheek against my chest, but I know she's not trying to get close. She's hiding.

I'll find out what my little wife is keeping from me, and I promise, there will be a reckoning.

Pushing back a fraction, I motion for one of my men, and he appears, placing a small square velvet box into my hands.

"What's that?"

"A gift." When I open it to reveal the thin diamond choker inside, she eyes it curiously, like it's going to detonate.

Though that *would* actually be a clever weapon. I may need to look into that.

"Wow. That's…uh, generous."

"Anything for my wife. Now turn around. Let's see how it looks."

When she does, I gently remove the choker from the box, placing it around her slender neck. She turns to show me, and for a moment, I can't tear my eyes away. My gaze drifts from the necklace to her face, and in this instant, I realize something deep in my chest.

I want this marriage to work, more than anything. I want more with her than I've ever had with anyone. For that to happen, she'll have to trust me, and I'll have to trust her. Though trust is hard to come by.

But from the way she makes me feel, the way she shifts something deep inside me, I know I don't have much of a choice.

No matter what happens, I'm not going anywhere.

And neither is she.

EMILIA

The soft clank of silverware and the murmur of the sea beyond are the only sounds surrounding us. The private terrace juts out from the restaurant like a secret candlelit oasis over the edge of the world.

A breeze kisses my bare shoulders, warm and scented with lavender and salt, but all I can think about is earlier, when he asked me about DeLuca. That wasn't a coincidence. He knew something, and I have to find out what.

My deception is slowly starting to catch up to me, and I haven't come close to finding out if he was involved in Nate's case or not.

From across the small table, I glance at Konstantin, sitting like sin incarnate in dove gray, his shirt unbuttoned just enough to hint at the body I know too well now. His forearms rest casually on the table, one hand cradling his wineglass, the other teasing the stem absently as if he's not entirely focused, but I know better.

He's always watching. Always calculating.

I smooth my hands down the sleek white silk of my dress, feeling its cool glide against my thighs, trying to ignore how tightly strung my nerves are.

"The view's amazing," I say, glancing out at the golden lights twinkling across the French Riviera, the water black and endless beneath the stars.

He tilts his head, a smirk tugging at the corner of his lips, and it's as though whatever was making him cold earlier is gone. "My view's even better."

My pulse kicks up a beat. Would a man who's thinking about throwing me into the ocean be commenting about how much he likes me?

I almost laugh to myself, because of course this man would.

"You look beautiful tonight, Mrs. Marinova." That familiar warmth spreads through my chest like wildfire.

God, when he's like this—relaxed, flirty—it's so easy to forget who he is. What he's capable of. So easy to pretend I'm just a wife out to dinner with her husband. Not a federal agent embedded in a monster's world. Not the sister of a man whose life hangs in the balance.

"I'm sorry I've been a bit distant today. I've had a lot on my mind."

His confession has me sitting straighter, focusing on every word.

"Is everything okay?"

"It will be." He reaches for the bottle of wine, pouring himself another glass while I sip on an iced tea. "Once I've gotten rid of the problem."

"The problem?"

Do you mean me? The DeLucas?

My God, I wish I could read his thoughts.

He eyes me for a long moment, forcing the invisible walls around me to tighten.

"The one making everything more complicated than it should be," he finally answers.

My stomach twists.

Well, shit. What does that even mean?

THIRTY-SIX

EMILIA

Five days later, and I'm happy to report that I'm still very much alive.

Not only am I alive, but Konstantin has been his normal self.

We actually had a nice time, walking the streets of Nice, eating ice cream at ten in the morning, laughing about silly things. And at night, when his body was tangled with mine, was the most alive I've ever felt. But that's how it always is when we're together.

In these past days, I've forgotten about my job, the mission that brought me here, and the tangled mess of secrets I'm still keeping from him. It felt real, like we were an actual couple, not just two people forced together by circumstances beyond our control.

But now, as we walk back into his home hand in hand, the reality of everything slaps me right in the face. It's then I feel my phone vibrate inside my handbag, and I immediately wonder if it's Riley.

"I'm gonna go up and take a shower," I tell Konstantin, throwing my arms around him and kissing him slow.

"Mm." He grabs a fistful of my behind and tugs me flush to him. "If I didn't have business to catch up on, I'd join you."

His lips trail hot, teasing kisses down my jaw, a low growl escaping him as a soft sound of pleasure slips from me. When he pulls back, his eyes are flooded with desire.

"Go. I'll meet you in the bedroom as soon as I'm done."

My teeth tug at my bottom lip as I take a step back toward the stairs, hurrying up, feeling the heat of his gaze burning into me the entire way.

As soon as I make it to the bedroom, I remove my phone, finding a text from Riley.

RILEY

Hey! I miss you! Call me so we can catch up!

A knot tightens in my stomach. Of course she doesn't want to catch up. It's all code for *call me ASAP because I have news.*

Heading for the bathroom, I start the water, hoping it blocks out the conversation as I dial Riley's number.

She answers on the second ring. "Tessa?"

The instant urgency in her voice is all I need to know that something's not right.

"What is it?" I whisper.

"We need to meet. Can you get away?" Riley's words are quick, almost frantic.

It's worse than I thought. She'd never ask to meet unless it was an emergency. I hesitate for a moment, like I don't want to know. What if this thing with Konstantin, this strange little bubble we've built, is about to pop?

"I can't today. We just got back from a surprise trip. What about tomorrow?"

It'll be much easier to pretend I need to go shopping tomorrow instead of today. Konstantin won't think much of it.

"Yeah, fine." A rush of an exhale leaves her, and my anxiety only increases.

"I'll text you when and where."

"Okay," Riley replies, softer now, like she's trying to mask the tension. "Talk then."

As I hang up, the sinking feeling in my stomach grows, and I can't shake the thought that whatever Riley's going to tell me will bring everything crashing down.

The bell above the door jingles softly as I step into the boutique where I told Riley we'd meet. When I step inside, Maksim and Dmitri behind me, their large frames cast shadows across the polished floors.

But I don't need them on my tail right now.

I turn to them. "Stay by the door and don't follow me around."

They exchange murmurs in Russian, but they know better than to argue. With a muttered response, they settle onto the velvet sofa, their eyes still trained on me.

I give them a smile, one that doesn't reach my eyes, before turning my attention to the racks of clothes in front of me. Pretending to shop is easy, though my thoughts are elsewhere. The adrenaline running through my veins is cold and the uncertainty in my chest won't fade.

I spot Riley moving to the back, her head down, focused on what she's grabbing from the shelves. She's doing the same as I am: blending in, pretending to be here for something else.

A saleswoman comes over, asking if I need any help. I shake my head politely, then gather a few more things, making my way toward the back.

I find an open door and slip inside, locking it behind me, and find her already waiting for me.

Time stretches on before she finally sits on the bench, pulling out a small notepad and pen, scribbling furiously. I stare at her, trying to keep my composure, but my body betrays me with its growing stiffness.

Finally, she peers up, her face pale and shows me what she wrote.

And her words? They're like a kick to the gut.

One so hard, it blows the air from my lungs.

No.

It can't be.

There's no way it's true.

Staring at what she wrote again, I read it over and over, turning it in my head to try to make sense of it somehow.

I think Gerardo's involved in what happened to Nate.

My head spins as I try to process. No. She has to be wrong. Gerardo has always been like a father to us. There's no way he'd do anything to hurt us. The more I think about it, the more I can't reconcile the image of the man who looked after me and my brother—the one who was a mentor, a protector—with the idea that he set Nate up.

Why? Is he the murderer? Is he covering up for one?

Grabbing the pad, I write back.

No way. What proof do you have?

Her gaze darkens as she grabs it back and writes something in return.

I found things. His financials link to the

DeLucas. He's been involved for years, and it's
a lot of money. He's dirty. No doubt in my
mind.

No. Nonono. This can't be happening.

My heart sinks into my stomach, the world around me suddenly spinning. If this is true, if Gerardo is really behind all of this, everything I've believed is a lie.

I clutch the notepad, barely able to breathe as I scribble another question.

Why would he set Nate up?

Maybe it has something to do with Nate's
dead partner. He was involved with DeLuca
too. Maybe Gerardo thought he was a threat.

The room seems to shrink as I stare at the paper. Her reply makes so much sense.

But there's just no way!

I swallow, my throat dry.

I need you to be sure, because there's no coming
back from this.

I am sure.

Her eyes lock with mine.

But I'll find more if that's what you need.

My hands curl, needing to be back in the gym, to punch something. It's been so damn long since I've done that. I take a moment before writing.

Keep me posted.

She takes the notepad, tucking it into her bag as she stands, leaving quietly, while I'm left alone with the storm of thoughts swirling in my head.

I can't believe it. Gerardo, the man who shaped so much of my life, the one who's been like family to me, could be the very one who betrayed Nate. Betrayed us all.

The panic begins to rise inside me, sharp and suffocating, and I sit there for a few minutes, trying to steady my breath, trying to hold myself together.

But it's hard. It's so hard.

The truth is a heavy thing, and right now, it's about to crush me.

THIRTY-SEVEN

KONSTANTIN

Tessa's off this morning, quieter than usual. The silence between us stretches thick, heavy, like a blanket smothering the room. She's been off since last night—lying in bed, barely speaking, her eyes distant, as if her mind is somewhere far away.

I didn't press, thinking maybe she just needed some space, but this morning is different. It's as if she's here physically, but emotionally, she's miles away, and it's driving me crazy. I hate seeing her like this.

Even as I try to focus on my work, my gaze keeps drifting to her office. Whatever's going on with her, it gnaws at me.

Getting up from my desk, I walk over to her office, the door already cracked. She doesn't hear me come in until I'm standing right in front of her.

"How's the progress on those files?"

She jumps, startled, and the smile she gives me is both forced and hollow.

"It's coming," she says, her attention flickering away for just a second. "Almost done."

I can tell it's a lie. I can see it on her face, in the way she avoids looking at me.

Closing the door behind me, I lower onto the chair next to her desk and take her hand in mine, forcing her to look at me.

"What's wrong, malyshka?" I ask gently, like I'm coaxing the truth out of her. "Anything I can do?"

Her shoulders tense, and she swallows thickly, like she's fighting something back. "What do you mean?"

My head shakes with disappointment. "Don't lie to me, Tessa."

She sighs, her chest rising and falling as she exhales. Her fingers twitch, and she releases a sigh. I can feel her hesitate, as if she's considering whether to let me in on whatever is haunting her.

"It's that dream. The one I told you about." She meets my eyes, and I'm still unsure if she's telling me the truth. "I had it again last night, and…it was worse than usual."

My hand squeezes hers. I can see how much it's affecting her, how deeply it cuts.

"When do you see your therapist again?" I ask, hoping that the process of talking it through will help ease some of this tension.

She glances at the clock on the wall. "In three hours."

"Good." I lean forward, cupping her cheek gently. "You *will* remember, Tessa. And you *will* be okay, because I'm here now."

Her eyes flutter, and for a moment, she leans into me, her proximity making every muscle in my body tighten. She loses herself in the comfort of my words, in my touch, and it stirs something deep within me, makes me feel more powerful than I've ever known.

Then, without warning, she throws her arms around me, and I pull her close, as if I can keep the world at bay just by holding her.

Her warmth sinks into me, grounding me in a way I've never

felt before. I breathe her in, feeling the way her body presses against mine, the way she melts into me.

I've never allowed myself to feel like this. Never let anyone get this close. This deep. I've always believed in love as long as it was for everyone else, not me. But holding her now, it's undeniable.

I don't just care for her. It's something deeper, something real. Something worth fighting for.

I know giving myself to her this way could destroy everything I've built, but I won't let it get that far. I'll protect her, be the man she needs me to be. And when the time is right, I'll tell her what she truly means to me.

Because for the first time in my life, I'm not afraid to want someone. Not afraid to admit that in ways I never imagined, she's everything I never knew I needed.

EMILIA

The waiting room is quiet, but the silence is heavy and oppressive. The soft hum of the bright lights above fills the space, and the steady ticking of the clock on the wall only makes me more anxious. I sit on the edge of the chair, bouncing my foot, reliving what Riley told me over and over again.

Maybe she was wrong. That's possible, right?

But she's never been wrong before, not when it comes to intel. Though I still refuse to believe it could be true, that Gerardo would hurt Nate or me this way. It makes no sense.

Glancing down at my phone again, I refresh my messages, hoping for one from Riley, maybe telling me she was wrong. But there's nothing there.

At least I can count on Konstantin showing me exactly who he is.

He never hides from it, and there's some honor in that.

I throw my head back, staring at the ceiling, my thoughts of him offering a strange comfort. His strong arms, the way he makes me feel safe despite everything I should fear about him. His touch is gentle, even though I know what he's capable of. Yet with me, he becomes someone entirely different.

There's something in him that makes me want to believe in the impossible, even when everything around me is falling apart. And when he holds me close, I feel… I feel like maybe, just maybe, everything will be okay.

But that's not true, is it? Because nothing will ever be the same.

The hypnotherapist's door opens, snapping me out of my spiral. I stand quickly and stride toward the entrance, stepping into her quaint space filled with a hint of lavender and the soft music I recall from last time.

I sit in the chair across from her, the burden of everything I'm holding in sitting heavy in my chest. She starts the session by asking how I'm feeling, if I've had a dream of the vision, and I have. What I told Konstantin wasn't a lie.

"Are you ready to try again?" she asks.

With a nod, I close my eyes as she gets me to relax, guiding me into a trance, the familiar darkness creeping around the edges of my consciousness.

I'm not sure how long passes before I'm back in that closet, the same place I've been stuck in for what feels like a lifetime. My chest tightens, my breath shallow. That same fear and helplessness is back, but this time, my senses are sharper.

"I can hear them better," I tell her.

"Good. Now tell the little girl it's okay to listen, to look at the man."

My body buzzes with this weird feeling, but I find myself taking the girl's hand.

Don't be afraid, I tell her, and it's as though she hears me because she looks my way. *They can't hurt you, I promise.*

She throws her arms around me, holding on tight, and I wrap mine around her in return, a strange sense of relief settling deep within me. As though she now knows it's okay, she removes her palms from her ears, inching closer to the door as one of the men speaks.

"You're threatening me?" He pauses. "You just never learn, do you?"

And I know what comes before it does.

A shot rings out, and the little girl shuts her eyes. My palm lowers to her shoulder.

It's okay. Remember, he can't hurt you.

She nods, and when the door rattles, she gasps, grabbing my hand.

Don't worry. I'll be here the whole time. Just look at him. That's all you need to do.

She doesn't want to. I can taste her fear—my fear. But something inside compels me to stare at the door as it starts to creak open.

At first, all I find is a tall shadow, but as the light creeps in and my vision adjusts…

"No, it-it can't be—I…"

My heart rate intensifies, my head spinning, my body like it's out of sync.

"You're okay," my therapist says. "Tell me what you see."

My body stiffens, the strain in my chest growing unbearable. The man steps forward, his hand reaching for the little girl.

She glances back at me as he takes her hand, but my eyes are pinned to his. I want to run, but I can't. I'm frozen in place, as if I'm being held captive by the memories I've been too terrified to face.

His hand is warm and steady as he pulls her out of the closet.

"It's alright," he tells her. "Come on out now."

And when he stares in my direction, there's no mistaking who he is, even as he appears much younger than I remember.

The world tilts, and for a moment, I can't breathe, can't move. Can't do anything but stare at him.

Gerardo…

No…

Nonono.

It was him? The whole time? How? Why?

He knew how desperately I wanted to remember, but instead, he made me believe it was just a dream.

My gaze shifts to the far left of the room, where a man in a cop's uniform lies on the floor, a pool of blood spreading around him.

That's why he's been lying to me all these years. He was terrified that I'd expose him. If Gerardo was dirty back then too, this cop must have discovered it, and it cost him his life.

The little girl starts to cry, and Gerardo's arms tighten around her.

That fucking snake! I wanna rip his arms off!

"It's okay," he murmurs. "He was a bad man. Don't worry about him."

No, you're the only bad man here. And I'm gonna make sure the whole world knows right before I destroy you.

THIRTY-EIGHT

KONSTANTIN

I'm in the middle of a meeting when my secretary steps into the room, and that familiar sense of irritation rises in me. I've learned to tolerate these interruptions, but only if there's a damn good reason.

"I'm so sorry, but I need a minute, sir," she says, an uncomfortable expression on her face, as if she's trying to conceal something.

"Excuse me, gentlemen."

Getting to my feet, I step out of the boardroom and into the hallway, locking the door behind me.

"What is it?" I try to keep my tone even but fail, frustration snapping through me.

This meeting is important, and I'm *this* close to getting them to see my way.

She hesitates, her eyes darting briefly to the door before she finally speaks. "It's about your wife…"

"What do you mean? Speak!"

She fidgets nervously. "Uh, her security detail…they've been trying to reach you. They say it's urgent."

As soon as she says that, my vision blurs, my mind spiraling with all the things that could've happened. If someone did something to her, the entire goddamn world will go up in flames.

"Tell them the meeting is cancelled. Reschedule it for later."

I don't wait for her to respond. My feet are already moving while my mind's racing.

As soon as I'm in my SUV, I turn on the car and press on the gas, looking through the missed calls and texts as I speed through traffic.

MAKSIM

SOS. Come home.

DMITRI

Gde, chert voz'mi, ty?

Where the hell are you?
I voice a reply.

KONSTANTIN

Chto sluchilos?

What happened?
When he doesn't respond, I call Dmitri, but he doesn't answer. My pulse spikes, adrenaline clawing at me. I try again, and still no answer.

The world around me starts to melt away, the engine roaring beneath me as I speed down the street.

If she'd been taken, they would have told me. This is something else.

I call her number, and it rings. And rings. Frustration burns through me, and I slam my fist into the wheel, the anger building.

I quickly dial the cleaning staff. When the voice on the other end answers, it's calm, but there's a subtle edge of worry beneath the words.

"Sir?" Flora says, and I sense that immediate fear in her tone.

"Is my wife okay?" Every syllable cuts through the air, my mind racing, desperate for answers. She needs to be okay.

"Um, I don't know much, sir. Only that she came home upset, and she rushed upstairs. But when she was there for a while, Maksim tried to get her to come out, but she wouldn't."

Blood pumps faster through my veins. Something is definitely wrong. Maybe her therapy session didn't go well.

"I'll be home soon." Dropping the call, I punch the gas and drive faster.

Every second, every heartbeat, feels like a lifetime. My hands grip the wheel until my knuckles turn white, and terror unlike anything I've ever known takes hold.

When I finally pull into the driveway, I don't even take the time to park properly. Flinging open the car door, I rush toward the house and enter as one of my men lets me in. I practically sprint up the stairs to find Maksim and Dmitri standing in front of the bathroom door in the hall.

"Chto proiskhodit?" I ask while I fight to suppress the pure panic in my chest. *What's happening?*

Dmitri's jaw clenches. "She came from the therapist's office upset, said she wanted to go home. When we got here, she ran upstairs and locked herself in the bathroom. We got worried when it was too long."

It's as if the air in the room has been sucked out, my lungs tight and burning with every breath. I don't even want to acknowledge the dark thoughts creeping in.

"Tessa," I call, my voice softer than I feel as I knock gently on the door. "Tessa, open the door. It's me, Konstantin."

No answer.

A sickening coil twists in my gut. A deep, dreadful feeling that something is horribly wrong.

Without hesitation, I slam my shoulder into the door, the wood cracking under the force before splintering open. And what I see before me knocks the breath out of me.

Tessa lies on the floor, unconscious, blood pooled around her, a razor resting dangerously close to her thigh.

"No! Tessa! No!" I roar, dropping to my knees beside her, frantically searching for a pulse.

There's nothing.

"BLYAT!"

My heart stops.

This can't be happening. I won't let it end like this.

But then I feel it: a faint pulse. Too weak, too fragile.

Panic surges through me. She can't die.

I won't let her die.

I tear my shirt off, tying it around the gashes on her arm, before I cradle her against my chest, yelling for Maksim and Dmitri to call my doctor to get everything ready for an emergency while I rush back out to the SUV.

"Tessa, please," I whisper, my voice hoarse as I pull her close, securing her in the back with me, Maksim focused at the wheel. "You have to be okay. You have to live, moya l'vitsa. I won't let you leave me."

My lips brush her forehead, a shudder of pure agony ripping through me as my heart explodes. My fingers trace her cheek, as if touching her is the only thing keeping me tethered to this world.

If she dies, I die with her. There is no future without her. Not anymore.

EMILIA

I wake up groggy, my head heavy and my thoughts muddled. The soft beeping of a machine beside me tugs at my awareness, but the warmth in my hand is what draws me fully back to consciousness. My fingers twitch instinctively, curling into the comforting pressure, and my eyes shift open slowly.

Konstantin.

His eyes lock on to mine the moment they meet. The relief that washes over his face is unmistakable, and it catches me off guard, knotting something in my chest.

For a moment, all I can do is stare at him, absorbing the worry and tenderness in his gaze.

"Where are we?" I ask, the words rough as I try to adjust to the unfamiliarity of my surroundings.

"Private hospital. One of mine." He takes my hand with utter gentleness. "Are you in pain? I can get you more medication."

I shake my head, my throat tightening as a sharp ache sinks deeper. But as I look down at my bandaged upper arm, it hits like a flash of lightning tearing through me.

I did this.

I hurt myself again.

The memories flood in. Gerardo's betrayal, the lies, everything falling apart around me.

I couldn't breathe, couldn't think straight. The world felt like it was closing in, and for a moment, I needed to escape it. I needed control over something, anything, when everything else felt uncontrollable.

After the session, I tried to ignore the darkness creeping in, but the pain of it all became too much to carry. My chest was tight with anger, sadness, fear. It was all clawing at my insides, fighting for space. My mind raced, caught in the chaos of too many emotions to make sense of. And in that moment, cutting felt like the only way to stop drowning in the flood of it all.

Some people wonder why. Why would someone hurt themselves?

But it's like the physical pain overshadows the emotional, like a way to center yourself when you're too overwhelmed to find a way out.

I wasn't thinking clearly, and it felt like the only way to breathe again. To make the pain in my heart match the one I could control in my body.

My eyes flutter shut as shame surges through me, leaving only the raw truth behind.

I undid years of progress in one single moment.

I stop the tears before they can fall, refusing to let them break through. I won't cry. But everything hurts. After all the effort it took to stop doing that to myself, I've fallen off a cliff, and now I have to climb all the way back up.

"I'm so sorry." His tone is thick with regret, a painful, vulnerable sound that breaks something inside me. His thumb traces the back of my hand. "This is my fault. I shouldn't have had any razors in the house." He buries his face in our joined hands.

"No, baby. Look at me." My heart constricts in my chest as I pull his knuckles to my lips, pressing a soft kiss to them, holding his gaze as I do. "This is on me. Only me. *I* did that. And honestly, in the state I was in, I would've found something else to do it with."

"Why did you?" The agony in his voice hits me harder than anything.

My mouth trembles as I try to hold back the overwhelming shame. It's hard to explain, harder to even face it.

"I couldn't handle what I learned during therapy." My lashes flutter to a close. "I'm a failure." The words feel like acid in my throat.

"No. Don't you ever call yourself that," he snaps, a protective growl that catches me off guard, cutting through the fog in my mind.

His hands cup my face, forcing me to meet his gaze, and the look in his eyes—so full of affection—makes my heart ache.

"It's okay, malyshka. It's okay."

He leans in and presses a soft kiss to my forehead, tender, yet charged with an intensity that cracks something inside me wide open.

"I'll never leave you," he vows. "I'll always be here."

Those words wrap around me like a lifeline, grounding me when I feel like I'm drowning.

I want to run with him. Take him and disappear back to France, back to when things were simpler. But I know I can't. This is my reality now, and I have to face it, no matter how unbearable it feels.

Gerardo was never a father to Nate or me. He was a liar, a murderer, a conman, and I fell for it all like a fucking fool. He probably thought I was pathetic for believing he was ever really there to help us.

That's why I did what I did. That's why I snapped. I couldn't face it. Couldn't face the truth of everything I had ever known about him and what it meant for me. What it meant for Nate.

"Please don't lock me up here," I whisper, panic creeping in. "It'll only make it worse. Please, I just need to go home."

If he forces me to stay, I won't survive it.

He hesitates, his hand tightening around mine. "I don't know if you're ready for that yet."

"I am," I say quickly, sitting up despite the heaviness in my body. "I'll go back to my regular therapist. I'll do whatever I have to do, Konstantin. I don't want to hurt myself, I swear. I'm done with that. This was just…a mistake. Please…" The back of my throat throbs.

"Do you know how hard it is for me to tell you no?"

My stomach turns to knots as the silence stretches.

"Okay," he says after a long pause. "You can come home. But…"

There's a hesitation, a moment of distress in his expression.

"But what?" My pulse hammers, already dreading what's coming next.

His fingers tighten around mine. "If I find out you're not going to your appointments, or if it doesn't help, I *will* admit you. You won't get the choice then. Because it's my job to protect you. Even from yourself."

I nod quickly, desperation and determination flooding through me.

"I'll do whatever it takes. I swear." My voice cracks. "I've been through this before. I stopped when I was seventeen. And believe me, no one feels worse than me right now. But I'll do the work. I can do this again."

"Yes, you will." He brings my knuckles to his lips. "You are strong. Moya l'vitsa." He leans in and presses another kiss to my forehead, this one somehow filled with more meaning. "You don't ever have to go through this alone. You have me."

I can't stop the tears from tumbling down my cheeks, and I lean into him, feeling the serenity of his embrace as his big strong arms hold me steady.

"This was just a slip," I tell him. "A bad one. And I know it went too far, but I swear I wasn't trying to die, okay?"

His jaw tightens as he pushes back, a muscle in his face twitching as if the words are physically painful for him to hear. "I hope not. Because if you die, I die. You understand?"

Emotions pound behind my eyes.

"Seeing you like this…" He chokes up. "It kills me. Do you know that? Watching you suffer, it's killing me."

I can't speak for a moment, the words stuck in my throat, the weight of everything pressing down on me. The guilt, the fear, the regret. But what's left in me is the truth.

"I'm sorry. I didn't want to do this to you."

He holds my chin between two fingers, his gaze warm and protective. "We'll get through this. Together."

"Thank you."

He shakes his head. "Don't ever thank me for being who I'm supposed to be. Your husband." Tugging my face to his chest, he holds me closer, silent for a beat before he asks, "What did you find out during therapy?"

I can't tell him the whole truth, not yet. Not until I'm ready to tell him everything. So I choose my words carefully.

"A man I grew up thinking was like a father to me was nothing but a liar, and now I have to live with that."

His eyes narrow. "I understand. Betrayal is a heavy burden to carry. But you're not alone anymore. If I can do anything to help, anything at all, you just have to say the word." His mouth curves into a deadly smirk. "You can even choose the method of helpfulness I employ."

A small laugh escapes. "No. Please don't do anything murdery. Not yet, anyway…"

He lets out a low chuckle, the sound infectious. "It's very difficult for me not to do murdery things when it comes to you, lubov moya."

My chest tightens.

"You're a good man, Konstantin Marinov." I cup his face, his stubble grating over my palm.

He arches a brow, a ghost of a smile playing at his lips. "Can't say I've ever heard that before."

I laugh, shaking my head. "There's a first time for everything."

This man—this brutal, crazy, infuriating, but sweet man—has shown me so much in this short time, and I wish we hadn't met the way we did. I wish everything was different, and I'm terrified that once he learns the truth, he won't want me the way he does now.

"In the last few days…" I say, my gaze fixed on him. "I've realized you've always shown me exactly who you are. And I just want you to know how much I truly appreciate that."

He pulls me close, his lips ghosting over mine. "You do know when I get you back home, I won't be able to take my eyes off you, right?"

"That's okay." My grin grows as I kiss him softly. "I like it when your eyes are on me."

He groans, his mouth crashing into mine with more intensity

before he pulls me back against his chest. As I snuggle closer, the steady rhythm of his heart fills my ear, each beat a reminder of how much I need him more than ever.

And deep down, I hope I don't lose him for good.

THIRTY-NINE

EMILIA

It's been three days since I returned home, and I kept my promise—saw my therapist the next day. I'm trying to believe I'm on the road to healing, but the walls of this house seem to close in on me, pressing into me with all the things I've been carrying. Things Konstantin doesn't know. Things I need to tell him. And soon.

To make it worse, Riley's been feeding me more damning information about Gerardo. Each new piece ties him deeper to the DeLuca crew, and there's no longer any doubt in my mind: Gerardo set Nate up.

He's been helping the DeLucas hide evidence and evade capture, manipulating the system for years to protect them. The fact that I can't confront him is eating me alive, and not being able to talk to Konstantin about it only makes everything harder.

I know I can't report Gerardo to the higher-ups until I get Nate out. If Gerardo really did frame him, nothing will stop him from killing my brother.

Sliding into my sneakers, I prepare for my run, a habit I've picked up since leaving the hospital. It's been the best way to release the frustration and anger building inside, since shooting things is no longer an option. Though, considering who I'm married to, I suppose it *could* still be an option.

As I lace up my shoes, I sense Konstantin's presence behind me—always there, always watching. His hand settles on my shoulder as I rise, solid and reassuring, and I sense the tension in him, the urge to protect me from even myself. I appreciate him for it, more than words can express.

"Off for a run?"

"Yes. Wanna join?" My gaze drifts over his sharp, expensive suit, knowing full well he's not heading anywhere other than to another meeting.

His eyes flicker with hesitation. "I'd rather you stay inside. There's a lot going on right now, and I don't want you wandering around."

"But I'll have my big, strong bodyguards with me..." My attention drifts to Maksim and Dmitri, their eyes widening for a moment.

Konstantin's jaw tightens and he steps closer, tugging gently on my chin. His lips brush mine, a warning wrapped in tenderness.

"Don't try to make me jealous, wife. That never ends well. And it would be a pity if I had to kill my own cousins."

"Hey, we did nothing!" Dmitri protests, but I can barely hold back a laugh.

"Irrelevant," Konstantin growls, his teeth catching my bottom lip in a teasing tug.

"I like it when you get jealous." My hands wrap around his neck, pulling him down into a soft kiss. The rich scent of his masculine, seductive cologne drives me wild. "You're not allowed to smell this good while I'm not here to fully enjoy it."

He smiles against my lips, a hint of mischief in his voice. "You're making it very hard to leave you as it is, katyonak. Don't tempt me." He nuzzles my neck, and I groan. "I should blow this billion-dollar deal and take you upstairs instead." He palms my ass possessively.

A laugh escapes me. "You could. But you'd probably regret it."

He eyes me with maddening intensity. "I would never regret you, moya lyubimoya."

"Have you ever been told you're a romantic?"

He shrugs, a half-grin playing on his lips. "A time or two. Some have even called me a matchmaker."

I raise an eyebrow, my smile widening. "I can see that. You're such a softie."

Maksim snickers from the side, and Konstantin shoots him a sharp look.

"Shto?" Maksim raises his hands in mock surrender. "Am I lying?"

Konstantin turns back to me, amusement flickering in his eyes as his hands tighten around my hips. "I'll miss you. Text me when you're done with your run."

"I will."

His lips fall to mine again, the pull of his touch almost too much to resist.

With a sigh, he turns to his cousins. "You'll go where she goes."

He holds me closer like he refuses to let me go, his lips pressing softly to my temple. The kiss is full of unspoken words, a promise to protect me even as he has to let me go.

"Be careful." His voice grows thick with concern. "I don't know what I'd do if anything happened to you."

A wave of emotion rises in my chest, and I fight to keep it down. Never before have I felt this much, not until Konstantin. "I'll be careful. I promise."

For a moment, as his eyes align with mine, it's as though the world stops spinning and everything else quiets in its wake. I can sense his worry, his affection for me, in the way he holds me, the way he's always there.

When he starts toward the door, I call for him.

"Konstantin."

He freezes and turns toward me.

"When you get back from your meeting, maybe we can talk about us."

His brows furrow for a moment, but then the corners of his mouth twitch. "Of course, my love. We can talk about anything you want."

My love.

I think that's the first time he's said it in English, and it hits me harder than I expected.

I like it. A lot.

He rushes back to me, like he can't stand the idea of being away from me. His hands cup my face as his lips press gently to my forehead and emotions flood behind my eyes, too overwhelming to name.

Damn this man—always making me feel too much, too fast.

Clinging to his arms, I wish for it to stay this way. This good, this happy.

But I know I'm only kidding myself.

The rhythmic pounding of my feet on the gravel echoes in my ears as I continue my jog, the cool morning air filling my lungs. I focus on the path ahead, the sound of my breath blending with the soft rustle of leaves in the breeze, but I can't shake it. Everything with Gerardo has invaded my thoughts, and I hate how much control he still has over me.

When my phone vibrates in my pocket, I instinctively think it's Konstantin, pulling me from my spiraling thoughts. But when I glance down, I see it's Fiona. I immediately slow my pace and answer the call.

"Hey," Fiona's voice rings in my ears through the earbuds, laced with an undercurrent of concern.

I keep running, forcing myself to push through the tightness in my chest. "Hey. Everything okay?"

"Did you forget what today is?"

I almost stop in my tracks, but I can't afford to, not with Maksim and Dmitri a few yards behind, watching my every move. They won't stop unless I do. So I keep my pace, my mind racing to figure out what I've missed.

Repeating the date in my head, over and over, I almost think she's messing with me. Then it hits me.

"Oh my God, Nate's trial!"

A wave of shame floods my face. How the hell did I forget? The hospital, the constant stress…it's all been a blur. But still, what kind of sister forgets when her brother starts his trial?

"It's okay. I know you have a lot going on. Can you talk? I wanna tell you some good news for once. Wait, are you running?"

"Mm-hmm, and please, I could use some of that. Tell me they dropped all the charges and that he's coming home."

"No, but his lawyer was able to get him an ankle bracelet, so he won't be in jail for the duration of the trial. Unless he tries to run, of course. Then he's fucked."

I nearly stop running, the relief rushing through me.

"This is amazing." My legs push harder, adrenaline surging through me.

He won't have to stay in that hellhole anymore. I smile, even though it's bittersweet, thinking of Nate finally getting a sliver of peace amidst all this chaos.

"Yeah, I figured you'd wanna know since you can't be there. He should be home soon."

Emotions flood my system, unable to wait to talk to him.

Fiona's voice softens for a moment as she asks, "Are you okay?"

I almost laugh.

No, I'm not okay. Nothing will ever be okay.

But I lie instead. "Yeah, I'm fine."

She sucks in a breath. "I can't wait until you're done with those damn Marinovs."

"They're not so bad…"

She's gonna take my head off for that in three…two…one…

"I can't believe you just said that! Have you met Aleksei? He's a real piece of work."

"Yeah, a few times, and I mean, I can tell why you like him. You two would have some amazing se—"

Her tone cuts through like a knife. "I swear if you finish that sentence, we are no longer friends. I'm cutting you out of my life."

I can't help but laugh. "You'd never. Don't lie to yourself."

"Seriously, watch your back with that one. He's the worst."

"You two are *so* going to sleep together, and I'm gonna say I told you so."

Her response is instant and sharp. "Never going to happen. It's just too bad I never managed to send his ass to prison. That still haunts me at night."

A teasing laugh rises in me. "I'm pretty sure plenty of other things about him haunt you at night too."

"Seriously, shut up. I'm getting off now."

"It's cute watching you deny this."

She groans before the call disconnects.

And as I continue my run, I wonder when Aleksei is going to force her into a marriage quite like my own. Wouldn't that be hilarious?

Okay, maybe not for her…

Hours later, on the bench out back in the garden, I dial Nate's number, desperate to hear his voice. My fingers tremble a little as I bring the phone to my ear, Maksim and Dmitri keeping a safe distance.

"Hello?"

My eyes pinch shut, a smile stretching as soon as I hear him.

"Glad to see you're alive." I try to lighten the mood.

"Yeah, almost thought I wouldn't make it." Nate laughs, the sound dry and strained. But it quickly shifts into a low groan, and I'm instantly on alert.

"Are you hurt?"

"I'll live. That's all that matters." He pulls in a sharp inhale, like even moving hurts. "Getting my ass beat the other day did help my lawyer make the case for the ankle bracelet, though."

"I thought you were in solitary."

"I was, but they moved me back."

"Fucking great…" Frustration builds inside me.

"It's fine. It worked out. I'm out for now."

My eyes squeeze shut. "I want to come see you, but I can't right now."

"Don't worry. I get it. I'm lying low in the apartment anyway. Don't worry about me."

I pause, unsure how to say what I need to. He deserves to know this too. That man means just as much to him as he does to me.

"What is it, Em?"

My God, he can see right through me.

"Are you okay? Did that Marinov fucker do something to you?"

"No, it's not that…"

"Then what the hell is going on? It can't be worse than me being framed for Tim's murder."

"Debatable…"

"Alright, Em, you're scaring me. Tell me what the fuck is going on."

My gaze drifts toward my bodyguards, stationed on the bench

yards away, watching me closely. I whisper the next words, just loud enough for him to hear.

"I've had Riley help me try to clear your name, and I found out some shit."

"Em," Nate interrupts, the frustration sticking to his throat. "I told you, I don't want you doing this shit for me. How many times do I have to tell you to let it go? Whatever happens, I've made peace with it."

"Well, I haven't. I'm gonna get you off, because you didn't do it."

"I know," he says, the fatigue in his tone matching mine. "The lawyer will help me. Gerardo set me up with a good one and—"

"Wait," I cut him off. "Did you say *Gerardo* got you one?"

"Yeah…why?"

The pulse in my head thuds, the words feeling like a slap to my face. "I thought you had a state lawyer."

"I did. But he got me a better one. What the hell is this about?"

I pinch the bridge of my nose, struggling to breathe. I can't hold this back anymore.

"This is hard."

"Just say it. Whatever it is, I can handle it. You know that."

I swallow hard. "When Riley was digging into things, she found a connection between your partner and the Russians, and also some small-time gang called the DeLuca crew. Ever heard of them?"

"Yeah, I have…" He pauses, the realization starting to hit him. "Wait, are you saying Tim was dirty?"

"Yeah, Nate. He was definitely dirty."

"Shit…" He huffs, his frustration clear. "I never saw him do anything shady."

I exhale slowly, gathering my thoughts. "There's more."

"Yeah?"

"Gerardo, he—"

"No." Nate interrupts sharply. "Don't even go there."

But I have to. He has to understand the depravity of the situation.

"Believe me, this is just as hard for me to say as it is for you to hear, but you have to know the truth, Nate."

There's a long silence, like he's giving me permission to go on.

"Riley found payments to Gerardo from the DeLucas, stretching back years—and not small amounts, either. He's been hiding evidence for them and using the system to protect them for a long time."

For what feels like an eternity, there's nothing but silence on the other end of the line. I can't hear him breathing, can't hear him moving, just the steady hum of my own thoughts filling the quiet. Then, finally, his voice breaks through, sharp and full of disbelief.

"There's no way, Em. No damn way!"

"I know this is hard to accept. Trust me, it's tearing me apart. But it's the truth. I had hypnotherapy to unlock that memory from when I was a kid, and it was him, Nate."

"What do you mean, him?"

"He was the one. The one who was there that night. I saw everything. How he shot the other man, a cop, how he led me away. But he never told me. Never let me know the truth. Because he didn't want me to find out."

A stretch of silence slices between us.

"Oh, fuck…"

"Yeah. We can pretend it's not real, but the facts are staring us in the face. Tim's dirty, Gerardo's dirty, and now you need to watch your back. This is bigger than we thought."

There's a deep exhale on the other end, followed by a harsh whisper. "Why the hell would he frame me?"

"Because you were just an easy mark. He needed to pin it on someone, so why not Tim's partner, the man who's around him a lot, someone who's had issues with him before? They have motive, opportunity, and a weapon."

"That fight Tim and I had a while back was nothing, Em. Plus, they've got no fingerprints."

"Yeah, but they don't need fingerprints to make you the killer. Sure, it would help, but they will say you know how to clean up a crime scene."

"Shit, I don't want to believe Gerardo did this to me of all people."

"I know," I go on, scared that something will happen to him. "Just please watch your back. I'll call you if I find anything else. I love you, Nate."

"Love you too."

When the call ends, I lower the phone and let out a shaky breath.

At least now he knows.

The truth is a cruel thing, one I wish I could forget. It would be easier to bury it and pretend everything's fine.

But life never offers us that luxury.

FORTY

KONSTANTIN

When I arrive home, my first thought is to check on Tessa. I don't care about the meetings or the business I've just left behind. All that matters is her safety and well-being.

I head straight for the living room, pulling out my phone to check in with Maksim and Dmitri, knowing she was out back when I called earlier.

"Maksim," I say once he picks up. "How is she?"

"She's fine. She finished her run, then spoke to a friend on the phone. Now she's reading a book outside, just relaxing."

"Good. Let her enjoy herself. Don't tell her I'm home yet."

"Horosho." *Okay.*

As I remove my shoes in the foyer, one of my maids approaches with a package in hand.

"Sir, this arrived for you." She hands it over before she leaves without saying anything further.

Staring at the large yellow envelope, I wonder if it's those contracts I've been waiting for. Taking it into the study with me, I head for the bar and pour myself a cognac, needing it after the stress of today's meeting. The moment I settle down, I rip open the flap, pulling out the contents crammed inside.

But as I flip through the first few pages, it becomes clear this has nothing to do with business and everything to do with my wife.

My world shifts, the crystal-cut glass nearly slipping from my fingers as my eyes race across the words, the photos attached.

This can't be happening.

My blood runs cold.

Who sent this? Svolichy!

As I flick through everything, my mind races, struggling to make sense of it all. The room shrinks, the air thickening as my grip tightens on the papers, crumpling the edges. Grabbing my phone, I dial my cousin again.

"Bring her to me. Now!"

I hang up before he can reply, my eyes still fixed on the documents. Fury surges through me, coursing like a poison through my veins.

Tessa will answer for this. And if she thinks she can hide behind her secrets, she's about to learn how far I'll go to make sure that doesn't happen.

EMILIA

I sit on the bench outside, my legs sore from the run, the sun warm against my skin. I try to lose myself in the pages of the book in my lap, but my mind keeps drifting, unable to focus.

Maksim's and Dmitri's shadows stretch across the stone path, and

I look up to see their stern expressions.

"Konstantin needs you back home," Maksim says, a sharp edge in his tone that sends unease crawling through me.

I close the book slowly, tucking it under my arm. "Is everything okay?"

Dmitri shrugs. "He just said to bring you in."

A knot tightens in my gut.

Something's wrong.

I force myself to walk calmly beside them, convincing myself that now is the right time to tell Konstantin everything, which is exactly what I had planned to do before he left.

Minutes later, we enter through the back door, and when I find Konstantin pacing in the foyer, a yellow envelope gripped tight in one hand, I stop short.

The second our eyes meet, my stomach drops.

He steps forward, taking my hand and pressing a kiss to my knuckles. His jaw is clenched, his touch gentle—too gentle. It's as though he's struggling to hold himself together, fighting not to snap.

"Let's go take a drive."

My pulse jumps. "Is everything okay?"

He doesn't answer, guiding me to his red coupe and helping me in. He slides into the driver's seat, the engine roaring to life as we drive in suffocating silence.

I glance at him, watching the sharp line of his jaw, the tension in his grip on the wheel. He won't even look at me.

"Where are we going?"

"Shh." He glances at me briefly, his mouth twitching in a way that only heightens my fear.

"Konstantin, you're scaring me."

Still, he says nothing, only lowers his hand to my thigh, squeezing until every muscle feels like it's being torn apart. As we pull onto the dirt road leading to the farmhouse, a wave of dread washes over me.

Did he find out who I really am? Is this it?

Fuck, this wasn't supposed to happen. I wanted to tell him. I should've told him sooner. But he could've killed me either way.

He parks the car, stepping out first and walking around to open my door. When he takes my hand, I shudder, his grip firm and almost deadly. Or maybe that's just how it feels because I'm quite certain I'm about to die.

I brace myself, hoping he makes it quick, though I've heard rumors he can calmly skin a man alive with a smile on his face.

I'm so screwed.

And here I thought being married to the head of the Russian Mob was going to be a walk in the park…

A bitter laugh's trapped in my throat. I always knew, deep down, that once he found out the truth, he'd stop caring. He'd stop wanting me. He'd see betrayal, and he'd want me gone.

It's too bad, though. I was actually falling for him. Falling so hard that it physically hurts right now.

He leads me up the porch steps, the boards creaking under our feet like a warning. When we enter, he gestures to the leather sofa.

"Sit. Now."

My legs feel weak, but I obey, settling on the edge, my heart pounding in my chest. He paces in front of me, his fingers twitching around the envelope.

"What's going on, Konstantin? What's this about?"

He laughs, a dry, ominous sound. "Do you know how many times I've imagined killing you?"

His eyes latch on to mine, his words cutting deep. His stare holds me captive, the intensity of it almost unbearable.

"But every time I saw your face, I forgot why I wanted to do it in the first place."

I'm frozen, every muscle tight, and it takes a moment to grasp the full meaning of his words.

"Do you know how difficult it's been falling for a woman I know is betraying me?"

Oh my God...

Dizziness swirls in my head, and I clutch the sofa, needing this to end, knowing he'll drag it out. He'll make it hurt.

He shakes his head, a sinister half-grin creeping in. "Just answer me one thing. Why?"

A bitter taste hits my mouth. "Why what?"

"Why did you save my life that day in Chicago? Was that part of your plan?" He steps closer, his knuckles grazing my cheek.

His touch, once a comfort, now feels like a cage, and I'm desperate to escape it.

"I haven't figured out what you were doing here exactly, Tessa. Or should I call you...Emilia Hayes?"

The blood rushes from my face, as if he's drained it all from me. My mouth opens, but no words come out.

What's there to say? He knows who I really am.

I was a fucking idiot for thinking I could deceive someone like him.

But if he knew and didn't kill me, why now? What's changed?

"How...how long have you known?" Each word feels like lead, heavy and painful.

He takes a shallow breath, his hand slipping away, and I immediately feel the cold in his absence.

"I knew who you were before you even begged me for that job the second time." His voice is strained, as if each word is a battle. "From the moment I saw you, you intrigued me. I needed to know everything about you. And when I finally uncovered the truth, I couldn't help but wonder what you were planning. What it was that made you want to get close to me. At first, I was going to end you..." His jaw tightens, his bicep flexing as his hand forms a fist. "But when I saw you again...I couldn't. I had to have you. You poisoned everything I ever thought I knew about myself until all I wanted…was you."

His confession shreds everything inside me—guilt, sorrow, and the bitter truth. I hate that I hurt him, but I know I had no choice. Nate needed me.

He moves in quickly, gripping my jaw and tilting my face up to his. "You betrayed me, my love. And now I have to decide what to do with you."

"Konstantin, I-I had no choice. You'd have done the same if you were me."

"We all have a choice, lubov moya." He tosses a stack of papers on my lap.

I look down, my stomach dropping as I see files and photos.
Oh my God…

Pictures from my FBI graduation. Me with Nate, laughing in his uniform. A full dossier on my life. My name, my face, my badge.

"Who sent this?" I glare up to find him watching me intently.

"Anonymous."

"Gerardo…" I whisper.

His head jerks, eyes narrowing. "Who?"

"Never mind."

But I know it was him. Who else could it be? Maybe he sees me as a loose end, worried I'll remember he killed that cop years ago. Maybe he got tired of waiting to see if I would.

In one swift motion, Konstantin's fingers tighten around my throat, cutting off my breath.

"Don't do that." His thumb grazes the underside of my jaw. "You'd better tell me everything before my devotion for you turns into something much, much worse."

I swallow thickly, closing my eyes.

He's right. At this point, I have no choice. I have to tell him everything and face the consequences.

He releases his grip, settling across from me with a calm that only irritates me. "Talk."

Glancing up at the ceiling for a moment, I start at the beginning.

"My brother, Nate. He's the cop in that photo." I lift it for a moment, releasing a sigh. "He was accused of killing his partner, Tim. My boss, Gerardo, made me believe one of your brothers, or even you, was the one who killed him, and I had no reason not to believe him, especially when we found a connection between your organization and Tim."

Konstantin's chest rises sharply, but he stays silent.

"You have to understand, Gerardo practically raised us. So when he said it was most likely you, I believed it too. That's why I came here, looking for proof to clear Nate's name. I was even ready to trade his freedom for yours."

He chuckles, sending a chill through me. "And how exactly were you planning to do that?"

Leaning back, I cross my legs and raise an eyebrow. "I was going to pin a cold case on you. Steal some of your DNA and plant it."

"Wow." He claps slow. "Bravo. You really are a lioness, aren't you? No wonder you impressed me from the start."

I fidget in my seat, unable to really gauge how mad he truly is.

"Please, continue. I'm deeply intrigued now."

"After I…" I hesitate, unsure if he'll believe the rest.

His gaze turns to a sharp slit. "Tell me. I want to hear it all."

Clearing my throat, I shift in my seat. "After I started to have feelings for you, I was relieved to find no proof linking you to Nate. It felt like I was waiting for permission to want you."

His body visibly tenses at that, but he says nothing.

"I'd say I'm sorry, but I'm not." I laugh bitterly. "Because Nate's the only real family I've ever had. Everything else I told you about my past, my mom, it's all true. She was shit, Konstantin. I spent my childhood imagining a different life, one with decent parents, but I didn't have that. I had Nate."

I run a hand down my face, waiting for him to say something, anything, to acknowledge what I just told him. But he doesn't, so I go on.

"Then my contact found proof that Nate's partner and my boss were tied to the DeLuca crew. They were both dirty, and Gerardo was the one who set up my brother."

"And this Gerardo, where do I find him?"

"Why?" Amusement flickers in my tone. "You planning to kill the head of a field office?"

"You insult me, moya lyubimoya." His arms stretch across the sofa.

I shake my head at his level of ego. "He's got bodyguards. He's never alone. And he's in deep with the DeLucas. He's been on their payroll for years."

"And you're telling me this like I'm supposed to be afraid?" He breathes deeply, his chest rising like the calm before a storm. "They're the only ones who have something to fear now." Then he says something that flips my world upside down, more than it already is. "You should know…the hit at the hotel in Chicago. That was meant for you, not me."

"What?" The word escapes me in a strangled gasp.

He nods. "Whoever sent those guys knew you'd be there."

My head spins.

"Only two people knew." My stomach drops as realization crashes over me. "It was him. It had to be. He knew I was getting too close. Knew I was going to remember that he was the one in my vision, the one I told you about."

"So, that's what you remembered? Why you did what you did…"

I nod, the words heavy. "He knew this whole time that I saw him kill that cop. He needed me gone. He…fuck!"

I pinch the bridge of my nose, trying to steady the chaos of emotions spiraling inside me. Everything's clicking into place, but it's all too much to process.

Then, suddenly, he's there beside me, his arms pulling me in.

"Emilia…you're okay. I've got you." His voice offers a sliver of comfort, but it doesn't last.

"No, just don't." I push him away, the need to protect myself overwhelming.

I know it's over. Why let it drag on any longer?

Konstantin's gaze sharpens, his intensity growing. "I know you're hurting. I understand. Because the ones who betray us are always the ones closest to us."

And I realize he's talking about me.

"What do you plan to do with me?" I ask, desperate for this to end. I just want it over.

"What I've been doing all along." He rises to his feet, pacing around me. "Try to keep you from getting killed. I know it may be difficult since I know how stubborn you can be, but this is the part where you thank your husband."

I scoff. "You're so generous."

"I'm glad you noticed." His lips curl as he slips his hand into his pocket, pulling out a flip knife and flicking it open. "Do you know what would've happened to you, to this household, if my brothers found out who you were? Any one of them would've slit your throat by now, and then I'd have to kill them." He flips a hand dismissively. "It would've been too messy."

He returns to me, dragging the tip of the knife slowly along my collarbone. "The fact that I didn't kill you when I found out about you? That's the most dangerous thing I've ever done."

"Like I said, generous." My tone is cunning, no longer afraid but filled with irritation.

He drags the knife between my breasts, his gaze never leaving mine. "Now, tell me…" He pauses, his breath steady. "What should I do with you, Mrs. Marinova?"

"Let me go. Forget I existed. I won't go to the feds. I only came here for Nate. He's all I've ever had."

His nostrils flare, his anger suddenly palpable.

"You had me." He slaps his chest with violent intensity.

My voice breaks, wanting to believe that with all my heart. "I never really did, though, did I?"

I grip his wrist, the urge to go back to those last few days, before everything fell apart, overwhelming me. But it's too late. The life we could've had is gone.

"None of it was real, Konstantin. You never truly knew me."

In an instant, he presses the tip of the knife to my jugular. "I knew you. I still know you." He fists my hair, dragging his lips and tongue across my mouth. "You think you can walk away from me after everything you've done?" His lips drop to my jaw with a growl. "After the way you slid into my heart? No, malyshka. You're mine now, until I decide otherwise."

"So, what's the plan? Drag this out, then kill me?"

His fingers tighten around my hair as he pulls back, his gaze cold. "I should. But I still can't do it. What does that say about me, dorogaya? Have I gone weak like my brothers think?"

"So, how does this end, huh? You keep hiding my identity and forcing me to stay as your wife? Because we both know it's over, right? You won't trust me after this, no matter what."

The words taste bitter, and my gut twists with the finality of it. I hate that it's over, that this is the end. All I want is to throw my arms around him and beg him to love me. For once in my life, I want to be loved with nothing in return, to have that unconditional devotion I never felt as a child.

His mouth curls into a twisted grin as he lets me go, and every inch of me turns ice cold. "You'll stay here until I figure out how to keep my brothers from killing you."

I shake my head, a harsh laugh escaping. "You're insane. You can't keep me locked up here."

My heart beats louder, fear and adrenaline racing through me. I can't stop him, but I won't let him think I'm just going to let him walk all over me.

His eyes gleam with dark delight. "Give me your phone."

He reaches for it, waiting. When I don't move, he shakes his head. "Either you give it to me, or I'll take it. The choice is yours."

I glare at him, but with a sigh, reach into my pocket and hand it over.

"I'll keep it safe for you while you reflect on your life choices."

"Go fuck yourself."

He chuckles, turning away. In that second, something inside me snaps. Without thinking, my body moves faster than my mind can keep up. I lunge at him, and the knife slips from his grasp, clattering to the floor.

My fingers close around the cold handle, and for a brief second, power surges through me.

But he's quicker. Before I can react, he's effortlessly twisting my hand, sending the knife flying across the room.

He towers over me, a smirk still playing on his handsome face. "What now, Emilia?"

My breath comes in uneven bursts, my chest heaving, skin slick with a mix of sweat and the violent energy rushing inside me. Without warning, I kick him in the chin, and blood bursts from his mouth as he lets out a sinister laugh.

"You always know how to excite me. Both in the bedroom and out."

I rush for the knife, fingertips grazing its tip, but he drags my legs before I can reach it. In the last second, though, I snatch it up.

He flips me over, teeth gritted, his fists on each side of my face. "Do you want me to bleed, Tessa?"

When he calls me by that name, I almost wonder if it's on purpose, if it was him reminding me of my betrayal.

"Then let me bleed for you the way I always have." Before I can process what he's doing, he pushes his abdomen onto the blade.

"What the hell are you doing? Are you crazy?!"

He laughs as his blood drips down onto my white tank top. Removing the knife from my hand, he tosses it across the room.

"You are mine, do you understand me? Mine!" In an instant, he yanks my shirt, tearing it violently, exposing my bra and bare skin beneath.

His fingers graze the cut on his abdomen, and without hesitation, he rips off his shirt, while his blood continues to drip, warm and sticky. The rawness of him stirs something dangerous inside me. He's fearless, his grin wide, as though nothing can stop him. Rising onto his knees, he cups my jaw, his lips meeting mine in a kiss that starts soft, but quickly deepens, leaving me breathless, my body strung tight.

One hand pins my wrists above my head, holding me captive as his grip tightens. With the other, he moves slowly, dipping his finger in his own blood before dragging it across my stomach. The motion is deliberate, sending a tremor through me, every nerve igniting with the sensation.

"Moya," he growls.

He begins drawing the letter *M* on me before continuing to spell out the rest of the word, each stroke igniting a deeper, darker feeling inside me.

"Mine," he finishes, his breath hot against my ear.

My body stiffens, but I can't move. I can't breathe. I shudder beneath him, my pulse thundering in my ears. He owns me in this moment, in every twisted way. And I don't know if I hate it or if I just want more.

His mouth crushes mine without warning. It's not tender. It's rough, frantic—like he's trying to take everything all over again. To ask me to stay, to love him, to need him.

But can he truly want me after this?

His lips bruise against mine—demanding, searching, as though this kiss is the answer to something neither of us can say aloud.

Every nerve in my body ignites under the force of him. The warmth of his body, the heat of his touch, consumes me. He tastes of blood, sin, and destruction, and I can't tell if I want to pull away or sink deeper into it.

But then, just as quickly as it started, he pulls back, leaving me breathless, gasping for air. My lips are throbbing and swollen, a sharp reminder of the battle that just unfolded. The echo of his kiss lingers, burning through me, even as he walks to the corner of the room and picks up some chains.

No. NO!

"Please don't do this. I'm begging you!" My voice cracks with desperation.

He ignores me completely, grabbing my ankle and fastening one end of the chain around it, securing me to the support beam. The cold metal bites into my skin, a cruel reminder of how powerless I am in his world.

When he begins to walk away, my heart races.

"Konstantin, wait! Please, just don't do this. Don't leave me like this!"

A rush of thoughts hits me: maybe I should tell him. Maybe it would change everything.

But the words stay trapped inside, and I stay silent. His back is all I see as he steps away, each footfall a hammer strike on the fragile wall of my sanity.

"Konstantin!" I call after him, wild and furious, my body straining against the unforgiving metal.

But it's useless. He doesn't care.

The door creaks open, followed by the cold, final click of it closing, echoing in the silence.

I'm trapped here now.

And as the desperation sinks in, the only thing left to do is figure out how to break free.

FORTY-ONE

EMILIA

It feels like I'm suffocating in this room, the walls closing in on me. My mind races back to the moment I first met him, replaying every interaction, every glance, trying to read his reactions, his expressions. But I saw nothing. He was too good at hiding the truth. I thought I was in control, but he played me.

He knew. He knew I was a fed this whole time and still let me live. Konstantin Marinov, the man who kills people for looking at him the wrong way, let me live.

Closing my eyes, I let the ache swallow me. He cares about me, and I care for him more deeply than I ever imagined. But what happens when all of this is over?

Still, I try to focus on what truly matters right now: finding a way to escape. With his men stationed at both the front and the back, there's no way out unless I can outsmart them.

But I have to get the hell out of here. And when the time is right,

I need to look Gerardo in the eyes and hear him admit everything before I haul his ass to prison. Killing him would be too easy. He deserves to rot for the rest of his life.

My eyes flick to a small shard of wood on the ground, some broken bit of a chair or something. Sharp enough to cut.

I reach for it, biting my lip as I position it just right and press it into my ankle. I don't want to hurt myself, not after everything, but this is different. I have no choice.

With a wince, I draw enough blood before I toss the shard to the far side of the room and let out a sharp cry.

The door creaks, and heavy footfalls shuffle closer. Here they come, just as expected.

Two of Konstantin's men appear, and when they see me in my state of undress, they quickly avert their eyes.

How cute. Criminals with a sense of honor.

"What happened?" one asks.

"Ow! This is cutting into me. I'm bleeding!" I force my voice to crack, sounding panicked. "Oh my God, it hurts so bad!"

They stop, eyes widening as they take in the blood.

"Please, just get something to wrap this with," I beg, my voice trembling with the pain I'm faking. "Just bandage it up, then chain me back. Konstantin wouldn't want me bleeding out on your watch. I'm still his wife!"

One of them hesitates before stepping forward. "Okay, we help."

My breath hitches. Now's my chance.

The second man mutters something in Russian to the first, too fast for me to catch, but I feel the tension radiating from him. The one who agreed to help steps forward, while the other disappears to grab supplies.

The guard kneels to unlock my ankle, and I hold my breath, every muscle wrung tight. He pulls out a set of keys, selects one, and releases the cuff around my ankle. I wince, pretending the pain is unbearable, but my focus is on the gun in his holster.

This is it. It's now or never.

In a split second, I snatch the weapon from him before he can react, aiming it directly at his face. His eyes pop, his arms shooting up in surrender as I jump to my feet.

"Your car keys. Now!"

Slowly, he reaches into his pocket, pulling out the keys and tossing them to the floor with a resigned sigh.

"Relax. I not hurt you," he says, his eyes crinkling into a small grin. "Boss kill me if I do."

"Great. So you'll let me go without being a problem. What a good boy."

He chuckles dryly, hands still raised. I start moving toward the exit, but then a door opens and my pulse gives a little kick.

The second man returns with the bandages, and when he sees the scene, he mutters something else in Russian. Probably something like, *I told you so, you idiot.*

His attention bounces between me and the guy with his hands up, the tension in the air suffocating.

The first one shakes his head at the second. "Otpusti yeyo. Boss skazal ne trogat yeyo, yesli ona popitaetsya sbezhat."

I catch a few words—something about letting me go, the boss having told them to maybe? My understanding isn't great, but when the second man raises his hands and begins backing away slowly, I know I got it right.

I glance between them with a cold edge. "Now, one of you give me your shirt."

They peer over at each other, but I don't have time for this nonsense. Konstantin could be back at any minute.

I raise the gun a fraction higher, the threat hanging in the air. "Your damn shirt. Now."

The first guy immediately pulls off his black T-shirt, handing it to me.

Taking the bandages from the other man, I say, "I need one more thing."

"Oy boji moy. What now?" the second man asks. "You need my pants too?"

They both laugh, but I don't. Anger pulses through me instead.

"If you say one more word, I'll put a bullet between your eyes. Now go find some fucking pliers. I need this removed."

Holding out my hand, I finger the bracelet Konstantin gave me, the one he uses to track my every move.

He laughs, thinking I'm joking, but when he reaches to remove it with his fingers, I'm ready. The shock hits us both at once when he unclasps it, the current jolting through my body, stealing my breath. He curses, yanking his hand back.

"I warned you."

Gun in hand, I rush backward toward the waiting SUV, slipping into the driver's seat and gunning the engine. When the guys at the first checkpoint see who I am, they don't hesitate. They let me through without a word.

He didn't tell them. He wanted to keep this hush-hush, just like I thought.

The plan is working. Now all I need to do is ditch this car, hotwire a new one, and get to Nate before Gerardo does.

He's not going to take my brother from me. Not if I can help it.

KONSTANTIN

I hate that I left her there chained up like that, but I had no choice. I couldn't afford to have anyone find out, and I couldn't afford her running while I leave for my next meeting. When I return, maybe she'll be more compliant.

I stare at the laptop screen, fingers hovering over the keyboard. The glow of the monitor bathes the dark study in cold, sterile light, but there's nothing sterile about the thoughts pounding through my skull.

Tessa's image flickers on the screen. No, *Emilia*. That's her name. The name she hid from me, or so she thought.

Doesn't she realize I'm always one step ahead?

When she told me about her brother, I almost understood why she did what she did. I've done worse for my brothers. Family is family.

Still, how can we reconcile this? How do I stay married to a fed? It's never been done in my world. It's unheard-of.

But there's no way I would ever let her go. It doesn't matter what she did or how. She's my wife, and I would never hurt her.

Now I have to figure out how to keep her alive.

My brothers will be really unhappy when they find out not only about who she is, but that I knew. That I let her stay. That I married her. They'll say I put all of us at risk, and they'll be right. But I don't care. What they think makes no difference. I do what I want, when I want.

She means more to me than anything. More than this empire, than blood, than reason. She's not just my wife. She's mine. *Mine*. My possession. A part of me embedded so deep, I couldn't get rid of her if I tried.

And I'll fight to the death for her. Burn every inch of this world if I have to.

When I drag the next image onto the screen, instant rage settles in my marrow.

Gerardo Peters. Her superior. The one she trusted. The one who tried to kill her.

I lean back in the chair, staring into his smug face. My fingers twitch. He doesn't know it yet, but he's already dead. And I'm going to make it brutal. I want him to *beg* before I end him. For daring to touch her. For thinking he could take her away from me.

My mouth twists into something that isn't quite a smile, unable to wait until he and I become good friends. Closing the laptop, I head toward the stairs, climbing two at a time.

When I push open the bedroom door, her scent hits me instantly. Sweet. Soft. Familiar. It's soaked into the pillows, the sheets, the air itself.

Crossing the room, I press my face into the pillow she slept on, dragging in a deep breath. Her scent may be here, but she's not.

And even though she's just down the road, her absence is like a blade against my throat.

I can't lose her.

Tessa, Emilia…whatever name she prefers, she's mine until my last breath.

I turn toward the bathroom, tugging a hand through my hair, when something catches my eye. A flash of pink in the trash can. Just a sliver of cardboard peeking out.

I reach in and pull it free, and almost stumble.

"What the hell?"

A pregnancy test?

Could she be…

The breath leaves my lungs in one sharp, panicked exhale. I freeze, staring at the box like it's going to morph into something else.

But it doesn't. It's real.

"Blyat!"

If she's carrying my child and I chained her and left her there, I will never forgive myself. I flip the can over, dumping its contents onto the bathroom floor. My hands search blindly through the mess until I find the test.

The one answer to a question I didn't even know I was asking.

I lift it and stare at the word written as clear as day.

Pregnant.

Everything stops. My world. My thoughts. My goddamn heartbeat. Pregnant.

She's pregnant.

With my baby. *Our* baby.

I'm going to be a father.

A smile stretches before panic grips me tight.

Staggering back, I almost collapse against the counter, gripping the edge to steady myself. My lungs can't fill. My chest can't contain what's happening inside. It's too much. Too fast. Too everything.

The thought of her carrying our child… I can't even fathom it, but it's real. My knees threaten to give way, too overwhelmed by what this could mean for us.

She wanted to talk to me before I left for my meeting, I remember that, but I never expected this. I thought maybe she was ready to confess who she really was. But a baby?

Taking the test and the box with me, I rush out of the room and down the stairs before the front door slams behind me. I'm halfway to my car when my phone rings, one of the men stationed to watch her on the other end.

I answer with a snap. "What?"

"Boss," he pants. "She ran. Took my keys and my shirt."

My jaw clenches. "You didn't lay a finger on her, right?"

Because you're already dead if you did.

"Net. I swear."

"Good."

I hang up, already cursing under my breath. I knew she'd do this. Of course she would. She's too smart to wait around. Too angry. Too driven.

It's okay. I planned for this. I expected it.

I pull up the tracking app for the bracelet.

But a harsh chuckle escapes me as soon as I realize it's still at the farmhouse. She removed it.

My blood turns to ice.

"Chorti materi!" I snarl, slamming my fist against the steering wheel. *Motherfucker!*

Throwing the SUV into gear, I fly down the road, tires screaming as I tear toward the farmhouse. My foot doesn't leave the gas pedal until I'm skidding to a halt in the gravel, leaping out before the engine even dies. The two men I left posted with her stiffen when they see me.

"Where is her bracelet?" I demand.

One of them points to a small side table just inside the doorway. "She wanted to take it off. Sorry, boss."

"Yeah?" I growl, pulling the remote from my pocket and powering it down. "You *will* be sorry." I tuck the bracelet into my pocket and face them again. "Don't tell anyone else about this, or you die. Understand?"

They both nod.

Rushing back to my car, I punch in the GPS for the SUV she stole as I race down the road.

She has a head start, but I can still catch her. I have to.

Because she's not just running toward danger. She's carrying our future with her.

FORTY-TWO

EMILIA

As I sit on the edge of the bed in the dingy motel room, the air feels thick and stagnant, carrying a faint smell of mildew. I grip the burner phone I grabbed from a shady convenience store while the clerk was in the back, my fingers trembling as I dial Nate's number.

The phone rings, and I squeeze my eyes shut, hoping my brother answers. I don't know how much time I have before someone tracks me down. The seconds feel like hours, but finally, I hear him.

"Hello?"

"Hey, Nate."

"Em? What's going on? What happened to your phone?"

I lean back, running my hand through my hair. "I-I'm on the run. I had to leave. It's bad." I pause, struggling to find the right words. "He knows. Konstantin knows everything."

Silence stretches on the other end for a moment, as if he's trying to grasp the full impact of what I just said.

"What do you mean he knows? How?"

"He got a file." My lashes fall shut. "One with my real identity. Your identity. He…he must have gotten it from Gerardo, though it was anonymous. But it had to be him. Fiona and Riley are the only other two who knew what I was doing, and they wouldn't do this to us."

"Shit…" He exhales sharply, his anger palpable even through the phone. "That fucking bastard."

"Yeah," I whisper, not sure what to do or say anymore.

I can almost hear Nate moving around, his frustration growing as fast as mine. "You have to lie low. Don't trust anyone, Em. We'll figure this out. Once we bring Gerardo down, we'll run. You and me. Somewhere far, just like we dreamed about when we were kids."

The idea of running, of leaving everything behind, twists something in my chest. The thought of not watching Konstantin become a father, of walking away from the family we could have, rips at me in a way I never expected.

Despite everything he's done, the way he chained me to the floor, there's a part of me that can't shake the sadness that settles deep in my bones at the thought of leaving him. Of the possibility that we could never be a family.

When I found out I was pregnant in the hospital, it felt surreal. So much so, I took a test at home just to be sure. I was on the pill, thought I was safe, but I was wrong. The doctor told me privately, unsure if I knew, but I didn't.

I hadn't even noticed I'd missed my period, too overwhelmed by everything else going on. Now, holding on to this knowledge, I want this baby. I want Konstantin.

But can I truly have it all?

"Are you listening to me?" Nate calls, snapping me out of my thoughts.

"Yeah. Yeah, I am. It's just all too much."

"I know, but look. You just lie low for a bit. I don't even wanna know where you are, just in case. We'll figure this out. Together." The way he says it takes me back, reminding me of when I first started living with him.

He was always the strong one, the protector. I looked up to him then, wanted to be just like him.

"I've gotta go, Nate. I'll be in touch if anything new comes up."

"Love you, Em."

"Love you."

As soon as the call ends, I'm dialing Riley's number, needing her to know what happened just in case.

"Hey, it's me."

"Em! Oh, thank God!"

The urgency in her voice sends a chill down my spine. "What's wrong?"

"I found something insane about Gerardo, and I've been trying to reach you."

"What?" Panic surges, sharp and immediate.

"I found out Gerardo isn't just helping the DeLucas. He *is* a DeLuca."

My head jerks back, confusion and disbelief swirling inside me. "I don't understand."

"His brother is actually Marco DeLuca. The boss. They're brothers, Emilia."

My lungs throb as I try to breathe, the words hanging in the air. "W-w-what?"

"Yeah. They have different last names because they have different fathers, but they're brothers, and Gerardo's just as deep in the organization as DeLuca himself."

My body locks up, a surge of shock running through me. "Holy shit..."

"That's not all," Riley continues, her tone dropping to a dangerous whisper. "I intercepted some texts between Gerardo and DeLuca. They want you and Nate dead. I don't know when, but they're coming for him first."

My breath stops. Everything goes still. My heart lurches painfully in my chest, and for a moment, all I can hear is the frantic pounding in my ears.

"I have to go. I'll contact you when I can."

"Be careful, Em. Please watch your back."

I end the call and immediately dial Nate again. I need to warn him. I need to make sure he's okay, even though part of me already knows he might not be.

When the phone rings, he answers immediately. "Hey, what's up? You okay?"

"I need you to listen to me. Riley just found something. Gerardo's brother is DeLuca, and they want you dead. They could be coming for you right now. Get the fuck out of there, do you hear me? Cut the fucking ankle monitor and run!"

"Wait, wha—"

The sudden crash of something sends my blood pumping.

"Nate, what the hell was that?"

"Shit. Em, they're here. They're fucking here!"

"Wait—what?" My stomach drops. "Nate, what's happening?"

"I've gotta go, Em!" His voice cracks, followed by a string of curses.

I register a loud crash, then nothing. The line goes dead. I press the phone to my ear, my pulse slamming in my temples so loudly I can hardly hear anything else.

"Nate?!" I scream.

But the silence on the other end only deepens the fear clawing at my chest.

I don't know if he's alive or dead. I don't know if he's trapped or somewhere safe. I only know one thing: the people who've been targeting us are here. And they're coming for us both.

Frantic, I swipe my finger over the phone to call Riley, but before I can even hit dial, her number lights up on the screen.

"Riley? They took him! They just took him!"

"Oh God. Em, listen to me right now."

Grabbing the car keys, I'm already heading out, needing to find him.

"I intercepted a text from DeLuca. Nate's not being taken far."

She rattles off the address, and I shut the door, the engine roaring. Icy dread fills my veins as I repeat the address to myself, committing it to memory.

"But, Em, there's something else. There were texts sent to Konstantin and you."

Adrenaline rushes through me. "What did it say?"

"I forwarded them."

My eyes focus on the phone, the knot in my stomach tightening as I read the message Konstantin got. The photo attached sends an icy tremor through me.

The image is of me—my face slack, eyes shut, making it look like I'm unconscious. How the hell did they get a photo of me sleeping?

When I open the other message, the one sent to me, my hand shakes so violently I almost drop the phone.

"Oh my God," I whisper, the words barely leaving my lips.

It's Konstantin. His face is bloodied, his eyes closed, and his arms are tied behind him to a chair.

I don't even realize I'm holding my breath until it escapes me in a jagged gasp.

UNKNOWN

Come alone. Or we kill him.

The address matches the one Riley gave me—the place they're

holding Nate.

I stare at the image of my husband, the father of my child, and the heaviness of it crushes me.

I know what I have to do. I have to save him. I have to save them both.

"Em, you're not thinking of going alone, right?" Riley interrupts, knowing me well enough to know she can't stop me.

When I'm silent, she goes on.

"You're not thinking clearly. This is a suicide mission. You need to call his brothers, tell them what happened. Get backup."

Konstantin would do anything for me. He's *done* everything for me, even when I didn't deserve it. And now I have to return the favor. I can't let him or Nate die.

"I'll call them now, but they're not as close as I am."

But first, I have to go back to my house. There's a stash of weapons there I'll have to grab.

"You're crazy," she mutters. "You need to understand that if you do this, you may not come back."

"I will come back, Riley."

And I mean every word, even as fear grips me tighter. Not for me, but for our baby.

"I'll talk to you soon." I end the call, and my thoughts flicker to Konstantin again.

This man—this ruthless, dangerous man—has somehow become family to me. He's saved me, he's protected me, and now I need to do the same for him.

Even if he decides he doesn't want me or this baby, I have to get him out of there. And most of all, I can't leave without letting him know how much I'm falling in love with him, as scary as that is.

I take one last breath as I make it to my home, jumping out of the car in a hurry.

I'll save him. I'll save Nate.

And once I do, nothing will ever be the same. Not for me. Not for Konstantin. And certainly not for Gerardo.

Because for the first time in my life, all the cards are on the table, and I know exactly what I'm fighting for.

FORTY-THREE

KONSTANTIN

Every second without her feels like an eternity, a blade digging deeper into my chest.

This is on me. I caused it all. If I hadn't locked her up, she wouldn't have had to run. She would've been safe.

But now she's out there, in danger, and I don't know where the hell she is. I've been hunting for her alone, using every resource at my disposal, keeping it quiet from my brothers. But she's vanished.

The SUV she stole? Abandoned in the middle of nowhere. No cameras, no trace. She's smart. Of course she is.

Teeth clenched, I fight to control the storm raging inside me. Finding her is the only thing that matters now before it's too late.

Her face won't leave my mind. The way she looked at me, that raw vulnerability in her eyes when she spoke about her brother. And like a bastard, I walked away. Left her alone when she needed me most.

My phone buzzes, ripping me out of my thoughts. I grab it from the cupholder, my fingers tightening around it as the screen lights up with a text from an unknown number.

When I read it, my blood boils. Tires screech as I rev the engine while two of my men trailing in a separate SUV try to catch up.

The message contains a photo. Of her.

Emilia.

Her eyes are shut, face pale. It's clear she's been drugged. The words beneath the photo burn into my mind.

UNKNOWN

If you ever want to see her alive, come alone.

"Blyat! Net!" *Fuck! No!*

A primal growl rips from my chest, my fist slamming into the wheel with enough force to rattle my bones. My vision narrows as my eyes lock on the address.

"I'm going to fucking tear your heads off!"

But then a thought shreds through me.

What if they've already killed her? What if this is all just a trap, luring me to the same fate? She and our baby could be gone, and I've been sitting here, useless, unable to save them.

I should've told her what she really meant to me. That I was falling in love with her. But I said nothing, and now it might be too late.

I don't know how long I've been driving, but when I pull up a few yards from the address they gave me—a house in the middle of nowhere—I don't see any bodies. Just two sedans sitting in the driveway.

With a gun in hand, I step out first. My men follow close behind, every nerve in my body on fire, ready to destroy anything that makes a sound.

We move cautiously, checking corners, scanning for any signs of life. But there's nothing. No one.

KONSTANTIN

Where the hell are you, lubov moya?

As we creep toward the back of the house, a bullet cracks through the silence, and a feral smile twists across my face.

So it's like that.

They want a fucking party? Good. I've been starving for one.

I whip around, scanning for the source, but before I can fire back, another bullet hits one of my men in the chest. Blood bursts out, splattering against the ground as he drops, dead before he even hits the dirt.

"Come out and fight like men!" I roar, releasing a few rounds toward the shadows, but no one shows themselves.

Another shot rings out. This time, it strikes my second man in the head, and he crumples.

They have a fucking sniper.

My rage flares, burning hotter, and I know what I need to do. Time to call my brothers. My fingers dig into my pocket for my phone, eyes still darting across the area, trying to pinpoint where the shots are coming from.

The phone rings when I dial Aleksei's number. But before I can hear a single word, a tear gas grenade explodes near me, the air thick and suffocating.

My phone slips from my grip, the world around me turning hazy as my lungs burn with every breath. I stagger forward, swinging wildly, fighting through the thick cloud that clings to me, but my legs are like stone, dragging me down. My chest tightens, the weight of it crushing me, and I can barely keep my eyes open.

Then, out of nowhere, a sharp pain sears through my neck, and everything goes black.

The last thing I see before everything fades is Emilia.

EMILIA

I sent a text to Aleksei, telling him where I'm going and why. I know they'll be here soon, but I can't just sit around and wait for that to happen. For all I know, the DeLucas could be killing Konstantin right now.

The thought of losing him, of never feeling his arms around me again, of never hearing him call me "katyonak" or any of the other pet names he's given me…it's a pain I can't bear to even entertain.

I want to see him again so badly, but the fear that I'll walk in and find him dead keeps gnawing at me. It twists inside me like a knife.

I have to save him. I *will* save him. I won't let him die.

Parking a few streets away, I make sure they don't see my vehicle. Because as soon as they do, they won't hesitate to shoot me down.

As I slip out of the car, my sneakers hit the pavement with a soft thud. A gun rests tucked into my waistband, another secured in the holster around my ankle. I've never been more ready for a fight, yet the fear of the unknown presses against me.

The colonial house looms ahead, completely unassuming, as I pull my gun free, keeping it low, my fingers wrapped tight around the grip. Each step is calculated, the air heavy with unease, every sound amplified as I move behind the cover of trees in the back, praying they don't see me.

Maybe they even assumed I wouldn't show up. That Konstantin means nothing to me. But I'm here, and I will take everything from them.

I reach the corner of the house, flattening myself against the stone wall. Every inch of me is strung too tight, like a coiled spring ready to snap. Taking deep, controlled breaths, I cinch my fingers around the gun.

When I get near a window, I freeze. Voices drift through the glass, low and muffled. I push my back harder into the cold stone, every nerve on edge.

Time seems to slow, each second heavier than the last. I'm so damn close now. The electric hum of imminent danger pulses in my veins, the taste of it sharp on my tongue. One wrong move, one sound, and it's over.

Approaching the back door, I test the handle. It turns with a soft click. I can't help the dark smile that pulls at the corners of my mouth.

Well, they do say criminals are stupid…

The door parts inch by inch, barely a whisper, letting the cold air rush in. I hardly feel it, too focused on the low sounds inside: the faint crunch of someone chewing, the click of a TV remote, the steady hum of a conversation. There are at least three men.

I move silently, step by step, across the threshold. The smell of stale air and cheap beer fills my nose. Suppressing the urge to gag, I keep my eyes on the figure sitting on the couch, the back of his head my only view. He doesn't notice me. His eyes are glued to the TV, completely oblivious to the fact that his life is about to end.

Creeping behind him, I already have the knife in my free hand, and with one clean slice across his throat, he doesn't even know what hit him. Before he can react, blood gushes from him, quickly soaking through his shirt and dripping down onto the couch as he falls limp.

I back away with hushed footfalls, knowing getting rid of the others will be more challenging. Wiping the blood on my pants, I flip the knife closed and slip it back into my pocket, praying they're actually keeping Konstantin here.

Moving silently toward the others, my body blending into the shadows, I'm consumed not by fear, but by an icy hunger for vengeance.

I sneak a glance around the corner, careful to stay out of sight. One man rummages through the microwave, slamming the door shut with a sharp bang that echoes, while the other lounges at the table, sipping from a glass, his attention elsewhere.

"You think the bitch isn't showing up?" one of them says, his voice thick with a mixture of boredom and anticipation.

"I don't see her. Do you?" The other man snickers.

As soon as he starts walking out of the kitchen, my heart rate spikes, adrenaline flooding my veins. Instinctively, I hold myself against the wall just out of sight as his footsteps grow louder, drawing nearer.

I stay perfectly still, listening to the sound of him moving past me, barely inches away. When the footfalls finally fade, my heart slams against my ribs.

Every second feels like an eternity. The quiet stretches on, broken only by the soft clink of glass and the low hum of the microwave. When I hear him return to the table, I slip back into motion.

Crouching low, I use the counters to provide me with a shield as I edge closer. All I need is two clean shots, and they're done.

When I inch forward, I see him.

Oh God. Konstantin.

Panic hits me like a freight train, my chest seizing, the pressure crushing my lungs.

He looks just like he did in the photo they sent, but also somehow worse. Slumped in the chair, his body is so still, it's almost as if he's not even there. His arms are still bound behind him, his head hanging forward—a lifeless rag doll draped in the chair.

For a moment, I can't breathe. The fury that crashes through me is violent, almost desperate. It ignites something inside me, something visceral.

They've done this to him. And they will pay for it.

My anger is now full-blown rage. They don't know it yet, but their time is running out.

The moment I step into their line of sight, they're finished. In seconds, I get to full height, firing a clean shot into the first man's head, and before the other one even realizes what happened, he's dead on the floor too.

Well, that was easier than I thought it would be. But I'm sure more will come. I need to get him out of here.

As soon as I rush toward Konstantin, I kneel in front of him, needing him to be alive so damn badly. I cup his face with one hand, the fingers of my other on his pulse. When I feel it, a rush of a breath leaves me, emotions clogging my throat.

He's alive. He's gonna be okay.

"Baby, wake up. I'm here." I shake him, hoping whatever they gave him starts to wear off.

Removing my knife, I cut off his zip ties, setting him free.

"Konstantin, please…I need you to wake up now."

"Emilia?" he groans, and relief hits me instantly. His eyes flicker, slowly opening. "Are you okay? The b-b-baby?"

Oh God, he knows. How?

I nod, my thumb running across the stubble of his jaw. "We're both okay. I'm going to get you out of this."

"I-I love you, Emilia."

The words hit me like a wave, crashing into my chest, and I choke back a cry.

He loves me?

When his eyes meet mine, hazy but full of something so real, I feel it. Deep in my soul, I feel the truth of his words. It's more than just the words—it's everything behind them. The sincerity, the rawness, the weight of everything we've been through together.

My hands tremble as I cup his face, pulling him closer, kissing him with everything I have. My heart is overflowing with love, with every emotion I can't quite articulate.

"I love you too, stupid."

The kiss lingers, a desperate need to feel him, to have him know how much he means to me. How much *we* mean, despite everything.

He manages a laugh, soft and pained, his voice barely there. "That's so romantic."

Even through the fog of the drug that clouds his mind, his gaze sharpens for a split second.

"You-you put yourself in h-h-harm's way for me again. I should punish you for this."

"But you won't." My lips hover near his ear, my breath warm against his skin. "Or you will, and I'll like it," I tease, trying to inject some humor into the moment, or maybe just to quiet the anxiety churning in my stomach.

His hand reaches up to touch my face, his fingers grazing my skin like he's memorizing the feeling of me.

"You are everything to me, lubov moya," he whispers. "I will love you until my heart gives out, and even then, I-I don't think I could ever stop loving you."

And before I can suppress it, my eyes well with tears. "I'm really glad we're expressing our feelings and all that, but right now, we need to get out of—"

A sudden creak grabs my attention, my pulse jumping to my throat.

The rest happens in a blur. One second, I'm standing in front of Konstantin, and the next, he's attempting to push me out of the way, but he's not strong enough.

"Look out," he tries to shout, but the words come out small.

As I turn, a man stands at the threshold, a gun drawn at me. And all the blood rushes out of my body.

Because I recognize him.

No, I *know* him.

What the hell is going on?

"What are you doing? Lower the fucking gun and help me!"

I wait for him to say something, anything that would explain what is happening and why he's not helping me.

Instead, he lowers the weapon just slightly, his eyes meeting mine with a hint of something like regret. Or maybe it's resignation. The expression on his face almost makes me feel…sick.

"It was never supposed to be like this, Em." He grabs the back of his neck. "Why couldn't you just stay out of it? Mind your own damn business? But no, you had to go snooping, stir up a hornet's nest. And now I have no choice."

No.

Nonono!

It can't be!

"What the fuck are you talking about, Nate?"

But I already know. I just need confirmation that he is part of whatever is going on.

"Don't touch her, you motherfucker!" Konstantin growls, as if a surge of raw power has just coursed through him.

My body instinctively moves toward him, but the gun stays trained on me. My mind races, trying to understand how I missed it.

Am I really this blind, or are they just that good? How long has Nate been involved in whatever this is? And what exactly is he here to do?

His gaze doesn't waver, but something in his eyes shifts. It's almost as if he's torn, like he's making a decision he's not even sure he wants to make.

"I don't know what you've done, but you need to put that gun away before you do something you'll regret."

"I don't have a choice anymore, Em. You did this to yourself." He says it like he believes it, like he truly has no other option.

Then he fires.

FORTY-FOUR

EMILIA

Time seems to slow, everything around me blurring into a haze. The deafening crack of the gunshot slices through the air like a bolt of lightning.

Konstantin's roar rips through the chaos as he attempts to push me backward.

Nate's bullet whizzes by, so close I can almost feel the heat of it. My heart slams in my chest, adrenaline pumping as my instincts take over. My hand moves, drawing my gun up in one fluid motion and pointing it directly at my brother.

I still can't make sense of it.

How can he do this to me after everything we've been through? How can he want me dead? And for what?

When he takes a step toward me, I aim the gun higher. "Stay back, Nate. I don't want to do this, but I will if I have to."

I'll do anything to protect my baby.

He laughs, a sick, twisted sound that feels completely foreign coming from him. "I can't believe you actually fell for him, Em."

Nate's words cut through the air, his eyes flicking briefly to Konstantin, who's trying to stand, but struggling, the drugs still working against him.

"I thought you were the *good* one," he continues with a sneer. "You always did the right thing. Arrested the bad ones. What happened? Fell to the dark side?"

Each word stings, each one sinking deeper than the last. My anger continues to build, but it's overshadowed by something heavier, something like grief.

Konstantin growls low, his body trembling with the effort of pushing himself up. "I'm going to rip your tongue out."

I catch his eye, silently pleading for him to hold back. There's still time to fix this, still a way to stop things from going too far. Nate will pay for his actions, but I don't want him dead.

He looks at Konstantin with a mocking grin. "You're not in a position to do shit right now, Marinov. I almost blew your brains out after I shot your men, but the boss wanted it this way."

The boss? Does he mean…Gerardo?

I shake my head, disbelief gripping me.

What the hell are you doing, Nate?

Confusion stirs with rage. "Are you working with Gerardo and the DeLucas?"

Then it hits me.

"Oh my God. Are you the one who sent Konstantin that photo of me?"

He snickers, the sound harsh and mocking, a reminder of how far he's fallen. "Maybe."

"I can't believe…after everything I did to try to save you! How could you fucking do this to me? You're my brother!"

"Yes, I am, and I fought for everything I had. And I'm not about to let you take it from me." He laughs dryly, shaking his head. "You never saw the full picture, you know that? You and Riley were *so* sure of everything, but you had no idea."

"What didn't I know?"

He blows out a breath, like he's already grown tired of this conversation, and I swear it hurts. I don't know who this is. Because this isn't the Nate I knew.

"Tim was never a part of this."

"What?"

"That's right, sis. Because I was! Me!" His eyes gleam with dark satisfaction, and it's like I'm looking at a stranger. "We just made it look like it was him. But he had it coming. He was gonna rat on us, so I had to take him out."

A cold shiver crawls up my arms.

"You actually did it? You—" I swallow the bile rising in my throat. "You killed him while I fought like hell to free you?"

My breath comes in sharp bursts, fury tearing through me.

"I know, and I am sorry about that, but it's not like I made you." His chuckle makes my blood run cold.

"So how the hell did you end up in prison if you had Gerardo's help?"

He hesitates, his eyes narrowing. "Well…" He scratches the back of his head. "They decided I was a problem too when I started collecting evidence on their dirty work. Only as collateral, in case they tried to screw me over." His gaze sharpens, his tone colder. "But I underestimated how far they'd go. Now if I want to stay out of prison, I only have one choice."

My gut twists, the power of his words choking me.

"What's that?" I barely manage to ask, the betrayal stinging deep within.

His eyes lock on to mine, cold and ruthless. "I have to kill you both."

An inhale sticks to my throat. I can't even process what he's saying, the air in my lungs freezing over. How can he even think those words, let alone say them?

"Kill me, but let her go," Konstantin mutters, gripping my hand tightly. He leans in, whispering urgently, "Give me the gun."

I shake my head, my clasp tightening on the weapon. Even if he wanted to, he can't shoot straight. But I can.

"I didn't want to," Nate adds, like that makes it any better. "I tried to tell Gerardo there had to be another way. But he said this was it. I had to prove my loyalty."

Every inch of me is ready to collapse. There's no one left to trust. No one but Konstantin.

"You kept making things worse without even knowing," Nate continues. "Once Gerardo found out you remembered about that cop he killed, he needed you gone."

I just didn't think you'd be the one to do it.

The thought hits with an ache so deep, I can't even comprehend it.

"Gerardo was Mom's biggest supplier back then," he goes on. "I get that you were young and didn't know, but yeah, that cop was our neighbor. He knew him because they worked together. He didn't want Gerardo giving her any more drugs and he was gonna rat, so Gerardo took care of him."

"Wait a minute…"

Something doesn't sit right with me.

"How did Gerardo know I remembered what he did? You told him?"

I mean, it wouldn't even be the worst thing he's done.

"Nah." He throws a hand in the air. "I didn't tell him shit. Your therapist, Margo, did."

"What?" I stumble back a step. "I don't understand."

Margo? The one I confided in? Trusted? The one I went back to after I hurt myself?

Oh God… I'm gonna be sick.

He raises a brow, his expression almost amused. "He's banging her. That's why he sent you to her. He sends everyone to her because she spills everything. She sent you to the other one she knows, that hypnotherapist, to get information for Gerardo."

"Oh my God." The room spins, but I force myself to stay upright.

"I'm sorry, Em," Nate says, his tone quieter now. "You know I love you. But I need back in. Showing them that I can take care of a threat, no matter who it is, is how I do it. This is how I survive."

The words hammer through me, digging deeper than anything he's ever said before.

"You're really going to kill me?" A part of me still hopes that maybe, somehow, this isn't real. That I'm dreaming.

Konstantin groans, words still rough and groggy. "Shoot him, Emilia. Do it."

He mutters something in Russian, but I barely hear it, the sound lost in the deafening rush of blood in my ears.

"I have to, Em," Nate says, his voice thick with something like resignation as he points the gun at me. "It's what has to happen. It's what they want."

"Sh-shoot him, Emilia," Konstantin cuts in, trying to take the gun from me, but I don't let him.

"Turn around, Em."

Aching emotions continue to pound through me, my heart literally ripping in two. I love him. I've always loved him. But this isn't him anymore. This is the monster Gerardo created. And I can't save him from that.

I almost pity him. But it doesn't change anything.

"No, Nate." I stand straighter, curling an arm around my belly. "You will look me in the eyes as you pull the trigger."

He pinches the bridge of his nose, his shoulders rising and falling with slow, shaky breaths. I witness the conflict in his eyes as he raises his weapon. But it doesn't matter. I won't turn away. He needs to face this.

As his gun lifts higher, as he's about to pull the trigger, I aim at his center.

And fire.

But it's not the shot that knocks the breath from me. It's the fierce instinct to protect my baby, something my mother never did for me.

Then I see Nate hit the ground, and everything inside me stops.

"NATE!" I sob when blood leaks from his stomach and he staggers back, his eyes widening.

And in that same instant, Nate's bullet finds its mark, tearing into my arm. Pain erupts like fire, but I rush toward him just as Konstantin screams.

"Emilia!" He forces himself to his feet, tripping back while I run toward my brother, dropping to my knees in front of him, tears pounding behind my eyes.

"Nate!" A sob breaks free as he lies there, blood spilling from his mouth as he tries to speak.

And all I see now is the young boy he once was, the one who protected me.

"Oh God, Nate!" I cry, my tears falling freely for the first time in what feels like forever. "I love you. I'll always love you."

His mouth trembles, but no words come out.

"I forgive you," I tell him. "It's okay. I forgive you."

His breath is labored, his chest heaving, until…

He's gone.

I bury my face against his, sobbing as his last breath fades, and all I feel is the emptiness of his body, refusing to say goodbye.

FORTY-FIVE

KONSTANTIN

The drugs have left my system. My blood is my own again, no longer tainted by whatever they used to keep me weak. And with that, my rage is back full force.

I can feel it in every muscle, every bone—an undeniable surge of fury. All I want right now is for that bastard brother of hers to still be alive so I could tear him apart with my bare hands.

The thought of Gerardo and the DeLucas still breathing, still out there, sends a hot wave of anger through me.

My body's fighting to fully recover, but I don't give a shit about the pain. I don't care about the throbbing in my muscles or the pounding in my head. What matters is that Emilia's okay. She's strong, stronger than I could've ever imagined, and she saved me, saved our family. And she didn't hesitate to kill her brother to do it.

As I walk back toward her hospital room with something for her to eat, I find my brothers marching over to me. As soon as Aleksei got her text, he said they rushed over, but only made it in time to catch the aftermath. But still, they came, and that's what family is.

Aleksei looks me over, his eyes flicking from my face to the bandages still covering parts of my body.

"How's she doing?" His tone's laced with concern.

"She's going to be okay. She's tough."

He nods. "She is."

My hand tightens around the bag of food I'm holding. "She's pregnant."

The words hang in the air until Aleksei's mouth twitches. "This is good."

I run a hand down my face, blowing out a breath.

"You won't be anything like Papa was," he adds, and I hope he's right.

Kirill's eyes flicker between me and the hospital door, a dry laugh escaping. "A fed, huh?" He smirks, shaking his head. "Didn't see that coming. But stranger things have happened."

That they have.

Anton walks closer, his gaze meeting mine. "She saved your life. There's honor in that. Honor's not something you find in everyone."

I know this is them accepting her, and I'm grateful for that. It's much easier than having to kill them…

But how could they not accept her? They saw what I see. Loyalty, even when it hurts. Love, even when it's hard. They saw a woman who risked her life for mine, and after that, how could they hold the badge against her?

Aleksei steps back, his expression hardening. "We're going to find Gerardo and the DeLucas. Bring them all to the farm and dispose of them."

A smile creeps up my face. "Save Gerardo for me."

He's dead the moment I lay my hands on him, but I want to savor it. I want him to feel everything I've been holding back. Everything he's done to Emilia, to me, to our family.

Aleksei nods, and with that, my brothers turn and walk away, leaving me alone in the hallway. But I'm not really alone. Not anymore.

As soon as I step into the room, I drop the bag of food on the table, my fist clenching when I see her propped up on the hospital bed, a doctor sewing her up while she stares at me with a faint smile.

"Hey, babe. That was fast."

"You're lucky I left at all."

Even with the men stationed at her door, I still hate to be away from her.

Blyat, her skin is so pale, and I know she still carries the shock of what happened. Every time I remember what her brother tried to do, my hands twitch, needing something or someone to break.

The doctor threads another stitch through the torn skin of her arm. And when she winces, I immediately see red.

Grabbing the doctor by the collar, I jerk him an inch away from her body. "You hurt my wife again, and I will do the same to you. Except worse."

His mouth goes slack, terror filling his eyes. "I-I'm sorry."

I drop my hand away. He works for me. He knows damn well I don't bluff.

Emilia shakes her head with a soft laugh. "Don't mind my husband. He gets a little sensitive when I'm in pain."

When I peer down at her, a hand around her stomach, I swear something in my chest cracks wide open.

I don't deserve this. Her. The child inside her. But I will burn the world to protect them both.

I should never have let myself get captured. I should've been smarter, played the game like I always do, but I didn't. I let my heart take the lead, and it almost cost me everything. It almost cost me her. The family we're trying to build.

But with Emilia, all I want is to feel—every moment, every touch. I want to love her through the darkest of times, to protect her with every breath I take. She's not just my wife. She's my equal. My queen. And nothing will ever change that.

This woman, this force of nature, risked everything for me. Again.

And I would die a hundred deaths to have her at my side.

Emilia. Tessa. My wife. My salvation.

She's strong, fierce, more independent than half the men I've ever commanded, and twice as dangerous. And yet she's mine.

The doctor finally leaves, muttering something about pain meds, but I don't even glance his way. As soon as the door clicks shut, I move to her side, lowering myself to the edge of the bed. My knuckles brush against her cheek, and I press my lips to her forehead, lingering there, still needing the reassurance that she's alive.

Her lashes flutter under my touch, eyes meeting mine, tired but full of light.

God, how did I ever live without this woman?

My palm finds her belly. The quiet promise of everything we have yet to become.

"I will love this child and you every day that I live. And I swear on everything I am, I will protect you both."

Her hand slides over mine.

"I know you will," she whispers. "And he or she will love you too. Because you'll be an amazing dad."

I search her face, every part of her, and I see it. The truth. The trust. The strength.

"And you know you'll be a good mom too, right, katyonak?"

She nods, tears glistening at the corners of her eyes. "I feel it already. This overpowering love I've never felt before. Not like this."

Dropping my forehead to hers, I exhale slowly. "It terrifies me, having you and this baby, but it's the best fear I've ever felt. Because it means I finally have something that matters."

She smiles through her tears. "You've always mattered too, Konstantin. Even when I hated you."

I smirk. "You're so good with your words, moya lyubimoya."

"I know." She laughs, and the sound fills the space between us, something pure and good.

Sliding down beside her on the bed, I pull her against my chest, her head resting over my heart. And for the first time in what feels like years…it beats in peace.

EMILIA

The following day, I'm home, tucked under Konstantin's watchful eye like I'm made of glass. He's everywhere, hovering, making sure I don't lift a finger, not even to walk to the bathroom without his help, and it would be quite adorable if it wasn't also a tad annoying. But I love him for wanting to take care of me.

I'm doing my best to cope with the aftermath of Nate's death, the betrayal that feels like it will take forever to heal, and the fact that Gerardo is out there, escaping the payback he deserves. But it will come. Konstantin will not let him live. He's going to make them all pay, and I will enjoy every painful second.

"Come, I have a surprise for you," he says, his voice laced with that excitement that hints at a secret he's eager to reveal.

I raise an eyebrow. "What kind of surprise?"

"You'll see."

He takes my hand, guiding me down the steps. "Careful, Emilia."

His grip tightens as he steadies me, and the concern in his eyes only makes me love him more. I let out a breathless laugh, even when that's the last thing I want to do.

"Really forgot who you married, huh?" I tease, pushing the

heaviness away for a moment.

"Never." His eyes darken, his intensity growing as we stand beside his Royce, already waiting for us.

In one swift motion, he grabs the back of my neck, pulling me in. The kiss is hot, demanding, burning with passion. It consumes me, pulling every bit of air from my lungs, leaving me breathless and raw. When he pulls away, his gaze fastens to mine with such force, it makes my chest tighten and my pulse race.

"I haven't forgotten who you are, Emilia," he says softly. "But I also know you're not okay. And that's alright with me. Trust me enough not to be okay around me."

His words hit deep. My throat tightens, a sharp throb in my chest, and I feel the sting of tears prick at my eyes. I quickly swipe them away, trying to hold it together.

"Jesus, stop making me cry. I never cry."

Konstantin cups my cheek, his thumb gently wiping away the remnants of my tears. "Maybe you should. You don't have to be strong all the time."

I shake my head. "What good would that do? I cried enough yesterday. I don't have anything left in me."

His expression softens, but there's a quiet anger behind it, anger I understand. "I'm sorry, malyshka. I wish I could take your pain away."

With a sigh, I wrap my arms around him and groan in satisfaction as my cheek hits his chest. "That's okay. This is enough."

My arm still throbs from the bullet graze, but it's nothing compared to the gaping hole in my chest where I once held space for my brother.

We stay like that for a while, comfortable in the silence, in the arms of one another, even when things are still unfinished. But in this moment, it feels like it's just him and me. And that's all that matters.

Gradually, he pulls away, still holding me close. He laces his fingers with mine and looks down at me.

"Come, let's go for a drive." He leads me into the back of the car with him as one of his men takes the wheel.

Konstantin's hand is warm around mine, his thumb brushing lightly over my skin as we drive up toward the farm, and something instantly catches my eye in the distance.

A slow-growing fire looms closer, something roasting over it. My heart skips a beat at the sweet gesture.

I turn to him, a small grin tugging at my lips. "Did you cook for us again?"

His smirk deepens, eyes lighting up with mischief. "Yeah, something like that."

Curiosity bubbles inside me, but I don't push it further as the car smoothly comes to a stop. Konstantin kisses my knuckles before stepping out and opening the door for me. He doesn't release my hand as he guides me toward the fire, his driver trailing behind us.

And when I see what he's actually making, the shock of it causes me to bounce back a step.

Because he's not cooking a meal. He's cooking…a person. Gagged, bound to a rod, spinning slowly over the flames. His body is burned and bruised, barely recognizable through the charred skin and open wounds.

I stop dead in my tracks. "Who is that?"

Konstantin smiles something cold and vicious. "You don't recognize your own boss, katyonak?" His voice drips with venom. "Gerardo was nice enough to come over for dinner. Except, of course, he'll be the dinner tonight. Isn't that right, my friend?"

Frozen, I watch as Gerardo groans, struggling against the ropes, a scream dying off in his throat.

Konstantin pats the top of his head, his eyes gleaming. "Good piggy."

I've wanted this confrontation for so long, wanted him dead. But now I don't even know if this will bring me an ounce of satisfaction.

"Where was he hiding?" I wonder, barely able to process what I'm seeing.

Konstantin comes to my side, sliding his arm around my back. "One of his girlfriends' basements. You made it easy, didn't you?" His gaze locks on to Gerardo, his irises flaming with fury. "Did you really think you could get away with hurting my wife? No one will *ever* get away with that."

Gerardo groans, the sound muffled by the gag, but Konstantin's rage only grows. He gestures sharply for his man to tear it away.

"Answer me!" he snarls, his features twisted with ferocity.

"Emilia, I-I-I'm sorry." Gerardo trembles out as he speaks, barely above a whisper.

My chest tightens as I step toward him, but I can barely look at him. "Not only have you lied to me my whole life, but you're the reason Nate is dead too."

"No," he mutters weakly. "Nate was…Nate. He knew what he wanted, and when I-I showed him how much money he could make, he went for it. That's n-n-not m-my fault."

He's gasping for air, his words stumbling over one another.

I want to scream, to say something else, but the anger, the grief… It's suffocating me.

He's right. I just want someone else to blame. But the truth is, Nate is just as at fault for his role in this. And Gerardo? Well, he's the monster I never knew he was, and now I'm watching him pay for it.

Konstantin's voice drops to an icy, unforgiving tone. "After I kill you, I'm going after your family and every member of your crew. Every single one. Because I'm feeling charitable with a baby on the way, I'll spare the wives and children. But no one else."

Gerardo doesn't respond. He doesn't get the chance. The fire crackles as Konstantin steps forward, picking up a heavy log and tossing it onto the flames. The fire soars to life, growing hotter, sending sparks flying into the air.

Gerardo screams, the sound echoing far and wide.

Konstantin leans in close, his breath hot against the shell of my ear as he says, "This is what I'll do to anyone who touches you. But you already knew that."

Gazing up at him with absolute adoration, I hold his cheek and nod. "I do know that, and I'd do the same for you."

Gerardo's screams fade, becoming muffled under the roaring blaze, while Konstantin pulls me against his side, his hand firmly holding mine as we walk away from the chaos.

The flames burn behind us, and all I feel is this sense of deep loss, but somehow, a new beginning too.

Because in Konstantin's arms, I finally feel like I'm home. Like everything I've been searching for has led me to this moment.

To *him*.

No matter what the future holds, I know one thing for sure: I'm where I'm meant to be. With this man. With our child. In this new life.

And together, we will survive it all, no matter the cost.

FORTY-SIX

EMILIA

The weight of the day hangs heavy on my chest as I stand beside Konstantin, my hand pressed to his arm, the only anchor keeping me from being swallowed by the finality of it all.

Saying goodbye to someone you love is already hard. Saying goodbye to the person you thought loved you too is even harder.

I needed to do this. To have a proper burial for my brother even when Konstantin didn't think he deserved it. But he respected my choice, and I'm thankful for that.

The priest's murmurs drift over me, his words drowned by the rush of thoughts in my mind. He recites verses about eternal rest, about the peace that follows life's trials. The words should comfort me, but they don't.

When he finishes, the silence of the graveyard swallows me whole. I gaze down at the casket and the dirt that will soon cover it, and I wonder if I'll ever find peace myself.

I never wanted to bury my brother like this, never wanted his memory tied to the pain he caused. But Nate gave me no other choice.

The priest blesses the grave while Konstantin tightens his hold on me, a quiet reassurance that I don't have to face this alone.

As the mourners begin to leave, saying their goodbyes, I'm left standing with dirt in hand, staring at the grave.

"I'm sorry it ended this way." I toss the dirt onto the casket before pausing to stare at it for a moment longer.

A lump hits my throat. I hate this. I hate every second of it, and I hate that I had to be the one to kill him, but I had no other choice. It was either him or my baby.

With a sigh, I walk away, returning to my place beside Konstantin.

Riley and Fiona look over at me with tears in their eyes, and when Konstantin notices, he kisses my temple, his lips warmly brushing my skin.

"I'll give you time to talk."

"Thanks."

He steps away, walking toward his brothers and leaving me with the two people who've always been there. They haven't seen me since it all went down, though we have spoken briefly and they were in as much shock as I was.

Riley pulls me into a hug first, her tears soaking into my jacket.

"I'm so sorry, Em," she whispers. "For Nate. For everything."

I hold her tight. "Thank you." I blow out a harsh breath. "I'll get through it. I always do."

Fiona steps forward next, her arms wrapping around me. "We're here for you." She pulls back just enough to look at me. "No matter what."

I smile faintly, my heart swelling with gratitude for the two of them. "I know you are."

There's a long pause before Fiona clears her throat. Her gaze shifts to Konstantin, then back to me.

"Are you really staying with him?"

I nod, my smile stretching, my body swelling with the love I have for him. "I am."

She raises a brow, almost like she doesn't quite believe it.

"I know, it's crazy. The old me would never have imagined being married to a mobster, but here we are." I shrug.

Riley tilts her head, her gaze filled with understanding. "If he makes you happy, then that's all that matters. Just…try not to die."

"I'll work on that." Laughing softly, I glance over at Konstantin, who's talking with his brothers. When his eyes meet mine, something in them grips my chest. "He does make me happy."

I turn my attention back to the conversation. "For so long, I thought I had everything figured out. We were the good guys, they were the bad ones. But things aren't so black and white anymore, as you two know. There's a lot of gray in between."

My hand moves to my stomach, instinctively protecting the child growing inside me.

Fiona and Riley freeze when they catch it, their faces draining of color.

"Oh my God." Riley presses her palm to her mouth. "You're pregnant?"

I nod, feeling my heart thud painfully in my chest. "Yeah. I am."

Fiona stares, her lips opening and closing like she's trying to find the right words.

Finally, she whispers, "Wow…this is insane!" Her hand cups my stomach. "But also exciting. Maybe we can have another lawyer in the family."

"Maybe." A small laugh falls out of me.

"I'm happy for you, Em." She curls her arms around me. "You deserve to be happy, even though I wouldn't exactly have chosen a Marinov for you."

"Believe me." I perch back, cracking a grin. "I'm fully aware of how you feel about them."

At that, her gaze lands on Aleksei, and his eyes lock with hers. I swear it's like they're caught in some kind of silent war, neither of them willing to back down.

"Just sleep together already, will you?" I elbow her. "I bet it'll be hot."

Fiona's eyes flick to me, and a flash of something passes over her face.

Girlfriend can deny it all she wants, but she wants him and hates herself for it.

FORTY-SEVEN

KONSTANTIN

A month has passed since everything changed.

A month since the dust settled. Since the DeLucas were all killed. Since Emilia quit her job with the feds and we began rebuilding what was broken.

The men who hurt her—every single one—are dead.

Lloyd, the one who begged for mercy as I carved him into pieces. The other svolichy from her past who dared to touch her when she was younger. They're all erased. Gone. Like they never existed.

It's what I do. What I will always do for her.

A husband's duty is to protect his wife, and I don't take that lightly. It's not just a promise; it's my purpose.

As I sit at the head of the dining table, my eyes drift to my wife beside me as she laughs at something Kirill said. Her hand rests on her stomach, a little rounder now. And every time I catch sight of her, something inside me swells with pride. I put that baby in her. I created life with her, and there's nothing I could ever do that would feel more meaningful than that.

The house is filled with warmth, the scent of dinner in the air, all the people I love around the table, and there's something in that. Because any one of them could be gone tomorrow.

My gaze drifts to Lev, whose little hands line up his carrots with careful precision. I watch him for a moment, a smile tugging at my lips. I'd do anything for him. I'd die for him, for his happiness, for the future of everyone sitting at this table.

My attention returns to Emilia, admiring her strength through everything she's endured. But there's still quiet sadness behind her eyes. I know she'll never truly be okay with the way things ended with her brother, but she's strong. Stronger than I've ever seen anyone be.

If that bastard was still alive, though, I'd kill him all over again. I'd rip him apart for even thinking about trying to hurt her. The thought of him trying to kill her—the woman I love, the mother of my child— fills me with rage, like fire burning under my skin.

She smiles at me when she catches my stare, and maybe because we've been through so much, I'm more in love with her now than ever before.

Thankfully, she's been keeping up with her therapy with someone new I found for her.

And her old therapists? Well, they're unavailable. Permanently.

The conversation drifts from one subject to another, everyone relaxed for the first time in a long while. But then Aleksei, of course, breaks the flow with his usual comments.

"I can't believe you knew Fiona all this time and I had no idea." He shakes his head slowly, that familiar smirk tugging at his mouth. "That woman…"

A muscle twitches in his jaw.

There's something in his tone, something dark, gritted, too sharp to be just annoyance. It drips with heat. Frustration. Obsession.

It's not just hate. It's *desire,* barely restrained, twisted up in everything he can't stand about her…and everything he clearly wants.

Emilia glances at him, lips quirking. "Yeah, I know she's amazing. It's perfectly acceptable for you to have a crush on her. I mean, I do, and I don't even swing that way. She's just—"

Aleksei cuts her off, his grin dimming like a storm rolling in. "An ice princess? Satan?"

Emilia turns to him fully, narrowing her eyes, and that flicker of the viper she is could incinerate kingdoms. "Listen to me, motherfucker. You mess with Fiona, and I will personally cut off your balls." She flashes a sweet, dangerous smile as she lifts the bowl in her hands. "More potatoes?"

Aleksei mutters something under his breath, clearly frustrated, but he knows better than to push her any further. She's my family now. And no one touches her. No one messes with her. Or they will deeply regret it.

Reaching under the table, my hand brushes against hers, a silent promise of protection. Bringing her hand to my mouth, I kiss the top of it, letting the moment linger between us.

Thoughts race through my mind, back to the days before she came into my life. I thought I had everything figured out, that I could keep control over it all, that nothing could break me.

But she has. In ways I never expected, she's cracked the walls I'd built up over the years. And I'm grateful, more than I ever thought possible.

I look at her, and it feels like everything is falling into place. When I think about how far we've come, how much we've fought through, it's hard to believe it's real. That we made it through it all.

But here we are. Together.

Aleksei leans back in his chair, sucking in a long, deep breath.

"Fiona may be a challenge," I tell him. "But you've never met a challenge you didn't like."

He gives me a sly grin. "You're not wrong about that."

I watch him for a moment, trying to figure out what's going on in his head. But I don't press, because when it comes to matters of the heart, we always tend to figure it out.

As dinner winds down, a sense of contentment hits my chest.

My brothers, my nephew, my Emilia—my family. Everything I've worked for, everything I've fought for, is right here.

And I know that no matter what happens, I'll protect them. Even if it means tearing the world apart to do it.

When the evening ends, I stay close to my wife, holding her hand the whole time, needing that constant contact, wanting her to know she's not alone. We walk outside together, the breeze catching her dress as we stroll across the grounds. I pull her close, guiding her against a tree, my heart swelling with the love I never thought I deserved.

"Do you miss it?" I tuck a stray lock of hair behind her ear. "Your old life? Your job?"

She shakes her head, a soft smile curling on her lips as her hand rests on her stomach. "No. What I have now with you…it means more to me than anything else."

Her words hit me hard, a rush of powerful emotion flooding my chest.

"I've never been prouder of anything," I tell her, cupping her jaw. "And I swear to you, Emilia, I will give you and our child the life you deserve."

She looks up at me, her eyes wide and filled with so much trust that it knocks the breath from my lungs.

"I know you will." Her fingertips trace the stubble of my jaw. "I love you, Konstantin."

"Ya tebya lyublyu, katyonak." The words leave my mouth with a force I can't control, because every part of me feels it. This need to make her understand, to make her feel what she is to me.

With a rush of need, my mouth crashes down on hers. Our kiss is fierce, desperate, full of promises of tomorrow. My hands round her hips and I lift her up in the air, her body pressed against the tree trunk while I roughly undo the zipper of my pants and yank them down, and she eagerly pulls her panties to the side. And with one hard thrust, I'm inside her.

I remain still for a moment, staring into her eyes, every inch of me belonging to her. With a growl, I thrust into her again and again, her cries reverberating in the silence, only to be swallowed up as I claim her mouth with another kiss, deep and desperate.

Passion pulses through me like fire—unrestrained, untamed—and I drown in the taste of her, the warmth of her body pressed against mine.

My hands cradle her face, tilting her head slightly to deepen the kiss. I lose myself in her, in the way she responds, her hunger matching mine with every press of her lips.

What we feel right here, right now… This is love. One that burns so brightly, it's impossible to ignore. I know it in my bones, what we have is stronger than anything I could have ever imagined.

It's unbreakable. It's ours. Nothing—not her past, not mine, not the danger that will always follow us—will ever change that.

And I can't wait to see where we go next.

THANKS FOR READING!

Want more Konstantin & Emilia? Scan the code below for a bonus scene!

I hope you're ready for *Aleksei* because his story is going to be so much fun!

While you wait, jump into the *Savage Kings* series to get more of the Quinn family!

PLAYLIST

- "Trouble" by Camylio
- "I Love It" by Croixx
- "Лунная ночь" by EMIN feat. JONY
- "I Know Your Secrets" by Katie Garfield
- "Devil I Know" by Allie X
- "Against Me" by Scout Speer feat. Austin Giorgio
- "Abuse Me" by Ex Habit
- "Fatal Attraction" by Reed Wonder feat. Aurora Olives
- "Love Is Going to Kill Us" by David Kushner
- "Poison in My Veins" by Elvis Drew
- "Let Me Fall" by Ex Habit feat. BURY
- "Scream My Name" by Thomas LaRosa
- "Dangerous Game" by Stellar feat. Camylio
- "September Trees" by memyself&vi
- "Good Girl (Praise)" by Nation Haven
- "Love Is a Bitch" by Dario Marcello feat. Mangusx and Dark Mage
- "Lament" by Tommee Profitt feat. Sam Tinnesz and Shaya Zamora
- "Sometimes" by Ashley Singh
- "Never Knew" by Shaya Zamora
- "Embers" by James Arthur
- "Hold Me Steady – Alt Version" by Valerie Broussard feat. Ronen
- "With the Devil I'm Going Down" by Steelfeather
- "Without You" by Omido feat. Bibi Silvija
- "Broken Symphony" by Rob the Sun feat. Roby Fayer

- "The Devil" by Dominic Donner
- "A Piece of Your Shadow" by Rob the Sun feat. Roby Fayer
- "Cold Touch" by Psylosia
- "Hurt Myself the Hardest" by Allegra Jordyn
- "Why Am I Falling for You" by Josh Alexander
- "Without You I Can't Dance" by Josh Alexander
- "Without You I'd Die" by memyself&vi
- "Work of Art" by Amber Ré
- "Hello Again – Acoustic" by Zoe Wees
- "Woman's World" by Steelfeather
- "Fatal Flaw" by Allegra Jordyn
- "Secrets Kill" by Ely Eira
- "Feel It" by JERUB
- "Masochist" by Empara Mi
- "Bonnie and Clyde" by Croixx
- "Love Me 'Til You Leave Me" by gavn!

ALSO BY LILIAN HARRIS

Fragile Hearts Series

1. *Fragile Scars* (Damian & Lilah)
2. *Fragile Lies* (Jax & Lexi Part 1)
3. *Fragile Truths* (Jax & Lexi Part 2)
4. *Fragile Pieces* (Gabe & Mia)

Cavaleri Brothers Series

1. *The Devil's Deal* (Dominic & Chiara)
2. *The Devil's Pawn* (Dante & Raquel)
3. *The Devil's Secret* (Enzo & Jade)
4. *The Devil's Den* (Matteo & Aida)
5. *The Devil's Demise* (Extended Epilogue)

Messina Crime Family Series

1. *Sinful Vows* (Michael & Elsie)
2. *Cruel Lies* (Raph & Nicolette)
3. *Twisted Promises* (Gio & Iseult)
4. *Savage Wounds* (Adriel & Kayla)

Savage Kings Series

1. *Ruthless Savage* (Devlin & Eriu)

2. *Brutal Savage* (Tynan & Elara)
3. *Filthy Savage* (Fionn & Amara)
4. *Wicked Savage* (Cillian & Dinara)

Marinov Bratva Series

1. *Konstantin*
2. *Aleksei* (Winter 2025)
3. *Kirill* (Spring 2026)
4. *Anton* (Winter 2026)

Standalone

1. *Shattered Secrets* (Husdon & Hadleigh)

For Lilian, a love of writing began with a love of books. From Goosebumps to romance novels with sexy men on the cover, she loved them all. It's no surprise that at the age of eight she started writing poetry and lyrics and hasn't stopped writing since.

She was born in Azerbaijan, and currently resides on Long Island, N.Y. with her husband, three kids, and lots of animals. Even though she has a law degree, she isn't currently practicing. When she isn't writing or reading, Lilian is baking or cooking up a storm. And once the kids are in bed, there's usually a glass of red in her hand. Can't just survive on coffee alone!